Fragile LIVES

Fragile LIVES

Little Hope Series, Book 4

ARIANA CANE

ISBN: 978-1-7338321-7-5

"You're the only thing holding me together. And they all know that."

To Chester.
And to everyone else.

Author's Note

I always use a sensitivity reader for my stories since every single one has some heavy topics.

I didn't need one for this book because I am that—the sensitivity reader for this topic. As many of you out there.

I contemplated for a long time if I should mention something but then decided fuck it, if I don't talk about that, it doesn't make the problem go away. I've been struggling with depression throughout my whole life. I've always been a sensitive kid with a way too wild imagination. You get the drift. When I grew up, my imagination became even wilder while depressions deeper.

Also, when I grew up, I understood that it's okay to not be okay. It doesn't make me any *less* or *different*, it just means that I'm tired and I need some time to myself. And that's okay. Archie is not okay, but he will get there, even though his 'okay' might not match your 'okay.' And guess what? That's okay too.

Also, I've had a very sad experience when my friend was about to commit suicide (shared with his permission without using the names). He was really close to doing something irrevocable, so I understand the feeling from both sides (you will get what I mean after you read the book). Do I want to forget about it? Maybe, but it keeps me grounded, so most likely not.

I am not an expert and not a medical professional, but it's my book, and I wanted to share it the way my heart told me to.

You will see a different side of Archie you probably didn't see before. I hope he won't disappoint you because he is my favorite broken boy.

The National Suicide Prevention Line in the United State as of winter 2023 is 988 or 1-800-273-8255. You can find extra information at the website https://www.samhsa.gov/find-help/988. I'm positive that other countries have something similar, so don't give up.

TW: mention of suicide, suicidal thoughts and actions, use of alcohol, mention of child mental abuse, adult language, adult situations, mention of masochism, pain play.

Please proceed with caution. And if at any moment you feel uncomfortable, stop reading. Archie's story ends with a happy ending, but it's quite a wild road on the way there.

With this being said, enjoy the ride!

P.S. I've been trying to sum up the story in one song, but couldn't. So I decided to put my top-3 for this one,
Citizen Soldier | Let it Burn
Linkin Park | Crawling
Bad Omens | The Death of Piece of Mind

Chapter One

L EILA

I'm driving home from Boston after a meeting with my newspaper. They want me to write more stories like the one I just submitted—exposing crimes. I don't know how I feel about it, considering the number of disgusting things I dug up in my research took a toll on my mental health. Knowing the inside scoop is never easy, and, depending on the crime, you don't come out the same.

I let out an aggravated groan as I see a figure walking on the bridge that connects the old and the new part of town. With no jacket on. In December. In Maine. My butt is freezing even firmly planted on a heated seat inside of my car, hidden away from the elements, and he's just...walking, hands in the front pockets of his pants.

It's dark, and there are not many lights around this part of town. If I hadn't been paying attention, there's a chance I could have hit him. Bridges are the most dangerous part of the roads around here, especially at night, in my opinion. Yet here, in this part of Maine, we like to live life on a cliff. Quite literally.

I want to drive by, I do. My intuition screams that something big might happen if I don't. Something that irrevocably will change my life. The desire to keep my foot on the accelerator is strong. But I was born and raised in Little Hope, Maine, and we small-town folks still care for one another, even in the twenty-first century.

As I drive past him, about to slow down so I can ask if he needs help, I notice how large he is and how wide his shoulders are. We're on the bridge. With no lights and no people. And it's closing on midnight.

It makes me think for a second. Yes, I know pretty much everyone in our town—not personally, no, but I've seen or heard of everyone—a perk of living in a small town—but I don't recognize this man. At least, not from inside my car with limited visibility. I slow down a little, hoping he'll let me know if he needs my help. Maybe his car broke down, and he needs a lift.

But as I'm driving by, I peer at him; his face is trained on the snowy road ahead of him. He has a purpose for being here that I'm not privy to.

I slow down even more now, and he moves to the side of the road, not lifting his eyes—a silent order to stay away from him.

Well, that's my cue, so I press the accelerator and speed up. An exaggeration, of course. I'm in Maine in December on a bridge—this speedy driver can only do thirty miles per hour tops without risking driving off this bridge right into the frigid water of our less than mighty river.

Letting out a loud sigh of relief, feeling I narrowly

avoided the unseen, I glance in the rearview mirror. A big mistake.

The stranger stands on the sidewalk, his elbows resting on the rails of the bridge. I slow down again, just a bit, so I can keep watching. His head hangs lower as if he's looking beyond the bridge.

He's not going to find anything but a fast river that may or may not be covered in thin ice. Despite the low temperatures every winter, the river only freezes mid-December when the cold hits the hardest, so we've got about two good weeks before then.

I come to a near stop, and the stranger's head falls even lower. His shoulders slump, and I pull my car over to the side, cursing my small-town upbringing. The bridge is behind me, the stranger about a hundred feet away, and I grip the steering wheel tighter, trying to decide what I should do. Instinct screams to run and talk to him, but my self-preservation slaps me across the face, warning me to not get involved.

The good prevails, so I put my white beanie on and climb out of my car, engine still running. Just in case.

A rush of cold air instantly chills my bones, and I hurry to zip my red puffy winter coat, shuddering.

The stranger hasn't moved.

I start slowly walking toward him. When I'm about fifty feet away, I call out, "Hey."

His head snaps toward me, and he looks around as if surprised to find himself on the bridge alone with me. *You and me both, buddy.*

"What are you doing here?" His voice is gruff and deep, coming from within his chest.

"I could ask the same thing," I counter, a little playfully, trying to lighten the situation. "Aren't you cold?"

He watches me for a few seconds. "I'm fine," he says, turning back to the deep waters.

I take a few tentative steps before he notices my approach and turns to me again. "What are you doing?"

"Sightseeing." I quirk a brow and start walking more confidently.

"Go home." He turns away again.

"Are you planning to jump?"

His head turns toward me so fast I think he's given himself whiplash.

"The fuck do you need here?"

I stop next to him. Only now do I notice how tall he is. Well, I'm five-four, and a lot of people are tall compared to me, but the top of my head only reaches his chest, and I have to look up.

His midnight black hair, a little longer on the top and shorter on the sides, is disheveled and wet from the falling snow. He has gorgeous eyelashes framing his brown eyes as if he's wearing eyeliner, and his clean-shaven jaw is so sharp —it feels like one could cut a finger by simply touching it. His cheeks are sunken. Tattoos cover the visible part of his neck, and I wonder how far down they go.

Why am I thinking that? Mentally shaking my head, I continue observing him.

Light wrinkles on the sides of his eyes tell me he likes to laugh, which is a far cry from his facial expression right now. He has a five-o-clock shadow and perfect lips, the bottom one a little fuller. His skin is clean of any blemishes, his cheeks a little pink from the biting cold.

I'd place him somewhere in his early thirties if I had to guess.

I look back up and find him pressing his lips together in a tight, angry line, his brow raised in question.

"As far as I've heard, Maine is still a free state, and I can be anywhere I want as long as I don't break any laws." I narrow my eyes at him.

"Be anywhere but here." His eyes narrow back.

"Why?" I squint even more.

"Because I was here first." His nostrils flare as he replies like a stubborn child.

I snort at his ridiculous answer and rest my elbows against the rails, mimicking his previous stance. I feel a hot glare drilling a hole into the side of my face, until eventually he sighs and turns to look at the river too.

"There are always reasons to not do it, you know," I say after a long stretch of silence.

"Did I ask for your opinion?" His tone is purposely rude, and the slightest hint of a British accent envelopes me in a warm hug—I've always been a sucker for accents.

"No. But you're still getting it." I shrug in the darkness, not looking at him.

He sighs tiredly, his voice void of any emotion. "I never said I wanted to jump."

"You never said you didn't."

He doesn't contradict or try to convince me otherwise and keeps looking ahead. I turn toward him, shamelessly staring at the side of his face. It's a work of art. All this anger and pain and longing...I can see all of it. He doesn't even try to hide it. How is he living like this? How did he end up here, on this bridge? His face is an open cry for help, hiding so much melancholy and tiredness—people would surely see his need for them.

They would, right?

"Why are you looking at me like that?" He shoots me an unhappy glare.

"I haven't seen you around here," I reply and pull my hat down over my ears before they freeze off.

"I'm visiting a friend." He grinds his molars, and I watch how his jaw works as he probably grinds them into dust.

"Is this friend a she?"

"Why do you care?" That draws his attention, and he turns to me, a lopsided smile finally showing on his face. I get the feeling this facade is something he knows how to utilize.

"I don't." I shrug—a half-truth. "But I want to know what pushed you to come here."

"I'm not planning to jump," he says, rolling his eyes.

"Alright," I agree too easily, and he groans.

"No, my friend is not a *she*," he says drowsily, undoubtedly hoping the nuisance (me) will disappear if he succumbs to my demands. "And I'm here because I need some time to clear my head. I'm fine; your conscience is clear. You can go now," he dismisses me and stares ahead again.

I let out a loud growl—inwardly. "Of course you do. Naked on a bridge at night while it's snowing."

"Don't throw things like that in the air. If I was naked, sweetheart, you'd never forget it. I can assure you I'm very much dressed." The arrogant notes in his voice clearly indicate that he's averted from the path I found him on. For now.

"It's cold," I say, ignoring him. "You'll get pneumonia."

He snorts, shaking away the snowflakes from his sleeve, and mumbles under his breath, "That'd be too easy."

I shut my mouth before I yell at him and go back to watching the river. This year it might freeze even earlier since the temperature is going psycho these days.

"I think—" I swallow before continuing, "I think my

brother had the same thoughts at one point in his life." I decide to share one of my deepest fears, hoping it will help him. "When he came back from the service..." I hear his breath hitch, and I don't dare to look at him. "He was...bad." The cold air bites my nose, making me sniffle. "Angry with the world and...with everything really."

I let myself drift away for a second, back to the time Alex returned from the Navy and was like a walking grenade with a short fuse. "He blamed himself for a lot of things. Thought that no one loved him, but it couldn't have been further from the truth. I don't know what we would have done if he chose that path. I just—" I cut myself off before I spill too much. My eyes water and I blink the moisture away. "What I'm trying to say is that there is always someone who will be devastated if something happens to you." It's the first time since the beginning of my speech that I dare to look at him.

His eyes are trained on my face. "What if not everyone has that someone?"

"Everyone does."

"But what if—"

"Everyone does," I cut him off, my voice firm. "It doesn't have to be family, but you've changed *someone's* life for the better. There is always someone out there." I hold his eyes, communicating my truth to him. "Always. Even if you don't know it."

The corners of his lips dip down, aging his face a few years. His neck moves in a rough swallow, and I notice the tattoos on his neck as the tail of something on the side of it—a dragon, maybe—shifts with the movement.

"Do you understand?" I press.

He swallows again and nods silently.

"Good." I nod to myself and bite the inside of my cheek, thinking over the situation.

"What's your name?" he asks carefully.

"Leila. Yours?"

He watches me before answering as if he can't decide if he wants to share. "Stephan."

"Glad to meet you, Stephan," I say and offer him my hand.

He eyes it cynically as if it'll grow a mouth and bite him, but right before I drop it, he envelopes it in his huge palm. My hand totally disappears in his, another indication of the difference in our sizes, being here alone with him. Strangely, I don't feel fearful. Well, I don't feel fear *of* him, but I do *for* him.

"You're freezing," he says as he brings the other hand to wrap around the one he's still holding.

"It's cold." I swallow. "How come you're not cold?" In fact, it's the opposite—his palm is on fire, and he doesn't even have a jacket on.

"I don't feel cold much." He drops my hand and nods toward my running sedan, "Go back to your car."

"No." I shake my head stubbornly. "Only if I give you a ride." My teeth chatter as I feel the cold air biting my cheeks, nose, and neck, slipping under my jacket.

"I don't need a ride. I'm fine." He steps back.

"Then, I'll stay." I turn to the river and lean on the rails again, trying to hide deeper in my coat.

A loud sigh nearly makes me smile. Nearly.

"Fine. Let's go." He rolls his eyes to the point where they might not come back, grabs my hand, and starts walking, dragging me along.

I'm trying to suppress my laughter at how easy it was to make him give up, but a cackle escapes me. Then another.

And then I can't help but laugh full force. He stops, drops my hand, and turns to me.

"What's so funny?" His voice is biting.

"Nothing," I say but keep cackling.

"I like a good laugh. But I like to be the one you're laughing with, not at." The corners of his eyes crinkle as I laugh even harder. I don't even know what I'm laughing about at this point. I think it might be a release of pent-up adrenaline and fear.

Bending over, I place my hands on my knees. "I'm sorry," I say breathlessly as I finally straighten. "I don't know what came over me." I try to take a few deep breaths when I notice his intense stare. A little unsettling.

A lot exciting.

His eyes suddenly turn hungry as they land on my lips, stretched into a wild smile. He's not blinking, just staring, and I stop laughing. I anxiously lick my lips, and his eyes snap to mine. He crosses the distance between us in the blink of an eye, his lips landing on mine, shocking me into a stupor.

I think he shocks himself, too, as he doesn't touch me anywhere but my lips. My eyes are wide open as I try to comprehend what's happening. His arms are noodles at his sides, and his lips are shy. They just touch mine, no tongue.

His eyes snap open, and he tries to rear back, but I don't let him. Instead, I grab the front of his sweater and pull him into me. He stumbles as he tries to regain his footing, but his hands land on my back. The height difference makes the kiss awkward, so he bends lower and moves his hands to my lower back, helping me to my tippytoes. Snaking them under my jacket, I can feel his warm palms through my sweater, despite him not having decent clothes in this freezing weather.

His tongue traces my lower lip, probing it. I reluctantly open, letting him slip in. The velvety feeling of him invading my mouth makes my breath hitch, and I part my lips wider on instinct. He groans as if in pain and dives deeper.

Pressing me into him, he intensifies the kiss. Our teeth clink, and I sink my nails into the buff muscles of his shoulders. He lets out another loud groan and grinds his pelvis into me. Even through my coat, I can feel his hardness.

Fuck. *Fuck! What am I doing?*

I push on his chest and jump away.

Chapter Two

A RCHIE

Fuck. Fuck! What am I doing?

I look at her swollen lips and crazed, glassy eyes. She stumbles back and stares at me.

"Fuck, I'm sorry." I wipe my face with my hand. "I don't know what came over me."

"That's okay." She averts her unusual gray eyes as if seeing me disgusts her, and I notice the specks of dark blue in them.

And oh fuck, do I understand her. Seeing myself in the mirror every single day disgusts me too.

"It's an adrenaline rush," she adds with a small smile, finally meeting my eyes. "Happens to the best of us."

"Right." I start backing away. "Thanks for stopping by."

"Where are you going?" Her voice rises slightly as her eyes narrow suspiciously.

"To my car." I point behind my back to my nonexistent car and turn to walk away.

"You're delusional if you think I'm letting you walk all the way to your car." A deep, loud sigh follows. "Wherever it is."

I keep walking, not paying attention to what she said. Feeling ashamed to my fucking core that she caught me *thinking* and somehow *read* my fucking mind, I wish more than anything to disappear and to never see this woman ever again.

Someone grabs my forearm, and I suddenly turn, ready to push whoever's next to me away. Not seeing her, I shove the hand touching me away, too rough and too fast, before I comprehend it's her. Shaking my head to clear it from the haze I'm in, I wipe my face again and groan.

"Fuck. *Fuck!*" I take a deep breath, reining myself in. "I'm sorry. I don't react well to people touching me unexpectedly." Another reason to be ashamed and hope to never see her again.

Her wary eyes dart between mine before she swallows and nods. Too *understanding*. "That's okay too."

"Okay?" I let out a sardonic laugh. "Are *you* okay?" I take a step toward her. "Stopping for a fucking stranger on an empty road?" I spread my arms wide. "I can be a serial killer, for all you know. I just fuckin' pushed you away, and yet, you're saying it's okay. It's not fucking okay." I get in her face, noticing that I let my accent slip a bit, being high on emotions. "I'm twice your size, if not more, yet you're here, eager to help. What's wrong with you?" Her eyes widen at the proximity. I'm an inch away from her.

"With me? What's wrong with me?" She presses her finger between my pecs, pushing hard. "What's wrong with you? Huh? Being here alone in the cold? Walking to your car," she mockingly mimics my voice and makes quotation marks in the air. "I don't know what kind of assholes people are where you're from, but where I'm from, we don't do this to people." She lifts herself up on her tippytoes and gets in my face, still poking her finger into my chest. Her wild, red hair frames her pale face and reddened cheeks like a sun wrapping someone in a blazing hug. "We fuckin' care." She pokes one last time, hard—surprisingly hard for such a tiny human. "Now get your ass in my car before we both freeze to death." Her little nostrils flare, and she begins walking toward her tiny sedan. There's a light jump in her step, a clear indication of irritation.

My cock jerks as my eyes widen. *Fuck.* I want to look down and ask the fucker what's happening and why he got so excited, but that would be too weird, well, *weirder*, because the situation is already awkward enough.

I didn't know I like to be ordered around like that, but I find myself smirking before following her like a puppy. She climbs into the driver's seat, her head barely visible from behind the wheel, and I find myself smiling at how cute she looks. Like a tiny, angry doll, her red hair sticking out from under her hat, her small hands tightly gripping the steering wheel, knuckles white.

The passenger seat is so close to the dashboard, I feel like a four-foot person sat here before me. Moving the seat back, I can barely fit my six-three frame into it as I crouch and knock my head on the ceiling in the process.

"Are you done?" comes a snarky voice from the driver's side, followed by a snort. I give her a side-eye and buckle up as she starts the car. "Where to?"

"Cat and Stallion." I name the local bar I left my car at, and she quirks a questioning brow. "I drove a friend who had too much. Happy now?" Why I am explaining this to her, I'll never know.

I don't tell her that I came to the bar hoping to get wasted, but instead, I met a dude who was suffering, forced to separate from the love of his life, apparently, and needed to get wasted more than I did. And that I shared my bottle of scotch—the last one in the whole damn bar, if you can believe—with him and drove him home, where I met his love outside his house.

I could tell it was her from her apprehensive eyes as she saw me dropping him off at home. We had a short talk but enlightening regardless. I don't tell her any of that. It's a small town, and I know better than to tell her that "the love" was Justin's sister, a dude I don't have a good history with.

To be fair, I don't think anyone does. Besides Alex, my friend and an old team member from our Navy years. He seems to be one of the only people with enough patience to put up with Justin, and the reason I'm in town today: we're trying to spend more time together since it seems to be helping him with his PTSD and guilt.

Unfortunately, it does nothing for mine.

The silence in the car is suffocating, and more than anything, I just want to jump out of it to be alone, but the raging ball of anger next to me is dead set on delivering me to my car without any jumping involved, so I grind my teeth, praying for the five-minute drive to pass faster. With the heavy snow packed on the road and her driving like a grandma, I'd get to the car faster by foot.

As the lights from the bar come into view, I let out a loud sigh of relief. I can *feel* her rolling her eyes next to me. She stops right under the sign and parks the car.

"Thanks," I mumble, and she grunts something, not turning my way. I climb out of the vehicle, hitting my head on the ceiling in the process. I want to walk away but pause, deciding to say my piece. I bend over the opening of the car, meeting her eyes. "For real, Leila. Don't stop to help strangers at night. You never know how far they're gone."

She turns back, staring ahead without answering, and I shut the door. She puts the car in drive and hits the gas. The rear of the vehicle swivels, and she hits gas harder, disappearing down the road.

I look longingly at the bar, deciding if I should go inside and fulfill today's dream of getting wasted and maybe take that pretty bartender Rory up on her offer to meet after her shift. But I find myself remembering those big gray eyes looking warily at me on that bridge, in the moment of my lowest low, and I decide that I can't do either.

I walk to my Rover and climb inside, grateful for the tall ceiling and enough space for my frame without breaking my back.

I'm supposed to meet Alex tomorrow for dinner and a drink, but for some reason, I find myself in Little Hope, Maine, today. Ever since I visited Alex a few years ago, my soul yearns for this place. I don't have a family or anything besides Alex here, yet I'm earlier than I'm supposed to be.

Since sharing a bed with the bartender and drinking bourbon at the bar are out of the question, I let out a heavy sigh and drive to the bed-and-breakfast I usually stay at. I guess I'll experience small-town life at its very core by turning in early.

The next day, I do some work from my laptop, move some investments around, and check in with my parlors. I have a few requests about franchising, but I'm not planning on expanding anymore, so I move them to the back of my priority list.

When the evening comes, I shower and head to the local diner where I agreed to meet with Alex. He invited me to his place at first, but I feel like an intruder every time I go to his happy home. He has a family, and it's no place for a morose asshole.

So I asked if we could meet at the diner. I don't know today's waitress, but Marina, the owner, gives me a wave and goes back to cooking.

I find an empty booth in the corner and take a seat facing the door. A few minutes later, the door chimes, and Alex walks inside. It takes him two seconds to find me, and he saunters toward our seat with a smile on his face.

"Fucker. Took the best spot," he says with jealousy. Facing the door lets me observe everything happening in the diner. Old habits die hard, and every little comfort helps break the everyday hell cycle. I'm not moving my ass from here.

"You snooze, you lose," I say with a laugh and push the menu toward him.

"I know what I want. Freya thinks," he's talking about his girlfriend, "I like this breakfast, the Lonely Kurt, that she keeps bringing me, but I just want my fuckin' steak." His eyes roll back in his head, and I bet if Freya was here, she'd smack him.

I laugh, understanding where he's coming from. He loves Freya too much to disappoint her, but a man needs his steak.

A young girl comes to take our orders. Alex orders a medium steak with extra sides for himself, and I mimic him, not bothering with being super creative today. When she leaves, Alex leans against the back of his seat.

"So, how have you been?" His eyes narrow.

"Good. You?"

"I'm good." He chews on his lips. "Have you talked to them?"

"Who?" I ask, confused.

"Their families."

And here comes the dark cloud, wiping any joy I felt away. I knew he was going to ask about it at some point, but I didn't think he'd start off with it. To be honest, I'm surprised he waited so long. And by long, I mean years.

"No." I shake my head firmly. "You?"

"No." He taps his finger on the table. "Not since that first time, no."

When we were both in the hospital after the explosion during our mission, we received calls from the families of two other people in our unit. They wanted to ask how their loved one's last minutes were, and I couldn't fuckin' bring myself to utter a word. I just breathed into the damn phone, listening to one of their mothers crying. Alex got our other brother's wife, and to this day, I don't know what he told her. And I don't think I'll ever be brave enough to ask.

We sit in silence, remembering.

Alex got burned pretty badly. Half of his body is damaged. When I was trying to get him out from under that burning truck, I didn't think he'd make it. Thank God he did. But he got scarred, inside and out.

And I got nothing. Not a fucking cut.

The waitress brings our food, but we both lost our appetites. Alex becomes grimmer, and I don't want his girlfriend coming after me for ruining his anti-anger strike, so I try to lighten the mood.

"So, how is domestic life going?" I chuckle. "Must be cool to have a willing woman by your side every night."

"You shut it, fucker." He laughs as his neck pinkens.

Hook, line, and sinker. Anything to change the subject.

"She's my girlfriend."

"I remember." I lean back with a toothy smile, glad he's moving away from that dark place he goes to when anger hits. "So, how is that?"

"Fuckin' amazing. Ten out of ten recommend."

I laugh louder. "Sure, whatever you say."

"No, for real. It's awesome. You have someone in your corner all the time. Every day. No matter what happens, she's on your side. It's amazing." He shakes his head in wonder, a look of pure awe on his face.

Then, a moment later, Alex digs into his food, missing how it's my turn for dark clouds to shroud my mood.

What he found isn't in the cards for me, ever. I'll never have that with someone. Ever. My life is written in the stars to be lonely and miserable. I just need to make sure it's not long.

Chapter Three

A RCHIE

I open my eyes to my phone ringing. Leaning over the sleeping body in my bed, I grab it from the nightstand. *An unknown number*. I usually don't take those and am about to put it back when something nudges my mind. The first digits clearly indicate that the caller is from Maine, so I hit 'accept.'

"Yes." I sound gruff, but that's not my problem since they got me half asleep.

"Archie?" An unfamiliar voice asks.

"This is him. And you?"

"It's Kenneth Benson, Alex's brother."

My blood runs cold, and my heart stops. I've heard of him briefly but never actually met the guy, and him calling me in the morning like this? It fuckin' chills my bones. Alex is a vet struggling with severe PTSD, and no one, trust me, fuckin' no one wants to get a call like this.

"What happened?" I push through the sudden dryness in my throat.

"Oh," he exhales loudly. "Sorry, didn't mean to scare you. He's fine."

I let out a breath of relief.

"I was wondering if I can ask you for a favor," he chuckles apprehensively.

"Favor?" Interesting. I barely know the guy. Alex hardly mentioned him during our years of service together, so Kenneth calling me must be big. "What sort of favor?"

He chuckles again, clearly not knowing where to start. "This is gonna sound weird."

"You think?" I lean back onto my pillows, and the female body next to me wiggles her ass in the air, stirring my dick.

"Fair." Another chuckle. "I'm kind of in a...how should I say? An interesting situation." I'm quiet, so he asks, "You there?"

"Oh, I am." I laugh. "I can't wait to see where this is going."

"Fucker." A loud groan follows, and I instantly begin liking the guy. "I know you're coming here tomorrow for dinner at our parents', but I was wondering if you could come tonight."

"Why?"

"I need you to be somewhere to wait for..." I can almost *hear* him thinking, "us."

"Us?"

"Yeah, myself, Justin, and another dude."

This is getting more interesting by the second, especially as the woman next to me places her hand between her legs, letting out quiet little moans.

"Do I want to know why I need to meet you all there?" I ask, eyeing the show at my side. "Considering I can't fuckin' stand that blond asshole."

"No one does. But they need—*we* need—an alibi."

I push from the pillows, swinging my legs over the bed to sit, forgetting about the woman in my bed. "Why would you need that?"

"Look," a deep sigh, "the only reason I called you is because Alex talks about you like you hang the moon and fuckin' stars, and I need someone not from around here who can keep his mouth shut, and I thought you could be that someone." He groans as if he's tired of trying to reason with me and says, "You know what? Never mind, forget it."

I know he's about to hang up, so I rush to reply, "I'll be there. Text me the address."

There's a weighted silence before he speaks. "Alright. Thanks. I don't know when I'll need you there, but I strongly suspect that it might be tonight. I'll text you the time as soon as I'm sure."

"Copy that," I say before hanging up. Interesting. There are not many people I'll do anything for, but Alex is one of them, and that means his family too.

A second later, my phone chimes with a text containing the address of a bar in one of Little Hope's neighboring towns. I check the drive time: about four hours, and with the snowy roads it might be longer. It's currently nine in the morning.

I still have time for a quickie.

Lying back in bed and turning to the brunette, I gently pat her shoulder. She turns around to kiss me, but I press my finger to her lips before she can. "No kissing, babe. That's the deal, and you know that."

She pouts and pushes on my shoulders, and I don't know why she acts so scandalized—I'm always open and strict with my rules: no kissing, no morning snuggles, no heartwarming hugs. I like a warm body next to me just like any other man, but it needs to be *next* to me, not on me, beside me, or any other variation. Don't get me wrong, I like said variations during the fun activities, but not after.

When I'm on my back, she climbs on top of me. I smile, ready for a good time.

If not for my flaccid cock. The gorgeous brunette— *Jannette? Jaqueline?*—pushes her boobs into my face, and still nothing. She moves over me, and nothing. *Fuck, here we go again.* I slightly push her back and lean over to the night-stand. Opening the drawer, I pull my knife out. Her eyes go round, and I rush to calm her down.

"Don't worry, sweetheart. It's not for you."

She lets out a relieved breath but watches me warily.

I flip the knife so the handle is pointing toward her and offer it. "Take it."

She takes it carefully, and I grab her hand, guiding her toward my chest. "Now, cut it."

Shocked, she looks from me to my chest and licks her lips. I think she's about to bolt when her eyes turn hungry, and she presses the blade into my skin, cutting it.

"More," I rasp, and she presses harder. The pain is familiar and welcoming. Now, my dick stirs, and I grab the condom, ready for action. That's another rule I always follow—always dress up. Never in my life did I go in raw, nor do I plan to.

As she makes another cut, going a lot deeper this time, I think about how it's getting more difficult to feel anything without pain with every passing day. When will I reach my limit?

———

It's seven in the evening when I park at the Dancing Pony, the Little Hope bed-and-breakfast. Getting my overnight bag out, I walk to the door. A slim elf-like woman with her ever-present long, fake ears greets me at the reception desk. She's the owner of this place. Emma has only ever been nice to me, a real ray of sunshine. But today, she greets me with a concerned frown.

"Archie, I'm so sorry! Your room got a radiator leak. It'll take a couple days to fix."

"Bummer. I'm okay with any room."

"I don't have any left," she says, her voice small, nearly ready to cry. She's one of those people who don't know how to just say 'no.'

"None?" I longingly glance at the hallway of the inn.

"No." She shakes her pretty head, her elf ears flopping a little.

"Oh, well." I sigh. "I guess call me when you have anything available."

"Will do. Sorry again!"

"Don't worry." I wave at her, walk out the door, and back to my car. Fuck, I can try another town, but it's like a thirty-minute drive on a good day.

Once I get inside, I pull out my phone and call Kenneth. He's the local sheriff, and he would know if something is available somewhere around. Plus, he's the reason I'm here today, so he owes me.

He picks up on the second ring. *"Benson."*

"Do you know of any other accommodations around besides Dancing Pony?"

He sighs. *"They're packed?"*

"Yeah."

"Nothing around here." He clicks his tongue. *"You can stay at my place; I got plenty of room."*

"You sure?"

"Yeah. I'll text you the address." He yells something to someone and then returns to me. *"Sorry, work. The extra key is on the beam at the back door."*

"Got it, thanks."

"Sure. I'm stuck at the station for another thirty minutes, but that thing we talked about? I think it's tonight. I'll give you the details when I'm back."

"Copy that."

The end of the line goes dead, and a message follows a moment later. I plug the address into my GPS and drive to his place. I could probably crash on Alex's couch, but something tells me he is unaware of the shenanigan his brother is up to. And I intend to keep it that way—Alex already has enough on his plate.

Benson's house is a suburban-style, two-story brick building with more character in its gutter than my whole gigantic mansion in Boston. I walk around to look for the back door, and, as promised, I find the spare key on the beam. Opening the door, I step inside.

It matches the outside. Clean cut, simple but tasteful. Looking around, I get a feeling that Benson must have spent a few years in the military, judging by how neat and tidy everything is and the ninety-degree angles everywhere.

I drop my bag on the bench by the door and take my shoes off. My mother would have a fit if she saw me walking barefoot in someone's house, but pissing her off is one of the last pleasures in my life. Even if she doesn't see it.

I wash my hands and plant my ass on the couch, scrolling through social media. Seeing new tattoos made by my crew warms my heart. My parlors are among the very few things that still bring me pleasure in life besides being a tool to my mother, and I treasure seeing the beautiful work my employees put out into the world.

Thirty minutes later, the front door opens, and a tall, well-built dude in a sheriff's uniform walks inside. I see the family resemblance right away. His hair is cut short, but besides that, he's pretty much Alex's twin, just a little older. A few stripes of silver mark his temples, and a few extra lines around his mouth and eyes. I stand up and walk to him, hand outstretched. He shakes it firmly and smacks my shoulder with his other hand.

"Thanks for coming."

"Don't mention it." I smile. "Though I might say I'm curious."

"I bet you are. C'mon, I'll explain everything." He takes his shoes off and proceeds to the kitchen. "Alex doesn't know you're here?" he asks, turning to me.

"No," I say, following him. "Figured if you wanted him to know, you would tell him."

"You figured right. Don't want to get him involved." He nods.

"And involving me is alright?" I ask with a smirk.

"It's not like that." He opens the fridge. "Want something?"

"Water."

He grabs a cold bottle and passes it to me. "You won't be mixed into anything that might cause you trouble, but if he knows, he will make sure to be in the middle since he knows the parties involved."

"Okay, you got me hooked." I unscrew the cap, toss back half in one go, and sit at the table. My hangovers always leave me dehydrated, so I'm always thirsty.

"You know Justin, right?"

"The asshole who treated my star artist like shit? Yeah, I know him, alright."

Kayla, Justin's fiancé, is my top artist. I discovered her a few years ago and paid for her classes to become a tattoo artist. The best investment I've made so far—she's booked for months ahead. She is an unbelievable success considering she's a brand-new name. Her signature phoenixes are getting well-deserved recognition around the world.

Justin did some shady shit and lost her there for a minute. She came to my house, ready for a new life. She stayed in one of my many empty rooms while she was studying and working part-time in one of my Boston locations. One day, he showed up at my place, demanding to see her. But the asshole realized she was better off without him for the time being and let her chase her dream.

I may have influenced his decision. A bit. I felt sorry for him, to be honest. He came to me looking like a beat-up, homeless dog. That's what love does to people, and that's precisely why I only do one-night stands. I can't get involved with someone and go through those highs and lows since I'm already so unstable. And I can't get anyone involved in my bullshit either.

"Yeah." He takes a sip and chews on his lip. "Well, his sister—and this stays between us, you got it?" He finds my eyes and gives me a death stare, so I nod. "His sister was assaulted eight years ago, and no one was punished."

"Fuck." I wipe my face with my hands, masking my anxiety.

So, that pretty blonde I met the night I dropped drunk Romeo off went through something horrible. That's why her eyes were permanently sad. It wasn't only because she lost her lover, but because she's been through hell and back.

After hearing this, I know I'm in, no matter what the hell he'll ask.

"Yeah. So, rumor has it, Mark, her boyfriend, found them."

"You're shitting me." I lightly smack the table with an open palm, too excited at the prospect of what he might do to them.

"What?" His brows arch.

"I met the guy a week ago at the bar."

Kenneth's lips quirk up. "You're the Samaritan who drove him home?"

"And how do you know it?"

"It's my town." He shrugs and adds with a smirk, "Rory told me."

Ah, the pretty bartender.

"Small towns." I shake my head.

"Yep. Gotta love 'em." He chuckles and looks longingly at the fridge. "God, I wish I could have a beer right about now."

"You and me both. I'm not used to being sober this late in the evening."

He gives me a once over and continues, "I have my suspicion that he and Justin are going after them tonight."

"After them as—" I let the question hang in the air.

"To deliver justice. And that's why I'm going. To make sure they don't overdo it."

"Alright. You want me to go with them." I nod, getting excited about fixing at least one injustice in this shitty world.

"Fuck no. Two psychos are enough. I can't rein you in as well. No offense." He shoots me a sympathetic smile, making me cackle. "I need you to wait for us at the bar and make everyone believe we were there the whole evening. Is that doable?"

I snort. "I'm offended that I'm left out, but I can do that. The drinks will be plenty, and the table will be busy. No one will notice you weren't there from the start."

"Glad that's covered. I hope they won't go too far."

"Would that be bad, though?" I mumble under my breath, but he hears it.

"I don't give a shit about those fuckers. God knows that's wrong to say, but it's the honest truth. They've done a lot of shit, if my..." he averts his eyes, *"research* it correct. But I can't let them go that far. That's not how justice is served."

"And yet here we are, securing an alibi." I lean back in my seat and fold my arms over my chest.

"It's complicated." He shakes his head and leans against the table. "It's been eight years, and not even one person came forward."

"How do you know they're to blame then?"

He levels me with a stare. "We always do. But our hands are fucking tied if there's no evidence. Or if it's getting swiped under the rug." His words are heavy; he looks tired, and I understand. I understand the system isn't perfect. I know that more than anyone.

His phone rings, and he answers it with a bark. "Yeah." Someone talks on the other end, and Benson groans. "Fuck, thanks, Jennica." He puts his phone away. "I'm gonna go change. It's definitely today. Go there now because it looks like our little vigilantes went on a hunt a little earlier than planned."

A few minutes later, he exits his bedroom dressed in civilian clothes. "Take the key. You can stay here while you're in town. I don't think Dancing Pony will have a room for a few days. They had a new movie come out or something, so they'll be swamped."

"You sure it's okay?" I grab the keys and shake them in the air.

"Yeah," he waves me off. "I have three extra bedrooms; take whichever you want."

"Thanks."

"No, thank you." He pulls on his coat and shoes and walks outside. "See you there," he yells over his shoulder.

I get dressed and lock the house up. The drive to the bar takes about thirty minutes. The place is super busy, and I take a table in the corner and make friends with a couple huge dudes who come to sit with me.

I pay for their drinks and make sure to constantly walk to the bar and back to my seat, bringing attention to our table and how drunk we are. Then three more guys join, and the party becomes so loud even I can't figure out who's been here from the start. About two hours later, when the guys at my table are wasted and barely remember their own names, Kenneth, Justin, and Mark walk inside.

To say that two out of three of the newcomers are surprised to see me would be an understatement, but they quickly regain themselves and start acting along.

A quick assessment shows Mark and Justin's knuckles bloodied, their pupils dilated, and their gazes crazed and rapid. I walk them over to our table, where our two wasted friends greet them like we're all a big happy family. Kenneth is collected and professional.

He scans the room and says under his breath to no one in particular, "Good job."

We all did well tonight, judging by the satisfied looks on Justin and Mark's faces.

I give Mark a side hug. "Now would be a good time to go and powder your nose." I nod at his hands. He follows my gaze and hides them under the table.

"Good idea. Coming, Justin?"

"Yeah," he says and rises from his chair.

"Are you gonna hold each other's hands?" One of our new friends' cackles, and Justin laughs back. It's forceful and unnatural—no Oscar for him, for sure.

"Yeah, can't let him out of my sight." He and Mark disappear, and Kenneth calls my name.

"I owe you one," he says firmly as I face him.

"No, you don't." I roll my eyes. "I came to the bar to get drunk like I usually do. It's just another Wednesday for me."

"I do," he repeats firmly.

"I'll never call in a favor for that. Forget about it."

He gives me a thumbs-up and sniffs a glass in front of him.

"You got anything lighter than this?"

I rise to my feet to grab us some water. "Coming right up."

<hr>

A few hours later, Justin and Mark are dropped off at their places. I saw a glimpse of Kayla through the window of

Justin's condo, but I sure hope she didn't see me. I don't want to lie to her, and I can't give her an explanation, as it's not mine to give. We reach Benson's home well past midnight.

"I'm gonna go to the station tomorrow. It's my day off, but we have to interview a new hire, and I'm going straight to my parents' place. I can pick you up on my way if you want."

"Sounds good. I'm still not quite sure why I was invited," I say, befuddled. I was somewhat shocked when Alex called me a couple of days ago and said that his stepmother had asked him to invite me over. She doesn't even know me; why would she want me in her house?

"Because you're Alex's friend, and he talks about you. A lot." Then he pauses. "Alex. Talks a lot." He raises a brow, letting his words sink in, and I smirk.

"Yeah, that's new."

"Exactly," he replies, taking off his boots. "Mom is impressed. So yeah, you can't get out of that."

"Wouldn't dream of it."

"You just wait." He lets out a tired laugh. "It's gonna be a mess. My father will make sure to fuck it up. He and Alex don't get along very well."

"That I've heard." I don't add that that's pretty much all I've heard about him.

Alex didn't really talk about his family much during our years in the Navy because he didn't consider himself a part of one. I know that his father had an affair with his mother while still married to his current wife. Alex's mother died when he was a teenager, and he came to live with his father and his family. I believe he just decided to reconcile with them recently, and I'll bet my left nut it was influenced by his girlfriend Freya. She's a foster child and wants to have a big family. Good for him.

"But you hadn't heard about us?" he asks half-hopefully, half-sadly. He already knows the truth.

I smile in response. "A little. I've heard about your little sister and brother. Mostly your sister, though." I don't know her name, but I don't say that. On those rare occasions when Alex talked about his family, he mainly mentioned some shenanigans his little sister or brother did. I believe they're close in age and used to get into trouble at school.

He said she had hero syndrome and wanted to protect every bullied kid starting from kindergarten, and her brother was the one who got his hands dirty when the message wasn't received. Every time he mentioned her, he called her one of those cute things a brother would call a sister, and I never questioned it. Neither of us liked to talk about home, so we took what either of us was willing to share.

"Figures. Alex adores her." Then he gives me a pointed look and adds, with a smirk, "Secretly. I think he only tolerated her because I was about the same age, and we didn't get along, and Aiden, the youngest, was a little shit and pissed everyone off." He chuckles at some memory, his gaze wavering. "Besides our sis. They did get in trouble together, for sure. Nothing's changed, by the way—Aiden's still pissing everyone off." He chuckles again, sounding oddly affectionate. "It got better, though. You should have seen our first dinner together. What a fucking disaster it was."

He shakes his head with sad laughter.

"Thank God Freya was there. She always acts like a buffer."

"You should have seen my family dinners." I walk to the fridge and pull out two bottles of water.

"Were they bad too?" he asks as I pass him one.

"Bad would be an understatement." My brows jump as always when my family is mentioned. It's like a damn tick, I swear. "My mother is a proper British lady. You know, those unrealistic ones you see on TV, where they don't have any emotions, drink tea twenty-four-seven, and don't accept any flaws." I take a sip from the bottle and let out a bitter laugh. "And I've got plenty of those."

"I wondered for a moment if your accent was Australian or something."

"Nah, British. Eighteen years with my mother left a footprint. I've been trying to ditch it, but it appears here and there." I shrug.

"Makes sense," he agrees. "What about your dad?"

"He died when I was nineteen." A lump forms in my throat at the mention of the only person who held me together.

"I'm sorry." He sounds sincere, so I nod, accepting it.

That's where the conversation dies, and I'm about to walk to the bathroom when Kenneth asks, "Wait, how did you serve in the Navy?"

I turn back to find him looking confused, his brows furrowed.

"My dad was American. Came from old money. I moved with him when I was eighteen."

"Why wait so long?"

"He didn't have custody." I bite back the bitter memories. "When I was old enough to leave, I did."

"Shit, I'm sorry."

"Yeah." I roll my lips. "I'd've left earlier, but my mother severed all communication between us, so I thought he just didn't want me, you know."

Suddenly, I feel uncomfortable with oversharing and

turn to head back toward the bathroom when Kenneth stops me.

"I'm sorry, man."

I turn to face him. "What are you sorry for?" He already said that, and I don't know why he keeps mentioning that.

"That you only got to spend one year with your old man." His voice is coarse.

I nod and hurry to the bathroom. That's gotta be one of the top things I'm sorry about, too—I wish I didn't listen to my mother and had gone to find my dad before she got to me too much. I've always been a difficult, rebellious kid, but she suppressed all the feelings I might have had, and I never learned how to deal with my emotions.

She has this ability to destroy a person just by looking at them, and she often used it on me just as my brain was developing. I guess I can 'thank' her for contributing to what I am now.

She used to hide me in my room like a freak whenever guests visited. Even during dinners with her family, she didn't utter a word to me, hating my very presence.

I still don't know why she kept me and didn't just ship me away to my dad. I guess it was a power play, because when I met my dad, he told me he'd been trying to contact me for years, and she prevented it every single time. Eventually, she even filed a police report, and he was banned from coming to the country.

Since I came to meet him a month—because that's how long it took me to find him in the States—after I turned eighteen, I haven't been back to England because of her, even though I miss the country and its great fuckin' beer.

She calls me from time to time when she needs something from me—usually money—and that's about it. She comes from money too, but her spendings know no limit.

I've stopped picking up the phone when any British number shows up on my screen because every minute talking to her brings me closer to the edge of insanity.

Yeah, that's a bad way to finish a day of small victories. *Fuck you, mother.*

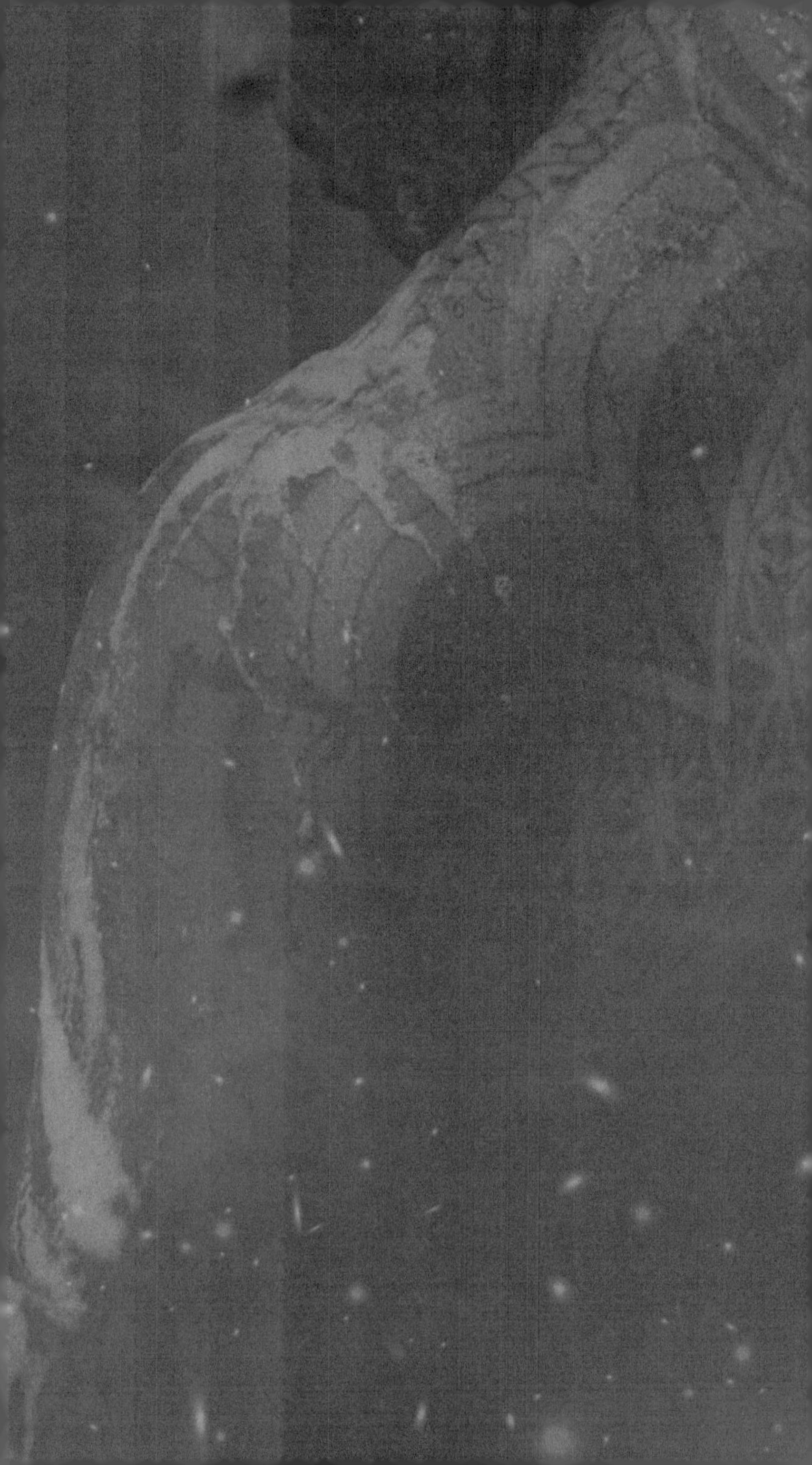

Chapter Four

A RCHIE

We drive to the house in Kenneth's police cruiser, and it's weird to be in the passenger seat and not in the back of it. I acted out a lot when I was a teenager and often found myself in trouble with the police. The type of trouble that gets you booked overnight.

To tell the truth, I'm a little nervous, and I don't know why. It's not like I'm some teenager meeting my girlfriend's parents—which I'd never done, by the way—but I'd imagine the feeling would be the same. Maybe it's because Alex is like family to me, and I've never met anyone from his real family besides Kenneth. And we served many years together. Or maybe it's because I don't actually know what a normal family looks like.

So, when Alex called and told me that I was invited to dinner at his parents' house, I took time with my wardrobe.

And that's precisely why I'm currently feeling like a total moron, wearing a dark-gray button-down and black pants while Kenneth wears comfy pants and a sweater.

When we park, he turns to face me.

"I apologize for anything that might happen here." He nods at the house with a slight wince.

I laugh. "You don't have any hope for your family?"

"I love them, but I stopped expecting normal meals a long time ago. So yeah, sorry for everything in advance." He sighs resignedly.

I take in the beautiful, homey house. White brick covers the front of the building, and a cute bench sits next to the burgundy front door. The perfectly shaped bushes lining the sidewalk are covered in snow. The front yard is adorned with Christmas decorations, and electric candles twinkle in every single window. It looks like the perfect home to me, so I don't know what Kenneth is talking about.

"Whatever happens, it can't be worse than mine. Trust me." I get out of the car and look around.

The neighborhood is just as perfect: Christmas trees and Santas everywhere.

"You might eat your words later." Kenneth draws my attention to him. Leaning against his cruiser, he sends me a funny look. I just smile and gesture to go inside.

"It's cold here. Let's go."

"I don't see you shivering." His eyes narrow, and I laugh again.

Fuckin' cop.

"Let's go." I keep laughing as we walk toward the house, and I feel his stare on my back, assessing me.

Once we're at the door, he whips it open, stepping inside. "Mom, we're here!" he yells.

A small ball of ginger curls, supposedly Kenneth's mom, rushes to greet us.

...And I get hit by a strong case of déjà vu—she reminds me of someone. Someone I've met recently but can't forget. Such a weird and unwelcome memory coming out of nowhere.

The woman wipes her hand on her stained apron and offers her hand. "I'm Stella. And you must be Archie?"

"Yes, ma'am," I reply and give her small hand a gentle shake. I feel like a fucking elephant next to her, and I eye Kenneth who's even bulkier than I am. It's unbelievable that such a tiny human could produce him.

"Everyone's already here," she announces cheerfully and gestures somewhere behind her.

"Are we late?" Kenneth glances at his wristwatch.

"No," she waves him off. "Everyone is early today for a change." She sends me a conspiratorial wink, and I smile back as if I understand what she means. "Let's go."

She puts her hand on my shoulder and nudges me forward, so I follow her lead. It's pretty quiet here for everyone to be "already here." I only hear one voice belonging to Freya. No one else is talking.

When we step into the living room, the tension is so thick that it can be cut with a knife.

Alex sits in a chair, a deep line between his furrowed brows, his hand resting on Freya's lower back. Planted on the armchair next to him, she chirps away some nonsense as she usually does when she's nervous.

An older man who looks a lot like Alex and Kenneth sits in the other chair, the same look on his face as on Alex's. His eyes are trained on the wall in front of him. A young man who reminds me of young Alex in both looks and attitude is planted at the table, glued to the phone in his hands. I can see the family resemblance among everyone here.

"You know Freya." Stella draws my attention back to her. "This is Keith." She points to the older man. "Well, and that's Kenneth." Then she adds with a cackle, "I didn't know you guys were friends."

"I didn't either," Alex says, eyes narrowed a little. It's the first thing he's said since we showed up.

I give him a half-smile, mentally urging Stella to continue introductions and save me from the incoming interrogation.

"Aiden is right there," she tells me, eyeing him. "Drop your phone," she scolds him.

He rolls his eyes but puts the phone face down on the table. "'Sup."

I nod at him, seeing so much Alex in him. He came to the service just like that, angry and bitter but able to follow the rules.

"And this is Leila."

...A bucket of cold water is dumped over my head.

And a second bucket follows as Stella points to the silent woman sitting on the low window. She's half-hidden behind a heavy curtain. Her long, red hair is thrown over her right shoulder and lies across her chest in soft waves. A thick book is open in her hands. Her eyes are wide, her mouth slightly ajar.

"Leila, this is Archie, Alex's friend from the military."

"Archie?" she asks, her voice small.

"Yeah. Archie. Hi," I reply firmly, not giving her any indication that I recognize her. It's an asshole move, but a needed one to survive this dinner. It's going to be tough. I should have listened to Kenneth's warning.

"Hi, *Archie*," she says, stressing the name. Her face is

full of disgust, and I can't tell if it's because she's mad that I pretended not to remember her or because of what she witnessed on the bridge and what happened after. I'd be pissed, too, if she forgot the kiss. Because I haven't.

"Alright!" Stella claps her hands excitedly. "Now that everyone is here, let's go eat. I spent the whole day cooking, so you all better clean your plates or else."

I don't remember when I last ate a homemade meal. I would be excited about it if not for the hot glare from the little ginger. She avoids looking at me, but every so often, her stare lands on the side of my face, and when I look, her nose scrunches as if she smells something foul, and she turns away.

At the table, everyone takes their assigned spots. I wait for everyone to be seated so Stella can point out where I should sit. Keith sits at the head of the table, and to his left are Alex, Freya, and Aiden. Opposite them are Leila, me, and Kenneth.

Fuck.

Stella runs around the table serving everyone food and chirping nonstop. I haven't seen her stop moving for a moment.

"Mom—" Kenneth wants to say something; his voice is annoyed, but he's interrupted by Leila.

"Ken," she calls quietly for only him to hear. When he looks at her, she subtly shakes her head. The sheriff purses his lips and nods curtly, surprising the hell out of me.

The food in front of me looks like a hill I'd be happy to die on, but I can't swallow a single piece because of the woman to my left. She's tiny, but her presence is large. She moves a carrot on her plate without taking a single bite of anything.

"You better start fuckin' eating because mom is getting upset that you don't like it," Kenneth hisses to my right.

Oh shit—that was never my intention. In fact, it's the opposite. I'm so grateful for the invitation to be included, yet I behave like an ungrateful asshole. So, I dig into my food, and for a moment, I forget that I should be embarrassed and uncomfortable. Because this, right here, is what heaven might taste like—like a homemade beef roast with crunchy veggies.

Besides that, the tension at the table is thick without me making it worse. Alex and his father clearly have never resolved their issues. Ever since the service, Alex never talked much about his family. I knew he was forced to live with his father and his family when his mother died, but Alex never shared much. Neither did I, and that's why we bonded there.

Right now, Alex is being Alex. Every so often, his father throws him a heavy stare, making him a beastly Alex—and that's someone I don't want to witness today.

I watch Leila through my peripheral like a hawk, expecting her to throw a fit at some point. That's what women usually do when guys upset them, but she's quiet. She just picks on her food and subtly watches everyone at the table.

Stella and Freya chat about Freya's PTSD center and how much it's grown since opening. Kenneth is devouring everything on the table. Keith's brows droop lower with every look he sends Alex's way while Alex methodically chews his beef. I must admit, it's an interesting dinner.

Finally, Alex places his utensils to the side and clears his throat, drawing everyone's attention. Then he drops a bomb.

"We are getting married."

Freya's eyes widen. She turns to him. "A little warning the next time, Boo Bear," she hisses.

He turns to her. "What next time? We are getting married fuckin' once. There will be no next time for you, woman."

Stella covers her mouth with her hands in silent excitement. Big tears run down her freckled cheeks.

Kenneth drops his fork on his plate with a loud bang and draws everyone's attention.

"Pay up," he says, stretching his arm out, palm open.

Leila rolls her eyes and digs into the back pocket of her jeans, produces a twenty, and reaches over me toward Kenneth. Her forearm grazes my chest, and she quickly pulls away as if it burned her. She drops the money into Kenneth's palm and retracts back into her seat, attempting to avoid touching me like the plague.

Then their father follows and does the same. Aiden groans and digs into his pocket, taking a dollar out.

"I'm nineteen bucks short."

I glance at his mischievous face—the dude is funny.

"Pay up." Kenneth wiggles his palm. Aiden rolls his eyes, takes a twenty out of his pocket, and drops it into Kenneth's hand.

"What the fuck is happening?" Alex asks with furrowed brows as Freya bites her lip, trying not to laugh.

"What is happening, brother, is that I am the only one who still has faith in you." Kenneth dramatically counts his money, folds the banknotes, and puts them into his pocket. Then with the satisfied look of a cat who just ate a canary, he leans against the back of his chair and crosses his hands over his stomach with a wide smile.

Alex shakes his head, trying to hide his amusement. I'd

expect an outburst from the old Alex, and this new one is clearly a stranger to me.

"Yeah, you're getting old, ya know. Shouldn't wait any longer." Aiden wiggles his brows at his brother and gets a smack on the back of his head from him.

I quickly glance at Leila, wanting to see her reaction the most. She has a beautiful, secret smile on her bright face as she watches their interaction without saying a word.

A loud sob stops everyone, and we all turn toward Stella, who's wiping her eyes with her linen napkin.

"Mom, what happened?" Alex asks, and Stella sobs even more.

My head whips toward Alex, and his good cheek, the one without a burn scar, turns pink. No, not pink—bright red. He just called his stepmom he used to hate 'mom.' One of the few things he said about his family during his time in the Navy was that he didn't want to go home because he had an 'evil stepmother' there. As far as I can see, the tables have turned, and Stella looks the furthest thing from evil to me. Trust me, I know. I grew up with one.

A subtle sniffle to my left makes me instantly switch my attention to Leila. Her eyes are watery, and her nose is red. But she looks happy, so I let out a sigh of relief. I can't explain why my heart skipped a beat when I thought she was upset and crying.

"I'm so happy!" Stella sobs. "So, so happy!"

"Alright, alright," Keith says, subtly wiping his pink nose. "Congratulations, son. You finally grew some balls."

Everyone at the table freezes, expecting Alex to go ballistic. My old muscle memory works, and my body tightens, preparing to drag him away if needed. There were too many stories from when Alex couldn't control himself, and shit hit the fan. But it looks like he managed it, since he lets out a loud chuckle, throwing his arm over Freya's shoulders.

"It was about time," he says.

I feel Kenneth and Leila relax next to me. Kenneth leans back in his chair, letting out a relieved sigh, and Leila wipes her palms on her jeans.

"That's right, bro." Kenneth cackles. "Can't say I don't agree with Aiden."

"You're older than me, idiot." Alex flips him off with a smile.

A cloud rolls over Kenneth as he thinks. "Oh shit, I'm not twenty anymore."

"And it's been like that for a long time, honey." Stella pats his hand on the table. "When will you find a nice girl and settle down too? I want grandchildren." Her face is twisted in a silent plea, focused on Kenneth while he manically looks around the table for support. None is offered. Instead, they're all happy he's at the center of the roast, so he clears his throat.

"So, when is the date?" he asks Alex.

I send Kenneth an appreciative glance—*sleek move, man.*

"Next Saturday," Freya spits out as fast as she can, blinking rapidly.

"What?" comes a chorus of voices, followed by "Why?"

"Well," Freya exchanges a happy look with Alex, "we're expecting."

"What?" exclaims another round of excited voices. Everyone seems surprised, but not Leila. She's sitting back in her chair silently with a knowing smirk plastered on her face as she sips her water. She's quiet again. In fact, I've never seen a woman so quiet. It's funny, considering she had so much to tell me on the bridge.

"Did you know?" I can't resist asking her, bothered by her ignoring me the whole evening.

She finally turns to me slowly, with a lifted brow. "I had my suspicions."

"Don't you always?" I whisper, a little more flirtatious than I intended, but it comes naturally.

Her brows stay arched. "Do you really wanna go there?" She licks her lips. "*Archie.*"

An inappropriate ping of excitement in my dick makes me clench my jaw, but she takes it as an act of aggression. "Yeah, didn't think so," she says, turning away.

Everyone is talking around the table, but my mind is far away. I'm fucking happy for Alex, but he was the last straw that connected me to the past. The last thread. The more I'm around him, the more I understand how much he's changed, and I can't use him as a crutch. I'll only drag him down because that's where I'm headed. It's time to check out from Little Hope.

I keep stirring in my unhappy thoughts until my name is called.

"...with Archie. What do you think?"

I lift my eyes and find everyone watching me. I clear my throat, "Sorry, what did you say?"

"I asked," Alex repeats, "if you would be my best man?"

My throat contracts and I look around the table, searching for any indication that I'm being pranked. "Me?"

"Yeah."

I find Alex's eyes, and he gives me a subtle nod.

"I thought..." I blink. "I mean, I thought Justin or Kenneth would be your best man."

"They'll be in the groom's flock. But I want you by my side," Alex states firmly.

I can't breathe. That's not what I expected. I'll fuck it

up somehow; I just know it. I want to refuse, but instead, I find myself saying, "Yeah, sure. I'll be happy to."

"Great." He nods again. "It's settled then."

They launch into a long conversation about the wedding and how small it will be. I'm only half listening since I'm trying to process the news. I never go to weddings since it's never in the cards for me. I don't want to be a Grinch and ruin all the fun, but also, I can only push myself so far—there is a limited number of smiles I have per day.

Soon I excuse myself and go to the bathroom. I wash my hands, lean on the sink, and look in the mirror. *What are you doing here? Why do you keep coming back to this small town?* I thought it would be therapeutic, but it's not. It's actually making things worse.

Here, I can see how lonely I really am and how much I don't fit in with anyone. Back home, alone in my mansion that I bought because I thought it would help me be less miserable—spoiler alert: it didn't—I can be myself. I don't need to stretch my face in a pretend smile, and I don't need to act happy all the damn time. Everyone thinks I have it all figured out, that I ride my life as a careless surfer riding a fuckin' wave, but none of those things are true.

I open the door and jump, startled—Leila leans against the wall, her arms crossed over her chest.

"All yours." I give her a lopsided smile and go to pass her by, but she stops me by calling my name. My *real* name.

"Stephan," she whispers, but she might as well be yelling.

I whip toward her and lean closer. "*Archie.* Call me Archie."

"Who is Stephan?"

"Not me." I feel my nostrils flare, and suddenly I can

smell her floral perfume. It's so subtle. Maybe it's her shampoo. I inch closer and inhale deeply.

She pulls away, her eyes rounded. "Did you just sniff me?"

"I did." I stand to my full height, dwarfing her, but she doesn't look affected by it.

"Why would you do that?"

I can flirt my way out of this, but for some reason, I don't want to do that with her. "I don't know," I answer truthfully.

Her demeanor changes instantly—she's *understanding*.

"You can tell him no, you know."

"What are you talking about?" I pretend not to understand, scared that she sees too much. She *had* seen too much.

"That you don't want to be his best man."

"Who told you I don't?" I narrow my eyes at her.

She shakes her head, disappointed, and I feel a knot form in my stomach. How the hell am I so attuned to this woman and her mood changes?

"I don't know what's going on in your life, and, actually, I don't even know you, *Archie*, but what I do know is that you're allowed to say 'no.' At some point in your life, you will have to drop this guilt-driven act and live for yourself." She keeps her eyes on mine the whole time she speaks, making me feel bare in front of her.

I breathe like a bull, not knowing what to say, and she turns to walk away, but I don't let her. I grab her hand and pull her toward me. Her back ends up pressed to the wall, my body flush to her front. It's a fuckin' bad idea—we're in her parents' house with her whole family in the dining room. It's a bad idea because I'm twice as big as her and act like a neanderthal.

The moment I think about that, I want to pull away. Making her uncomfortable is the last thing I want to do, but she surprises me—as usual—by rising on her tippytoes and getting into my face, challenging me.

"This man right here," her eyes roam my face, "can offer so much more to the world than the carefree bad boy you pretend to be."

"Pretend to be?" I inhale sharply, cursing myself for enjoying her smell too much. "Want to talk about pretending? Don't pretend to know anything about me. You think I pretend to be a bad boy?" My hand drops down and lands on her hip. "Well, I don't pretend." I press my nose into her cheek, and she lets out a gasp. *Good.* She should stay away from me, and this interaction should ensure it. "And I don't think I asked your opinion about anything. Go stick your nose in your book instead of my life."

With that, I find the willpower to push away from her, feeling like a piece of shit. It was needed, but that doesn't mean I don't regret it.

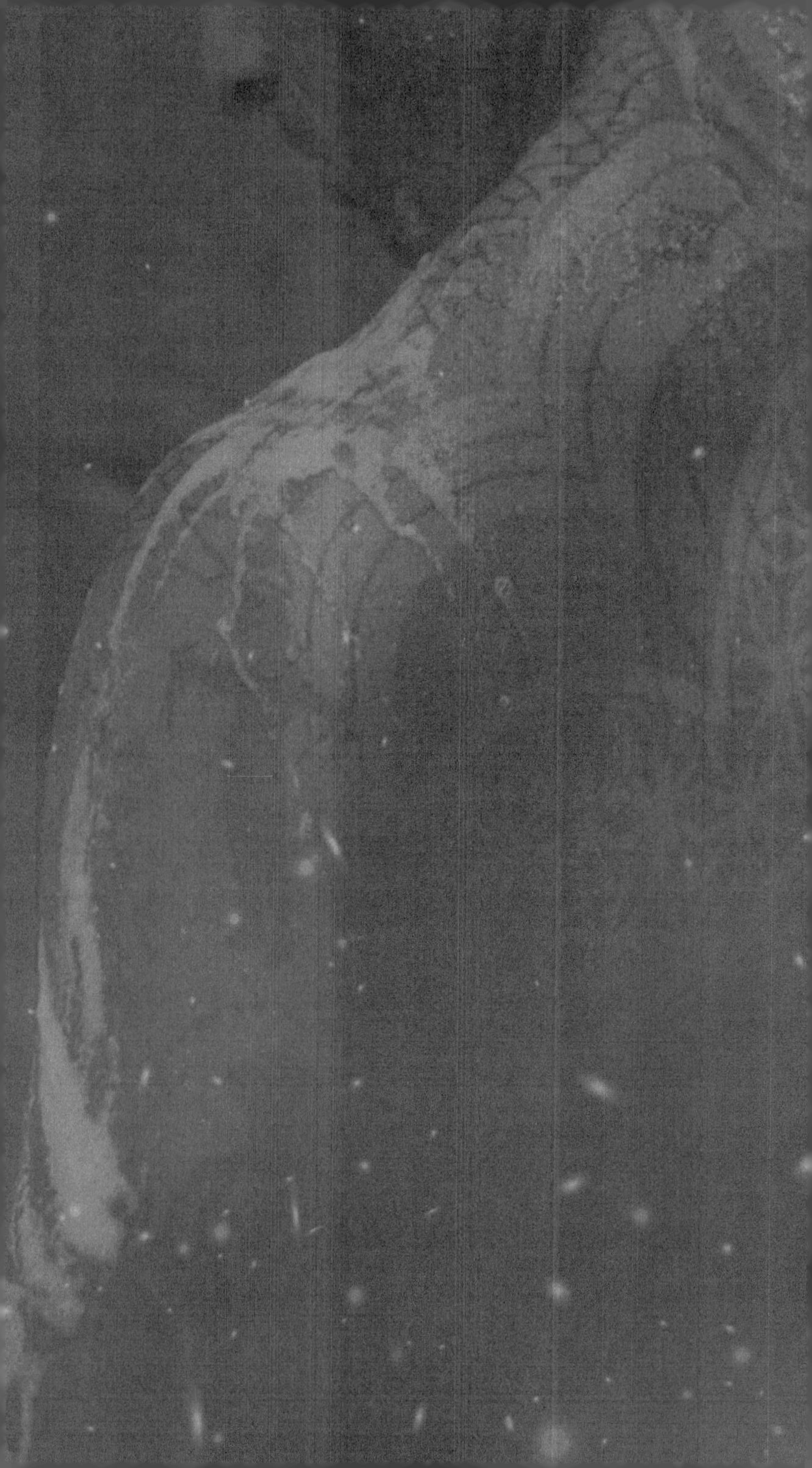

Chapter Five

L^{EILA}

The nerve of that jerk, I fume as he walks away.

To be completely fair, he didn't ask for my opinion or my help, but he got me involved regardless of what he might think when he was alone on that damn bridge, and I was driving by, not knowing that he was the man my brother talks about all the damn time. How would I, anyway? He introduced himself as *Stephan. Stephan my ass.*

God, I hate that bridge, I think as I look at the ceiling. Like truly hate that bridge. When I was a kid, one of the girls at my school wanted to jump from it because her boyfriend cheated on her. Then there was a kid who was bullied and came to the same bridge. There was an old guy who came there when his wife died. I've seen my own brother eye that bridge a few times before Freya came to town.

The thing is, even though there were a lot of bad thoughts on that bridge, nothing bad had ever actually happened, and I want to keep it that way.

The girl with the cheating boyfriend? She met a guy whose car broke down at the same time, and as far as I know, they married and moved to New York.

The bullied kid? A coach from the karate school in Springfield drove by and noticed him. Now, the bullied kid is our very own karate kid, and he won some federal-level championship. The whole town celebrated.

Then that old Irish guy. It was Kayla who noticed him. He was the regular patron of the diner she worked at, and she knew him well enough to know he needed help. Turned out the guy had a grandson. Well, before, he had a son, but it was actually his grandson who came to town and stumbled upon the diner since it's on Main Street.

When the old guy was young—*can someone give me a Pulitzer for the mind-blowing phrasing here*—his high school sweetheart moved out of town when he came back from WWII. And guess what? She was pregnant with his baby. His son died a long time ago, but his grandson had been looking for him ever since.

A great story I wanted to write about at some point, but when I met the old man, I felt like he didn't want his story to be told—he was too settled into his quiet happiness. And a good reporter should know when to back down.

The point of all of it is that I hate that bridge. Good stories with happy endings come from it, but I don't want to get involved in making it someone's end. It's too much responsibility, and I can't carry it.

And yet somehow, somewhere, I got tangled with this man who refuses to let anyone call him by his real name (even though he introduced himself to me with it) and who talks to me like, well...that.

Like *that*. Like I'm a woman and not just someone's sister. The fact that everyone around seemed to miss it.

My phone pings in my pocket, and I take it out. When I read the notification, I frown—a few weird messages have come in recently. The sender's phone number is hidden, so I can't see who it is.

I tried to ignore it at first, assuming it was some prank, but the more I get them, the more uncomfortable I become, feeling like they're sending it to the right person, and I just don't get the meaning.

> You still don't get it, do you? They told me you're smart. But I don't think you are. You like to stick your nose in places where it doesn't belong. And you must pay for it.

I look around as if hoping to find the person who's pranking me, but I don't find anyone, of course. I'm at my parents' house, after all.

Archie and his antics are immediately forgotten since I have more pressing matters.

Putting my phone back in my pocket and returning to the dining room, I can't help but notice how slowly time is moving. I just want to go back to my place and wallow in my misery alone—brought upon myself, I should add. Some people just can't help themselves, and I'm one of those people. I know I shouldn't have grated on his nerves when he was clearly on edge, but I just couldn't help myself. He was sitting there, surrounded by us, yet alone at the same time. He must be thinking he doesn't belong when in reality, he does.

And then this secret sender with that ominous message. Yes, I'm so ready to go so I can openly freak out without setting off my family's alarms.

When I get back to the table, Archie is sitting in his spot with a plastic smile on his face. My mom is sending him curious looks, but she's curious about Stephan's enigma. Well, *Archie's*, my bad.

Up until seeing him here, I thought of him by the name he introduced himself with. I think it suits him better. To be fair, it suits better the person I see, but Archie is the one whom everyone else seems to see, and I don't understand why.

His eyes scream for help when he smiles. They scream when he flirts. Even when he seems relaxed and so confident in himself, his eyes are full of melancholy. How do they not see it? I make a mental note to speak to Alex about him when I get the chance.

"Where have you been?" Aiden asks, brows furrowed.

I roll my eyes. "In the bathroom. Peeing. Am I allowed?" My brothers have always treated me like a baby. I'm older than Aiden, and I'm still questioned about bathroom breaks.

He scratches his nose with his middle finger and sticks his nose back into his phone. I wonder what's happening with him recently—I've never seen him anywhere without his device for the last couple of weeks. Another mental note to check on him. My mental list of things to do is never-ending.

When I sit back in my chair, Archie shifts his weight, so his body is facing Kenneth. I shouldn't feel offended, but I do; plus, this whole secret sender situation is playing dirty tricks on my mind, so I decide to take off. While everyone is chatting, I go to give my congratulations to Freya and Alex.

When she gives me a hug, she asks, "How did you know?"

"P-p-please!" I pull back. "Your glowing face, a widening waist while you run five miles every single day, and your aversion for Lonely Kurt." Freya loves Lonely Kurt, absolutely adores it. It's the heavy breakfast from Marina's diner she's been religiously eating for years. "Yeah, I wonder what tipped me off."

"You are too attentive to everything around you for your own good." She laughs and pats my shoulder.

"Don't I know it," I mumble, smiling. She gives me a quizzical look but lets it go. Thank God.

Then I say bye to Alex, still unsure of how much sisterly affection he wants to receive, and give Aiden a peck on his cheek. When we were younger, we used to be very close. He might be a little shit, but he is my little shit. Then I move on to mom and dad.

Finally, I go to give Kenneth a hug. He rises from his chair and envelopes me in a big, brotherly bear hug. The same one he gave me when my first boyfriend dumped me. The next day, the ex miraculously had two shiners. Or the secret one he gave me after mom and dad yelled at me for failing an exam—completely my fault, by the way. That type of hug.

"Are you alright?" he asks into the top of my head. Every man in my family dwarfs me.

"Yeah." I sniffle into his shirt. It smells like family.

"Didn't sound so," he chuckles.

"I'm really okay, Ken." With that, I pull away. "Just a little tired."

His piercing eyes watch me for another moment, and he lets go of me with a slight nod. "Let me know if it changes."

"I will." I smile at my big brother and turn to Archie, just so my attitude toward him won't raise any suspicion. "It was nice meeting you." I give him a weak smile and walk away.

When I'm inside my car and start the engine, a body shows up by the passenger window, making me scream.

"Sh-sh, chill." Archie's eyes roam my face, puffs of air coming from his mouth with every word he says.

I roll the window down. "What do you need?"

"I feel like an asshole." He rakes his hand through his hair, looking sheepish. "It wasn't my intention to end your family's dinner. I should be the one to go if you're uncomfortable."

"If I am?" I quirk a brow.

His eyes squint. "*When*. When you are uncomfortable."

"You're off the hook." I pull my hat off and place it on the passenger seat. "I didn't leave because of you."

"You left because you're tired?" He waits for me to look at him. "Yeah, I heard that part."

"Eavesdropping?" I ask accusingly.

"Not when you're practically shouting into my ear." His flirty smile is back.

I sigh loudly. "I'm tired, Archie." He winces at me using his name, and I wonder why—after all, he wanted me to call him that when he introduced himself to me today. Again. "I need to go home."

"I thought you live here." He glances at the house.

"I don't," I reply, staring ahead.

"Surprising," he says.

"Why?" I glare at him.

"I don't know." He shrugs. "Maybe because you're so young."

"I'm twenty-four. Where were you when you were twenty-four?" I challenge.

"In Iraq." His face darkens.

"Yeah, exactly. Go inside." I nod toward the house. "You'll freeze to death."

His cackle is too happy at the prospect, and for the umpteenth time I remind myself that Archie's brain works differently—his own value is nonexistent in his eyes. He suddenly leans through the window. "Go back, Leila. I was about to leave anyway."

I lean closer to him. Seems like all we do is lean toward each other. Like magnets.

"Contrary to your belief, my life doesn't revolve around you, pretty boy."

"Pretty boy?" His voice sounds seductive, and his tongue peeks out to lick his lower lip. "You think I'm pretty?"

I pull backward. "I think you like to play with fire."

"How so?"

"With all my brothers in one," I point at the house, "place. They might not like the way you speak to me and teach you a lesson."

"And I might just like that." His face stretches in a wide smile. A very scary one. Something clicks in the back of my mind: I think Alex had mentioned at some point that Archie doesn't bare visible scars; his are of a different kind. *What are they?*

I start rolling the window back up, but he puts his palm on the top and stops it. "Really, Leila. Don't leave because of me."

I let out a tired sigh and take pity on him. "It's not

because of you. I'm just—" I chew on the inside of my lip, thinking about what I can tell him, and then I decide on nothing. I can tell him nothing. "I just really need to go home."

His face changes. He becomes Stephan in front of my very eyes, the man I met on the bridge. The one who doesn't hide behind a sexy smile and swagger.

"Is it because of the message you got? What did it say?" His nostrils flare as he squeezes his jaw tight.

"How do you—" Then I stop myself and shake my head. "You know what, never mind. I really need to go."

I roll the window up, and he lets me this time. Then I hit the gas, and the front of my car slides to the side, nearly hitting him. Good thing he has quick reflexes and jumps out of the way. My heart squeezes as I dare to glance in the rearview mirror, but he's standing there watching my tail-gate with a maniac smile on his face.

Chapter Six

A RCHIE

I watch her leave, and an uncomfortable feeling settles in the pit of my stomach. Something wasn't right. I wanted to leave her opinionated self in that corridor, but something made me stay. She received a message, and after that, her whole posture changed. She became defensive, anxiously looking around, and quickly ran away. *Who was it?*

A heavy hand lands on my shoulder.

"Don't go there."

I turn to Alex, whose eyes are focused on mine.

"Don't go there, Archie. You are my brother, but I don't want you near her."

"Why?" I square my shoulders, even though I know the answer, and I know he's right—we don't go for our brothers' families, no matter what. My body language is just a dumb bravado for nothing—I don't know who I'm trying to prove anything to.

"You and me," he shakes his head, "we're not the same as the others. We didn't come back whole, and she is too young to deal with all of that. That's why I stay away—I love her from a distance. And that's how you should too." His stare is filled with heavy meaning. It screams 'stay away.'

"Don't worry; she is safe from me." I switch my attention toward the direction her car disappeared.

"I still do."

I glance at him.

"Worry," he continues. "She likes to fix broken things, and you're just about as broken as they come."

I quirk a brow—we've never beaten around the bush, but it's a little harsh even for two vets chitchatting.

"Don't give me that look," he chuckles. "You know I'm right. I came back half a man."

I shoot a glance down his front, and he punches me in the chest, laughing. "Not there, asshole. Everything is man enough there."

"You sure?"

He snorts. "Just ask Freya."

"I just might." I smile, not intending to ever start that particular conversation with his soon-to-be wife.

"Yeah, you actually might. Forget I said it." He shakes his head, most likely trying to erase the image he pictured in his mind. He looks at me, his expression somber. "But Archie, don't go there. I'm serious. She tried fixing me, but I just barked every time she said something. I just can't talk to her because she just—" he wipes his face with his hands, pressing into his eye sockets with the heels of his palms. "She's just so damn intuitive and stubborn, and she sees so fuckin' much. And when she speaks, it's always a fuckin' bull's-eye. I just don't know how to behave around her."

"Yeah, man," I side-eye him, "smooth you are not."

He gives me a heavy stare. "We both know that you've got a kink."

I raise a brow, curious how he knows about it. We sure as fuck never shared partners. To be clear, I've never shared partners with any other men I know, nor will I. Two women on the other hand...

"And what do you know about my kink?" I challenge.

"More than I care to, and I don't want my sister near it. Are we clear on this?"

I hate being ordered around—it never sits well with me. It's one of the reasons I always got in trouble in the Navy. But Alex is like family to me, and I don't want to lose him because my dick leads me the wrong way. I'd never disrespect his family like that even without his warning. Even if the temptation is strong. So strong.

I've seen beautiful woman in my life—and Leila *is* beautiful—but she is also something else. The air around her is of a different color. It's bright but has little, dark engravings, not visible to everyone. She has this aura of confidence and calmness. It clashes with her youth and purity, making her so unique. I like unique things. I like to collect them on my body in the form of art.

She is vibrant.

"We are." I finally nod, deciding to end this conversation because otherwise, it won't go anywhere good. He made his opinion known, and I accept it.

"Good," he says, looking between the house and the road she disappeared on. "Something is up with her."

"Yeah," I agree easily, as I was thinking the same thing.

"You noticed that too?" He sends me a curious look. "She came back to the table acting differently."

"Yep." I cross my arms over my chest, hoping he'll stop questioning.

No such luck. Well-deserved. "I thought it was because you said something to her," he says, voice full of snark. I bite my tongue, trying not to let out a smart-ass remark.

"I thought so too," I say instead.

"Really?" He turns to face me. "And what did you say to her?"

"Nothing that concerns you, Alex." I meet his stare with one of my own. "She's a big girl."

"And she's my sister." He gives me one just as heavy.

"I know," I say slowly, showing him I *get* it.

"Alright. Let's go back inside." He shivers. "It's fucking cold out here. I don't know how you're never cold. Fuckin' beats me, man."

"It's my British blood talking," I laugh. "It's made of ice."

"I doubt that," he mumbles under his breath, but I still hear it and decide to let it slide. Too many deep conversations for one evening.

"You're gonna be a father, huh." I eye him as I say it— I've never thought of him as a dad, but now I see it's happening. The right partner and the right time.

"Yeah." He scratches his damaged cheek. "I'll be the worst fucking dad on the planet."

I laugh and smack him on the back. "You'll be the best. I know that. Let's go."

With that, we go back to the house. Everyone moved to the living room. When I lean against the doorframe, Kenneth walks over to me, a steaming mug in his hand.

"Do we need to have a talk?" he asks tiredly.

"Alex already did."

"Good." His tone cheers up. "Saves me the trouble. I just want to add that you wouldn't be the first guy whose nose I broke for her. I'm sure you wouldn't be the last."

I send him a curious stare, surprised to hear that. Not that she got around a lot, but that whoever got her first let her go. If I was younger and cleaner and had someone like her, I'd hold onto her with all my might. No number of broken bones would stop me.

"Did she date a lot?"

Even though I think she can date anyone she wants and shouldn't be ashamed of her sexuality, the thought of her being with other people irks me. It's fuckin' hypocritical, considering the notches in my belt, but I can't help it.

"The opposite. I mean, look at us." He glances at Aiden and Alex. "No one stood a chance. Everyone was too scared to mess with the Benson's sister." He laughs quietly to himself, probably remembering something. "But there were a couple times she came home from college for holidays looking sad." Then he winks at me. "It was a fun road trip for us." He shifts his attention to Aiden. "That was the first time I saw Alex when I looked at my little brother. A damn beast, worse than him." He looks at me with a twinkle in his eyes. "Warned you our dinners are weird."

I laugh because, it's a different sort of weird than I'm used to, but weird regardless.

"It's alright."

A few moments later, Stella brings out a steaming cup and offers it to me. I look at her hand like it's a snake about to bite me. She smiles understandingly and pushes the mug toward my hand. "It's my special tea. We gather and dry herbs with Leila every summer."

I swallow the saliva and accept the offering. Leila made it.

Scratch it, fucker, her mom Stella made it, and you are in their house. You're a sick fuck.

I take a sip, and flavor bursts in my mouth. "What is that?" I ask, looking inside the mug, expecting to find the answer.

"It's lavender, mint, chamomile, and something very special." She winks.

I sniff the steam. "What's the special ingredient?"

"Love, my boy. It's love." With a huge smile, she walks away.

An annoying cackle sounds to my left—Kenneth watches me from behind the brim of his cup.

"What?" I ask.

He shakes his head and chuckles, not giving me the answer.

A couple hours later, we pull into Kenneth's driveway. I'm about to open the door when he starts speaking.

"I don't know how much you guys saw there." His sigh is heavy. "But I see that you've changed. Even though I didn't know you before, I assume whatever issues you had before the service multiplied when you came back."

I keep quiet; I don't think my answer is needed here. We both know he's right.

"I know that because my brother came back worse than he left, and trust me, that's saying a lot." The chuckle that follows is sad. "And I'm not talking about his scars. I'm talking about this." He taps his temple with his finger. "I did a couple tours and sure as fuck don't want to go back there, but you both did. Alex wanted to escape his life here, and from watching you and that story you shared, I can tell you did the same." He grips the steering wheel with one hand, and the other keeps tapping his knee. "But I just want to tell you that you've got a place here. No matter what. We know how to deal with the demons of the past. We get it." He avoids looking at me while squeezing the steering wheel tighter. "You found the right place. Little Hope does that for people."

"Does what?" I ask quietly.

After a long moment, he finally looks at me. "Gives hope."

I swallow a sudden lump in my throat the size of a basketball and nod, showing my appreciation for what he just said. I fear that my voice would waver if I spoke now.

"Still, stay the fuck away from my sister," he adds with a cackle.

I flip him off and climb out. It's going to be a fun night.

Chapter Seven

A RCHIE

It was a fun night, indeed. We got wasted on bourbon Kenneth had stashed, and I'm fucked by the queen of all hangovers. I should have gotten used to it by now, but I feel like shit every morning after drinking. It's getting worse and worse every time. I'm getting old, it seems.

Taking a few pills helps me survive the morning. And a gallon of coffee. The wedding is in a week—I didn't intend to stay that long since I have a business to run (such a pitiful excuse since I have Cherry for that), so I talk to Alex on the phone and tell him that I'll be back in a couple of days.

He doesn't want a bachelor party, saying that Freya would give birth too soon if she heard that he went to a strip club, so we opted for a chill night with drinks at Kenneth's place the night before the wedding.

The whole drive back to Boston, my mind drifts to Leila

and how she changed once she read that damn message. I need to know what it said.

When I pull into my driveway, a big empty house greets me with its cold, unwelcoming windows. I paid a shit ton of money for it, hoping it would bring me peace since it was in my father's family for many generations until he sold it.

I still don't know why—money was never an issue for him. But I'm beginning to get an idea—maybe he felt as shitty as I did here alone. I wish I could spend that one year with him in this house instead of his flat in the city. Maybe this house would feel different to me now.

He left all his money to me in the will, and the first thing I did was buy this house. He always talked about it. How he grew up here, but when his parents died, the house felt too lonely, and heavy shadows of the past lurked around every corner. He was an artist too and very sensitive to changes in the air, so he sold it. And I bought it, like an idiot, hoping to feel a bit closer to him, settling in my American roots.

Spoiler alert, though—it didn't make me feel closer to anyone. Quite the opposite, actually. I feel even lonelier here. I was thinking about getting a dog because that's what everyone does, but then I decided against it since I don't want to make the poor creature suffer in my absence.

I park my Rover and go to unlock the door. Silence greets me. It always does. I don't turn on the lights—no need; I know this house like the back of my hand, and light won't make my mood brighter. I walk to the liquor cabinet and pull out a bottle of bourbon. Dropping two ice cubes into the glass, I pour more alcohol than I probably should and drink half of it in one go. Alcohol helps me forget, but the relief is temporary. I find myself wanting to forget the very next day. So, I drink again.

My phone starts ringing. Who even calls these days? But I have a suspicion, and she would be the only one who expects an answer.

"Yes," I answer, grouchy because I'm right—it's her.

"Hello, asshole."

"Why are you calling, Cherry?" I ask with a sigh.

"Because you would never respond to my text anyway." Her tone is extra bitchy today—I must be in trouble.

I chuckle—she's right. I probably wouldn't. "What happened?"

"What happened? What happened?" Then she asks someone next to her, *"He's asking what happened? Can you believe it?"* She speaks into the phone again. *"What happened is where the fuck have you been? And why the fuck did you avoid my messages and calls?"*

"I was in Maine."

"A-a-ah, pining after the hot chick again," she singsongs.

I nearly spit out my drink. "For fuck's sake, Cherry, how many times do I have to tell you that I've never pined after Kayla."

"Well," she sighs, *"maybe you should. It would do you a ton of good."*

"Please, not you too," I groan.

"I mean, sex never hurt anyone, you know. Especially good sex."

"I get plenty of that. Leave it alone." I force a fake laugh.

"Alright," she chuckles. *"But really, boss. When are you coming back? I need you to sign some shit, and clients have been asking about you."*

"We have seven top artists in Boston, Cherry, and a few really good ones scattered across the country." I regret her not seeing me now because I'm rolling my eyes so hard. "They can manage without me."

"*Nah, boss.*" She loudly pops her bubble gum—a habit of hers I hate. "*They want your hand and your art.*"

"I haven't inked anyone in years, and I'm not planning on ruining the strike," I reply firmly, praying she'll leave me the fuck alone about it finally. We've been having this conversation at least once a week.

Another bubble pops.

"*Will you ink me?*"

"Nice try. No. Does anything need my immediate attention?"

"*We miss you.*" I can hear her pout even through the phone. "*Though you pay me handsomely to avoid complications, we just miss you. Will you stop by?*"

"Yeah," I sigh in defeat. "I will tomorrow."

"*Cool beans. See ya.*" She blows a kiss into the phone and hangs up.

Cherry has been with me for a long time—I'm talking a decade. And I don't know how I would manage my business without her. She's the sister of one of the guys who served with us and didn't make it.

We emailed back and forth while I was there, and when I came back, I made sure she was taken care of, knowing their living situation sucked. And that's how I found myself ten years later with the most loyal person in my life. I also know that she's destined for bigger things, but she doesn't leave to explore them. I'm dragging her down along with me.

And the thing about Kayla? Yeah, Cherry has been crushing on her since the moment Kayla stepped foot into my parlor. It was hilarious to see how Cherry tried to sway her, but Kayla was too in love with her dickhead of a now fiancé and didn't pay her much romantic attention.

Good fucking thing Cherry moved on because she lost her sleep over it. She legit had cartoon eyes every time Kayla walked in, and I need this woman because she's the only thing that's holding my business together at this point ever since I lost all interest in it.

Since Cherry is doing everything, there was no need for me to come home, but I couldn't stay in Little Hope any longer during their pre-Christmas chaos. Everyone has a family, and I don't belong there. I belong here, in this empty, cold house, with a bottle in my hand. And when, if not the holidays, does a lonely person feel the loneliest? Never.

I rise from the chair I'm sitting on, and the dog tags click under my shirt. I grab them with my hands, remembering why I'm still here and why I do what I do, so I go to my laptop and initiate another wire transfer to the organization that supports fallen vets' families. It makes me feel better. Well, not better, but less shitty.

Then I pick up my phone and browse the names of women I hook up with when the mood strikes.

Well, maybe this one. She is a feisty redhead. Nope. This one. Redhead too. I browse two more before I realize I'm stopping on redheads only. I didn't know I even knew so many. But every time my finger hovers over the 'send' button, I pause.

I don't want just any redhead. I want one redhead who radiates fuckin' sunshine that pisses me off. I want to swallow and absorb all that light, hoping it will make me see in color too. I want to drink her purity, hoping it will free me of my darkness.

And then a wave of hate sweeps over me for the thoughts I'm having. Everything that pops into my mind is selfish and aims to make *me* feel better, with not a thought about how *she'd* feel with such a shithead like myself around. Alex was right to warn me off. He was so right.

I throw my phone on the couch and lean my head against the back of it, looking at the ceiling. How long can I go like this? Why do I need to go on like this?

These questions are not new to me, and as usual, they don't come with answers, so I take the bottle I brought with me and don't bother with a glass anymore.

Chapter Eight

L EILA

It's been four days since the dinner at my parents', and I still can't stop thinking about it. My brother finally pulling his head out of his ass and getting married before Freya changes her mind came unexpectedly.

As a family who likes to make bets because life in a small town is boring, we made a bet about when Alex would finally man up, and my vote was on him asking her before Halloween. He seriously let me down by waiting longer, so Kenneth won. Bummer for me since Kenneth never wins any bets, and here he came out victorious with that smug look of a big brother who's always right.

I don't know if her being pregnant had something to do with the decision, but it didn't come as a surprise. Well, to most of us. Kenneth and I talked about it; he noticed little signs way before Freya did. It's part of his job that's engraved so deep into his bones he can probably deduct anything in his sleep.

I still got a surprise at the dinner, though—officially meeting Archie. *Stephan, my ass.* Now I want to know what his real name is. Is it Stephan? Is it Archie?

Those are two completely different men. Completely. I like Stephan more, and I got a glimpse of him in the corridor. No mask on—a real person with real feelings, not that artificial shit he puts on for show. No. He showed a bit of the real him I connected with on the bridge.

But he also has another side—a scary one. Intense. Fearless. Crazy. He evokes fear deep inside my belly. The type of fear that excites and grades on your nerves in a good way, making you tingle in all the right places, like the anticipation of unfolding his layers and seeing what else he's got. It excited me on some primitive level I didn't even know existed.

Don't get me wrong, I love good sex; I just never had it *that* good that I forgot about everything, including my family in the dining room. And when he pressed me into that wall...that moment woke something in me, and I suddenly remembered that I've dreamt about having a night with a man like that. Something new has awakened. I wanted to push him back and aggravate him just so I could see how far he'd go.

I'm one hundred percent positive sex with him would be unforgettable. That bad-boy slash tortured-man vibe he has going is my kryptonite. I didn't expect him to rip my clothes off and press me into the wall in the corridor of my parents' house, of course, but the anticipation was so delicious, I couldn't help myself from poking the bear.

Okay, fine. Maybe I *was* hoping for the ripping of clothes part a little. Just a tiny bit.

So, that was an interesting find for me, and now I crave the feeling he caused. Did I do the right thing by leaving? Did I look immature in his eyes? He probably got used to other types of women: self-confident and sophisticated, who followed the plan they started—everything I am not.

But that night was just full of different sorts of surprises, and what didn't come as a good one was him being *the* Archie, the very same friend my brother adores. Well, as much as Alex can adore, you know. They served together for many years in the Navy.

To be honest, I don't even know how long since Alex never talks about his time there. He enlisted after high school when I had just entered the teen stage, and I assume the same happened with Archie. They both got caught in that explosion that damaged about thirty percent of my brother's body. And while my brother's self-hatred is somewhat understandable to regular folks with his burns all over his face, Archie doesn't wear visible scars. Maybe he has some too—I don't know—but his whole presence is dark, screaming of a different sort of damage. His scars are on the inside; I feel that.

Also, Alex has a lot of survivor's guilt. I don't see Archie being any different. Especially considering he's the only one who got away alive and unscarred, at least on the outside.

Enigma indeed.

I sigh loudly and look toward the entrance door of my house. Since that dinner, I get more and more uncomfortable with every passing hour. The messages keep coming, and they've turned threatening. I rake my mind, trying to figure out who it might be, but I'm drawing a blank. The texts have made me paranoid, though—I check all doors and windows ten times before I go to bed. When I come home, I check all the rooms, ensuring there are no hidden guests in any of them.

I glance at the door again before opening the fridge to grab a bottle of apple juice and instantly bang my forehead—very lightly, because I still have two brain cells left to rub together, which may come as a big surprise—on the stainless steel.

What have I become? A paranoid, timid creature, constantly checking the entrance door as if a SWAT team is about to burst through it. What's next? Getting a security system in our small town? I mentally roll my eyes, imagining the looks from my neighbors when men in black come to install cameras on my property (well, my rented property).

Mrs. Ludwig, the lady living to the left of me, will have to stop throwing her dog's shit into my backyard, and Mr. Crocks to my right will have to stop stealing the newspaper I'm paying a subscription for. He drops it back off a day later with coffee stains all over it.

I have charming neighbors.

Today we're having a bachelorette party for Freya at Marina's diner. They're closing an hour earlier so we can eat some nice, greasy food and talk crap about everyone. Well, everyone else will talk, and I'll be listening as usual.

I shower and get dressed four hours before the agreed-upon meeting time since I promised Kayla that I'd pick her up to drive to Springfield to get the penis-shaped cupcakes. We decided against ordering local because we didn't want to give our eighty-year-old town baker a stroke with our unusual order.

By the time I park in front of Justin's garage and honk, I'm a nervous wreck. Kayla has been working for Archie in his parlor for a couple of years now, and I think they've known each other even longer. And her being in my car with all that knowledge seems to unsettle me.

It's not like I plan to interrogate her, but people tend to spill secrets in my presence. A very useful power for a reporter, but not so much for my personal life—I'm like a vault of town secrets. If even a tenth of it ever gets out, the whole town will go down.

With a wide smile on her face, Kayla parks her butt in the passenger seat and smacks the door shut so hard the whole car shakes. She looks at me, her face made up in full glam, her hair is artfully braided in some style I'll never be able to manage.

I eye her back carefully, mentally apologizing to my dear, loyal car for her. "Jeez, who pissed in your cereal this morning?"

"It's Cherry," she says, clicking her tongue and throwing her braid to the front of her chest.

"Who's Cherry?" I pull off the curb.

"She's Archie's friend," she answers and digs into her bottomless bag. I'm grateful she doesn't notice how the car nearly swerves at her words.

My hand squeezes the steering wheel harder.

"His girlfriend?" I try to ask as calmly as possible.

"No," she snorts, and I relax. "She's his manager. Cherry oversees the chain of his parlors. Don't know how they work it out, but she's a dog with a bone when it comes to business."

"He has a chain of parlors?" I ask, surprised, glancing at her in wonder.

"Yeah." She gives me a dubious look. "You didn't know?"

I shake my head.

"Yeah, like, he has a ton of locations in the States and franchises in a few countries."

I quirk a brow at her, and she laughs.

"What? The dude is rich. You didn't know?"

I shake my head again, and she continues, looking impressed with me falling out of the rumor mill, "Did you know that he paid for my classes in full?"

I send her a curious look.

"Yep." She leans her head back on the leather seat. "We agreed to a contract that I would be working exclusively for him for five years after I graduate. That was the only term. But we actually never signed anything, and he just paid in full for the whole thing anyway." She waves her hand in the air. "I was shocked."

I'm not. I knew he was like that.

"Not anymore, though; I'm not surprised," she continues, oblivious to me side-eyeing her. "I mean, for the time I've known him, he's donated to so many charities. I'm surprised he has anything left at this point. And he buys gifts for everyone all the time. And pays for everything. Like, everything." Her eyes widen to accentuate how amazed she is as she looks at me. "Hank's son, the guy in the Boston salon," she clarifies since I have no idea who Hank is, "needed a hip surgery because he got hurt during his football game at school. Boom." She snaps her fingers. "Archie paid for it. So yeah, he does a lot of things like that."

Makes total sense to me—besides being a genuinely good guy and wanting to help people, he's trying to pay off some sort of moral debt he's tied himself to.

Suddenly Kayla frowns. "How did I get to telling you this story?"

"You started talking about Cherry," I answer with a chuckle.

"Right." Another snap of fingers. "So, we kind of became friends." Kayla's voice wavers a bit, and I send her a curious look. "What?" she asks, a little too defensively. "Well, she might have a tiny crush on me." Her cheeks turn red, and I can tell Kayla is enjoying it. Good for her, I hope Justin sweats a little—he sure deserves it; the whole town would agree on that. "But anyway, she called me this morning and asked to keep an eye on Archie."

"Why?" My head whips toward her, and she cries out, pointing ahead,

"Watch the damn road, would ya?"

I instantly turn back to the road, mentally rolling my eyes at the drama queen next to me.

"Why did she ask you to keep an eye on him?" I repeat the question.

"I have no idea." She shrugs. "It's Archie, you know. He has everything figured out, so I don't see how I can help."

I glance at her, trying to figure out if she speaks this way so I don't suspect anything. Nope, she really thinks he's put together. *Oh, Archie, you need an Oscar for your performance in fooling everyone.*

She lets out a heavy sigh. "Justin was bummed he wasn't the best man."

"Yeah?"

"Yeah." She looks out the window. "He wanted to do this huge bachelor party with strippers and all that."

I cackle, imagining his crestfallen face when Alex told him. "Maybe that's the reason he wasn't chosen?"

"I told him the same." Her laugh is contagious, and I find myself joining her. "I still think he'll do the party."

"Freya will kill him."

"Told him the same." She waves her hand in the air.

"The man doesn't listen." She sits silently for a few seconds before speaking again. "Though I understand why Alex chose Archie."

I don't interrupt, letting her find her own words, feeling like she needs to talk it through.

"They lived through something out there that irrevocably changed them both. I think they both need closure, and that brotherhood, or whatever it is, will help them."

I agree, nodding. But what happens when they find this closure? Alex will move on with his life, and what about Archie? I'm a little scared to venture down that road.

We don't chat about anything of substance the rest of the way. Well, again, Kayla chats, and I nod and shake my head at all the right places, preferring to let her carry on the conversation. Especially when she just wants to vent about certain things. People do that around me.

When we arrive at the diner, we place little cartoon dicks everywhere. A full-sized shirtless cardboard cutout of Freya's favorite actor with steely abdominal muscles, a wide toothy smile, and a blond ponytail greets everyone at the door. I eye him suspiciously—he is the furthest thing from Alex as they come. To be honest, he reminds me of Justin. A little too much, and I shudder.

Cupcakes of all different penis shapes, sizes, and colors are artfully displayed in the shape of—you guessed it—a penis on the bar table. Drinks are ready to be served: a pitcher of virgin Margarita for Freya and a few alcoholic ones for everyone else. Marina cooked a few appetizers for everyone when she closed the diner. We are all set for a quiet, family-like celebration.

Soon ladies begin coming in. Donna, the owner of the local coffee shop—well, a Dunkin' that may or may not deal some of the best home-roasted beans you'll ever find under the table—walks in first. My mom—weird but okay. Alicia, Justin's sister, comes in, looking super sad, with their mom.

Emma from the Dancing Pony, wearing an elegant elvish outfit and ears, of course. She's a few years older than me, and I don't think I've ever seen her without those ears, even in school. It all became a part of her personality. I can't imagine her without any of it, and I respect her for standing her ground even when school bullies deemed her weird.

There are a few other locals that Freya became friends with, plus a few people she probably doesn't know, but others invited them. But that was expected, so we got extra food and drinks.

Everyone brought gifts even though we told them that it's not a wedding but a bachelorette party, and we'll just be drinking. No one listened, of course. So, here we are, loading gifts in the trunk of Freya's new SUV. Since the weird situation with Freya's first car when she showed up in Little Hope, Alex can't stop changing her vehicles. He buys her a new model every single year. I can't imagine what will happen when the little one is born—he'll turn into a grizzly papa bear, buying out every single minivan in the state.

Everyone takes pictures with the shirtless actor, and by the time the Margarita pitchers dry out, the pictures become risqué. So far, me and Freya are the only people who don't drink. When my mom throws her leg over the actor's waist, I regret not having a glass. Or five.

I longingly glance at the leftovers of Margarita and then at Freya, who looks like she wants to bury herself under a pile of blankets in her house and be done with this party. Leaving her the only sober person to watch after everyone else would be cruel, so I let out a loud sigh and go back to watching my mom and another respectful lady of our fine town humping the cardboard dude.

Two timid, elegant women my ass. I cross my arms over my chest and laugh to myself. We should have events like this more often so people can let go and have some fun—a thing we lack in this small town. So far, gossip, coffee, and good pancakes are our main weaknesses.

Everyone left, and only a few people stayed to help clean up. It's actually better this way; otherwise, we would be bumping into each other.

We're all cleaning as Kayla smacks her forehead with an open palm, scaring the ever-loving crap out of me—I'm so on edge these days. "Oh shoot, I forgot!" she exclaims.

"What?" I ask.

"We were supposed to pay the rest of the money for the order."

"And you didn't?"

"I forgot." Her cheeks turn pink. She's a very responsible person. Usually. But not today. Today, her brain checked out, and she's already tipsy.

"Can you pay online?" I ask, hopeful.

"Have you seen the place?" She quirks a brow.

True. The place was very clean and nice, and the penises were delicious, but the owner sure hasn't gotten with the times, as her place doesn't even accept cards. Cash only. Gotta love it.

"Fine," I sigh, knowing where it's going. She's tipsy, everyone else is nearly drunk, and Freya is pregnant. I was the only one who didn't drink, so I have no choice. "I'll drive."

"Thank you, thank you!" She claps her hands. "I'll get you the money."

She disappears into the back room, and I keep wiping the tables.

"Thank you," comes a quiet voice.

"For what?" I turn to Freya.

"For doing all of this." She smiles and keeps collecting glasses from the tables.

"It's not me. It's everyone."

She sighs and straightens her posture, rubbing her lower back. "You know what I mean."

I glance at her tired face and decide not to beat around the bush. "No problem," I say with a smile. "You're stuck with us now, a part of our weird family. That's what we do." Then I point at the chair behind her. "You should sit. We'll finish this—it's your party, after all."

"You're probably right." With that, she wobbles to the chair like she's twenty months pregnant and leans on the back, rubbing her belly this time. "I'm very happy to be a part of your family." Then she looks down at her still flat stomach with a slightly widened waist. "This little guy will be very lucky to have so many uncles and a kick-ass aunt."

"A guy?" I ask excitedly. We've never had a baby in the family, and the prospect of spoiling a little munchkin makes everyone happy. "You know it's a boy?"

"No," she laughs and hugs her stomach. "But I think it is. What do you think?" She narrows her eyes. "You're never wrong about anything."

Oh, Freya. I'm plenty wrong.

"I don't know." I shrug with an easy smile. "But we're going to love this baby like it's no one's business. Just like we love you."

Her lips spread into a wide smile, and she whispers, "Thank you."

I want to say that we're the ones who are very thankful to her for helping Alex and giving him back to us as a whole person, but I'll get all misty-eyed, and I don't like that. So, I just smile and keep cleaning.

Chapter Nine

ARCHIE

Tomorrow is the night I rid Alex of me. Meaning he's getting married, and I will have to stop coming here to drag him down.

Today is his bachelor party. Justin wanted to go to Springfield to get strippers—I didn't even know small towns had those—but Freya warned me before that if Alex quote *"sees someone's ass other than mine, I will hold you responsible."* By 'you' she meant me as she solely distinguished me as the most responsible of the bunch (a totally false assumption, but I didn't tell her that), and I don't want to get on her bad side—it's never a smart idea to aggravate the significant other of your friend. Even if you're planning on disappearing from their lives. Leave a good impression, that's all I'm saying. So, we're going to go to a bar to get drunk.

Maybe shoot some darts and play pool. No strippers or naked asses.

By the time we get everyone together and arrive at the bar by a taxi, it's way past seven. Kenneth assured me that local bars don't close at two like in Boston—they serve till the last client. I open a tab under my credit card, and we do rounds and rounds of drinks.

By eleven, Justin is sleeping on the table, his face resting on his crossed hands, his not-so-gentle snoring comes in waves. Kenneth is arguing with some bearded dude by the bar, clearly trying to prove something judging by his furrowed brows and narrowed eyes. Mark isn't here since he told Alex he's not coming until he makes amends with his girlfriend, Justin's sister, and it's scheduled for Christmas eve, which is just around the corner.

Aiden wanted to come too, but he's not twenty-one yet, so he stayed home, stewing in anger. Poor guy. As for Alex, I never thought I'd see him looking so happy. With a silly smile on his very drunk face, he leans against his chair and looks ahead without seeing anyone. Well, I bet he's seeing Freya. Lucky fucker.

We all drank about the same amount, but they're all lightweights, and I'm the only one who can still comprehend our surroundings.

Kenneth's gesticulation gets more articulate, and I feel like it's a good time to get home. I get Alex and Justin into a taxi first. They're both huge dudes who take up the whole backseat of the regular sedan. I could drive with them in the front, but I can't leave Benson here since he's evidently looking for trouble. So, I pay the driver and send them home.

I call Kayla and let her know that I just sent two drunk people her way. She laughs and tells me that she's tipsy too but ready to receive the precious cargo, and she'll figure out how to send Alex home. Then I call the same taxi service, and they tell me they are out of cars.

"What do you mean out of cars?" I ask, dumbfounded. How can a town run out of taxi cars?

"It's not a big city here, mister," the dispatcher tells me with an attitude that may as well translate to 'you're a piece of bear shit.' Let me tell you, I tried ordering Uber or Lyft or anything online, but there were no cars available. None. It didn't even show one. So, I had to ask the bartender for a local taxi service, and here I am, speaking to a local taxi over the phone, and the lady sure is not happy to talk to me. That rarely happens, and I feel bummed. Charm gets me everywhere, but it's wasted on her.

"Okay," I sigh, thinking we should have squeezed into the car with Alex and Justin. "How long is the wait?"

"Two hours." Even more attitude.

"Okay. Thanks."

And then she hangs up without even seeing if I want to wait two hours. Yeah, small-town hospitality is charming.

I go back to the bar and find Kenneth trying to prove something to the bearded dude who brought three equally bearded friends. I mentally roll my eyes at this primitive flock culture and walk to them.

"Hey." I place a calming hand on Kenneth's shoulder. "Everything's okay?" I'll never turn down a fight, but Benson is a sheriff known by a lot of people—I don't know how it will look for him, so I try to avoid figuring it out on my watch.

"Yeah." He looks at me, swaying a little on his feet. "What's up?"

"There are no taxis available. Do you have anything like that in Little Hope you can call?" I ask him quietly, ensuring his new friends don't hear me through the bar noise.

"Yeah," he slurs and pulls his phone out of his pants. He shoots someone a message and chuckles when he gets an answer, putting the phone back in his pocket. "Taxi will be here in about ten minutes."

"Okay."

"So, this is your *girlfriend?* I see he's wearing eyeliner." The bearded dude cackles and turns to his friend to wait for their reaction to his joke. "Is he gay?"

I roll my eyes because it's so 'hilarious' I just can't take it —a fucking homophobe with a groundbreaking sense of humor.

"He is not." Kenneth puffs his chest. "But even if he was, what the fuck is wrong with that?"

The bearded guy stops laughing and steps closer to Kenneth. "We don't need faggots in this bar."

"Oh really?" he says as he inches closer to the dude without actually touching him—*smart move, man.* "How about stupid ass punks like yourself and your friends?"

If I got a cent for each time I was called gay, I could build a fucking house by now. Everyone thinks I wear eyeliner—I don't. My eyes have naturally thick lashes, and it looks like I might have eyeliner on. But even if I did wear eyeliner, what the fuck would be wrong with that? The coolest dudes who can rock like no one's business have always worn eyeliner.

Wear whatever you want. But these guys either think differently or are just looking for a fight, because the one I assume is the leader pushes Kenneth's chest. Benson's gaze drops to where the man's hands are before slowly returning to his face. A maniacal smile spreads across his lips, and I see a kindred soul. He was waiting for the guy to make the first move.

He pushes the dude in his chest and tilts his head, inviting him to make another move. The dude's nose flares, and he charges at Ken. Three of his friends follow his lead.

I catch the first one with a fist to his solar plexus, and he doubles over, attempting to catch his breath. The second one swings at me at the same time, and I duck down, avoiding his fist to my temple. Instead, I introduce my fist to the painful spot under the ribs on his side, and he doubles over too. Yeah, graceful they are not.

The third guy tries to attack Kenneth, and I want to go and stop him because the sheriff is undeniably more intoxicated than I am, but even in his drunk state, he makes me proud by grabbing the man's hand and bending it behind his back. He presses him into the bar as the first bearded guy rises from the floor—I missed how he ended up there—and swings at Kenneth.

And the scariest moment of my life happens. It takes two seconds, but to me, it feels like it lasts for hours.

A little figure with flaming hair jumps out of nowhere and starts hitting the bearded guy with her purse.

"Get off my brother!"

The man turns around and blindly swings at her. I make a jump to stop his hand, but before I reach them, his hand connects with her shoulder.

"Oh shit!" he yells as she stumbles back.

I don't breathe.

I can't breathe.

I can't think.

She gets herself together. Her face is a mask of anger, and before she attacks him again, I lose my shit.

Before, I was collected and controlled, but now, all bets

are off. I see red. Quite literally—I have tunnel vision with him as my target. He's not leaving this place alive.

I launch at him. Shifting my body halfway through, I duck and meet his stomach with my shoulder, tackling him to the ground. He's easily fifty pounds heavier, but he doesn't stand a chance.

The first hit to his face results in a broken nose. I feel it shifting under my knuckles. The second hit covers my fist in blood.

I rear back to deliver a third one, but someone pulls me back. Large arms wrap around my shoulders and squeeze tight.

"Stop," the voice says, but I see red and black only. I don't acknowledge the person and try to break free so I can finish my task. "I said stop, Archie!"

I don't give a shit. None. I'm on a mission.

"Stephan, stop."

I freeze.

Her voice is like a cold bucket. My name on her lips is a soothing balm over the internal wounds I'm hiding from everyone.

I stop struggling to break free and let Kenneth pull me back. When I'm standing, I let him know with a subtle nod of my head that I'm in control again.

"You fucker! You broke my nose!" the guy on the floor yells, clutching his face in his hands. "I'm pressing charges! You all saw that, right?" He looks around, and when a few patrons hesitantly nod, he points his finger at me and adds quieter, only for me to hear, "You're fucking done, faggot."

"O-o-oh!" Leila suddenly yells and drops to Kenneth for support.

My heart freezes.

"My shoulder. What have you done?" She starts rubbing her awkwardly positioned shoulder.

"I—" the guy on the floor mumbles. "I—"

"My shoulder!" she cries out and hides her face in Kenneth's chest.

My blood rushes through my body, getting ready for a fight.

She's hurt.

She's in pain.

He must pay. I go to lunge at him, but I'm stopped by a sudden grip on my shoulder. Kenneth's fingers squeeze into my flesh while he gives a small shake of his head.

"It hurts so bad!" she cries into his chest, and I attempt to take deep breaths and calm myself down. I don't know why he doesn't let me go after him.

"So bad!" Another loud cry as her face stays hidden in his chest.

Her shoulders are shaking. She's crying.

I go to lunge again.

"For fuck's sake. Stop," Kenneth mumbles, stopping me.

I give him a quizzical look but stop, keeping an eye on her the whole time.

Everyone around watches the situation unfold. The guy's friends look lost, not knowing how to behave as he's sitting on the floor with a bloody, broken nose.

"I'm pressing charges. You broke my nose, fucker, and you will pay for it," he finally throws at me.

I give him a death stare, daring him to bring it on.

"Oh, it *hu-u-urts!*" Leila cries out again, and I tilt my head at her perfect timing.

I look at Kenneth and find his face red, his lips pressed tight. He doesn't look as murderous as I'd be if someone touched my sister, and she was in so much pain. Instead, he looks like he can barely hold back a laugh as his arm is wrapped around her back.

One of the man's friends steps closer and leans over to whisper something into his ear. Beard's eyes dart around the bar before landing on Leila, who shakes against Kenneth, crying. The same people who nodded in support of him don't look so sure anymore.

The man clears his throat. "I mean, I guess my nose is alright."

"Are you sure, man?" Kenneth asks. "Because I'd be happy to call the cops. My sister got hurt pretty badly."

He looks around tensely before nodding. "Yeah, I'm 'lright."

He takes a second to get himself together, and they scatter away from the bar. My eyes are trained on Kenneth and Leila. I want to be the one to comfort her, but I can't, so instead of doing something stupid like going to them, pushing Benson away, and enveloping her in a hug that'll hide her from the rest of the world, I walk to the bar and tell the bartender to close my tab.

I leave more than a generous tip—because bartenders and waiters don't get paid enough to deal with all this bull-shit—for the troubles we brought and follow Kenneth and Leila. He's still hiding her face in his underarm as they walk.

Outside, we silently walk to her car and get inside. Kenneth goes to the back seat and plants his ass behind Leila, stretching his legs out on the seat, leaving me to take the passenger side.

When the doors are shut behind us, I demand answers.

"What the fuck was that, Benson?" I look back at him. "Why didn't you let me go at him?"

"Because you were ready to kill him, idiot."

"And?" I still don't get why he stopped me.

"Wanna spend the rest of your life in jail for the murder of a homophobic asshole who doesn't deserve the time of the day?"

"He hurt *her*." I nod toward Leila as she silently watches me with wide eyes. "He deserved that. She was in pain." I hiss the last words, and her eyes widen even more.

"He accidentally swung at her, but the hit was tiny. He didn't do any damage."

"She was in pain. She *is* in pain." I shift my attention to her. "How is your shoulder? We need to go to the hospital."

"I'm fine." Her voice comes out as a squeak. I've never heard this tone before.

"You're not. You were crying." I gesture back to the bar.

"I wasn't crying." Her big gray eyes do two slow, adorable blinks.

"What was that, then?" I narrow my eyes.

"A performance for your benefit," Kenneth explains with a raised brow. "And if you weren't so engrossed in your," he clears his throat, "feelings, you'd have seen it too."

"What do you mean?" I look between them. I don't think Leila's blinked once since those two times—she just watches me, her mouth slightly ajar—as her brother stares me down.

"You attacked a man in a bar, full of patrons, and broke his nose, and it all happened in a span of a second. Not everyone saw him hitting Leila. I don't know if anyone even did because we were standing pretty close together. So, to everyone else, you went off the rails and attacked a regular back there. Do you catch my drift?"

I shake my head.

"She pretended to be in pain, so the man would direct his attention to what he did instead of calling the cops and pressing charges." He raises his eyebrows. "Get it now?"

"Oh." It finally clicks.

"Yeah, *oh*." He stretches his hand out and grabs a water bottle from between Leila and me. "Can we go home now? I'm too old for that shit." With that, he leans back.

Leila snorts loudly and starts the engine. "I bet you were the one starting the fight."

"I was not!" he exclaims, trying to hide his smile.

"Sure you weren't." Her light laugh tickles my chest from the inside, making me all warm and fuzzy. I write it off on the adrenaline surge. "I told you, you need to find a woman already—you're getting too restless," Leila continues, unaware of the weird feeling I'm having.

"Not you too," he groans and looks at the ceiling. "Mom has been on my ass for years now."

"That's because you're clearly not getting laid enough." She switches gears and takes off. "The whole county is terrified."

"Stop!" he cries out, hiding his face in his hands. "I don't need sex advice from my twelve-year-old sister."

Leila lets out a loud snort but doesn't respond. The atmosphere in the car is light, even though the situation a few minutes ago was anything but. Their sibling bickering worked its magic as usual.

When Kenneth leans his head back on the seat and closes his eyes, I turn to Leila.

"I saw him hitting you. It wasn't light. Are you really okay?" I ask quietly.

She sends me a brief glance before returning her attention back to the road.

"Yeah, I'm fine," comes her quiet reply.

I stare ahead, hoping she's telling the truth. I can still

see the moment when he swung at her, and his fist connected with her shoulder. I'm so happy it wasn't her head because he was nearly three times her size. A hit to her head would be damaging.

When I feel hot eyes on the back of my head, I turn back expecting to meet a judgmental, warning glare, but instead, I see a sad look of understanding.

Everyone in this damn town is too *understanding*. Or is it just the Benson family?

The drive to Little Hope is uneventful—thank fuck. I occasionally throw looks at Leila as she tries to subtly rotate her shoulder. She's hurt. I know she is. When we're back, I'll check on it.

Back at Kenneth's place, Leila comes inside to use the bathroom. When she's out of sight, Kenneth walks toward me. I expect another warning because he definitely saw too much, but he surprises me. Again.

"I'm going to take a shower and go to bed." He glances at the bathroom door, looking troubled. "You should go to bed too. Today I saw something I'm not sure how I feel about. I'll sleep on it before I decide to break your face. Night." He slaps me on the shoulder and disappears into his bedroom.

I'm not sure how I feel about it either, but it's not the time to stew in my feelings, so I go to the kitchen and get ice out of the fridge. Leila comes out a minute later and looks around.

"Where's Ken?"

"Went to bed."

"Really?" Her forehead wrinkles in surprise as she watches the bedroom door through the hallway.

"Yeah." I chew the inside of my cheek. "Take off your sweater."

Her brows shoot to the stratosphere, and she lets out a surprised laugh.

"Without foreplay?" Her teeth sink into her lower lip while her cheeks stretch into a smile.

"I need to take a look at your shoulder." I try my best to hide the pinkening of my cheeks. I bet it went down to my neck. Good thing my tats cover everything.

"Oh." Now her cheeks turn pink. "I'm fine."

Smooth move, asshole. I could have played it off with a joke like I usually do, but for some reason, I can't think straight knowing she's hurt. Can't joke. Can't focus. But her slumped shoulders and worried lip make me reconsider, so I try something new and let the real me show.

"You are not." I point at the chair. "Please, sit, Leila. I need to see that you're okay."

Her neck moves in a rough swallow at my plea, and she decides to obey. She pulls her sweater off, revealing a black cami, the straps of her lacy, red bra showing. I'm nervous, like she's the first woman I've seen in her under-wear, but the moment my eyes land on her shoulder, I curse.

"Yeah," she winces, "he got me a little."

"A little?" I grab the ice and put it into a bag before covering it with a towel and pressing it to her shoulder. "It's a huge fuckin' bruise, Leila."

Her head whips to face me. "Are you British?"

Hell, I guess I let my accent slip a little. I got too emotional.

"My mother is."

"Makes you British too. Genetics, you know." She smiles but winces when I move the ice pack around.

"Sorry," I murmur. She moves too much, and I grab her other shoulder to make her stand still. Her skin is warm under my touch, her breath fanning my neck—that's how close we are. "Yes, I guess it makes me British."

"You don't sound too thrilled," she notices quietly.

"It's not something I'm exactly proud of."

Somehow, she knows I'm not talking about my nationality, so she switches her attention to what she assumes might be a safer topic.

"Where is your dad?" Her tone is careful, probing, like with a cornered animal.

"Dead."

"Oh." An awkward silence. "I'm sorry."

"Yeah, me too." I take the ice pack off and see that the bruise has settled. There's nothing much I can do at this point.

But I press the ice back on and hold her shoulder with my other hand, unwilling to let her go just yet.

"You should have let me go at him," I complain as I see the color it's taking.

"It wouldn't change the fact that my shoulder was already hurt. If you were let loose, you'd end up hurting yourself and me more."

I rear back, shocked to my very core. "I would never hurt you."

"Hurting yourself would hurt me." She shrugs and pulls her shoulder away from the ice. "I'm cold; it should be good now."

"Yeah." I drop the ice on the table but don't step away. She doesn't either.

"I was scared for you when your face changed."

"My face changed?" I repeat, confused.

"Yeah," she nods and licks her lips, "your face went blank. You know, like you weren't even there. I didn't like it."

"Sorry, I didn't mean to scare you." I make a move to back away, but she grabs my forearm and stops me.

"I wasn't scared *of* you, I was scared *for* you," she whispers, her eyes focused on mine.

I look at her—she's so much smaller and so much younger. Her light is bright, and I'm too dark for her. No matter how much I want to bathe in the rays of her sunshine, I have to step away just so I won't overshadow it with my darkness.

Alex was right; I have too much baggage for someone like her. The temptation is too strong, she is too desirable, and I just know that she easily can be *that* reason for me. The reason to live. But I can't do that to her. I'm the definition of toxic at its worst. Eventually, I'll dim that light in her eyes, and we'll both hate me.

So, I take a step back and gently remove my hand from her arm.

"You shouldn't have been. You don't know me enough to worry." Another step back. "You should go home, Leila. Keep icing your shoulder and go see a doctor if it still hurts tomorrow."

Her face changes: her little nostrils flare, and her lips turn thin. She grabs her sweater and pulls it back on before grabbing her purse and marching away, sending me an evil look on the way out.

"Coward," she says under her breath as she passes me.

I can't even blame her. I am a coward, but sending her away was the bravest thing I've ever done.

Chapter Ten

L EILA

Asshole! Jerk! Coward!

This is the second time in a row I'm leaving Archie with curse words in my head. The nerve of the guy! I know we had a moment. I know he likes me. Is he scared to act on it because of my brothers?

Dang cockblockers. Little Hope is too small for all the Benson siblings.

But maybe it was a good thing since you don't need the complications of a relationship? Especially with one of your brother's friends, my inner voice suggests helpfully, but I shut it down. For a man like Stephan, I could make an exemption. Not Archie. Stephan. 'Complications' next to his name don't look so scary.

I pull into the driveway of the tiny house I'm renting. I've been living here for two years now, and every neighbor knows what time I go pee in the morning. So, it takes me by surprise to find a note stuck to my door. Every neighbor has my phone number, so why didn't they just shoot me a message?

I take the note and open it.

Hey, hun. It's Mrs. Roberts from 22 Pine St. Your boyfriend came around, asking for you. He said he has a surprise for you and will be back. I thought I'd let you know so you can get dressed all fancy like young people do. Xo xo!

Oh, Mrs. Roberts. Good intentions never pave the road to heaven. I know it's not the saying, but it sure represents me better.

I nervously look around, scared 'the boyfriend' will jump out at me from the dark. Finding no one, I quickly unlock the door and rush inside. Once I'm in, I lock both locks and run around the house, checking the back door and all the windows. Feeling a little safer, I get in the shower and blast the hot water, washing the dirty feeling off my suddenly cold body.

I have a feeling that 'the boyfriend' and the sender of the messages are the same person, and it terrifies me. Now I'm not just paranoid; my fear came true—they know where I live. The security system sounds like a real necessity now, and not a vague idea in the back of my mind.

I'm contemplating texting, but I don't have a choice, so I

pull out my phone, find *his* number, and shoot him a message.

Is he still in prison?

The reply is instant. I'll never know how he can reply so fast when he has so much stuff to do.

Yes. Why?

Nothing. Just making sure.

A couple of minutes later another message comes through.

Just double-checked. He is still locked up.
Let me know if you have any problems.

Thanks. Will do.

Will not. I want to be as far away from that world as possible.

I force myself to push my worries away, quickly wash myself, and get into bed, considering I have to be up in three hours. Young or not, the lack of sleep will surely show on my face tomorrow, and I want to look at my best.

The next morning my shoulder aches, my eyes are red, and my whole body feels like it's been hit by a truck. Not my best day, for sure.

I take two aspirins and get myself ready for the wedding. Today, I put extra care into my make-up and lingerie. Even though no one will see my undies, beautiful stuff always makes me feel better, so my dresser is stuffed with lace and leather. I truly believe confidence comes from within. And from under your clothes, so to speak.

I arrive at the Dancing Pony at ten, one hour before the ceremony. I wasn't asked to do anything special, so I wasn't needed early, but still, if you're not early—you're late.

Mom meets me at the door, hands covering her mouth.

"Honey, you look so beautiful!" She touches my hair and looks at me in wonder. "Did you curl it?"

"I didn't." I pull the curl back. I totally did. *Just for myself, alright?* That and the lingerie act as a double weapon.

"Anyway, it looks beautiful." She kisses my cheek and flies away to oversee some tasks in need of micromanaging.

"She's right, you do," comes a low voice from behind me, and I turn around, nearly giving myself whiplash as my eyes find Archie standing two feet away. He's smoking hot in his black suit, crisp white shirt, and red tie that Freya picked for the groomsmen.

His hair is pulled back away from his face, but a few wayward strands keep falling over his forehead. He's clean-shaven, and a dark tattoo plays peekaboo from behind his collar, making him ten times more handsome—a nearly impossible feat, considering he's already a hundred on a ten-point scale.

He owns this bad-boy vibe, barely restrained by social stigmas, with enough class to shame any of the royals. His dark eyes hide a mystery that I instantly need to solve.

And I'm not the only one who wants that, judging by the thirsty looks the women present send his way.

I've never liked a guy enough to be in a relationship with him. I've had casual partners, but no actual relation-ship where we go to dinners and meet each other's friends because I never craved it, so I don't know what exactly it entails. But what I didn't think it entailed is the wave of jealous rage burning my chest when I see all those looks. Does it mean I like him so much that I want to be in a relationship with him? In what capacity?

In any, my subconsciousness suggests sardonically, and I nearly roll my eyes at myself.

I'm a levelheaded person, and I deal with unwanted emotions with grace. I repeat the mantra so I won't forget it.

"How's your shoulder?" he asks while rolling back on his heels. One might say he looks a little uncomfortable.

"It's fine." I shrug to prove my point.

"Leila," he sighs tiredly.

"It's fine, Archie. Hurts a little, but it's just a bruise." I sigh in return, giving up on pretending. "I took some meds. I'll be fine."

"Okay, good" is all he says, and I expect him to walk away, but he stays, watching me.

"Oh, damn it," Kenneth's voice booms through the room when he enters from another door. "My head is pounding." His eyes are bloodshot and barely open.

"I picked you up and went to bed later than you, so why do *you* look like shit?" I ask humorously.

"It's the age, sis. It will get you too," he replies with a laugh and comes to stand next to us. "Are you okay?" He wraps an arm around my shoulder and pulls me into him. I fall into his familiar, safe hug.

"Yeah, I'm fine," I muffle.

"You didn't get hurt, did you?" he asks quieter, but Alex hears it—from *the other* side of the room—and his head turns so fast, I'm sure he gave himself whiplash.

"What are you talking about?" his loud voice booms throughout the room, drawing everyone's attention to us. A few curious heads move between Ken and Alex, but Alex doesn't notice them as he barrels toward us like an icebreaker through Antarctica. I'm almost positive he would have knocked down that little old lady over there if she hadn't stepped to the side. He stops in front of me, crosses his arms over his chest, and levels me with a heavy stare. "What is he talking about, Leila?"

"Be quiet! It's your wedding." I punch him in the arm. "Freya will be upset that you're scaring guests."

That seems to do the trick—always does—and he quiets instantly. "This talk is not done." He points at me and starts backing away. "I'll be back in a minute."

"Sure!" I reply enthusiastically, and he pouts like a little baby while walking backward.

We all want to warn him that there's a little accent table right behind him that he's about to back into, but we don't get a chance. He makes contact with it the second he turns around, knocking the beautiful vintage piece to the floor.

I groan. Kenneth groans. Everyone around groans. Only Archie looks confused and amused, not understanding what's happening.

"On it!" Out of nowhere, Justin rushes over to us with a broom. He quickly starts wiping up the broken pieces of glass while talking to Alex in a baby voice, "That's alright, Boo Bear."

I feel Kenneth's chest shake under my cheek as he laughs silently.

Alex gives him an unamused look, but Justin just keeps going. As usual. Gotta love the guy. If you don't take him with a grain of humor, you'll want to murder the dude after five minutes of meeting him. "Freya told me to take care of you today, and I'll do just that, Boo Bear." He places a gentle hand on Alex's chest and bats his eyelashes at him. "Taking care of you."

Alex's cheeks turn bright red, one second away from murdering Justin. And I don't think anyone will stop him if he tries.

I glance at Archie, who's watching everything with a slight tilt of his head, a look of pure wonder on his face as if he had just stepped into some alternate reality.

A minute later, Aiden is there with a plastic bag to help Justin clean up. But Justin keeps going. "It's gonna get better, Boo Bear. You just wait."

His voice hitches, and I think he can barely refrain from laughing. Kenneth lets out a loud snort, bringing his fist to his mouth, trying to cover it with a cough.

Aiden jogs away with the bag in his hands, super-duper red cheeks, lips pressed tight, and suspiciously shaking shoulders. Justin follows him, coughing into his fist on the way. Everyone around us starts going about their business, getting the ceremony ready.

"What did I just see?" Archie blinks and looks around.

"Ah, this is nothing." Kenneth dismissively waves his hand. "Alex tends to break lamps anywhere he goes, and we told Emma to get rid of them before he did. She didn't listen." He shrugs. "Her fault."

"Breaks lamps?" Archie asks, not getting it.

"Yes," I explain. "He really doesn't have a good record with them."

"I'm fine with lamps!" Alex exclaims, throwing his hands in the air.

"Really?" I narrow my eyes at him. "How many did you break in the last year?"

His lips purse, and two red blotches color his cheeks.

"What about in the last three years?"

His lips turn white from how hard he's pressing them together.

"We need to open a lamp store here in Little Hope—Alex will make sure they'll never run out of business," I add with a laugh.

He doesn't find it amusing, pointedly scratching his chin with his middle finger. But his eyes are smiling. He likes the teasing. He likes to be included. *Oh, my big brother. I'm sorry for the damage our father did to you.* I try to say I'm sorry with my eyes, and he must see something because his own soften, and the corner of his lips quirk in a half-smile. Then his eyes shift to something behind us, and he rushes forward with a loud, "Hey! I hope you are not trying to get my fiancé to change her mind!"

We all look behind him and find Kayla sneaking around the room, a guilty look on her face.

"No-o-o! Don't you worry!" She nervously looks around. "Freya sent me to ask what the noise was about?"

"Alex broke the lamp," Mom offers helpfully, and Kayla's face brightens.

"Gotcha. We're almost ready. Can you come here for a second?" she asks my mom, who likes to feel useful, and gladly follows Kayla.

"She's happy," Kenneth says in an equally happy voice, and I don't even know who he's talking about. Everyone here seems to be genuinely happy. That's what happens when two really good people decide to tie the knot.

"Yeah," I say and glance to the side, feeling someone's eyes on me. To my surprise, I find Archie watching me with heavy intensity. His lips are tight, his eyes dark. I expect him to look away when I catch him staring, but he doesn't. If anything, his stare intensifies.

"Archie!" someone calls to him, and he shifts his attention to one of the townspeople organizing the wedding. "We need you here."

He gives me one of his flirty smiles and says as he leaves, "Duty calls."

I watch him until he disappears.

"Leila," Kenneth sighs next to me, "you're one of the smartest people I know and the most observant. You know he's got fucking' baggage. Make sure that's what you want before you go there."

"Why? Because I should be scared of it?" I'm surprised to hear it from Kenneth. Alex would totally say something like that because he sees only black and white with no spectrum in between, but not him.

Kenneth is levelheaded and careful about the things he says. He is a rule follower with a good-boy complex, even if sometimes it doesn't seem that way, and he would never degrade someone just because they have baggage. I'm really surprised at his prejudice.

"No." He shakes his head. "That man has nothing left to lose. Do you understand me?"

I meet his intense eyes and begin to comprehend that it's not prejudice he's showing, but care.

"Nothing," he continues. "And he's looking at you as if you might be his lifeline. But if he loses you, that would be the last thing he loses. Do you understand me?"

I slowly nod my head, not quite believing what he's saying. But also, it makes sense. It also makes me feel a little better that he cares about Archie too.

"It's a lot of responsibility," he says, kissing the top of my head. "I want to give you advice, but I won't."

I feel lost. "But what if I want your advice?" I whisper.

"You don't." He shakes his head with a warm smile.

"You're wired differently, sis. You're the one who gives advice, not the other way around, my little big sister."

My eyes swell, and I blink away the tears. "That sounds awfully like you accept me as an adult." I tilt my head back to look at his face.

"Fuck no," he snorts. "You'll always be my baby sister. Don't push too far."

Everyone is shedding tears at the ceremony. Well, my mom is a waterfall, and the rest of us all have misty eyes. For different reasons though. Every single soul here has a different reason to cry. Some are happy tears, and some are not so much. Mostly happy, though.

I'm for once happy for my brother. When he went full hermit in that cabin deep in the woods, I tried visiting him, but he never let me inside, so eventually, I stopped trying. Not because I gave up on him, but because I believed he needed to come home on his own terms. I didn't see it happening without a woman pushing him. It's sad but true. I didn't think he'd find a reason to on his own until he wanted to do it for someone else.

Enter Freya, a force of nature that shifted this town with her sudden appearance. The first time they came to dinner together at our parents' house, I knew she would stay, and he would be different. Some people just click together; it's like they are lost pieces of the same puzzle that come together once they're on the same board. I saw those pieces and got a little jealous.

I knew it wasn't in the cards for me—Ken is right; I'm wired differently. I've never connected to a man or a woman. Some might say I'm just young and all that is in the future for me. But it's not. I see too much. More than I care to, and the moment my partner's attention shifts somewhere else, I'll know. Even in a moment of weakness, I'll know, and I won't be able to live with that, so I'll leave. Damn my observance Ken praises so much.

My father had this moment of weakness and strayed from my mom, and that's how Alex came to our family. His mom was my father's lover, and when she died when Alex was just a teenager, he came to live with us. I love my father, but I can't forgive him for doing that to mom. I'm very grateful to have Alex from that affair, and I can't imagine our lives without him, but he did *that* to mom. I'm very sensitive about the matter. So yeah, daddy issues here, just of a different kind.

I don't know if someone made specifically for me exists out there. What I need is a little toxic. I want my partner to be one hundred percent devoted to me. To breathe for me. To breathe with me. And I'm ready to do the same for him. Who would agree to that? It's pretty much like losing a part of yourself. I know it's what I want, and this is what I can offer, but people don't like restraints. It's natural and normal, which is why I know it's a bit toxic. And that's okay too.

And that's also why eventually, I'll get myself a dozen cats to surround myself with unconditional love. Wait a minute, cats won't work here. They don't do devotions. I'll get dogs; they know a thing or two about loyalty. Yes, dogs. The plan is now set in motion.

Vows are made, and kisses are shared. Now it's time for dancing and drinking. I don't drink much because I personally don't like the taste of alcohol, but I take a glass of champagne in spirit.

"Hey."

I turn toward the male voice to my right—a handsome guy in his late twenties with a flirty smile and super white teeth shoots me a shy wave.

"Hey," I reply with a polite smile.

"Are you on the bride's or groom's side?"

"Both." Then I ask, just to be polite, "You?"

"Bride's." Then he rakes his hair with his hand and adds, "I guess."

"You guess?"

"I just checked into her PTSD center, so I'm not sure." He chuckles nervously and looks around. "Shit, I'm out of practice. Probably not the best way to start a conversation?" He rubs the back of his head, looking completely lost.

"Yeah," I let out a surprised laugh. "Probably not the best."

"Do you want, I dunno," he shrugs his broad shoulders, "to ask me something?"

"About what?" I quirk a brow.

"About PTSD and all that. I mean to ask why I'm there and all that." His eyes dart around the room.

"Do you want to tell me?"

"Not particularly, no," he cackles.

"Then don't. Freya is good with people. You're in the right place." Then I shift my attention to the dance floor. But not before I notice the surprised look on his face.

"Do you wanna dance?" he asks shyly after a few minutes of silence. It takes me a minute to gather the courage, and I don't want to discourage this small step.

"Sure," I say.

I accept his outstretched hand, and he leads me to the dance floor. There, he places his hand on my waist—very gentlemanly—and leads me in the dance. And he does it very well, may I say. His movements are sure, his feet are left and right (I have two left feet, so I'm happy he knows what to do), and his hands are never leery.

"I haven't done it in ages," he laughs nervously.

"Could have fooled me," I say and stumble over my own feet, and he catches me, lifting my body a little off the floor. The situation brings us closer, I'm practically squashed into him, and he quickly places me back on the floor.

"Thank you," I mumble, my cheeks flaming.

"Don't worry," he chuckles. "I'm just so irresistible that you can't take your eyes off me."

I look up at him, and he winks. The air around us is lighter. People with a sense of humor can make another person feel like a king, when in reality they feel like a fraud. And that's what I am right now, a fraud. Among my own family and friends today, I feel like an imposter, unable to be completely happy. *What's wrong with me?*

"May I?" A low voice interrupts our dance, and we both look at the intruder.

Archie—because that's his name now—stands next to us, his shoulders squared, his eyes narrowed and trained on my partner's hands on my body.

"May you what?" my dance partner asks, a little attitude creeping into his voice.

"Have this dance." Archie's lips purse and his eyes lift to meet the guy's.

"No, we're dancing." The guy's voice gets angrier, and I can't even blame him, considering Archie was the first one with an attitude and a pissed-off face.

But if I thought he was pissed off before, now he turns into a murderous figure, and I get a little scared for the guy. I take a step away from him, giving the most apologetic smile I can muster.

"I'm sorry, I already promised this dance to him."

He looks between Archie and me, throws his hands in the air, and says, "I so don't need that right now. Have at it." With that, he walks away, leaving us alone in the middle of the crowded floor.

"What do you want?" I ask, chewing on the inside of my cheek.

"A dance." He steps closer and places his hand on my waist and takes my hand in his other. Then he pulls me closer, not so gentlemanly as the guy before. No. Archie's hand possessively moves from my side to my midback, and he pulls me into him by my other hand. His chin touches my forehead, and my face smacks into his chest. His lips lightly graze my skin for a brief moment—*or did I fantasize about it?*—before he pulls away. Just a little, but it's enough to make me feel an instant gush of coldness.

"Why did you pull away?" I blink away the haze he put me into in exactly five seconds.

"You know why," he murmurs into my skin, and my breath catches.

"You can't do that."

"Why?" he asks breathily.

"You know why." I throw his own words at him.

"Tell me anyway," he whispers. His chest heaves hard. His inhales are uneven. Every time my hair gets stuck in his five o'clock shadow, his mouth falls open, and he makes very deep breaths. It's unsettling.

It's arousing.

I can't control my body, and my own breathing changes to match his.

"You won't have me, but you don't let anyone else have me either. It's not fair."

"It's not," he agrees too quickly.

"Then make a move, or let me be," I challenge and look up at his face.

His hand tightens its hold on my back.

"I will."

"You will what?" *Please, tell me you'll make a move.*

"Let you be." With that, he drops my hand and takes a step back.

"You're a fuckin' coward," I growl, watching his nostrils flare in challenge, but he quickly puts out the fire, turns around, and walks away.

I feel like an idiot being left in the middle of a dance floor like that. I look around, and sure thing, quite a few curious looks are being thrown my way. I can already see the local rumor mill begin its work. Just great.

When I walk away from the dance floor, I find the guy from before with a sad look on his face. Awesome, now I'm the object of pitying.

I say goodbye to everyone, congratulate Alex and Freya one more time and wish them a happy honeymoon, and leave. Before I go, I catch Kenneth's understanding stare, and I want to roll my eyes.

At home, I find a note stuck to the door. It's not my neighbor this time. The note says just one word, and I don't recognize the handwriting.

Hello.

I would have been scared out of my wits by this find, but I'm so numb that I can't even comprehend the seriousness of the situation. I go about my routine of checking the windows and doors, but not as thoroughly as I should, considering the haze I'm in.

I need a break from all of this. Being invaded in my own

place like this is unsettling. I don't know who it is. Well, not *for sure*, anyway. I could speculate because c'mon, I'm a reporter, that's what we we're taught to do, but I try to be another kind of reporter. The one that uses only facts and doesn't write clickbait.

Regardless of that, I still need to know who the fuck my stalker is. My only suspicion turned out to be false because the guy is still in prison, so I truly have no idea who's been shadowing me.

But I'm overwhelmed with the wedding and my weird newfound feelings for a certain bad boy, so my head isn't in the right place. I need a break, and I know just the place.

Chapter Eleven

L EILA

"Are you sure you cleaned the sheets?" I ask into the phone for the tenth time while trying to drop groceries into the cart.

"*Of course, we did, weirdo,*" Kayla replies, and I can almost hear her roll her eyes. "*You asked me so many times, I'm about to punch you through the phone.*" Then she adds with a chuckle, letting it trail off, making me gag, "*The walls, though....*"

Alex bought this cute little house for Freya a while back when she *thought* she wanted a home away from the house, but when she found out how deep in the woods the place was, she changed her mind and put it up for sale. But no one local wants to buy a place in the middle of nowhere when they already live in the middle of nowhere, so the house has sat without visitors for a few months. And it's not like it's even a real house, more like a tiny cabin that can protect from the elements, but I'm not sure if it's good for all the seasons or long-term.

About five months ago, Justin and Kayla went there for a little getaway slash fuck party for two, and she still happens to have the keys. While Freya and Alex are honeymooning—they left right after the wedding—I don't want to bother my brother with my problems. I'd have to explain why I need the keys to such a remote place, therefore ruining his vacation. Kayla having the keys is such a convenience for me.

"You are nasty." I gag, throwing a bottle of bleach into my cart.

"And you're a prude." She laughs, and something clicks on her end. *"Okay, I gotta run. We're swamped here. Make sure to get some gas; it starts snowing soon."*

"Will do, thanks." And I hang up.

Adding gas for the generator to my already long shopping list since I don't know how long I'm going to stay there, I browse the shelves, deciding what else I should get.

Kayla is right; it's starting to snow, and I'll most likely be there for a few days until the snow stops and the roads are cleared. And I'm totally okay with that. This scary situation I found myself in won't go away on its own, but it'll stay in the background since no one but Kayla knows I'll be there, and the ownership of the house isn't connected to my name. So yeah, I should be good.

Not knowing what's in the pantry and how long ago it expired, I fill the cart with everything I might need (or not) and move to the register. If the fridge there doesn't work, I'll just store the perishables outside in a bag.

Standing in the line, I glance at the condoms on the right and suppress the urge to giggle. I don't remember the last time I had sex. Was it last year? The dating pool of Little Hope is not deep to begin with, but when your brother is the sheriff, it makes it even shallower. All my adventures were done in college and during occasional trips to the big city.

Yeah, I don't need those, I think as I give the condoms the stink eye as if I have personal beef with them.

Loading the trunk of my sedan, I look around, assessing my surroundings. It has become a sad habit of mine recently. Happy to not find anything or anyone, I get in the car and punch the address of the house into my GPS. It's an hour drive deeper into the woods and closer to the Canadian border. Is it a smart idea to stay remote like that by myself in my current situation?

It's probably better that I stay in town where everyone knows everyone. But that can also be a problem since everyone likes to gossip and spill all the beans about everyone's business and whereabouts. That's precisely what happened to Freya and her ex—"helpful" locals. *Yeah, it's a good thing,* I decide and drive off. Probably not the smartest move on the other hand, but I'm getting too overwhelmed, and my ability to think doesn't exist at this point. I don't like the feeling, so staying in the mountains while no one but Kayla knows doesn't sound like such a bad idea after all.

A quick stop at the gas station to get some gas for a generator in case the power goes out and a shitty macchiato from the vending machine makes my mood brighter, and I switch my playlist from melancholic to cheerful. While my fellow ginger sings about how he loves the shape of me, I sing along and tap on the wheel, not noticing how bad the snow gets.

It's only when I turn off the main road that I notice it. Here I can see how the snowflakes become one big mass, pouring down from the sky, quickly covering the road that was obviously cleared before.

Hmm, I hadn't thought about that before—someone must have plowed the driveway since it's pretty snow-free considering the amount of snow we've had. Alex most likely paid someone to take care of the house in case Freya changes her mind about visiting the place.

I'm glad he did, because even my four-wheel drive sedan wouldn't be able to drive through anything more than what we have now. Yeah, not very smart of me after all, but there is no going back, since I'm not planning on sliding down the slippery mountain road all the way down to Little Hope.

I've never seen the house in person, to be honest. Only the picture Freya showed me, her eyes horrified. I expected some half-broken shed, its windows falling out, but in reality, it's a cute mini version of a fairytale house.

I climb out of the car and look around—Maine is beautiful, but here, it feels even more untouched. It's preserved in its raw ferocity with tall mountains and never-ending forests. I feel so small and yet so big. I don't need to share this beauty with anyone here. It's all mine.

I don't understand why Freya wants to get rid of this place—it's gorgeous. If I had money, I'd buy it in a heartbeat.

As I walk to the house, I notice that the walkway and the stairs are clean from snow as well. Interesting. Someone must have cleaned it very recently. Weird since it's a *remote, seasonal* cabin. I don't know why Alex would pay someone to maintain it, but he clearly does. Kudos to him. I make a mental note to thank him later.

An ounce of sudden dread washes over me as I try the keys—*because you never know*—but they work. I step inside and let out a loud sigh. The place is amazing. I mean, don't get me wrong, it's a shithole, but the potential of it, the feel I'm getting...It's unexplainable. It feels *right*.

As soon as you enter the cabin, you pretty much step on the sofa in front of the fireplace. Two beat-up chairs are by its side. The tiny kitchen on the left takes probably a fourth of the whole house. It has a decent sized round breakfast table and two wooden stools. Further into the cabin, there is a bed with two wooden nightstands. Two doors by the kitchen are probably a closet and a bathroom.

I unload the groceries in the kitchen and start making coffee. It's four p.m. and it's already getting dark, but it's never too late for a cup of joe. There's an old drip coffee maker, and I wonder how Justin, the resident coffee snob, survived here for a whole weekend without a fancy espresso maker. Any coffee will do for me as long as it smells good— I'm not picky.

As I start pouring myself a cup, I hear the engine of a car outside, and lead settles into my stomach. I peek through the window and find a black Range Rover parking beside my sedan. I don't know this car, which means only one thing.

My stalker has found me.

I look around for my purse and rush to grab it. Nervously digging inside, I look for the gun I purchased recently and don't find it. Shit! I must have forgotten it in the car. And Kenneth calls me smart—I want to facepalm myself. I start running around like I got stung by a bee, looking for a weapon.

After digging through kitchen cabinets, I find a cast iron pan that weighs a ton. Perfect! I grab it and run to the door. If the intruder tries to get in, a big, heavy surprise will be waiting for him on this side.

But the intruder uses a key that works.

I swallow a dry lump in my throat and quietly take my position by the door, ready to attack. When it flies open, I swing the pan with all my might.

"Fuck!" the person yells and grabs the pan from my hands.

I blindly jump on him, attempting to claw his eyes out. The man is so tall, I have to keep jumping to reach them. He must have dropped the pan because it hits the floor with a loud *bang*.

"Jesus fuck, stop," he yells, trying to hold my arms still. "Leila, stop!"

He knows my name.

So what? The other one knows it too.

"Leila!" He gets ahold of my shoulders and shakes them.

And only then do I see the person in front of me. Stephan. *Archie.*

"Fuck," I say and jump off. "Shit, I'm sorry."

"Are you okay?" He eyes me warily, eyeing the pan on the floor.

"Yeah, sorry." I glance at him and see him rotating his right shoulder with a wince. "I'm sorry, I didn't mean to hit you."

His eyes twinkle with humor. "You have a mean hook."

"The pan does." I smile weakly.

"That it does." Then he looks from me to the kitchen. The whole place is tiny. "What are you doing here?"

"Me?" I step backward, looking offended. "What am I doing here?"

"Yes, you," he repeats, not getting my sarcasm.

"I'm staying at my brother's vacation home for a few

days." I pop a hip and fold my hands across my chest. "And what are *you* doing in here?"

"I am staying in my vacation home that I bought from your brother two months ago." He quirks a brow.

Oh shit.

"Ah-ha. Sure." I roll my eyes, knowing I'm in deep shit. "And why haven't you changed the locks if you own the place, huh?"

"Because I didn't know someone would want to steal something here." He looks around pointedly. "And I didn't expect an intruder." His dark brow quirks up.

Embarrassment creeps up my neck and settles on my cheeks, making me look like a big carrot, I'm sure. Quite often, red hair and skin that's too white can be a punishment.

His eyes rake over my face, and the corner of his lips lift in a mocking smile. It drives me crazy, so I go to get my phone.

"You made it up. Alex didn't tell me anything; you're lying."

"Yes, he tells you *everything* about what's going on since you guys are *so* close."

I whip around to face him, wanting to tell him all the ways he can go and fuck himself, but my lower lip quivers. He hit a nerve—my relationship with my half brother has been estranged at best in the past, and I'm still trying to build it back up, so I shut my mouth and change my direction, trying to collect all of my things.

"Shit," comes a loud sigh behind me, and I choose to ignore it. "I'm sorry, Leila."

Yeah, he can be sorry all he wants since he knows my own brother better than I ever will.

"Leila," he calls out, but I keep fidgeting with my clothes, shoving my stuff inside my duffel bag.

"Leila." He sounds closer, and I turn around to tell him to go to hell, but I freeze when I find him a few inches away from me. So close I can smell his soap in the air, a hint of alcohol on his lips. "I'm sorry, I didn't mean it like that."

"Oh no, you meant it just like that." I grab my bag, my laptop poking out of it, and angrily walk around him toward the exit.

"Where are you going?" He follows.

"Off your property." When I'm at the door, I grab my puffy coat and open the door.

And instantly stumble back, hit by the gush of wind in my face. It's cold. It's really cold. And the snow is everywhere. It has to be about half a foot deep already.

"You can't go now."

I ignore him, walking toward my car—a difficult feat.

"The road is dangerous."

"That's not your problem," I call back over the wind.

"You are *my* problem while you are *here*." His voice drops lower.

"Watch me disappear then." I climb into the car, turn around, and flip him off. It's then I notice his face...He's frozen, his eyes dark. I don't think he's blinking.

I don't have time to analyze his behavior or his reaction to my words—the snow is getting bad, and if I don't get out of here now, I won't for a few days. Or worse—I'll get out now and get stuck on the road or slide off of it. Scratch that —I don't know what's worse.

I shut the door, and the sound brings him back to life. He sprints to the car and knocks on the window.

"Leila, you can't go out there now. It's not safe."

"Not your problem," I singsong, taking off.

To be fair, the takeoff looks less impressive than I intended, since the road is snowed in, but I still manage to do a little sliding and drive toward the side road. The snow is still soft, so I manage to get through, but to be completely honest, it's not easy and a little scary. Every so often my ABS system kicks on, and I slide to the side. And I'm not even on the highway.

Praying that the main road gets cleaned fast, I look in the rearview mirror. I don't know what I'm expecting to see there, but I feel a little unsettled leaving him there. I don't know the man, and the last time we saw each other, he acted like a dick toward me while being sweet as candy to everyone else. I don't know what gets his panties in a twist when he sees me, but something sure does.

I glance back one last time before returning my gaze to the road, and I don't have enough time to react when I see a deer running across the driveway. Acting on instinct, I hit the brakes. Never a good idea on a snowy and icy road. My car starts spinning, and when I'm nearing sideways, two wheels take off on the surface, and I think I'm flying.

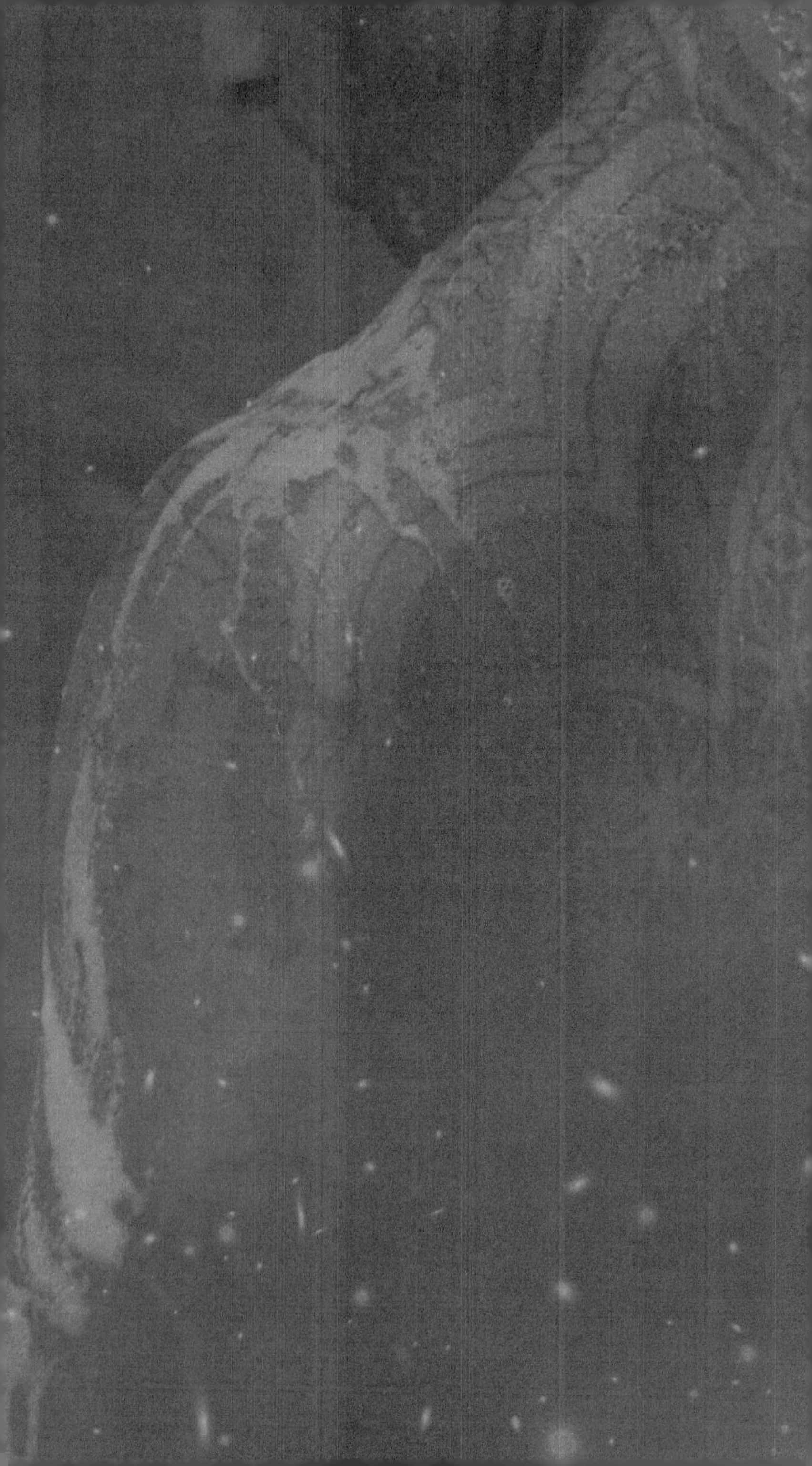

Chapter Twelve

A RCHIE

I watch her leave in this snowstorm that's only getting worse and worse by the minute. I look up at the sky—it's low and heavy. The snow won't stop falling for many hours. Even though she has a pretty decent sedan and Leila is a careful driver—when she's not taking off in a huff—I don't trust these mountains. I love them, but I don't trust them.

I look toward where she disappeared and sigh. She said it herself—she's not my problem. And it's not like I can follow her just so I can stop her car, drag her out, and throw her over my shoulder. And then lock her here with me... Even though the idea begins sounding better and better with every passing second...

No, don't go there. I shake my head, throwing the crazy idea out of my head, repeating what she said herself—she is not my problem.

Trying to convince myself that it's true, I turn to walk back into the house. I left this morning to go to Little Hope for more booze, a necessity for the storm, but ran into this old guy at the grocery store. Everyone knows he has dementia, but I find him extremely intelligent on a different level than anyone else. So, I took him to dinner at Marina's place and asked her to call his son to come pick him up as we were chatting. When his son showed up, we ended up chatting even longer, and that's how I found myself home later than I anticipated.

When I saw her car parked by my new house, I knew trouble was waiting. Ever since I met her, she brings nothing but disturbance to my brain and weird aches to my chest. This was no exception. The moment I saw the car, the dull pain started in the middle of my chest and moved to my stomach. And then she added a literal fuckin' bruise to the bunch.

On cue, my shoulder reminds me of the pain with a dull throb, and I rub it. Shaking my head, I remember how vicious she was when she attacked me and how fucking hard I got in an instant.

And how embarrassed.

I touch the doorknob when I hear a horrible sound I've heard before—metal hitting something hard. Most likely a tree.

And my blood runs cold. I whip around but don't see anything. The driveway is long and curves a few times on the way.

Fuck.

I sprint to the back of the house where I have a snowmobile covered with protective gear. I keep the keys in the ignition because I honestly don't expect visitors here—I doubt anyone but bears will go so far into these woods.

It starts on the first try, saving me from beating the shit out of it with my fist in rage, and I drive toward where the sound came from, dreading what I might find. Squeezing everything this snowmobile can give, I reach her car in a minute, wrapped around a tree. Smoke is coming from under the hood.

I stop on the road and run to the car, attempting to rip open the drivers-side door. Thank God most of the damage is on the passenger side. I try the handle, but it's locked, so I knock on the window.

"Leila. Leila!"

But she doesn't hear me. Her head is hanging to the right, and she doesn't move. I don't think anymore. I can't. Instead, I smash the window with my fist, hoping the flying glass won't hurt her. Then I unlock the door from the inside and open it with a screech.

"Leila," I breathe out. "Are you okay?"

Of course, she is not okay, you moron. She's not responsive.

I bring my shaking fingers to her neck and let out a loud sigh of relief when I find a pulse.

"Thank God," I mumble and start inspecting her arms and torso under her coat for damage.

When I touch her ribs, she lets out a groan and opens her eyes.

"What—" She stops midsentence and looks around. "Oh fuck. That's embarrassing."

I let out a loud chuckle while continuing to check her for injuries. "What is?"

"Getting hit by a standing tree while driving twenty-five miles an hour."

"It's not." I wink when she looks at me with a doubtful look. "Alright, maybe a little."

I touch her ribs again, and she mumbles, "Ouch."

"Might be broken."

"Nah, I think it's just a bruise from the seatbelt." She wiggles her body a little and winces, "Yeah, just a bruise."

"Okay. Can you get out yourself, or do you need help?" *Please tell me you don't. Please tell me you are okay.*

"I'm good." Her next wince makes me wince too as if I'm feeling her pain myself. Such a weird sensation. "Actually, I think I might need your help." Her big eyes shift their attention to my face, and something inside me breaks.

I lean over her and unbuckle the seatbelt. Then I place one arm under her knees, the other behind her back, and carefully pull her out of the car.

"Oh!" she exclaims. "I didn't mean like...you know, carrying me. I meant like to give me your hand or something," she mumbles but still clutches her arms around my neck.

"It's not a problem. Better be safe than sorry."

"I'm okay, really," she argues weakly.

"Okay."

"Really."

"Yep." I walk to the snowmobile, holding her small body in my arms. She weighs nothing, even in the amount of ridiculous clothes she's wearing. This red, puffy coat completely hides her body from view, like seriously. It's the same one she wore at the bridge, and it annoys the hell out of me because it makes her even more noticeable and hard to ignore. If I wanted to ignore her, that is.

I place her on top of the snowmobile and ask, "Do you think you can ride behind me?"

She lets out a loud snort and winces instantly. "Of course, I can. Or did you want to put me in front of you like a child?" Her forehead wrinkles as she pouts her lips. "I'm not a child."

Do you think I haven't fuckin' noticed that?

I ignore her tantrum and jump on the seat in front of her.

"Hold onto me," I say, turning my head slightly.

When I feel her arms fully wrapped around my torso, I take off. The ride back is twice as long since I'm carrying precious cargo. Alex and Kenneth will kill me if anything happens to her.

Back at the cabin, I jump off and offer her my hand. She takes it and carefully climbs off, wincing on the way. I want to scoop her up and carry her inside, but my adrenaline begins wearing off, and I don't know how much of a good idea so much physical contact with her can be at the moment. I might just wrap her in a hug and not let go until my heart settles. I gesture for her to head inside the house instead of following my instinct of securing her in my arms.

After stepping inside, she timidly leans on the door and looks around. She doesn't seem like the sure woman from ten minutes ago who wielded a whole cast iron skillet. Instead, she behaves like an unwelcome guest. I made her feel that way, but I had my reasons to. She took me by surprise. It's like when you dream of seeing someone—and maybe even rub one or two out at the thought of them as well—and then they suddenly show up at your doorstep, surprising the ever-loving shit out of you. You begin thinking that you drank too much and that it finally caught up to you, so you go insane.

"Are you going to keep standing there all night?" I ask casually, trying not to sound like a prick.

She shifts her attention from the floor to me. "I was hoping I could use your phone."

"There's no reception here."

"At all?" she asks, confused.

"At all." I poke the inside of my cheek with my tongue. "No phone, and electricity is a rare occurrence. The power went down twice in the past couple of days. I thought you knew."

"I didn't." Her voice falls. "When I came here, I was so excited that I didn't even check it."

"Why did you need a phone anyway?"

"To call a tow company," she says as she keeps looking around.

"When the snow stops, I'll drive you down the road. You can get a bar or two closer to the highway."

"But what should I do now?" She finally looks at me.

I meet her stare—*yeah, we're in a pickle here.* To say the place is small would be an understatement. Three hundred square feet, if that. One queen bed with two nightstands, one tiny sofa, two worn out chairs, and a small breakfast table with two stools. I longingly look at the closet I haven't dug into yet, hoping it has an air mattress or something similar because I don't fancy freezing my ass off on the floor. *Please, let it have an air mattress.*

"What you were planning to do here when you showed up, I guess." I shrug, pretending that staying with her in close quarters like this doesn't bother me. It does. More than I care to admit. And my heart sure as fuck shouldn't be racing so much in excitement.

She looks around again and then at me. "But—" Her throat moves in a swallow, and I follow her slender neck, or what I can see of it before disappearing under her monstrous coat. "But I wasn't planning on having you around."

"I wasn't planning on it either, but here we are." I

gesture for her to come to the table and sit. "C'mere, I need to check your wound."

"My wound?" she parrots, confused.

I reply by touching my temple. She repeats the same motion with her hand and finds blood on her fingers. "Oh. Oh! Shit, I'm bleeding."

"You are, but it's not a lot. You probably hit the window. Might have a concussion. Come sit here so I can check it." I point at the stool in front of me.

"Okay." She takes off her boots and walks to the table in white socks. I bet the soles of her feet will be dirty by the time she reaches me. I briefly glance down and feel a ping of guilt about wearing shoes when she doesn't. *What the fuck is wrong with me?* It's my house—I can wear whatever I want.

She plants herself on the stool and lifts her head like a good girl so I can see. I go to wash my hands and grab a clean towel. With a newly wet cloth I clean her wounds. Like the little soldier she is, not a sound comes out of her mouth as I dab the blood away, even though a big, purple bruise begins spreading from the center of the wound. But it's just a scratch. Thank fuck, because I only have alcohol here, no medicine. That's about it.

I walk to the bag I just brought from the store, unscrew a bottle of bourbon, and pour it on the dry side of the towel. Returning to my little soldier, I place it on her cut without warning, waiting for a wince—that shit should sting. I can't explain why I did it. Maybe I wanted to see her react to something. Or maybe my desire for pain has expanded to inflicting it too.

Once I'm done, I go back to the sink and take a sip from the bottle.

"Can I have some?"

"No," I bark back and glance at her. A big mistake—her wince, and not from physical pain, is visible. "You might have a concussion. It's not a good idea to mix it with alcohol. Alright?" I add, softer this time.

She nods, averting her attention from me, and I take another sip out of spite. Fuck it, but now she's taking the last pleasure away from my life with her judgment. Not here, not now. I loudly take one more sip so she can hear if she refuses to watch.

And that fucking sip refuses to go down, and I nearly choke on it. My damn body refuses me, siding with the little witch. I give her the stink eye, force the gulp down my throat, and place the bottle in the cabinet. Just great, alcohol was the only thing holding me together, and now I have to give that up because her *feelings* are hurt. She should want me drunk and abstinent while we're stuck here together because the things she wakes in me...she might not like them when they surface.

There's not much to look at around here, so Leila watches the wall ahead of her, stubbornly refusing to look at me as I go through this internal crisis.

"Your brothers told me you're super smart. So, how come you ended up here, in the middle of nowhere," I spread my arms, "alone."

"Alone?" she snorts and finally shifts her attention from the dot on the wall to me. "My brother also told me you're super friendly and cool, and here I am, stuck in the cabin with an asshole."

I smack the table with my open palm, expecting her to jump, but she doesn't flinch. Instead, her eyes are trained on me as if she's about to jump off the stool and attack me with her little claws. Or find the skillet again and use it on my other parts. My shoulder suddenly begins throbbing once more.

"What's your problem?" I ask with narrowed eyes.

"My problem?" She lets out an angry chuckle. "*My* problem?" She stands from that stool and comes closer to me, poking her finger into my chest. I didn't even notice that I moved toward her simultaneously, meeting her halfway. "What's *your* problem, huh?"

"I don't have a problem," I tell her.

But she doesn't let go and steps closer, poking her finger harder. "R-r-right."

I grab her hand in mine and press it to my chest, stopping her poking. "I don't have a problem." It comes out as a hiss.

She lifts herself on her tippytoes and hisses back, "You might not have a problem with anyone else, but you sure as fuck have one with me."

Her eyes feverishly dart between mine while the muscles in her jaw move.

"I don't have a problem with you," I repeat, leaning closer.

"You're an asshole."

"That's not what everyone says." The corner of my lips lift in a mocking half-smile.

She grabs the front of my shirt and uses it to leverage herself while she inches her body closer. Her eyes shine with barely restrained anger. "Exactly. You're a coward."

She annoys me. She drives me crazy because she makes me out to be an asshole while I've never been one. People like me. They gravitate toward me. Everyone likes me but her. What's wrong with her? And this thing she makes me feel deep inside my chest? This stupid desire to...*live.*

"You're the only one who has a problem with me."

She gets in my face. "That's because I'm the only one who sees the real you."

I feel a tick coming, and the muscle below my right eye starts jerking.

"Yeah?" I lean closer, and we're a breath away now. "And who is that?"

She bares her pearly teeth in a snarl like a wild fox I've seen around this place. "A lost boy who is scared to show the world the real you." Her nose touches mine, her voice shaky with anger. "Who is scared to show everyone that you are not the freak you want everyone to see."

My free hand jumps and snakes behind her lower back, dragging her up my body. I doubt she's touching the floor anymore, but I don't feel her weight on my arm—I'm too pumped.

"I am," I spit the words in her face, "exactly the freak everyone sees," nearly pressing my nose to hers, I add, "and worse."

She squeezes my shirt in her fists and pulls down on it until our noses are squashed together. "You aren't. You're just an imposter."

Her pupils are dilated, and I can't even see the color of her eyes. Her chest is rising in rapid movements, pressing into me with every breath. We're so close that when she licks her lips, her tongue accidentally touches my lower lip. It's been many-many years since anyone did that. Many years. Besides that one kiss on the bridge...

My mouth falls open slightly, and she launches for it. Her lips cover mine, and her tongue darts inside my mouth without giving me half a second to think. Her tongue is hot. It touches mine but not timidly, no. It touches the same way she fights—angrily, passionately, and with no restraint.

One of my hands is still holding her hand between us,

and I drop it. Instead, I let it snake to her back, pressing her small body into mine. This ridiculous coat is in the way, so I get rid of it in a second without breaking the kiss.

The sensation is too strong. The reaction of my body is unpredictable. It's taut with anticipation and desire. My dick is hard in an instant, forgetting all the problems we've been having. My hands are shaking as I grab her ass and lift her up, encouraging her to wrap her legs around me.

And she does just that. Her strong thighs squeeze my torso while her fingers dig into my neck with the faintest feeling of pain. Her tongue is ruthless. It takes no prisoners as she explores my mouth. To be honest, I'm so out of the game, I'm embarrassed. I don't remember how to kiss. I don't remember how to do it right for her, but I want to hear her mew with desire. But judging by her grinding her pussy over my stomach, she's getting what she wants anyway.

When she bites my lower lip, all common sense leaves my head, and all the blood officially rushes south. I angle my face to kiss her deeper and follow the feeling. She lets out a low moan and arches her body into mine. I squeeze her ass and start moving her over my hard dick, and even through my pants, I feel how hot she is. As I squeeze her harder, she lets her head fall back. Her mouth is slightly ajar, her cheeks are dark pink, her breathing shallow. Her fingers move from my neck and dig into my shoulders, using them for leverage.

She's constantly licking her lips, and every time her little tongue plays peekaboo, my cock gets harder. When her fingers squeeze my shoulders tighter, I know it's time. I bring my mouth to her neck and bite it while increasing the tempo.

And she comes apart. I watch her teeth sinking into her

lower lip, silencing the moan that was about to escape. It's enough for me.

And I reach the finish line, jerking my hips while moving her over myself.

Her head falls on my shoulder, and a sense of dread descends upon me.

I just fuckin' humped Alex's sister. My brother from the service. We don't fuckin' do that. I humped Kenneth's sister, the one man who seems to get me. I humped the woman who's been haunting me since the moment she found me on that fuckin' bridge. The same person whose light draws me like a damn moth. What the fuck did I do?

I slowly let her down to the floor. Her legs are still shaky, so I hold her elbow until she's stable again. She regains her composure, completely avoiding my eyes. Good —we're on the same page. It's easier this way.

"That should have never happened."

"Tell me about it," she mumbles under her breath, clearly not intending for me to hear. "Like I need another problem right now."

That nips at me. "What other problems do you have?" I didn't mean to sound like a total ass, but it came out that way anyway. I genuinely want to know what bothers her so much, and besides that, I still remember the text she received at dinner and the worry that came over her face. But of course, around her, my ability to speak normally evaporates, and I come out sounding like a complete tool.

Sending me a stink eye, she goes to the sink to wash her hands. Making a dramatic show out of it, she silently shakes her hands and goes to dry them with the towel. It all takes a good two minutes, and I nearly laugh. Which, of course, would probably earn me another beating with the pan.

Trying to shift her attention to something other than

hating me, I decide to go with a safer choice. "I'm gonna go get your stuff from the car. What do you need from there?"

She finally meets my eyes, instantly forgetting. "What do you mean?"

"I mean," I point at the window, "it's going to snow your car in soon, and I wouldn't be able to get anything out of it."

"Oh." Her mouth forms an O, and my eyes instantly dart to it.

Fuck it.

"My duffel bag, please."

"Alright." I nod. "Wait here."

"It's not like I can go anywhere."

Another grumpy mumble makes me almost smile. Almost.

"That you can't," I say with a sigh, and she shoots me an angry glare.

Barely containing laughter, I put my warmer jacket and snow glasses on.

Outside, I take a deep, cleansing breath and look up at the sky. The storm won't be stopping anytime soon. And I mean a couple days, for sure. Down the road, off the mountain, it's not as severe, but here it can get bad, and no one will be cleaning the roads until it's done. I had a plow come here yesterday to clear everything before I came back, but he's not coming again until the main road is clean.

And that's precisely why I'm here. That was my plan—to be alone and snowed in without anyone knowing where I am.

And she ruined everything. Again. I think I'm beginning to understand that that's my problem with her, besides the obvious issue of blood rushing south every time she's around.

I hop on the snowmobile and drive to her car which is

already covered in a decent layer of white flakes. Seeing the bent passenger side again, my heart starts beating faster, anxiety settling in the pit of my stomach. What if something had happened to her because I kicked her out? Well, I didn't technically kick her out, but I wasn't welcoming either, knowing well enough that the roads got bad. It just wasn't an issue to me—I was never scared to slide off the road in some mountain and never be found. But when I imagine her at the bottom down there, I nearly get a panic attack. Even this little fender-bender could have ended up badly with her getting serious injuries. And how would I get her to the hospital? On a snowmobile all the way down there? I'd get a chopper, perhaps. But I'd need to drive to where reception is stronger, meaning I'd have to leave her alone. What if she got worse during this time? What if she needed my help and I wasn't there? What if I fell off the road while she was waiting for me here, injured and in pain, and no one would ever know she needed help?

The overwhelming scenarios let my anxiety tightly squeeze my chest, so I get off the snowmobile and bend over, resting my hands on my knees to try to catch my breath. After a few deep inhales, I manage to get a grip on myself and walk to her car. Her duffel bag is pretty full; I assume she probably considered staying here for a few days. Why would such a young and beautiful woman like her want to be stuck alone in a tiny cabin in the woods for the New Year?

I take the keys from her car and secure her duffel bag and her purse on the snowmobile behind me. On the drive back, I wonder what I'm going to say to her and how we are going to survive these next couple of days.

I also wonder how I can sneak inside the bathroom without her seeing the wet spot on my pants, now fucking frozen from the cold. I was so eager to run away that I didn't even take care of it while I was inside the warm house with a bathroom nearby.

But then it dawns on me...with all this commotion, I chose to ignore the fact that I was able to come without inflicting any level of pain on myself. I was just...there, watching her. And that was enough.

I shake my head, trying to get rid of the image of her red hair falling behind her back as her mouth opens in pure ecstasy.

I try to erase it because I have no business thinking about her that way. She's nearly a decade younger. She's way too pure for me. She's my best friend's sister. She's bright and colorful, whereas I'm only one shade of boring gray. She really doesn't know what kind of freak I am. And she's wrong saying I am not.

Because I'm the worst of them all.

A loud mew right on cue proves my point. I look into the woods and find Midnight sitting by a bush and looking at me, his eyes accusing. His head tilts a little before he gets up, turns away, and walks back into the woods, angrily flicking his tail on his way. Great, somehow I managed to offend the cat too.

Chapter Thirteen

L **EILA**

Crap. Crappy crap!

I think as I run around the place, trying to come up with a way to get out of here. There is no way I can stay in this shoebox with *him* sleeping next to me. I just freaking humped his leg! How embarrassing is that? Now he clearly knows how I feel about him, and that's a whole lot of feelings overwhelming me at the same time. I'm usually very good with suppressing my emotions and letting logic rule me, but when he's around, it's like my nervous system goes haywire and completely out of control.

I provoked him one hundred percent, making us both uncomfortable. We're stuck here together, in this awkwardness, because I couldn't control my emotions and keep my big mouth shut. Just great. I was looking for a quick escape from my big problems, but it feels like I've got even bigger ones here. No-o-o, I didn't *get* that; I brought it on myself. And I don't even have anything to say in my defense—the moment his face turned ferocious, I knew I was a goner. I wanted to see what his experienced hands—and mouth—could do to me, and he was so close to becoming unhinged. I saw that. I *felt* that.

With every angry word falling from his mouth, I yearned to inch closer and feel his sheer, unrestrained power. I yearned to feel his anger directed at me. I wanted to feel how far his emotions could bring him, because he was absolutely right: everyone loves him. *Archie this, Archie that, he did this, he did that.* He's always all flirty smiles and lopsided grins. But not with me, no. I get angry stares, flared nostrils, and a heavy stare from under his thick lashes as if I'm his biggest enemy. So, I just snapped...and wanted him to snap too.

When I felt those waves of the *real him*, I just acted. *Stupid, stupid, stupid Leila!* I sit in the chair and grab my head in my hands. *Stupid Leila!*

The engine of the snowmobile outside tells me he's back. I nervously look around as if I'll run away through the window or something. Nope, I can't. We're truly stuck here.

A moment later, he comes back inside and drops my bag and my purse on the floor by the door.

"I grabbed them both. I didn't know if you need the little bag," he says, avoiding my eyes.

"I do, thank you," I answer politely, and he just nods.

I rise from the chair—and not very gracefully since I lose my footing and nearly fall back.

He looks around, clears his throat, and finally faces me. *Oh-oh, this can't be good.*

"Look, Leila. I'm sorry, it was my fault. I shouldn't have

let it go that far." His voice is full of remorse, his face a picture of self-loathing.

"Stop it right there." I can see the desire to argue flash across his face, so I raise my hand to stop him. "I was there too, and I was the one to make the first move. It was consensual." I pause, brows furrowing. "I hope." I add since I was the one who pretty much forced him into our unfinished coitus. Such a shame; I wouldn't mind going further.

"I'm older and should have—" he continues, berating himself, oblivious to my words. I want to growl so he can snap out of this state he's in.

"Oh, shush." I wave my hand at him, and his brows jump. I have a younger brother, and yet everyone treats me like the child of the family. I hate it. "I made the first move, and we leave it there. It was no one's fault; let's move on."

He leans against the wall and crosses his big arms over his chest. He looks positively curious about what will come out of my mouth next.

"I don't know how long we'll be here, but to survive, we need to forget this," I point at him and then myself, "ever happened. Do you agree?"

He nods.

"Great," I sigh in relief. "Also, thank you for letting me stay here."

He quirks a brow in amusement, keeping silent.

"I know you didn't have a choice, but still. Thank you." I start chewing on my lip, finished with what I wanted to say.

He nods again and pushes from the wall. Taking off his goggles, he hangs them from the hook by the door.

"So, what do you want me to do?" I ask nervously, trying to figure out how to pass the time without getting in his face too much.

His eyes dip to my lips, and his nostrils flare at my question before darting back to mine, but I saw it. I saw it the moment it crossed his mind.

"Can you make some coffee?" he asks.

"Sure," I reply eagerly, happy to have something to do. "Do you want me to make yours or mine?"

"I don't have coffee," he glances at me sheepishly, "but I smelled yours when I came in."

"Sure." I jump to action, grateful to be useful.

He goes for the doorknob and twists it, and on some instinctual level, I sprint after him and grab his arm. "Where are you going?"

It's not me; I don't behave like this. I'm usually a picture of calmness and common sense. Until he showed up on that bridge all those nights ago. Now all bets are off, and I turn into a hysterical, illogical banshee every time he enters the room.

His attention switches to my hand on his and then returns to my face. He doesn't try to shake me off. "I need to get some wood for the fireplace. It's going to be a really cold night, and the generator won't stay at max heat for long. I'm usually okay with the cold, but—" He doesn't finish, but it's clear that he meant with me here, he'll need to use more heat considering I'm always cold. I don't even think he owns a warm jacket.

I instantly feel guilty.

"I got some extra gas; it's in the trunk of my car."

"Okay." He nods, still not attempting to remove my hand. "But we still need firewood. I'll be back."

For some unexplainable reason, I still clutch him. "I promise," he adds firmly, keeping his eyes on mine.

"Alright." I drop my hand and hide it behind my back, embarrassed by my weird reaction to his proximity.

He opens the door again and walks outside. When the door is shut, I rush to the window to see where he's going. The dim light on the front porch allows me to follow his figure to the side of the house. He comes back a minute later, and I rush to the kitchen as if I were there the whole time. He drops the wood by the fire and goes to hang his coat up before proceeding to the bathroom, disappearing for a few minutes. When he comes back out, he's wearing different jeans and the same shirt. *Hmm, what was he doing in there?*

He returns to the fireplace and squats.

His ass is taut in his dark jeans, his shoulders looking impossibly wide in the gray turtleneck sweater he's wearing. How can a guy be so hot wearing a turtleneck, for fuck's sake? And yet, he is. Even from the back. His hair is short, but the black strands at the nape of his neck touch the collar of his sweater, where I see a tiny part of his tattoo peeking out. When he stretches to arrange the wood in the fireplace, his sleeve rolls up, revealing more ink. It's colorful and large, and I instantly want to roll his sleeve up more to see what he's hiding. I've never seen Archie shirtless, and I don't think I can survive the sight, to be frank. My libido gets crazy with just a sliver of his corded forearms showing. What will it do when his abs and chest are on full display? I just know it'll be epic. I hope he sleeps in long sleeve shirts and wide pants.

Gosh, I hope not.

He suddenly turns to me, catching me checking him out. I jerk back and nervously move around the kitchen, making coffee. I'm sure my cheeks are aflame, matching my hair color. Just awesome. Now he thinks I'm a stupid, horny teenager.

I rummage through the tiny cabinets, making more

noise than possible considering they're practically empty. As the coffee drips, I keep myself busy, scared that if I stop for even a second, I'll continue ogling him. It's an arduous task because the man is gorgeous.

I mentally roll my eyes and start putting away the groceries, noticing that we only have the things I bought at the store, a few cans of cat food, and bottles of alcohol.

"Where's all your food?" I ask, surprising myself more than him. "Your human food?"

"You're looking at it," he replies without turning to me.

I glance back at the shelves, expecting food to magically appear, but there's still nothing. "It's just booze in here."

"Exactly," he replies with a smile.

"Were you planning on eating anything while you're here?"

"Are you auditioning to play my mother?" He throws me a funny glance.

"No, jerk." I suffocate the desire to go and shake him so hard his teeth clack. "That's what normal people do."

"Ask each other about their eating habits?"

"No," I reply with a growl. "They care about other people."

With that, I turn away, expecting some snarky remark, but it doesn't come. Instead, I feel his stare on the back of my head. The man is weird.

Once the coffee is done, I pour a mug and ask him, "How do you take it?"

"Black."

Figures. I fill the mug to the brim and carry it to him. He's still squatting by the fire, staring at the flames. His hands hang from his knees.

"Here." I push the mug toward him.

He looks up at me and carefully takes it from my hands, avoiding contact with my skin.

"Thanks."

I should go back to my task as far away from him as possible, but instead, I sit on my knees and hide my palms under my butt. He sends me a curious look but doesn't say a word. We're watching the fire in comfortable silence until I open my big mouth to make it a little less comfortable.

"Why are you here, Archie?"

"I'm here because I bought this place. Your turn." His side-eye is heavy.

"No, I mean, *why* are you here," I stress my question, hoping he'll drop this annoying persona for a moment and be real with me. We've met before, so I don't know why he's so dead set on hiding behind this mask. "It's such a remote location. And you knew it was going to snow, but you have no food." I gesture toward the kitchen. "And yet here you are, expecting to be snowed in. So, why are you here?"

He stares ahead. The fire mirrors in his dark eyes, the muscle in his jaw ticks, and his usually plush lips form a thin line.

After a moment, he looks at me, and when he finds whatever he's looking for on my face, he speaks. "If we're going down this road, you'll have to tell me why you're here." I want to say something, but he quickly adds, "Oh, stop it. We both know there's a reason you're here. A reason you don't want to share. Just like I don't want to share." His eyes roam my face. "With anyone."

I watch him darken before my very eyes. I know that last comment was meant to hurt on purpose by showing that I'm no one, just like everybody else, but it comes from a place of pain where he'd rather push someone away than be hurt. I noticed it the first time I saw him on that bridge—it was so obvious to me that I thought it was obvious to everyone. I thought he must have a lot of friends and good people in his life that could help him get out of that hole he found himself in. But the more I look, the more I understand that they don't see it at all. Not like I do. They don't see a man lost in his pain; they don't see someone in desperate need of help, one who hides behind flirty smiles and quick humor. Even my brother doesn't see it. And for the love of everything, I can't understand why.

"I'm glad I'm here," I say, watching his face contort again.

His jaw sets tighter, and his eyes narrow. "I'm not."

"That's okay. I don't want to be liked by everyone. One person somewhere out there is more than enough." I shrug my shoulders. "It's not like I can do anything to change the situation, so, yeah," I shrug again, "I'm glad I'm here."

"Why?" he croaks.

"Because this is where I should be." I smile and turn back to the fire, still feeling his eyes on me.

"You're weird," he says in wonder.

"I know." I smile again and push my palms deeper under my butt, attempting to warm them.

He rises to his feet and walks to the bed. Grabbing the white, fluffy comforter from it, he returns and carefully places it over my shoulders.

"Thank you," I whisper, surprised he picked up on my discomfort.

I expect him to leave, but instead, he plants his fine butt on the floor and sips his coffee.

"Did you talk to Alex?"

I shake my head. If I talked to him, I wouldn't be in this situation now.

"Right." He takes a sip. "You wouldn't be here otherwise."

I shoot him a look, scared he read my mind. He notices and lets out a laugh. It's coarse and low and so damn sexy. The place between my legs tingles, making my eyes widen —I just got turned on by the *tone* of his laugh.

"If you talked to him, he wouldn't let you anywhere near me. He'd be warning you away from this place," he explains.

"Why do you say that?" I tilt my head curiously.

He lets out a gloomy chuckle. "Because he knows me, and he was the one who sold me this place."

"Are you, like, a sex addict or something?"

He chokes on his coffee and starts coughing, trying to stop his laughter. "Why do you say that?"

"I don't know." I shrug. "Why else would he warn me off?"

He stops laughing and turns to me. "Leila, I'm not the guy you think I am. I'm really not. And you can't save me. I don't need saving."

"Why do you think I want to save you?"

"Because Alex told me about you." He smiles dispiritedly and turns back to the flames as if he can find the truth in them.

"Right," I snort. "He talked about me so much that you didn't even know my name."

"He called you Squirrel," he says quickly before adding with a chuckle, "Among other things. Now I can see why."

I hate the childhood nickname that Kenneth gave me when I was little, but that's not the point. Kenneth called me that, and Aiden did too. But never Alex. In fact, throughout our whole childhood, he purposely ignored me.

"He told me," Archie continues, "that you like to bring

home broken projects and fix them. People like you have a big thing here," he taps the left side of my chest, right under my collarbone, "and they want to help everyone. But you need to understand that some people don't want to be saved. You'll just end up hurting yourself. Do you understand?"

I keep quiet, so he adds, "I'm one of those people. I don't need to be saved. I know you see me as one of your projects, but you shouldn't. Put your energy somewhere else."

With that, he turns away again, sipping his coffee.

Is he wrong, though? I love fixing broken things, and he is that—broken. Is that why I'm so drawn to him?

"Why did you kiss me?"

He whips his head toward me, looking offended. "You kissed me."

"No, on the bridge when we first met. Why did you kiss me?"

"You're not beating around the bush, huh," he murmurs with a chuckle, but I don't return the humor.

It's been a question bothering me ever since that night, so I wait for him to respond.

He stops laughing when he notices my stare. I guess he expected me to drop it, but I don't.

"Because you were too bright, and I wanted to dim you." His eyes are trained on my face. He said it for a reason, we both know.

He wants me terrified and running for the hills. Or at least to the opposite wall under current circumstances. He tells me he's a monster, and as the smart girl my mom claims me to be, I should listen to him and make our interactions minimal. His words tell me to run away, but his whole being tells me to stay. I can't understand why, yet.

It's definitely not for my good looks and charming

demeanor considering I don't have much of those. Well, I'm not ugly per se, but I've heard about Archie's escapades from Kayla while she was living at his place, plus Alex's remarks about him being a man who could get any woman—I'd have to be an idiot to think he wants to get in my pants because I'm just *so irresistible.*

Then what?

Maybe he's telling the truth about his desire to dim my light. But why does he need that? It's an unnatural reaction for a human. Is he so used to being alone in a room full of people that when someone sees him, he becomes uncomfortable?

I hate my love for analyzing absolutely everything, but I can't help myself when the biggest enigma is stuck with me for the time being.

"Why are you like this?"

"Like what?" I blink.

"All nonchalant." He waves his hand at me. "I just told you something horrible, and here you are, looking at me like you just found a lost puppy and want to adopt it."

"Not used to women looking at you like that?" I lift a brow.

"Yeah, they're usually looking for the way to get into my impressive pants," he replies with a lopsided smile, easily sliding into his charming character.

"Why do you put on this mask?"

"What?" he asks, confused, rearing back.

"Why did you pick this mask?"

"Which mask?"

"That." I make a circle in the air around his face with my finger. "A carefree boy who never grows."

His eyes narrow. "And Alex told me you don't talk much."

"I don't."

He turns toward me and quirks a brow, silently mocking me.

"I really don't. Usually." My brows draw together in confusion.

He's right. Well, Alex is right. I don't talk much, preferring to stay on the sidelines and watch people. Their body language usually tells me so much about their lives. And since I don't have my own, I people-watch.

Archie lets out a loud sigh and longingly looks at the bed.

"You sleep there." He nods toward the unmade bed he just took the blanket from. "Take the comforter. It'll be cold."

I look around, hoping for a couch to magically appear, or a second bed, but my Fairy Godmother clearly took the day off.

"Where will you sleep?"

"On the loveseat, maybe." He looks at the short couch and winces as if the piece of furniture personally grew legs and came to punch him.

"You're too big. You won't fit," I deadpan and realize too late that it's Archie I'm talking to.

He quickly turns to me with the flirtiest half-tilt of his head. "You think?"

I roll my eyes. "We're both adults and can sleep on the bed."

"Yeah," he clears his throat before continuing, "I don't think so." He glances at the floor in front of us. "I can sleep by the fire."

"It's going to be really cold on the floor. Does the closet have anything useful?"

"I don't know. Let's go check it out." His face turns serious. "I didn't bring much stuff with me—didn't need it—so I didn't even check the closet and dropped my bag straight in the bathroom."

He rises to his feet and offers me his hand. But it's not to impress me or to show how gentlemanly he is, no. He's not even looking at me. Instead, his attention is focused on the closet as if it contains the last hope for humanity. His outstretched hand sits there, and I can't stop looking at it. It's such a simple gesture, but I'm about to cry. Every time someone offers me their hand to help, it feels meaningful.

Guys in college wanted to show how polite and well-mannered they were so they could get more girls. They made me feel used.

My brothers offered their hands when I fell on the ground while everyone was playing rough. Every time I was reminded that I should stay back so I wouldn't get hurt. They made me feel small.

My coworkers wanted my hand so they could give it an extra hard shake to show how big and manly they were compared to me. They made me feel undeserving.

So eventually, a hand became something symbolic I chose to refuse every time.

Until now.

I put my hand into his. He easily lifts me, and once I'm fully up on my feet, he lets go and heads to the closet, leaving me in the same spot, looking at my open palm.

He opens the door and steps into the tiny closet. I walk up to him and peek inside. There are a few white towels, a change of sheets, and some old pants hanging on a hook.

Archie sighs heavily. "The loveseat it is."

"Stop." I instinctively put my hand on his back and feel his muscles flex under my palm. I drop it, feeling awkward. *Really, Leila, when did you become so touchy-feely?* "We'll share the bed. I suppose we can behave ourselves and not hump each other for a night."

He chuckles and sends me a funny look over his shoulder. "We don't have a good record of that."

"We don't." I return the smile and go to inspect our nest for the foreseeable future.

It's a standard queen bed with a rustic wooden headboard. It's got four pillows, a sheet, and the comforter Archie draped over me when I was cold.

I glance at Archie and back to the bed. Then back at Archie.

Yeah, maybe it wasn't such a good idea after all. He'll take a lot of space, and at some point, we'll end up on top of each other, I just know it. And as it turned out, I can't be trusted around the man. Just to be sure that there will be no incidents, I'll wear my big pajamas.

The big pajamas that I left back at home. I hate sleeping with my legs covered, and I wanted to be comfy, so I packed my favorite white T-shirt that is very much see-through. So, it's either that or sweater weather in bed. I groan inwardly.

While I'm fighting my inner demons, I don't notice him watching me with a look of pure torture on his face.

"I don't snore if that's what you're worried about."

He lifts his head to the ceiling, murmurs something under his breath, and walks to the bathroom. "I don't know how long the luxuries of civilization will last, so I'm gonna take a shower."

"Why? Are we running out of gas?" I look at the kitchen in horror. I grabbed a few extra water bottles, but not enough for two people to survive out here.

"Not yet, but if the temperature drops more than this, the water pump can freeze or burst; not sure how it works in this weather, so I'd rather be prepared," he says over his shoulder.

"Sure." And before he closes the door behind him, I call out. "Are you hungry?"

"No, thanks. I'll get a drink later."

I purse my lips like the midgrade teacher everyone hated at school. He's got a large frame on him, but he looks like he's just been drinking and fucking all his life—you know, cardio with some weightlifting. A delicious picture if you ask me, but he's almost as large as Alex, and Alex is a mountain of a man who consumes an insane number of calories every day. And yet, Archie probably weighs a few dozen pounds less while staying in amazing shape. And even with that, I still can't help but worry: he came here without any food. Did he plan to drink himself to death?

I walk to the kitchen but suddenly stop, shocked by my own thoughts.

Did he?

I look at the bathroom where the water turns on, trying not to think about the most intriguing man washing his naked body right now. Then I remember how I met him for the first time, and I don't like where my thoughts are going.

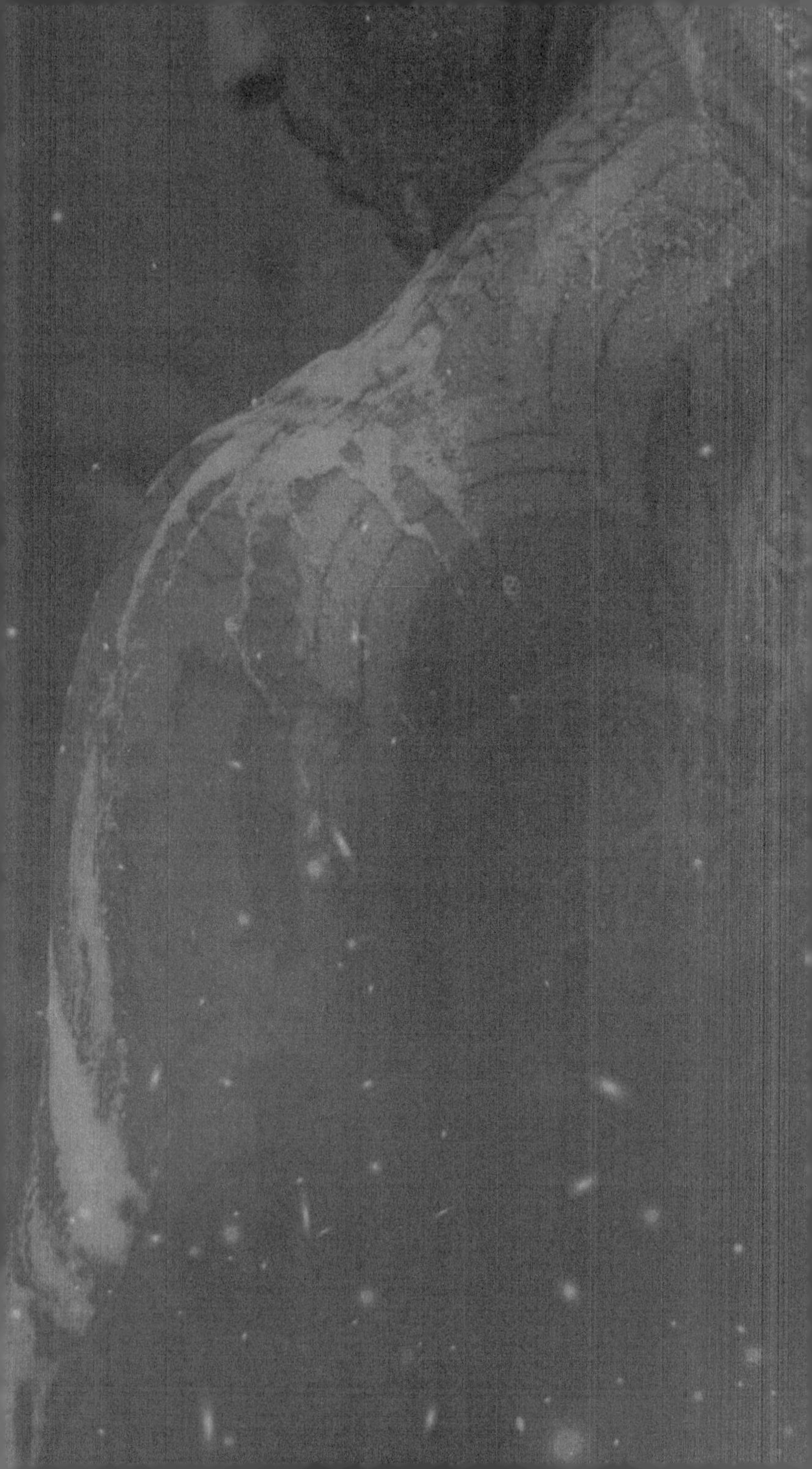

Chapter Fourteen

L^{EILA}

He's been in there, *not* preserving water and our pump—
fine, his pump—for the past twenty minutes. Both my
brothers spend at least thirty minutes in the bathroom every
single day. Archie has just proved my point: I will fight
anyone who will argue that women "spend hours in the
bathroom, doing God knows what." How about men
spending hours in there doing God knows what?

As I stir in this unfairness, I chop my salad with the
ferocity of a serial killer. Am I imagining Archie's dick?
Maybe. I wish I could imagine it without murder coming to
mind after our little humping session. And the worst thing
is that I'm only angry with myself. Does he annoy me? Yes,
he does. But I'm an intruder and a provoker, so this one is
on me.

Digging into the stocked cabinets, I realize, to my utter

horror, that I brought cans upon cans of beans. What else would you bring to eat while staying in a remote location alone? Beans. They're safe. They're nutritious. But I didn't plan on having a roommate. Now, beans are a horrible option, as I don't want to be walking around bloated. Torturing the man is on my priority list, and I can't do that if I'm not feeling sexy. Because no matter what other people say, I truly believe that if you see yourself as desired and sexy, others will see you the same. And no one feels sexy when they're gassy, let's be honest.

I let out a loud sigh and move to the fridge. Liar, liar, pants on fire has some frozen meat. Pulling it out of the freezer, I pray that it was indeed purchased by Archie and not left here from Kayla and Justin's escapade; otherwise, our dinner might turn into a very sad one. I can chop some simplified ratatouille since I brought so many veggies and cook it with meat.

After more digging, I discover a big pot that might be good for stewing, and I fill it with the needed ingredients. We'll be able to eat for a couple of days.

The water in the bathroom stops. I stop too.

A few minutes later the door opens, followed by a gush of steam, and he steps out.

Shirtless.

Steps out of the bathroom shirtless. In a towel. A towel wrapped around his hips. Shirtless. Towel. Hips.

The chain with two dog tags is hanging from his corded neck, making his tattoos pop even more.

I always laughed at women who lost their ability to think when they saw a hot body.

Well, I am those women now. My brain completely checks out, and I swallow a very dry lump in my throat. An arid one. I'm suddenly *very* thirsty.

"Hey. Have you seen my bag?"

"Your bag?" I blink like a dummy, my eyes fixated on his torso.

"Yes," he repeats slowly, "a bag. I had a bag this size," he spreads his arms wide, "in the bathroom," then he points at the cloud of steam, "over there."

"Oh! The bag!" I smack my forehead a little too forcefully. "Ouch!" I exclaim. It brings me back to reality, and a low chuckle reminds me that I'm not alone in the room. "Yeah, bag." I feel my cheeks heating up. "I moved it to the closet. Sorry. When I went to use the bathroom, I nearly fell over it, so I just, you know, moved it. Over there." I point at the door. "In the closet."

"Alright. You moved it? Where?"

"To the closet." I point at the door again. "In the closet."

"Over there?" He points the same way, and his right, very developed pectoralis jerks in response, making the dog tags click.

His nipple jerks too, and my eyes catch on the little rays of sunshine on his tattooed chest. Because yes, Archie has pierced nipples. Two shiny, golden rings. And yes, it *is* a dragon with its tail adorning his neck. It wraps around his front, hugged by dozens of other artful tattoos, the meaning of each I hope to find out.

His abdominal muscles are taut and ripped. It's like someone painted those little grooves with a brush, so they'd look more pronounced.

"Leila, are you there?" His voice is low, and the chuckle at the end lets me know he's having fun with this.

"Yes." I blink twice again. "What?"

"Where did you move my bag?" he repeats and bites his lower lip. Specs of laughter twinkle in his dark eyes.

"In the closet," I respond quietly, tucking my hair behind my ear and looking down, embarrassed.

"Over there?" He points again, clearly knowing exactly what he's doing to me, and I narrow my eyes at the jerk, aware of the game he's playing.

"No, over there." I flip him off and march to the bathroom. My stew will be fine for a few minutes without me while I, myself, stew in my anger.

Loud laughter follows me, and I flip him off with my other hand too. Okay, now we've established that I'm a thirsty fuck around this man, and he knows it. We're stuck here, and he just made it harder on the both of us. Well, I'll make sure to make it *harder* on him too.

I turn the shower on, and...*Dang it,* are there any towels in here? I look under the vanity and don't find any. They might be in the closet, because I haven't seen any specially dedicated areas for linen.

I march back out and straight into the tiny closet.

And one person is already there. Standing naked. The towel pooled around his feet. His legs are almost fully inked, a humongous phoenix graces his back, wings spread over his shoulders. It touches the dragon's tail, entwining together. I know for a fact that phoenix is Kayla's design and is probably much newer than the dragon. It's such a beautiful and tasteful piece of art, that I just stand there, admiring the view.

Until he bends over.

Then I get another view, but not less exciting. Archie is ginormous in more places than one. I can't take my eyes off of him as I imagine his balls slapping against my ass with every thrust he makes, and I clear my throat because it's suddenly the Sahara. No one could blame me for it.

He slowly turns to face me, his eyes finding mine. Soft,

gray pants in hand, one brow arched in silent question. He's not ashamed to be on full display. Why would he be? With a body and art like that? I'd be walking around Little Hope naked every day if I looked like him.

Naturally, my eyes dart down, but he covers the goods with his pants.

"Did you forget to look at something else?" he asks mockingly. His tongue pokes inside his cheek before a boyish grin stretches across his face.

I step forward, and his eyes widen. I stretch my arm toward him, and his throat moves in a rough swallow. I take another step, and he licks his lips. I grab a towel from the shelf beside his shoulder and walk backward.

"I've seen enough." I give him a once over and click my tongue in disappointment before turning and retreating to the bathroom. A bark of laughter behind me warms my already heated heart.

I forgot my clothes in the closet. I took a towel, but no clothes. Just great. He'll think I'm playing his game, but my copycat move makes me look stupid. I don't have a choice, though; I'm not putting my dirty clothes back on, especially after our not so dry, dry humping session.

I wrap the towel around my torso, fluff my hair and throw it over my shoulder so it looks artfully disheveled, and step outside.

Archie sits on the sofa, his arms across his lap. Gray sweats and a black T-shirt cover most of his art, but his full sleeves are still on full display. Now that I know he has nipple piercings, I can clearly envision those golden rings under the thin material. His head leans against the back of the couch, and his one leg rests on the tiny coffee table.

His cheeks look sunken, his brows furrowed, and I instantly drop the idea of torturing him back—he looks too tired to deal with anything right now. So, I quietly slip into the closet, get my stuff, and move to the bathroom. He hasn't opened his eyes in a moment, and his chest moves in a steady rhythm. I think he's sleeping.

I sigh deeply, get dressed, and go to the kitchen. His eyes are still closed; he doesn't stir. I check on the stew—it still has a good thirty minutes to go—so I grab my phone and go to the chair by the fireplace. No internet or Wi-Fi—I could use a good electronic detox—so I put the phone on the table, curl my feet under me, and focus my attention on the sleeping man in front of me.

He's not having a pleasant dream, that I can tell for sure. His eyes move left and right with crazy speed under his eyelids, and his fist squeezes at his side. I consider waking him, but I don't want him to know that I'm witnessing this—I remember Freya told me that Alex used to be embarrassed of his nightmares, and I don't want Archie to feel the same, especially when he doesn't have anywhere to go here.

But then his jaw shuts so tight, I'm sure he broke a tooth, and I can't take it anymore. I jump from the chair and call his name, "Archie."

No reaction. I repeat it louder, "Archie!"

Nothing.

I walk over to him and carefully touch his tight fist. His eyes fly open, and he propels forward so fast, pushing me back with so much force that I stumble back, barely catching myself in time to land on the coffee table and not the floor behind it.

"Leila?" he asks groggily. "Fuck, Leila! I'm sorry. I'm so fuckin' sorry!"

His voice takes the British turn—he's been taken by surprise, unsettled.

"That's okay." I force a smile, attempting to reassure him that it's okay. Of course, it's all fruitless considering he's intent on finding reasons for self-loathing. He's just like my brother who loves doing that. I can see clear similarities.

"Okay?" he asks quietly. "Okay?" Louder this time. "It's not *fuckin'* okay! I knocked you down!"

"But you didn't. I'm sitting on the table. I'm fine." I give him a genuine smile because he will sense anything else.

"For fuck's sake, Leila. Stop doing that. Please."

"What?"

"This." His hands come out in front of him. "Stop fuckin' explaining everything I do. I knocked you down, and who the fuck knows what else I could have done to you." He grabs his hair, pulling it. "I gotta fuckin' go."

He moves from the couch to the door, and I sprint after him, grabbing his hand as he's nearly outside.

"Where do you think you're going?" I pull on his arm, drawing his attention.

"Out of here. You're not safe with me here." He looks anywhere but at me.

"Oh, c'mon!" I roll my eyes. "Fucking look at me already!" I tug on his arm with all the strength I can muster, and he turns just enough to *look* at me. "You stop with this bullshit. I've seen it all my life with my father, then my brother, then another brother, and then guess what? Another brother! So give me a damn break!" I nearly yell and instantly catch myself for being so hysterical for no reason—voice of logic my ass, I wish Kenneth could see me now—so I take a deep breath, drop his arm, and take a step back. "Now, if you'll excuse me while I go and use the restroom. I'll be back in a moment, and I expect you sitting over there," I point to the kitchen table, "waiting for me. Because I cooked us dinner, and we *will* be eating it."

I raise a brow, inviting him to question my demand, but his pupils dilate and he nods, agreeing with me without a fight. *Huh, interesting.*

A few minutes later, I come back to two place settings set up on the table and Archie perched on the stool. *Good boy.*

I fill his plate with three times more food than mine and place it in front of him. He takes the fork and carefully tastes it.

I see the exact moment it hits his taste buds because he digs into the stew with the intensity of a starving man. I push the bowl of salad toward him, and he lifts a hefty portion onto his plate. I smile inwardly, counting it as a small win—better this than a glass of bourbon. He can have that when I'm not here, but with me, he'll get the right nutrition. Well, as much as I can get him from our small pantry.

When our plates are clean, Archie surprises the crap out of me by taking both of them to the sink and washing them before walking back to me and placing a kiss on the top of my head with a quiet "thank you." And when I say "surprised the crap out of me," I mean it—an unexpected tear escapes my usually dry eyes and sneaks down my cheek. I sniffle from the sudden burst of overwhelming emotion in my chest and go to get some water from the fridge just to make myself busy.

I think Archie is uncomfortable too, because he goes back to the small couch and sits. It's not like we have a TV or the use of our phones for mindless games. I have my laptop with me, but I'd prefer not to use it—I kind of enjoy this rustic vibe going on. I've seen a few books on the small shelf by the bed, and I think it could be a good time to relax. So that's what I do: I go to check what we have.

The shelf is practically on the floor, so I bend over to check the titles.

"What the fuck are you wearing?" comes a low, growly voice behind me.

I slowly rise and turn around. Archie stands behind me, a piece of wood in his hand. I bet he was ready to feed the fire as I decided to grab a book.

"What's wrong with what I'm wearing?" I look down at myself. I don't know what got his panties in a twist. I'm wearing a big hoodie over a cami and shorts.

"This freakin' thing." He points at my shorts.

"This?" I look down again, just to make sure I'm not standing here in my underwear. "They are shorts."

"They're not!" His neck reddens a little as he grips the firewood tighter.

"They are," I repeat stubbornly, blood boiling at his stupid antics.

"Don't you have normal pants or something?"

"They're shorts!"

"They're fucking panties; they don't even cover your ass."

"Don't look at my ass," I nearly hiss, mad at him for being a hypocrite as he walks around, assets on full display.

"I can't not look," he takes two steps forward, now standing right in front of me, "when you're flaunting it right into my face."

"My ass was very far from your face. Maybe you're just having a *hard* time staying away?" I take a step toward him, and now we're a foot apart. I'm expecting a joke, but his eyes darken as he leans closer.

"Maybe I am." His voice is a low grumble. And promising. Very promising.

"Is it really that *hard?*" I ask on an exhale.

"Very." He swallows. "Very hard."

"Then don't." I move, so we are flush against each other. "Don't stay away."

His face drops to mine, and he takes a deep breath. His mouth falls open like he's enjoying the scent, and his lips land on my temple.

"Your skin is so soft."

"Yeah" is all I can manage; I'm too focused on the anticipation of his next move. Archie is unpredictable. And I love that.

He gives my temple another gentle kiss and goes to step backward when I grab his shirt and lift to my tippytoes.

"Stop pussying around," I whisper into his mouth. "We both know we're gonna end up fucking here like rabbits. Why waste time?"

He pulls his head back and looks into my eyes. Really *looks.* Deep. Searching for something that will determine the course of the next few days.

"It would be a shame to waste it," he finally says. His voice sounds predatory. Forewarning. Mouthwatering.

"We shouldn't," I agree quickly; I've been dreaming about this since the moment I met him—the mysterious, dangerous man on the bridge that night.

His face stretches in the broad grin of a cat who just ate the canary. Taking off his shirt, he drops it to the floor. My eyes move up his body, taking in his gray sweats that hide nothing, up to his tattooed chest and the dog tags he keeps on.

His smile turns wicked, and he lunges at me.

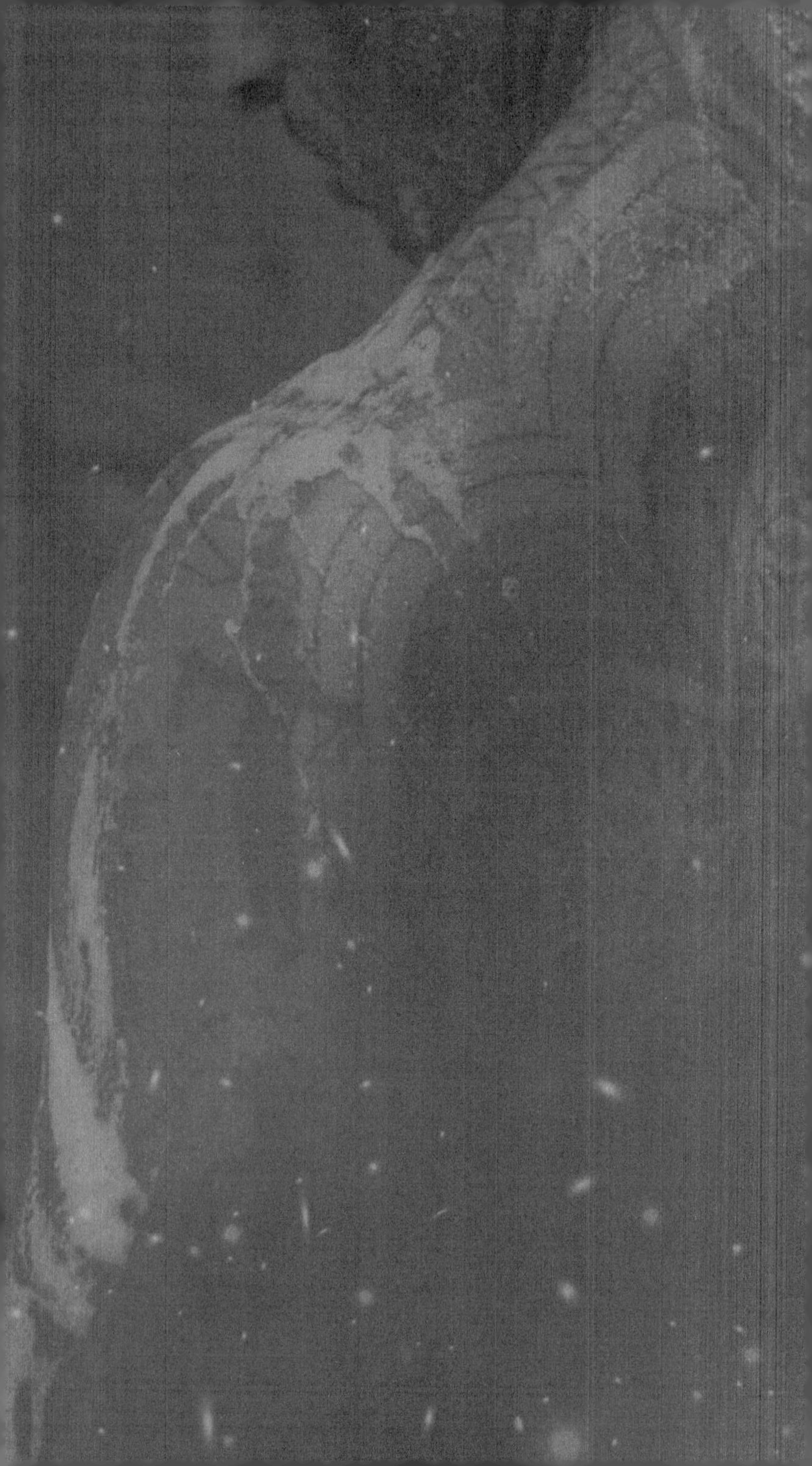

Chapter Fifteen

A RCHIE

I grab her ass, lift her in the air and move to the loveseat—the name is so fitting for what I'm about to do.

When the back of my knees hit the cushions, I fall backward into the softness of the old piece of furniture that's about to witness my ascension to heaven.

I know it'll feel like a quick descension to hell after it's over and the high subsides, but it sure as fuck will be worth it, I just know that.

I pull her on top of me, and her thighs land on both sides of mine, her pussy right above my cock. Her tongue slips inside my mouth, needy, teasing mine with every stroke. Her hands roam my chest, shoulders, and neck, and my body becomes sensitive, everything around me fading until only she remains.

I pull the zipper of her hoodie down and throw it to the side, leaving her in a white cami without a bra.

Fuck me sideways. Her taut, dark nipples stretch the thin material and make my mouth water.

My hand aches to feel the softness of her breasts, the hardness of the tips. And I think she wants the same, because she lets out a quiet moan and arches her back so her tits are in my face. I'm happy to oblige.

I lean down and cover her nipple with my mouth through the cami. And bite.

She moans louder and arches her back even more. *My little bird likes a pain game, huh.* So, I bite her nipple again, and she squirms on my lap, making me painfully hard.

I grip the edge of her cami and pull it down, exposing the tight little tips of her gorgeous tits. They instantly harden, and I lunge for them again. Biting and sucking, I pull back and lunge forward once more. She throws her head back, her fingers digging into the flesh of my shoulders. Women's breasts are so sensitive, and it's so easy to overdo it, so I just have to find the right rhythm.

In the meantime, she finds her own rhythm as she grinds on my rock-hard cock.

"What do you want, Leila?" I ask coarsely.

"Come. I want to come." Her reply is breathy, and I like how she doesn't shy away from what she wants.

"How do you want to come, Leila?" I place my hand behind her back and pull her into me. "Do you want my mouth on your pussy?"

Please say yes.

"No," she whispers, and I nearly whimper in disappointment.

"What do you want then?"

"I want your fingers." Her voice is low and unapologetic.

"My fingers?" I repeat. "You want them deep in your pussy?"

"Yes. I want them to fill me." There's a pause. "Do you think you can?" the little minx adds.

I let out a loud chuckle, enjoying the way she can be shy and forward at the same time.

"Archie." Her tone is pleading.

I graze my teeth along her chin. "Say my name, and you'll get them."

"Archie," she says loudly. "Archie, make me come with your fingers."

"No. Say my *name*, Leila."

I don't know why it's so important to me, but it is. She understands it too, because her eyes sober up, and she pulls away just enough to see my face.

"Make me come with your fingers, *Stephan*," she breathes out, and my name on her swollen lips does something to my heart. To the place it's supposed to be. That empty void I've long but given up on.

I don't want to pretend with her. I just want to *be*.

A beast awakens within me, one I've been scared she'd see, and my hand snakes inside the shorts that started it all. I go lower and find her completely drenched. Pulling my hand away, I look at my glistening fingers in wonder. She watches me, unmoving. I meet her gaze as I slowly bring my fingers to my mouth and lick them clean. For a moment, I close my eyes—she tastes so fucking good. Until this very moment, I never knew how much I could love the taste of someone. The woman in my arms tastes like sweet nectar on a hot day. Like hope in a desert.

I let out a loud, unapologetic moan, and her ass clenches

on my lap. I can feel her muscles contracting, and she begins squirming.

"No fuckin' way." I push my hand back in her pants. "You're only coming with part of me inside you."

My finger dips inside her wet center. I pump inside her a couple of times before adding another, but she instantly pulls her body up.

I freeze. "Are you okay?"

"Yeah," she breathes out. "Don't stop." She pushes herself back on my hand, and I start again while pressing my thumb to her throbbing, swollen clit. My free hand wraps around her lower back and pulls her to me so I can control her movement. When she whimpers again, I lunge at her neck. And I bite. And suck. And bite. Not caring if I leave bruises.

In fact, I want bruises on her; I want evidence of my lips and teeth on her skin so everyone will know to stay the fuck away.

When she starts pushing onto my hand harder, I increase the tempo, and she falls apart on my fingers. I feel a gush of liquid in my palm, and I keep pumping my fingers. She pushes away, clearly too sensitive, but I know that right behind this moment of increased sensitivity, there's a moment of intense pleasure, so I pull her to me, press on her clit harder, and continue for a few more moments.

And I'm rewarded with the sexiest moan I've ever heard and another gush of liquid onto my lap.

Feeling like a fuckin' king, I pull my hand away and lick it clean again. It tastes so fuckin' good, I swear.

When she stops shaking, she falls onto me. Her skin is wet and flushed. She looks satisfied, and I pray to anyone who will listen that she will stand up and go to the bathroom so I can finish here by myself. This situation in my pants won't let me think straight.

But no one listens to my prayers as usual, and Leila leans back on my lap and looks down.

"What are we going to do about that?" Her eyes are flirtatious.

I let out a tortured laugh, "I need to take care of it. I'm gonna go to the bathroom," I say.

"Why?" Her brows draw together, her head tilting to the side.

"Because this kind of wood doesn't disappear on its own," I say with a chuckle, getting uncomfortable. "Not after the most gorgeous redhead just squirted in my hand."

Her cheeks turn an even darker shade of pink. "But I'm here. Why would you need to take care of it yourself?"

I cover my face with my hands and think about how I got myself into this hell of my own creation.

"Because I need to come, Leila," I muffle into my palms. "So my blood can go back to my brain."

"I can help you," she says with a smile and scoots to the side a little. Her hand goes to the waistband of my sweats, and my hand shoots out to stop her.

"No." I hold her hand firmly.

"Why?" she asks, looking even more confused.

"Leila," I hold her gaze, "you've heard about me, right?"

"That you have kinks?"

"Yes." I nod.

"Alright," she replies carefully. "What's your kink?"

"I like pain, Leila." The confession brings me shame, even though it shouldn't. "And I don't want you anywhere near it."

Her voice takes a questioning tone. "You like causing pain?"

"No. I like to feel pain."

She watches my face intently. "But you like normal stuff too, right? You know, boring stuff."

I shake my head.

"Never?" she asks, her eyes wide.

"No." I press my lips tight. "I can't get off without pain."

Her eyes assess me as she observes me carefully like I'm a frog she's dissecting—a good way to bring my wood down. But then she surprises me by saying, "I'll do it."

And just like that, my dick jumps again.

"No, Lei, I don't want you anywhere near that shit." And I don't mean my straining cock.

"How did you think this would unfold?" She points between us, referring to what just happened.

"I didn't think," I answer with a chuckle.

"Let's do it. I want to see how far you go."

"No—"

"Yes," she cuts me off. Her hand sneaks into my pants and squeezes my hard cock. My head instantly falls back, and I moan.

"It feels so fucking good," I say, stretching my arms out on the back of the loveseat. "So good."

Her hand moves up and down my dick as she pulls me out of my pants. She squeezes it at the base, lets go a little in the middle, and squeezes again at the top.

It feels so good.

But not enough.

"Dig your nails into my shoulders."

She places her free hand on my shoulder and digs her fingers into my skin. Not deep enough. Just grazing the top.

"Harder."

She presses them in deeper. Still not deep enough.

"Harder, Leila."

Her nostrils flare, and she puts a tiny bit more force behind it.

But it's not fucking enough.

"Break the skin," I breathe out as the sensation in my cock intensifies.

"What?"

"Break the fuckin' skin, Lei. Make me bleed."

She drops my dick and jumps back. I open my eyes, realizing I'm fucked. Everything is fucked. I should have never opened my big mouth. I should have pushed harder when she said she wanted to try, but as I said, my blood wasn't in my brain.

Her burning eyes are focused on my chest.

"Those," she points at my scars, "are from those who liked to hurt you?"

"Don't talk about other women now. Don't."

"I don't give a fuck about other women right now, Stephan." To my utter surprise, I relax a little. "What I give a fuck about is you and your fucked brain." She points at her head.

I chuckle angrily. "Yeah, everyone is aware of that. I'm fucked up."

My dick is deflating, and I put it back inside my pants. She gets even angrier and jumps closer to me.

"No, you idiot. You are not fucked *up*. You are just fucked by your own guilt. And you've gone so far down this road of self-hate that you don't even see reality anymore." She hisses as she leans closer, "You're the only one who hates yourself." She inches toward me even more. "Your obsession with letting others cut you is your fucking guilt talking, and I hate that."

"That's my fuckin' kink, Leila. You wanted to know, and now you're shaming me. How fuckin' hypocritical."

The death stare that follows is aimed to kill. "You think I'm shaming your kink?" When I don't respond—*the answer is obvious*—she continues, her voice rising, "You can be a masochist as much as you want." She throws her hands in the air. "Hell, I love pain. I like my hair pulled to the point my eyes sting."

My dick deflates even more. The idea of her finding this out at the hand of some dickhead, pulling her hair behind her back, makes me cringe.

"But that," she points at my chest, "is not masochism, Archie." She called me fuckin' *Archie*, and my nostrils flare in anger. "It's punishment you're inflicting on yourself. Deep here," she taps her temple, "you only let yourself go when you bleed because guilt doesn't let you go otherwise."

"Oh yeah." I push away from the couch, getting into her face. "And you got me all figured out after the five seconds you've known me?"

"Yep," her face is so close, "that's all it took because you're not as complex and bad as you think."

"Then," I breathe into her face, my nostrils flared, my heartbeat crazy, "you're dead fuckin' wrong."

With that, I grab her waist and try to move her away from me just so I don't do something stupid—again—and make a move to stand up, but she presses my shoulders and pushes me back.

"Sit the fuck down." Her voice takes a tone I've never heard from her before, and for some reason, I freeze on the spot.

Then she saddles me. "Sit the fuck down, and don't you dare move while I'm fucking some sense into you," she orders.

My heart rate instantly doubles when it's already at its limit, and I drop my hands by my side, not touching her. My dick returns to full mast in a matter of two speedy heartbeats. I didn't even know it was possible to beat that fast—my heart is putting in some serious work. I rest my head back on the couch and watch this beautiful piece of pure fury unravel on top of me.

Fuck common sense. Fuck logic. Fuck the consequences. For once in this lifetime, I'm letting myself just be, because she ordered me to.

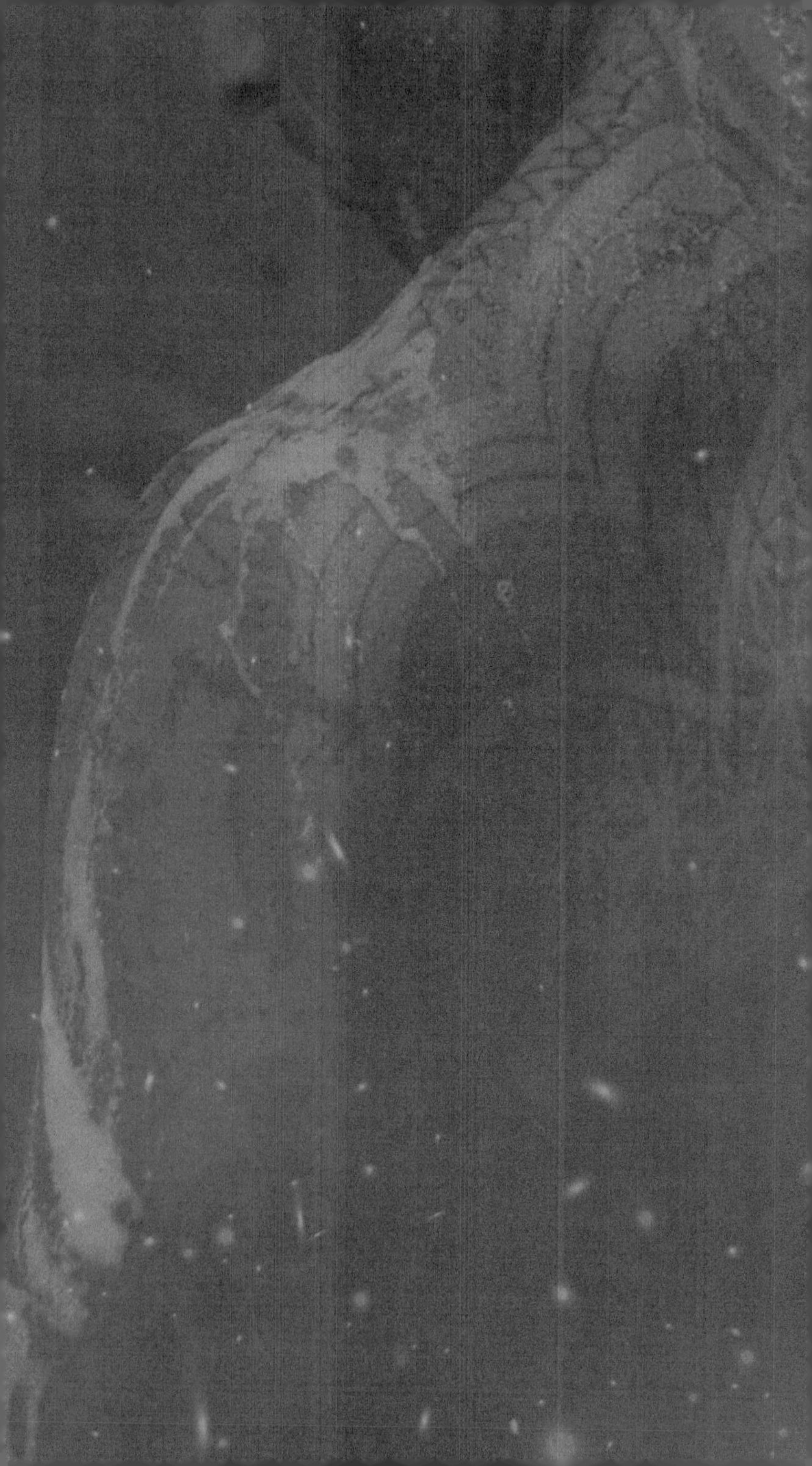

Chapter Sixteen

L EILA

I'm so mad at him right now, I just want to deliver a few hefty punches into his too-handsome face. I hate the disdain he has for himself. I can't stand him at this moment. I don't know how to show him that he's wrong.

I'm so pissed that I almost miss the moment his eyes flash when I command him to sit down. Just like the moment I told him to wait for me in the kitchen. And I almost miss how his hands drop to his sides without touching me. I decide that I can fume later, and in the meantime, I can explore this new revelation and maybe prove him wrong and invoke a few orgasms while I'm at it. Sounds like a total win to me.

"Don't talk, Stephan." I lean in close, calling him his real name—I noticed how his face contorted in anger when

I called him Archie, the name *everyone else* uses. "Not until I'm done. You got it?"

He nods, and I feel another pang of excitement in the pit of my stomach.

"You can't touch me; only I can touch you."

Another nod.

His cock twitches under my ass, and I feel a very unfamiliar tingle of power. A very new sort of power for me, as this strong alpha man is at my mercy. Stephan is as alpha as they come. And he chooses to be this way with me.

It's overwhelming.

It's empowering.

I start exploring his face with my fingers, tracing the sharp line of his cheekbones, and the edge of his jaw, his stubble tickling my skin. I trace his heavy eyebrows before moving onto his straight nose and ending on his lips. I push my finger inside, and he starts sucking. I feel every pull from his mouth deep in my core, and my inner muscles clench in thirst.

I pull my finger out and lick his saliva from it as he watches my every move, his pupils dilated.

My hand goes to his chest, my nails grazing his pierced nipples. I give one ring a tug, and his breath catches. I pull on it again, and his mouth falls open. I lean to give him a quick, wet, open-mouthed kiss and suddenly pull away. Right when he's ready to dive deeper. His chest rises in a deep inhale, and I lick my lips, still tasting him on me.

"Fuckin' witch," he murmurs with that British accent of his, dropping his head back in anguish, and I shush him.

"I told you to be quiet."

"You didn't—"

"Sh-sh." I press my finger to his lips, and he bites it.

My smile is evil as I pull on his nipple. "Be quiet, or I'll stop doing this."

His grin is so wide, I'm scared his face will break in two. "Yes, ma'am."

I give him a quick nod of approval and begin trailing the dragon tattoo around his torso, exploring every scale with my tongue. The second it touches his skin, he inhales loudly, and his hands move toward my waist.

"No!" I exclaim loudly, and he drops his hands with a muffled curse.

I dig my hand into his sweats and wrap my fingers around his thick cock. It's hard and throbbing. The head is weeping with precum. I begin stroking the sensitive skin with my fingers, and his dick jumps.

"Please," he begs, "I can't fuckin' take it anymore."

I thought I wanted him to beg, but as it turns out, I don't. I don't like his pleading tone, so I quickly take my pants off and help him pull his off too. While he watches me with wide eyes, I center myself over him.

"Leila—"

"No, you don't talk. Every time you talk, you think. So just...don't." I press my lips to his, and his tongue sneaks out, meeting mine. Just at that, I take his dick in my hand and push it inside me.

He inhales sharply as his eyes roll back. Mine do too.

I knew we'd have unforgettable sex, but I didn't think it would be so good before we even started. I have to move a few times so I can adjust to his large size.

I open my eyes to look at him and find him watching me, unblinking. His arms by his sides are strained, the veins and muscles popping. His mouth is slightly ajar. Every breath he takes comes out faster and shallower.

"Do you want to put your hands on me?" My voice is hoarse, like I've been screaming his name for days.

I didn't even finish asking before he brings his hands under my ass and pulls me into the air. Rising from the couch, he walks toward the bed, still connected at our cores.

"Can we do it like this?" I ask him before we reach the bed.

His eyes turn bright. A feverish light in them makes me think I asked the wrong question, but the stupid thought lasts for only a second: there are no wrong questions in sex —you can explore anything you want.

"Hold onto me," he instructs and shifts his hands from my ass to my thighs as I wrap my arms around his shoulders. It's an awkward position, and I almost regret asking until he moves me for the first time.

His palms under my thighs move me up and down his cock, but not like he would do it on the bed. No. He drops me down every time, and I get impaled on his dick with every forceful descent, nearly knocking me unconscious. Every time he hits that spot deep inside me. Too deep. It's painful. But the pain lasts only a moment, instantly replaced by pleasure. And then it all repeats.

His movements turn needier, the muscles on his neck, arms, and chest more pronounced. The vein on the left side of his neck beats with a crazy speed that matches my own.

Every time I rise up and down, my oversensitive nipples touch the rings on his, making the sensation stronger. I dig my nails into his shoulders, holding onto him and giving him what he likes—a healthy portion of pain.

He starts dropping me onto his cock faster. It hits the spot inside me harder, and after one of the drops, I fall apart. Literally.

I'm a blubbering mess, making incoherent mews of pleasure. I hold onto him, trusting him to carry me somewhere—*anywhere*—because I can't even think straight. Wave after wave after wave hits me harder and harder. After impaling my quivering, pliable body onto his hard cock one more time, he starts shivering too. I wrap my arms tighter around his shoulders and start sucking on his neck. His fingers dig into my thighs as he pushes into me a couple more times, and I feel a warm stickiness inside of me, quickly sluicing onto my thighs.

Once the waves of pleasure subside, he shifts his grip, and his hands go back to my ass. He walks me to the bed and falls backward, and I land on top of him. He pulls the comforter over us and tucks me under his armpit. My cheek rests on his hard chest as I throw my arm around his torso.

He lets out a chuckle. "May I speak now?"

I giggle at his question and hide my face in his chest, a little embarrassed.

"Yes, you may," comes my muffled reply, and his chest shakes in quiet laughter.

"You're fucked now, Leila."

I giggle. "I'd say so."

"No," his voice is void of any humor, "you're truly fucked." He pulls back a little so he can see my face. "You shouldn't have been so open with this invitation because now I'll never ever let you go."

I stop giggling and watch him.

"Never, Leila. Do you understand that?" His eyes are serious.

I slowly shake my head, hoping he'll elaborate.

"I've been searching for something to hold me together for a long time. And I just found it."

Kenneth's words resurface from memory. *Go away,*

Kenneth! Not now, when I'm lying naked with the man I just fucked.

"Are you sure it's not your orgasm or your newly discovered kink talking?" I try to bring some humor, but he ignores it.

"You're mine, Leila, and no one else can have you."

I should be scared of a declaration like that, but I'm not. I'm a woman of the twenty-first century, and it sounds too possessive, archaic, and unhealthy.

And I'm fucking loving it.

"Don't you want to ask my opinion?"

"It doesn't matter." He pulls me closer and kisses the top of my head. "I'll change it in my favor."

His body suddenly turns rigid. "Lei," he says in a whisper.

"What's wrong?" I ask, confused.

"We didn't use..." His words trail off as he looks down at my legs.

"Oh, don't worry," I wave him off. "I'm on birth control and I'm clean."

"I'm sorry, I should have asked before." His voice is full of self-loathing again.

"You didn't have time because I was holding your cock hostage." I chuckle at my own phrasing. It's not far from the truth.

"That you were." His chest rumbles with a laugh. "But I'm clean too. In fact, never done it without protection, and quite frankly, wasn't planning to. But you can be distracting."

I turn into his chest and laugh, tickling his skin. Nibbling on it, I feel a stir under my thigh thrown over his most manly area. Because yes, Stephan is all man, but *that*, right there, is something extraordinary.

"Really? Already?"

"What did you expect?" His arm squeezes me tighter.

"We had sex a few minutes ago. Your balls should be empty."

His chest rumbles with quiet laughter. "I love when you talk dirty."

I smile and relax, feeling content deep in my bones as I trace the cut scars on his chest. They're barely visible because of his tattoos, but I can feel them with the tips of my fingers.

"How long have you been doing it?"

I don't need to explain what I'm asking about because he knows. Sighing heavily, he says, "A few years."

"And everyone was okay with it?" I hate that I ask about the women in his life, because I know for a fact there have been plenty. Kayla used to tell horror stories about how he came home every night with a new lady on his arm but was always a gentleman about getting them a taxi the first thing in the morning.

Bile rises up my esophagus, but I need to know.

"Yes," his reply is curt.

"I hate them."

"Lei, they're not anym—"

"No." I push away from him and sit, covering my chest with the blanket. "I mean, yes, I hate them for touching you. And don't tell me anything about it being stupid and all that since they were before me and *blah blah blah*. I know it's illogical, but that's not the point." I silence him with my finger as he opens his mouth to speak. "The point is I hate them for making you hurt. For making you bleed. I hate them, Stephan. And now I hate you a little bit too, for letting them do that to you. How can you hate yourself like that?"

He watches me silently, an unreadable look on his face.

"Why aren't you saying anything?"

"Do you really need me to?" His voice is curt. "I thought you were just ranting."

"Ranting?" I feel my nostrils flare like a bull's. "I'm trying to talk to you."

He pulls himself up too. "No, you're sprunting hate. Everyone has their kinks, and you can't blame someone for liking something just because you're too scared to try it."

I rear back. "Too scared to try it?"

"Yes, *little girl*. Too scared. I've lived longer." His nostrils flare as he leans closer. "When you live as long as I have and try everything that's out there, you get tired of vanilla sex eventually."

"Longer? Vanilla sex?" I blink a few times, trying to understand if this is really happening. How are we here after the mind-blowing orgasms and his declaration of owning me? And as far as I remember, it's not like he's one hundred years old and already tired of everything.

"Yes, vanilla." He leans back against the headboard with a bored sigh. "That's what you do, vanilla. Right?"

"Vanilla," I parrot and blink again. "Vanilla." I glance around, searching for my clothes. They're nowhere to be found, so I pull the comforter from the bed, wrap it around myself, and climb out.

"Leila," he calls out with a sigh. "Leila, wait."

"Fuck you, Archie." I throw him the middle finger without looking back.

"Wait, Leila." I hear footsteps behind me. "I didn't mean to offend you."

"Offend me? Offend me?! You think that's what I am—offended?"

"Yeah, with my comments about being vanilla," he questions, looking a bit unsure now.

"And you're calling *me* the child here?" I raise a brow and turn away from him to go find my clothes. Why are all women thrown under the same stigma of being easily offended creatures with fragile egos? We've gotten a bad reputation for no reason at all.

"Leila, fuck. Wait." He grabs my hand, spinning me around to face him. "What do you mean?"

"I see you, Stephan," I spit in his face. "I see *you*." I press my finger between his hard pecs and hiss. "*Stephan*."

His eyes darken, and the muscle in his jaw pops.

"Pushing me away when things got too real."

His lips thin at my words.

"Throwing insults, hoping I'll run away screaming." I wave my hand behind my back.

His right eye ticks.

"Is that what everyone does, runs away from you?"

He doesn't respond. Obviously.

"What was that declaration when you were high off the orgasm? That *I'm yours*." I parrot his words. "I'm not yours, Stephan. Because you really don't want me. I don't think you want anyone because you're a coward."

"Why am I a coward?" he asks through gritted teeth.

"Because you're scared to feel anything other than this all-consuming self-hatred and disgust for yourself." I nearly spit on the word 'disgust' because that's how I feel about it. "I mean you even turned defensive when you talked about what you like. Why? Screw everyone—you like what you like, and don't be ashamed to admit it. I don't. And I'm *oh so young* and *oh so vanilla*." I mimic his tone, mocking him.

His jaw moves from side to side, but he doesn't say anything. His chest heaves with every breath, his hands balled into fists by his sides. He's nearly three times my size, but I don't feel an ounce of fear.

"I can't help you with that. You should find a way to love yourself and let other people do that too."

With that, I turn away and collect my cami from the floor. I half expect him to rush after me, but he watches me move around the room for a few moments before he goes to the bathroom, shutting the door behind him. Soon the water starts running, and for a second I think it would be a good idea to not waste hot water and jump in with him. But then I instantly give myself a mental smack for my over-crazed libido and get dressed.

Ten minutes later, he comes out, wearing new gray sweats and a tight white T-shirt. Fuck me if he didn't dress like that on purpose. Every muscle in his strong body is on full display. Full sleeves of his tattoos look striking in contrast with the white. His hair is wet and disheveled like he didn't bother with a brush. He probably really didn't—the whole time I've been here, I've only seen him use his hands to manage his dark mane. I can see his sharp, pierced nipples poking through the thin material of his T-shirt. And as the nail in the coffin, he doesn't wear any underwear—I can see his huge dick swinging with every step.

Evil bastard. Evil pants.

I give him a side-eye and walk to the bathroom. *Game on.*

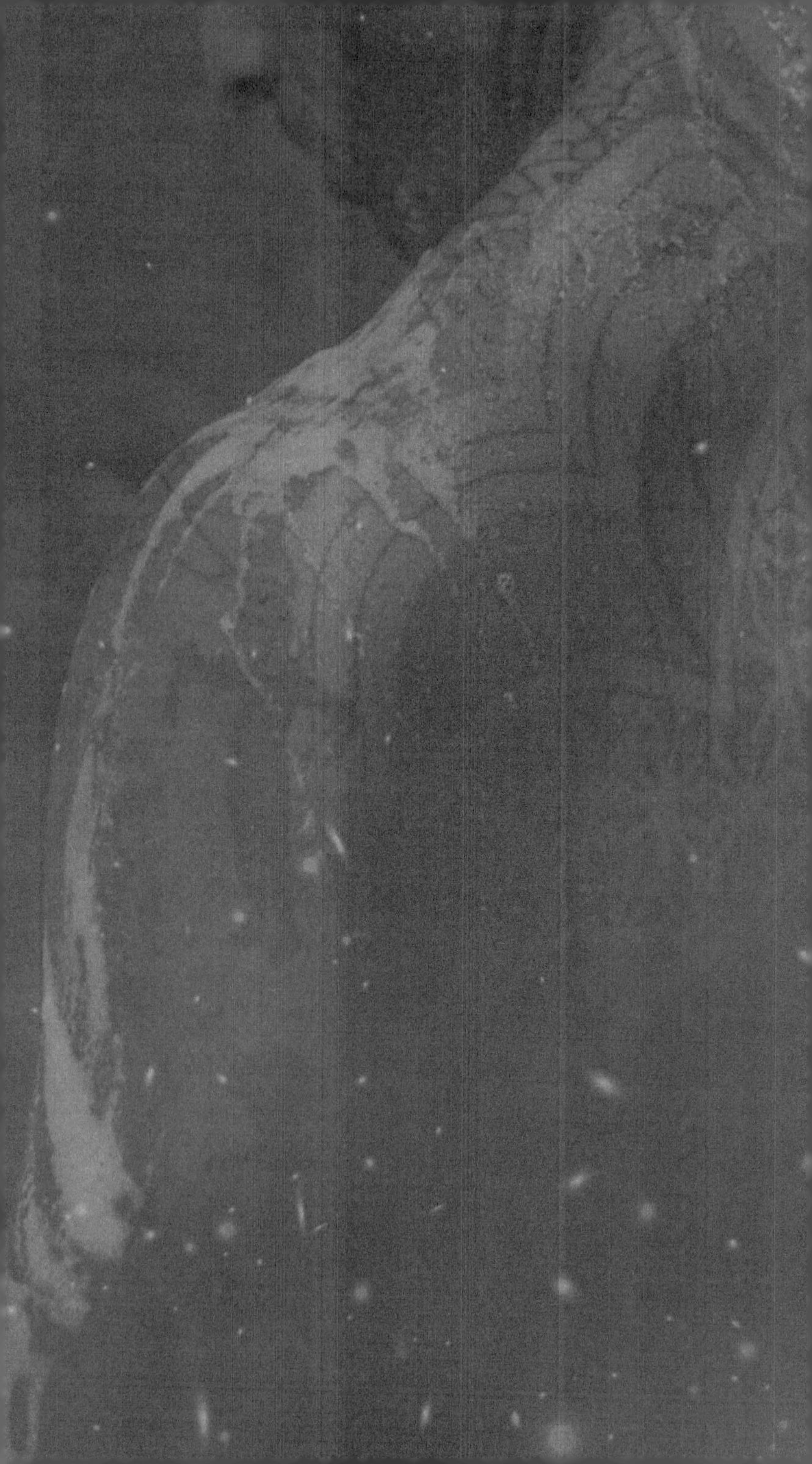

Chapter Seventeen

ARCHIE

I hate that she's right.

I hate myself for losing my cool and having sex with her.

I hate myself for letting what I like in bed slip.

And I hate myself for announcing that she's mine. She can never be mine. Never. And it was a low thing to do—she's young, and she might be living in a fairytale. I don't know anything about her experience with love and how she may take my words. Fuck, she's nearly ten years younger than me. What type of an asshole am I?

At the moment though, she doesn't feel younger. The way she thinks? The way she processes things? And the way she took charge? My dick stirs just remembering it. I'm an alpha in bed. Always have been. But the moment she told me to shut up and do as she said, my body listened. It was an out of body experience. I had never let anyone take control in bed like that. Never.

When it all started, I was ready to go to the bathroom and finish what we started because there is no way I was going to share my kinks with her, making her cut me. Well, in my defense, all the blood left my brain, so I blame my slip on that.

And then she proved me wrong on all accounts—I rocketed like a fucking volcano without drawing any blood. I don't remember ever having such a strong orgasm. And my words about being vanilla? Yeah, bullshit. That was anything but vanilla.

When she told me she wanted 'to try it like that,' I nearly came on the spot. I'd never admit it, but I love that position. Every single thrust brings me deeper than any pose ever could. Every move in is effortless. No woman has ever loved it the way I do until her. It's a hard position for a guy, but it takes a physical toll on the woman as well. But she met my every push with one of her own to match. Her arms wrapped around me while her little moans tickled my ear.

I groan and glance at the bathroom door—she's been in there for a long time. What is she doing? Is she crying?

No, I can't imagine Leila crying. The way she called me on my bullshit when every other woman would get offended and run away, locking themselves in the bathroom, not ever speaking to me again. Yeah, I've been there before. But she didn't. She just got mad. I was a second away from throwing her over my shoulder, carrying her into the nearest cave, and fucking her into oblivion like a madman. Harder this time. Longer. I'd prove to her that after time with me, she wouldn't want anyone else.

Anyone else...

Fuck, even the idea of that makes my skin crawl. How will I survive when she finds some asshole to be in her bed? A woman like her has a large appetite, and not everyone can satisfy it. I know I can. But my sex skills come with a side of issues that I will never be able to resolve, and I wouldn't do that to her. Plus, it's hard to forget Alex. What I did is a slap in his face. If he didn't warn me against doing anything with her, this situation would be a little more bearable, but he saw it coming and told me not to. And yet, here we are. And now Kenneth has been added to the list of people I'll disappoint—the asshole wormed his way into my life.

It was bullshit to say that she judged me for my masochism. I knew she didn't, but I needed to push back when she got too close to the truth. I've always liked my sex with a bit of pain involved—woman's nails digging into my skin, pulling hair, an occasional ass slap—but after I came back, it changed. Every time I felt pleasure during regular sex, I felt guilty that I was enjoying my life while my brothers lost theirs. So, I stopped having sex for a while. But urges won, and I found a way to coexist with them. I began inflicting pain on myself.

But at some point, it stopped being enough—I was still here, enjoying my life, while *their* families couldn't see their husbands and sons. I was lost for a year and couldn't deal with that, deciding to refuse sex again. But I had people relying on me, and without sex or even jacking off, I became unbearable to be around. Even Hank, my top artist, told me to get laid, and he never gets involved. Ever.

I'd always been a sexual creature, and refusing sex felt like a good punishment to myself. Until it became a punishment to the people around me; I had to come up with another solution. One which came to me one night in the face of a very sadistic partner I picked up at a bar. She had a knife and cut me pretty deep—I couldn't stop the bleeding after she left—but it worked. By the time she was out the door, my balls were empty, but my thirst wasn't satisfied. I didn't get any pleasure from the act, but my hormones calmed down a bit. And that's how I eventually found myself in this circle of self-hate only I was privy to.

But when Leila said it out loud, it became all too real, and she was right. She really read me like a book, and I attacked her for it, being an asshole instead of just agreeing with her. Because agreeing meant accepting the problem and then *healing* (fuck that word away from my vocabulary), and I will never be ready for that. So, here I am, a jerk extraordinaire who just told the woman he dreams of making his own, that she's pretty much a piece of shit. *Way to go, Stephan.*

Suddenly the water stops, and Leila comes out, wearing skimpy shorts (even skimpier than before, those tiny offensive shorts that made my dick hurt) and a tiny see-through shirt with thin straps. It's pink; I think they call it blush or something. Her long hair is down, and it moves with every step she takes toward the kitchen, completely ignoring me. There, she proceeds to put a kettle on the fire and grabs a mug from the cabinet. Still ignoring me.

It pisses me off, so I rise from the couch where I've been waiting for her to emerge from the bathroom and walk over to her. Tea sounds good right about now.

I walk past her to grab a mug for myself and graze her shoulder with my arm. She shoots away like I just burned her and gives me a death stare. I lean my butt on the table, waiting for the tea to boil. She takes the same pose opposite me, leaning on the counter.

Our eyes meet, and she quirks a brow. I want to smile, but I keep my cool. I cross my arms over my chest, knowing that the muscles in my arms pop. I've seen her ogling me before, so I count on that. True to my assumption, her eyes dip down, and her cute nostrils flare. But she quickly catches herself and crosses her arms over her chest too. Her tits threaten to spill from the top—two perfect globes I had in my mouth just an hour ago. I feel a stir in my dick, but I keep staring at her, not acknowledging it.

She drops her hands and brings them to the back of her neck, kneading her muscles. A low moan follows as she drops her head forward, and I shift my feet uncomfortably, suddenly not so sure of myself. She tilts her head to the side, gliding her hand over the side of her neck.

I swallow.

Her finger gets stuck in the strap of her shirt, and she pulls it aside, fanning herself.

My eye twitches.

She puts her hands on the table by her sides and pushes herself up. Now, she's sitting on top of it. Her gorgeous hair falls over her shoulder, and she pushes it back.

My dick starts forming a tent in my sweats.

She spreads her legs and places her palms on her thighs. Her shorts are tiny, and she doesn't have underwear on. I can see her pussy as her shorts slide to the side. She starts rubbing her thighs with her palms, up and down, up and down, letting her fingers graze over her slit.

My breathing becomes heavier. I drop my hands to my sides and watch her next movements. My intention of driving her crazy is completely forgotten.

She brings her middle finger to her mouth and sticks it inside, giving it a few good sucks, all the while watching me. She takes her wet digit out with a pop, moves her shorts even more to the side, baring everything to me, and presses her wet finger to her clit.

It's wet, and the air already smells like sex—I don't think I'm just imagining it.

My mouth opens as I attempt to steady my breathing. My nostrils keep flaring, trying to catch her scent.

But she just keeps rubbing her clit with her finger.

And then her eyes close. Just for a second, and I know she's close. I want to be there with her, but I also want to watch.

I can see her putting more pressure on her clit as she increases the speed. Her mouth falls open, and her breathing turns shallow. The top of her chest is pink, her cheeks too.

On another rub, she drops her head back and lets out a long, loud moan. Her pussy glistens, wetting her silky shorts, and she claps her thighs shut with her hand still between them. It's the hottest fuckin' thing I've ever seen. I push away from the table with the full intention of going to her, but she opens her eyes, already sober, and jumps from the table. Raising her hand in the air, she stops me halfway.

"I'm sorry. I guess it was too vanilla for you. I don't know what I was thinking." She blinks innocently a few times and goes to turn off the kettle. Pouring the water into our mugs, she takes hers from the table and marches to the living room like a little soldier going to war. My dick salutes her, and I look at the ceiling, asking the universe why I deserve such torture.

Such pleasure.

The rest of the evening proves to be the former—some sort of prolonged, painful torture.

When she takes a seat on the loveseat with her mug and

a book she found on the shelf, a little stash someone left here, she doesn't just sit there. No. She aims to kill.

She brings her feet up on the couch and keeps her knees together. It would be a very innocent pose if not for her moving her feet to the side slightly, so I can see the result of her self-play in the kitchen—the wet spot on her silky shorts. Plus, those tiny shorts don't leave much to the imagination, so the tent in my pants has no plans of going away anytime soon. And that's what she wants.

So, I cover my lap with a pillow and take my phone out to play mindless games since there's no reception here, and I can't make any phone calls. Nor can I focus enough to make one should we get service at some point. That was what initially attracted me to this place, but now I could sure use the distraction.

I glance at Leila from time to time, and she seems so engrossed in her book while she's anything but. Her eyes are trained on the pages in her hands, but her finger is in her mouth, making slow, sucking motions, and unless she's reading pure porn and getting really excited, I think this show is for me. *Yeah, this woman is not vanilla.*

When she feels my eyes on her, she pushes her finger deeper into her mouth and hollows her cheeks, imitating real hard sucking.

I swallow the dry lump in my throat and press the pillow to me harder. She notices and squeezes her knees tighter while placing her feet wider. *Little minx.*

I decide two can play this game since she's putting on this show for me, so why waste the resources I've got? I throw the pillow away and pull my dick out.

Her eyes go wide, and she forgets to keep sucking.

Good. Now I have her attention.

The next thing I do is place my dick in a comfortable

position by pulling my sweats down a little and freeing my sack too. I place my palm over my angry-looking cock and grab my balls with the other. They're fucking heavy, even though I just emptied them an hour ago. They would feel so nice slapping against her ass...

My dick twitches, leaking with precum, and I squeeze it at the base, willing it to chill a little so I can prolong this torturous pleasure.

Now it's her turn to squirm. She moves her butt, pushing herself deeper into the chair.

I give my dick a lazy pull.

Her finger falls out of her mouth while her lips stay parted. Her eyes are on me. *Good girl.*

I move my palm along my shaft, and I could use some lotion for sure. Running to get it would ruin the mood, so I spit into my palm and cover the head with it.

Her breath hitches and she leans toward me. *Interesting.*

I slowly move my hand up and down, and she licks her lips. *Oh fuck,* I can imagine her full, red lips wrapped around my dick while I fist her gorgeous mane.

Another tug on my cock feels too good, and the muscles on my stomach contract, nearly sending me into a full-body shudder. She lets out a loud sigh but quickly catches herself and clamps her mouth shut.

Fuck, I want it open. I want to imagine her on me.

I keep running my palm over my shaft while squeezing my balls. It feels so fucking good, but I'm at the point where I need pain to come, or eventually I'll deflate and embarrass myself. So I squeeze the base, making my whole dick darken. Then I feel the ping of that pleasure I was waiting for. I glance at Leila so I can live my fantasy and find her sitting on the edge of the couch with an angry look on her face.

"Drop the hand," she hisses.

I tilt my head, confused by her request, still high on the feeling I'm experiencing.

"Drop. The fucking. Hand."

And my hand drops. Both of them. Fuck me, my body listened to her without even listening to my own brain.

She moves so her ass is nearly hanging from the edge of the loveseat, then spreads her legs wide. I can see everything.

"Eyes on my face, soldier."

"I'm not a soldier."

"You are when I say you are." Her voice is rough and low, one I haven't yet heard from her.

And with that, my eyes shift to her face and find her licking her suddenly swollen lips. Her eyes are half closed, her cheeks are red. She's a sight to behold.

"Wrap your big hand around your giant dick," she orders, and my hand moves to do as it's told. I didn't know she could talk like that, and I squeeze my shaft, excited.

"Gentler."

"No, I can't, Lei. I ca—"

She raises her hand, shutting me up, and stands from the couch. Moving toward me slowly, she keeps her eyes trained on mine. Warning me to not move. And fuck me, but I love her treating me like this.

When she's next to me, she kneels on the side of the chair I'm sitting on and places her hand on top of mine, grazing my fingers with hers.

"You can." Her eyes find and hold mine. "You don't have to punish yourself every time you feel good."

I swallow the rough truth I've been running away from,

unsure of how she managed to get it out of me in the short time she's known me.

Her hand helps mine move, and I notice how mine is twice the size of hers, and I love how small she is and yet how she can mold me into something new without any effort other than being herself. Letting someone else control me relieves me of responsibility for the time being. I didn't know it could be so liberating.

Her hand slowly moves with mine, and even though it's my hand touching my dick, it feels so fucking good. Then she takes my hand, brings it to her mouth, and gives it a long, wet lick. My eyes go droopy, and when she places my hand back on my cock, I'm ready to go.

We move a few more times when she leans down to my ear and whispers, "Let me."

I instantly drop my hand, and hers replaces it right away. It's small and barely covers anything but fuck, it feels so good. She licks her hand, and I follow the movement of her tongue with my eyes. When she puts her hand back on me, my whole body goes rigid, the muscles in my stomach twitching. She feels it too, because she quickens the tempo and inches her mouth closer to my ear.

"Let yourself go." Her whisper tingles my brain, and when she bites my earlobe, I explode, shooting cum all over my stomach and chest. She's walking me through the whole orgasm and slows down at the end when it gets too sensitive. I don't want to think about where she knows so much from —I just want to erase the moment the question ever popped into my brain.

When I'm done, she trails light kisses from my ear, onto my cheek, before giving me a peck on the mouth.

"Go clean yourself, soldier."

"I'm not a soldier." My voice comes out coarse like I've been yelling at some rock concert for hours.

"You are when I say you are," she repeats with a challenge and a sneaky half-smile.

A smart man knows how to pick his battles, so I respond with, "Yes, ma'am."

She rolls her lips, trying not to laugh, and stands up. "Since we're stuck here, I want to get a Christmas tree."

"But it's not Christmas anymore." I look out the window.

"Who cares?" She shrugs. "It's New Year's soon. Can you help me get one?"

"Yeah." I nod. I'll get her the moon if she wants it. It might take longer, but I'd reverse gravity so the shining ball could be in her magical hands.

"Cool." She looks outside. "It's getting dark even earlier here. Like we're on a different planet."

I follow her gaze. "Yeah, I didn't expect that, but I like it."

"Me too." She smiles and looks at the bed. "I guess we've solved the problem of sleeping arrangements. Even though this bed doesn't have a good track record of conversations held there." Then she adds with a quirked brow, "But if we manage to keep our mouths shut, maybe we'll manage?"

I let her have this moment because I totally deserve that.

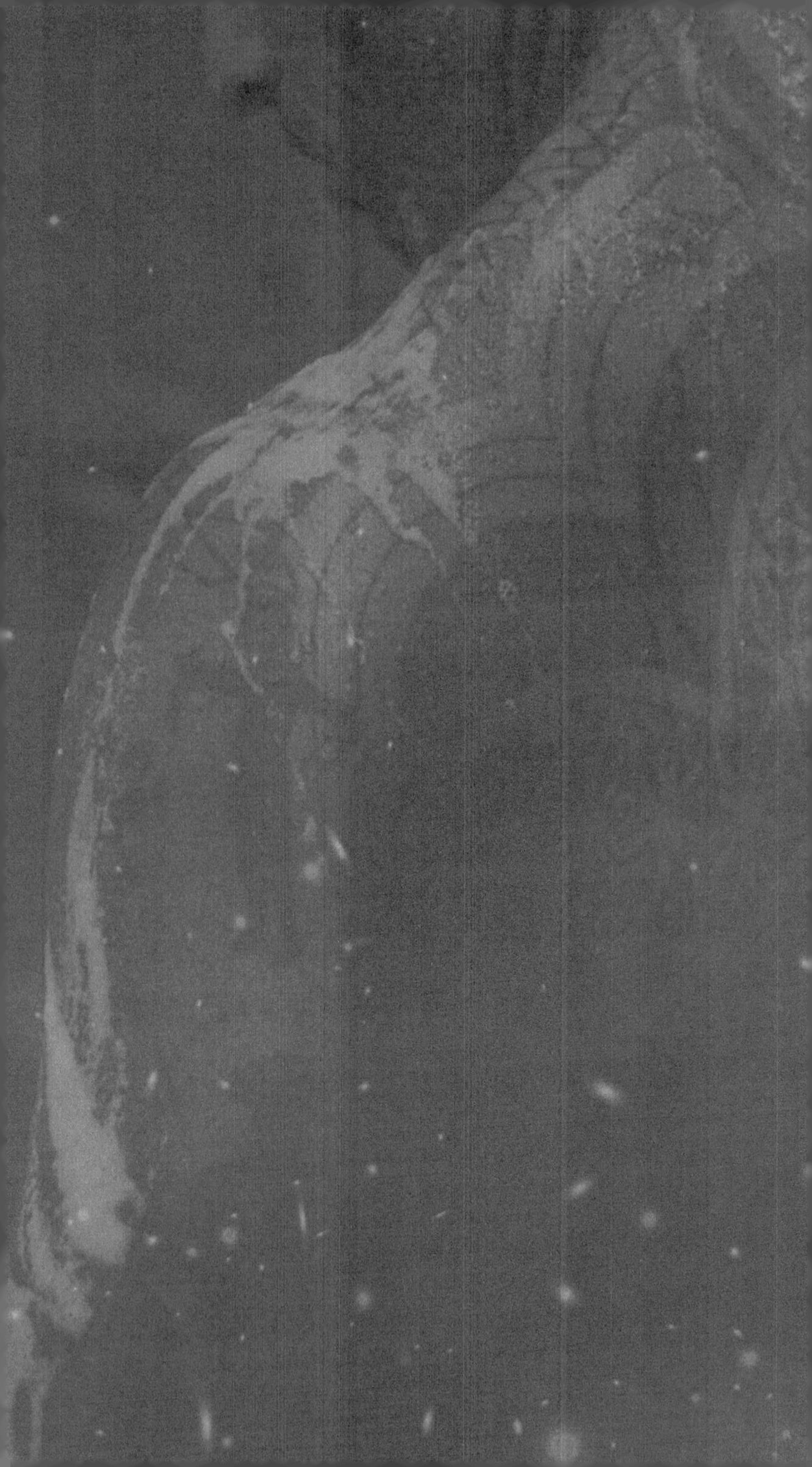

Chapter Eighteen

L **EILA**

Last night was...interesting.

The convulsing muscles of his tattooed stomach will get me through many lonely nights in the future, that's for sure. The moment I imagine him spasming under my touch, my own muscles contract, and I smack the tiled wall of the shower. The physical sting grounds me, bringing me back to reality.

I went too far.

I dove too deep.

I didn't listen to Ken's warning and got hooked on Stephan's powerful presence. And he was so right—there will be no coming out of it. One thing he got wrong, though —there won't be coming out of it *for me*, because I'm too deep. I *see* him. I *feel* him.

And I'm addicted to him as if he's the best drug out

there. I don't think Stephan is the one in danger here—I am. At some point, he'll get tired of me. He will see me as I am—his friend's little, inexperienced sister. And I don't mean just in sex, but in life in general—he's seen so much while I've seen so little. That's not self-pity talking, no. It's the reality of the situation.

Stephan is a drifter, and he'll never settle down, nor would I want him to. He's too large for me and our small town—I understand that, but I can't make myself stop gravitating toward him. So, I decide fuck it, I'll ride this wild horse as long as he'll let me.

Besides that, I wasn't joking when I said we would end up fucking like rabbits. The chemistry in the air around us was palpable, and from everyone's warnings, they all knew it. It was a matter of time before it was too much in this small space, and we'd explode. I'd prefer sooner rather than later.

Finishing my shower, I step into the chill air and instantly shiver. Are we running out of gas? Why is it so chilly?

I quickly dry myself, get dressed, and walk out of the bathroom.

And find no one. The place is small, so it's hard to lose a person in here, but Stephan is nowhere to be found. I'd be lying if I said my blood didn't turn to ice when I don't find him. I run outside, not bothering to grab a jacket.

I rush to the porch, my fuzzy socks sliding on the slippery surface. I wail like a banshee as I slip, but a strong hand grabs my elbow and steadies me.

"Are you insane? It's cold out here." Stephan's voice chides me as he reaches for me. "And you're not even wearing boots."

His arm wraps around my torso from behind and pulls me into him.

"Put your feet on my boots, or you'll freeze to death."

I do as I'm told, and he wraps the front of his jacket around me, enveloping my shivering body into his warmth, smelling delicious and cozy. My heart palpitates with the adrenaline of not finding him and nearly falling, beating against my ribcage. Right where his arm is placed.

"What are you doing out here?" I ask, my breath coming out in white puffs.

"Came to get more wood."

"Where's the wood?" I ask as I lean back onto his shoulder.

"On the side of the house."

"You're not going to get it?"

"I will."

Even though his hold on me is gentle, his whole body is taut and rigid. So is his voice.

I turn to look at him. "Are you alright?"

His narrowed eyes are trained ahead of him. "Yes."

"Then what's wrong?"

"Someone is watching us, Leila."

It's my turn to go rigid. I start looking around wildly, pushing myself into his frame and looking for assurance and safety, I guess. Because I do feel safe with him. Sheltered and reposeful. Along with the general overdrive my body goes into when he is close, I also feel content and...happy.

"Do you know who it is?" His voice is careful but probing. Like he feels the sudden shift in my mood.

I shake my head in refusal.

"Leila." He's more insistent.

"I don't know who it is." And I'm not even lying—I

don't know who's been stalking me in town, if this person found me here. "Did you see someone?"

Stephan's silent for a few moments before answering, "No. And no footprints either. At least not around the cabin."

"Then what it is?" I look back at him.

"Just a feeling."

Suddenly, a twig cracks somewhere in the forest, and Stephan instantly moves me so I'm standing behind him. His whole body is a sheet of steel.

Another twig snaps, and we both turn toward the sound.

A large figure appears from behind the thick pines. First —his antlers. Widespread and magnificent. Then his big head with his big dark nose. Then that whole beautiful body of his.

"Frank!" I cry out and try to move around him, but he pushes me back. "It's okay, Stephan. It's Frank."

"Who's Frank?"

"That is," I point at the moose, "Frank."

"The moose?" He turns to glance at me. His forehead wrinkles in confusion, and he looks positively adorable.

"Yes, Frank the Moose."

"Hold on a minute." He finally lets me go. "You know this moose? This particular moose?"

"Yes, everyone knows him. It's Frank. He lives with Kayla." I look back to Frank. "I will be back, Frank. Don't go anywhere," I call to him.

He snorts loudly, so I rush back inside, put my shoes and jacket on, and run back outside. Stephan stands on the porch, head tilted, watching as Frank watches him. The moose moves toward the cabin, and now only a few feet of deep snow separate us.

The moment I jump from the stairs, I sink into two whole feet of fluffy snow. Obviously, my boots are not equipped to deal with this, and my feet are instantly cold. But it's not a big deal if I can pet Frank. He's a special soul and shows up only at the most convenient, important moments. Some people have started calling him 'the Little Hope angel,' and I agree with them.

I walk to our guest, arm outstretched, letting him sniff me. When his wet nose touches my palm, he snorts and tilts his big head, letting me scratch his ears.

"How did you find us here, Frankie?" I coo as the good boy snorts and pushes his head into my hand for more affection.

The footsteps behind me make Frank strain and pull away from me. Now, his accusing eyes are trained on Stephan, who couldn't resist staying away.

"This is the moose that lives with Kayla? *The* Frank?" His voice is full of wonder.

"Yep."

"When everyone talked about Frank, I assumed it was some homeless dude, living in the woods that everyone loved. Not a moose."

"Yep. That's what everyone thinks."

"And no one thinks to mention it to people who don't know?" A note of irritation clear in his voice.

I turn to face him before I respond. "You weren't local, so people were wary. But you're one of us now." I feel my brows draw together. "To think of it, you became one of us a while ago."

He swallows roughly. "Since when?"

"I think since Frank spotted you at Kenneth's house before."

"What?" His eyes go round.

"Yeah," I nod, "when I dropped you off at his place, I saw Frank marking your car. He does it to people who belong."

"Marking my car?" His face looks horrified. "How?"

"You don't wanna know." I smile widely and turn back to the moose. "Thank you, Frankie." I pet his nose and add with a whisper, "I know what you did, so thank you."

His intelligent eyes blink a few times, and he beats his hoof on the frozen ground before jogging away back into the woods.

I find Stephan behind me with a look of pure wonder on his face.

I tap him on his chest. "Let's go, soldier." His shining eyes move to me. "There goes your lurker. He does that sometimes."

I feel so much better knowing it was Frank and not the same person from Little Hope. Well, if it's a real person with malicious intent and not just some stupid prankster leaving notes on my door and sending messages. These days, it's a likely possibility since a lot of people are too bored to be useful.

We walk back inside, and I take off my jacket and wet boots, heading straight to the fireplace and kneeling in front of the dying fire. Stephan follows me there.

Crouching next to me, he calls my name. "Leila."

"Yeah," I say too cheerfully.

"There was a moment there where you thought someone was in the woods besides Frank."

I keep my eyes on the fire, a plastic smile, hating that he noticed that. I don't want to talk about my little fuck up of a situation. He brings his finger under my chin and turns my face toward him.

"Look at me, Leila." His voice is gentle but firm—he's on a mission.

And I do, unable to resist the warmness of his call. Looking up at him, I find worry lines marring his handsome face.

"I just want to be prepared, that's all," he says gently. "Who did you think was out there?"

I swallow a lump in my throat, worried he's going to look at me differently if I tell him. "I thought it was someone from Boston. Maybe."

His jaw clamps shut, and I hear his teeth scraping against each other.

"Your boyfriend?"

I roll my lips, deciding how much I should tell him. I came here hoping to get away from this person. I don't even know if he's really who I think he is, but my sixth sense is screaming it might be him. Even though I was told he's still in prison, I can't get rid of this feeling. And besides, the ex-Navy man who went through professional training and years of real-life combat felt like we were being watched. Why am I hesitating to tell him that I've got a stalker? There is no one better to help me than him.

"No," I answer with a sigh. "Possibly someone I upset with my work or something." I shrug, trying to look nonchalant. "I don't have a boyfriend."

"That better be fuckin' true." His nostrils flare, and anger fills his voice. He grabs my chin with both hands and leans closer to me. "I. Do. Not. Share."

"Really?" It's so not the time to drag out all the things I've heard, but out of nowhere, I turn into a petty bitch. "That's not what I've heard."

I shouldn't start this by attacking him, but if it'll get me out of my little predicament...

The muscle in his jaw ticks, and his eyes turn bright. "Really?" His tongue peeks out to lick his lips. "What did you hear?"

We're playing again, so I make narrow my eyes, looking up at him through my lashes. "That you love to share. That you like threesomes. Of all kinds."

He slowly pushes into my space. Inch by inch.

"What else did you hear?"

I let my eyes roam his torso slowly before returning to his face. "That you like a good cock too?"

I don't know how I braved up enough to ask that question—it's so very personal—but I'm curious.

"Will it change anything if I did?"

I think before I answer. "No. It wouldn't."

"Good." The corner of his lips quirk up. "But I don't like a dick in my ass. Nor will I like any dick other than mine in yours."

"Presumptuous," I say on an exhale, his face still near mine. "Do you think yours is so good I'll want to stick with it?"

His smile turns mad. His hand shoots behind my head, and he wraps my hair around his fist, pulling my head back and exposing my neck. I try to swallow, but it's hard in this position.

"Too bad for you, because that's the only one you'll be getting." He presses his lips to my jugular and nips at the taut skin. My pussy clenches, loving the feeling. Or maybe his words.

"And what if I don't agree with that," I breathe out, expecting an outburst from him. Hoping it'll be directed at me.

He lets out a guttural growl, and a gush of liquid runs down my thighs. I don't remember ever being so aroused that my body produced enough liquid for a month-long sex marathon for ten people at once.

"Then I'll fuck you until you change your mind," he says, and my body liquefies.

He yanks my head back, bringing his lips back to my neck and sucks. Hard. It's not for my pleasure, it's for his. The primitive marking of a man.

And I'm loving it.

"Promises," I croak, and he yanks my hair harder.

Grabbing my chin in his hand and holding my head back by my hair, he kneels beside me. It's a vulnerable position for me, and I've never been in it before—so dominated —but I'm curious to see where it will go.

"Do you think you can take it?" He leans down to me.

"Do you think you can deliver?" My throat is dry. My nostrils full of his scent. My insides too empty.

"We shall see." His lips graze over mine.

I'm anticipating the kiss too much, and I open my mouth, hoping he'll meet me there. But he doesn't. Instead, his lips tease mine with butterfly-like kisses before he retracts. I want to follow, but he's holding me firmly in place.

"Not so fast," he breathes, fanning my rapidly sweating temple with his breath.

He squeezes his fist tighter, making my scalp hurt. My lips part, letting out a tiny moan. His mouth lands on my chin, and he begins tracing the line of my jaw with light kisses. He bites my earlobe and blows cold air on it.

A shudder quakes my body.

He traces the line of my throat with his free hand down to my chest and stops between my breasts. I'm wearing an oversized T-shirt—*his*—with no bra, and I imagine how good his hand would feel if he only moved his hand a bit to the left or to the right. I've never been into guys playing with my boobs before. I never felt anything and had to pretend to be aroused just so it wouldn't be awkward. But with Stephan, it's different. My whole body is taut and electrified. It's like if he touches any spot below my neck with his bare hands, I might combust in flames.

In the meantime, his hand comes back up, pulling on the collar of my shirt.

"How do you like to play?"

"Vanilla." My throat is dry, so my voice comes out rough. "I like to play vanilla."

His low chuckle is the sexiest sound I've ever heard. "I like vanilla."

I try to laugh, but it comes out as a moan as his hand moves back down and dips under my shirt. He moves back up and lands on my ribs. He spreads his large palm over the front of me, his thumb grazing over the bottom of my left boob. *Just move it a little higher, damn it.*

I squirm, reminding him to move, and he chuckles again. This sound...He should do it more often.

"Impatient, I see."

He brings his mouth close to mine, a breath away...But not touching.

"I can fuck you the way no one else ever will." His voice is coarse. Restrained. Patient.

"I don—"

He presses his lips to mine and quickly pulls back before I can even understand what's happening.

"Sh-sh-sh." Another quick peck. "You had your chance to talk. Now you'll be quiet. I'm talking."

I keep my mouth shut, excited at the prospect. A few hours ago, this powerful, dominant man let me have all the control, and it felt so good. Now I want to experience being on the receiving end of his dominance.

"Nod if you agree."

I go to nod, but he yanks my hair again, sending a shot of pain through my scalp.

...and I can feel how wet I get in an instant.

My mouth falls open in surprise, and his chuckle into my ear causes another shudder. Fuck it, he didn't even do anything, and I'm already so fired up.

He kneels in front of me, still holding my hair in his fist. He opens his hand and places his palm on the back of my head. My hair falls down, cascading over my shoulders.

"You are so beautiful, Lei. You don't even know it."

"It's the hair." I glance to my right, seeing the long, heavy waves resting on my shoulder. I've been told my hair is pretty.

"No." He shakes his head, suddenly grabbing my face in his hands. "I mean, yes, your hair is gorgeous. But it's more." His eyes dart between mine. "It's you. You're just...." He takes a deep breath before continuing, "I would give everything to keep you, but I got nothing left to give."

"Don't say that..." I whisper. This moment of sexual tension quickly turns into something else.

His lips cover mine in a gentle kiss. Very slow and gentle. I wrap my hands around his wrists, feeling his pulse under my fingertips.

He pulls away and touches his forehead to mine.

"I went too far with you and promised too much I can't deliver."

I know he's not talking about sex, because that's something he sure can deliver.

"But you're addictive. Better than any drug I've ever tried." He inhales deeply and closes his eyes. "But I can't stay away from you. Not when we're in close quarters like this. How can I stay away from you? Tell me how."

"Don't," I whisper, because him staying away is the last thing I want.

"I can't, Lei. I can't be with you." His voice is full of agonizing torture.

"Just with me? Because of Alex?"

"God, no. I'm an asshole for breaking a pact with him, but I'll gladly take my punishment for that." He chuckles and then adds seriously, "I can't be with anyone, Leila. I'm not built for that. And frankly, dealing with relationships might be my last fuckin' straw."

I think for a moment, trying to figure out if there's a way out of this for the both of us.

"What if we make a pact?"

"A pact?" he asks, rubbing his nose against mine.

"Yes." I swallow. "We can pretend that nothing else exists while we're here. Just you and me. We can give into everything we're feeling."

"And then?" he breathes out.

"And then," I lick my lips, desperately wanting to taste him again, "we go our separate ways when we're back to real life."

"No strings?" His nostrils flare, and I can't tell if it's because he's mad or he's smelling me. He does that quite a lot, actually.

"No strings," I confirm. "What do you think?"

Please, say yes.

"We can do that," he whispers and licks his lips.

"Yeah" is all I manage to say—his masculine scent enveloping me. He doesn't wear cologne or special soap. It's all him: pure and intoxicating. *Stephan.* I wonder if Archie smells differently—I can always feel the shift when he puts that mask back on.

"Okay," he says with a sigh, but I have already lost track of our conversation.

"Okay," I parrot.

"Alright," he replies with clear amusement.

"Yeah." I'm not even slightly embarrassed by my current lack of brain power.

He laughs, fists my hair once again, and smashes his lips to mine.

Fucking finally!

His tongue checked all gentleness at the door and now invades my mouth like a warrior on enemy land. His free hand grabs my thigh and pulls me toward him. His fingers begin kneading my flesh, and my hips buck. He intensifies the kiss, angling my head so his tongue can dive deeper. I've never been a fan of deep kisses like this. Never found them even remotely arousing. But with Stephan, I seem to find something new about myself every single time he touches me.

My hands go to the seam of his shirt and try to pull it up. He helps me, but unfortunately, he has to stop the kiss to pull it off of him.

Fortunately, I can admire him as he does.

His eyes are on fire with passion, dark and focused. His strong body moves in sleek, precise movements. With every move, the tattoos on his body move along with it, as if every single one of them is alive. His lips are swollen, and it's my doing. I feel unexpected pride rising in my chest.

In a moment, he's in front of me, wearing only gray sweats, tattoos, and piercings—the way I like him the most. He looks around and leans to grab the blanket from the couch. Throwing it in front of the fire, he grabs me by my waist and pulls me onto him. I wrap my legs around him, and he crawls to me, kneeling on the blanket as he lowers me on my back.

"You're awfully overdressed." His wicked smile promises insane orgasms—something I think I'm already addicted to.

I quickly remedy that by pulling my T-shirt off. Lying in front of him in only my slutty black panties, I bring my hands under my head. "Not anymore. Whatcha gonna do about that?" I say playfully.

The right corner of his lips lift in an evil smile as he lowers himself on top of me and rests on his elbows. So close —I can feel his body heat—yet so far away. I want to touch him.

But in the next moment, he's on me. Trying not to crush me—even though I wouldn't mind his whole weight on top of mine, just for a moment, just to feel it—he begins peppering my face with kisses.

Alternating between licks, kisses, and bites, he moves on to my neck. My hands roam his back, feeling his bulging muscles under my palms. They move as I glide my hand over his sweaty skin. And I love the feel of him under my fingertips. I love the power he's withholding. I savor it.

And I want it.

I want him to let go of control and show me the real him.

"I want you to fuck me," I whisper into his ear.

His kisses skip a beat.

"I want you to fuck me so hard I can't walk tomorrow."

His breathing quickens.

"I want you to fuck me so hard every time I fuck someone else, I'll compare them to you."

He lets out a guttural growl and bites my neck. That

one will bruise, for sure. And I'll gladly wear his mark on my skin as long as it will stay.

I want to mark him too. I want everyone to know that I changed something deep inside of him, just like he did in me. So I sink my teeth into his shoulder. Deep. Too deep. I may have broken his skin. But he loves it. He stops biting me for a moment, letting out a loud exhale. He brings his face to the crook of my neck and begins breathing me in. His arms are tight around me.

I squeeze his torso with my thighs and bite him again. A little gentler this time.

His breathing is erratic. His heartbeat crazy—I can feel it in his chest, threatening to knock his ribs out. His arms are a little too tight around me.

But that's what I want—the real him.

"Don't you," he growls into my ear, "talk about others," he bites my neck again, "while you're with me."

"But I—"

"*Fuckin' don't,*" he hisses as he pulls himself away from me.

Oh no.

But he grabs my panties and rips them apart.

Oh yes.

He grabs my thighs and finds my eyes. "Never."

I can't utter a word, so I just nod, excited for what he'll do next. He's at his most primitive state, judging by his face and jerky movements. His own brain has checked out too.

He lowers his face to my stomach and dips his tongue into my belly button.

My breath hitches. It's not like no one has ever licked it before, but my body is so fired up that I nearly come from just that. He places one of his hands between my breasts and presses me down while he licks my belly button once more.

After, he wraps his other arm around my thigh and secures me in place with his hand. I look down and find his face between my legs. His eyes are half hooded and crazed, his hair disheveled, and his shoulders rise with every breath he takes. It's a sight to behold.

He slowly lowers his face and gives a long lick from the back to the very front, and my body spasms as I try to clamp my thighs shut. He doesn't let me, though. He presses his hand to my belly, keeping me flat as he holds my thighs with his hand. He starts licking again, putting pressure in all the right places. My clit is throbbing. My belly spasming. My back arching.

But he keeps the pressure firm, holding me in place. His tongue presses harder onto my clit.

I moan and arch my back despite his hand pushing me down.

He lets go of my stomach and slides his finger inside my pussy. It's drenched. I look down and find him watching me as he moves his tongue up and down. His cheeks are wet with evidence of my desire, and red from restraining his own.

He adds another finger and starts pumping. I moan again.

He moves his mouth back to my clit and starts sucking.

My hands act on their own and grab his hair.

He begins alternating sucking on my clit with flicking his tongue over it while his fingers keep pumping me, hitting that sweet spot.

"Stephan," I moan his name, begging him to put me out of my misery and let me come.

He sucks harder and pumps deeper.

And I come all over his face. My body quaking. My thighs squeezing his face while he helps me ride my high.

I'm not all the way down when he brings his body back up, spreads my legs wide, and smacks himself into me in one fast go, holding my legs at the shins.

My body arches again.

And he starts fucking me mercilessly.

It's the real deal. Not gentle. Not caring. But primal and raw.

With every move of his body, mine moves on the floor, and very soon, we end up off the blanket. And I don't care. My back can be bruised and scratched and totally ruined—I don't care as long as he keeps fucking me like this.

He lowers his body to mine and kisses me. It's messy, sloppy, and perfect.

And I come again. Out of nowhere. When he hits something inside me, I feel the pressure build and release so fast I don't have time to prepare. I've never been a squirter, but I guess no one before him could find the right button.

His nostrils flare, and he wraps his arms around me. Lifting the lower part of my body, he angles it the way it suits him while proceeding to impale me with his enormous dick. I've always known that he wouldn't be small—that swagger and big dick energy can't lie—but he exceeded all expectations.

I'm lost at this point. My body is overstimulated. I can't think anymore. I've entered that state of bliss where my brain can't think, only acts. So I follow his lead, digging my nails into his corded forearms. Scratching his skin. Invoking pain.

His eyes are focused on me, the veins all over his body strained. Especially the one on his neck, where I can see his crazy heartbeat.

"I need you to come for me again." His voice is barely human at this point.

"I can't." It comes out as a whine, and I want to crawl away from this overwhelming sensation and sleep for a week.

"Of course you can."

He puts his finger on my swollen, sensitive clit and presses down as he speeds up his pumping.

And I come again.

My whole body is convulsing, and he joins me a moment later. He tilts his head back and lets out a gravelly growl, making my heart stop beating. It's still the sexiest fucking thing I've ever seen in my life. The muscles all over his body are strained. The veins popping. He's sleek with sweat and my arousal.

It's so messy.

It's so perfect.

This is how real sex should be—two animals lost in each other.

He pumps into me two more times and slowly lowers his body on mine.

I wrap my arms around him, holding him as tight as I can.

He mumbles something into my neck.

"What?" I ask.

He pulls away a little, just enough so I can hear him. "I thought my soul left my body."

I chuckle quietly. "Is it back?"

He pulls his head away and looks me in the eyes. "I'm not sure yet."

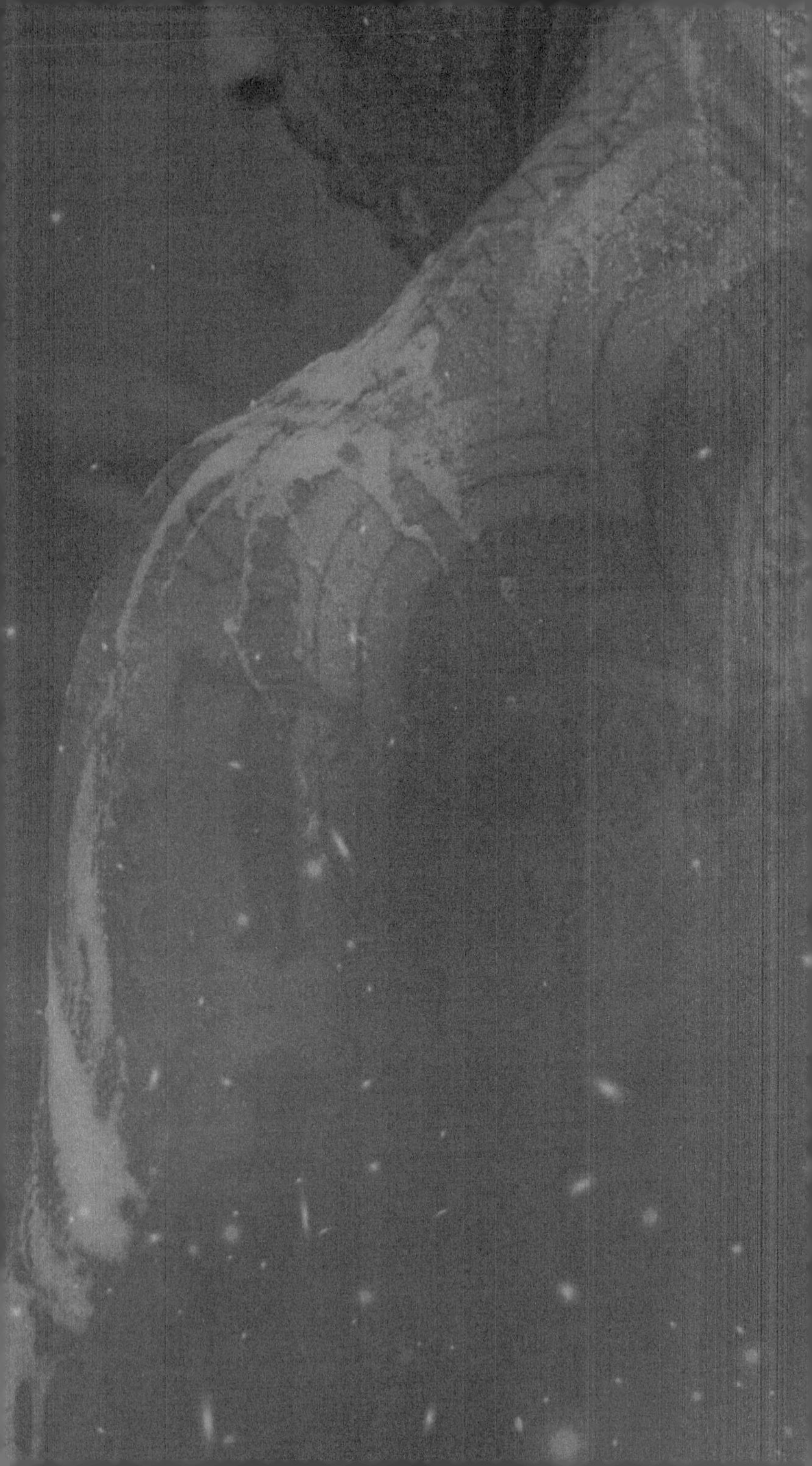

Chapter Nineteen

L EILA

When we wake up from our nap, there is no awkwardness. I don't feel an ounce of shame for anything I do or say around him anymore. It feels...good.

We have a quick bite and get dressed to go find a Christmas tree. Christmas itself has passed, and today is New Year's Eve. But we can still celebrate. Plus, I'm feeling jolly, which isn't a surprise considering the number of orgasms I've received in the past twenty-four hours.

Stephan seems happy too. His face is relaxed, the worry lines on his forehead gone. The corner of his eyes crinkle from smiling.

We're walking deeper into the woods on a mission to find the perfect tree because I don't like anything on our way—I'm totally lying, I just love spending time out here, in the middle of the woods, with snow falling around us—

when I hear the sound of a twig under someone's foot. We both freeze, and Stephan instantly positions himself in front of me, and I get squashed against a big tree.

Another twig breaks, and the sound of a large, loud animal comes closer.

"Damn it, Frank!" I push Stephan away, unable to breathe. "You scared us half to death!"

The magnificent moose appears from behind the big trees and heads straight toward us. He pushes into Stephan's shoulder, moving him out of the way, and stops in front of me, looking for affection. I scratch between his eyes and behind his ears, slightly pushing him back. He presses his wet nose into my hand, snorts as he passes Stephan, and slowly meanders back into the woods.

"See, it was just Frank." I turn to Stephan and find him watching where Frank disappeared, his gaze intense.

When his worried eyes turn my way, there is no humor in them. "I feel someone watching us."

"It was Frank. Trust me, he'd know if someone was around." Frank is notorious for beating up bad guys. As an animal, he has way better senses than we do, so I rely on him here. "Don't be paranoid." He doesn't listen, so I tug on his hand. "Stephan, it's okay, don't worry. It really was Frank."

His dark eyes dart between mine. "Yesterday, you thought someone was around. Who is this person from Boston?"

I thought this conversation was settled, and I've dreaded more questions. But there's no reason to hide it anymore. "Someone has been pranking me, sending me weird messages."

"Do you have them saved?"

"Yes."

"Show them to me when we're back," he demands sternly.

"Okay." I shrug easily. "We don't have service, though. What would you do with them?"

"I'll check them out when we leave."

"Okay," I say with a nod. "But it's real—"

But I'm interrupted by a black furball smashing into Stephan's legs, coming seemingly out of nowhere. He instantly crouches and pats the creature. It looks almost like a cat if it wasn't so skinny, missing an eye and an ear, and not covered in so many battle scars. Cats don't look like that. And besides, I doubt a domestic cat could survive out here.

But it's indeed a cat. A very hungry one.

"I left you food on the porch. Why didn't you come?" Stephan coos as he scratches behind the furball's ears.

"Okay, now the cat food I found makes sense." I nod, checking off one of the mysteries of the cabin. "Do you want to introduce me to your friend?"

When Stephan looks up, his cheeks are blushing, and I bite my lip, trying to hide a smile.

"Sure. This is Midnight." He pats the cat one more time and rises to his feet.

Now it's my turn to crouch. I take off my glove and offer my outstretched hand to the cat, who sniffs it once, lets out a loud hiss, and instantly walks away. "What just happened?" I blink as he disappears.

"He stopped coming for food. He needs to eat." Stephan's voice is worried, like he's a father talking about his child. It's so cute that my nose starts stinging.

"He'll come around when he's ready." I touch his arm for reassurance, but he just keeps watching the cat. I get the feeling the little thing became jealous when I showed up at the cabin, and I can't say that I'm *not* feeling bad about it—it looked so hungry and pissed, and I don't want to be the reason it starves to death.

"You remind me of that cat, you know."

This draws his attention, and he looks at me with a raised brow because that animal is definitely not the best looking one.

"What? You do. All this dark and mysterious." I circle my hand around his face. "Like a black panther or something. This small version," I point toward where Midnight disappeared, "works too. It's like a mini panther, but not even slightly less lethal. *Grr.*" I giggle and mimic the cat's claws with my fingers.

He lets out a loud snort and gestures for me to keep moving.

When my face is so frozen, it threatens to fall off, and I finally find the perfect tree (miraculously), we both hurry back home. I never doubted for a moment that he couldn't find his way back. Throughout our whole walk, he never lost his sense of the land, and we never walked in circles despite the heavy snow. I probably should have thought about the possibility of being lost when I asked to go on this trip, but I always feel less responsible around him. It's like his presence takes the worry of being an adult away.

When we get back home, I shiver in pleasure at how cozy the place is. I cook us dinner while he heads outside to change Midnight's food since he didn't eat it, and now it's frozen.

We celebrate the New Year with two orgasms and a glass of bourbon. I offer Stephan another one, but he refuses with a smile, letting me know he really doesn't need it anymore. I'm happy. I don't like him intoxicated and unable to enjoy his life fully.

We sit by the fire, cuddling and watching the dancing

flames. If there is anything out there better than this, I haven't found it yet. His arm is wrapped around me, and my head rests on his shoulder.

"Will it be okay if I ask you why you changed your name?"

He lets out a loud laugh and answers, "I haven't."

"What?"

"Haven't changed it. Well," he chuckles, "at least not myself."

"What do you mean?" I glance up at him and find a beautiful, content smile on his lips.

"When I went to my first training in the Navy, they took one look at me and called me Archibald." His eyes twinkle at the memory, reliving his past.

"Why Archibald?" I ask, still confused.

"I wore a black turtleneck and high pants—really high pants—and still had a really thick accent and looked like a butler from some British show one of the guys saw. So just like that, I became Archie." I feel his shrug. "And I was cool with it, considering I was there to escape my old life. And trust me, some guys didn't get so lucky with their call names." His chest shakes with quiet laughter. "Like your brother."

"What?" I pull away and start laughing. "What was his call name?"

"Speedo."

"Why Speedo?"

He begins cackling hysterically. "His whities were the tightest in the whole station. Like so tight, your eyes might bleed."

"Okay, stop, stop, stop!" I cover my face with my hands. "Forget I ever asked!"

This is way TMI for my liking, and my ears and eyes are

about to bleed. I don't want to imagine my brother in tight underwear. *Oh no, why did I go there?*

We spend the rest of the night sharing funny stories from our lives, and when morning comes, we move our cuddling to the bed.

The storm stopped sometime during the night, way earlier than anticipated, but we don't talk about it. Talking about it means our little agreement coming to an end, and neither of us is ready for that.

And that's why we spend the following five days in the cabin, eating, fucking, and talking. At some point, someone came to clear the roads.

We drove to Springfield to get some groceries and to find a tow truck. Stephan entered the body shop to ask the guy to come get my car. When he came for it, he told us it's salvageable, but it might take a hot minute to fix. I wanted to pay for everything, but Stephan shut me down, almost offended, and gave the guy his phone number so he could take care of everything. I don't know how I'll explain the lack of a vehicle to my family. I can always tell the truth and just withhold the part about Stephan. Accidents happen all the time, and Kenneth is familiar with it more than anyone.

Today is the day we go our separate ways. In the morning, we had the laziest sex possible, enjoying the moment and memorizing each other's bodies. Three times. I could say the man is insatiable, and it's all his fault, but that would be a lie—I love it just as much as he does. In fact, the third time was totally my doing.

We clean the cabin, pack our stuff, and walk outside. Stephan loads our bags into his trunk and walks around the house.

"What are you doing?" I call out.

"Looking for Midnight."

I don't even try to hide my smile. "What are you planning to do when you find him?"

"Take him with me, of course," he responds, as if it's the dumbest question on earth. Stephan has such a soft heart, I can barely contain my emotions. God help me if he ever mentions a kid or something?

A kid?

Where did that come from?

I shake my head, attempting to erase my unwelcome, illogical thoughts, but it's too late; the seed has been planted, and now all I can think about is Stephan as a father. Of someone else's child. My mood drops even lower than it was. Thank God he's too engrossed in his cat search that he doesn't notice it.

When he finally gives up and walks to the car, we silently climb inside and, as if on cue, look at the cabin together.

"I'll miss this place," he says quietly. A note of longing clear in his tone.

"Me too," I agree and take his hand. He gives it a squeeze and starts the car.

We don't talk much on the way to Little Hope, but he holds my hand the whole time. When he parks in my driveway, I turn to face him.

"I loved our time together. It's what I needed."

"Me too," he says sadly. "Take care, Leila."

"You too, Stephan," I sigh his name, and he swallows roughly.

He turns to look ahead and drops my hand, which is my cue to leave in order to avoid any embarrassing moments like jumping onto his lap and begging him to become 'us' for real. I open the door and silently slip out. Our time in paradise is over, and harsh reality is back.

Chapter Twenty

A RCHIE

I promised myself I wouldn't go to Little Hope under any circumstances. No matter how much I want to. No matter how bad it gets.

And that is precisely why I'm currently parked at the damn diner, watching Leila through the window like a creep four days and fifteen hours after I dropped her off at her house—I promised myself I wouldn't, and I can't keep a promise, apparently.

I looked into the messages she'd been receiving and couldn't find anything. And that's a good thing, of course. But if I had found something, I could have used it as an excuse to show up. The messages were sent from an internet browser, so it's impossible to trail them. I even checked all her recent articles that might have made someone wish her harm, but the only guy I found is still locked in prison. So that was a dead end too.

I sure hope it was just some stupid prank, because the uneasiness I felt back there was alarming. But no matter what I did, I couldn't find anyone who could physically cause her any harm. Of course, they could hire someone to do the deed, but the guy we both suspected is in a high-security facility with no visitors. I was thinking about installing a security system at her place; that will be my next move.

I glance back at the diner windows.

She's alone even when she's surrounded by people. Freya and Alex are back from their honeymoon, and she's chatting with Kayla, who's pouring coffee for everyone. Justin's head rests on his crisscrossed arms—I hope the fucker is having the worst hangover. I can see Marina through the door to the kitchen, and there are a few other people in the diner I don't know.

A knock on my window startles me, and I turn to look, feeling like a peeper who's been caught red-handed.

Kenneth motions for me to roll my window down, looking between me and the diner with furrowed brows.

"What are you doing here?" His voice is stern.

I look ahead, respecting him too much to bullshit.

"What do you think?"

He sighs deeply and looks up at the sky, murmuring, "Heaven, fucking help me. This is gonna be a shitstorm." He looks back at me. "Let's go."

"Where?"

"Inside, dickbag. Let's get this over with."

With that, he heads for the diner, expecting me to follow.

I can do that. Or I can put my car in gear, hit the gas,

and hightail it out of here, away from these problems. I've been doing that for far too long, though, and besides that, I don't want to leave Leila alone under the circumstances. No matter how much we wanted to stay there, we couldn't, and it's time to face reality. Kenneth saw me lurking here in the car, clearly watching her, and now I can't leave her to deal with the questions alone. We might not be able to repeat what we had in the cabin, but we must face reality and move on with our lives.

And I want her to be able to do that. Once she sees me in her close circle, her brothers going crazy, she'll know there's no place for me here and will move on to someone else.

Someone else.

My blood turns hot when I imagine her with someone else, and a shudder rocks my body. *But that's what you wanted,* my fucker of a consciousness helps out, *for you to have her for a few days while you were both far from reality, and then you both move on.*

"Are you coming?" Kenneth yells, standing by the door.

I stare longingly ahead, imagining myself driving away and avoiding all that is about to come, but I man the fuck up and climb out of the Rover to follow Kenneth. He waits for me, a shocked look on his face as if impressed to see me actually coming in. I'm not sure why he isn't smashing his fist in my face, since he clearly knows something happened. And he knows me—no brother would want me for his sister. Not one.

He opens the door and gestures for me to go in first. As I'm walking past him, he smacks my back—a little harder than necessary—and says, "Good luck. You'll need it."

When we enter, everyone cheers up. By everyone, I mean the company I know. Kayla squeaks something. Freya feverishly waves her hand, holding her other to her still tiny belly, and Justin lifts his head and gives me a small wave. I nod to them with a tight smile—I can't muster anything more.

Alex rises from his chair and walks to me, his hand outstretched. "I didn't know you were coming to town."

"It was spontaneous," I answer, shrugging.

As we talk, I glance at Leila, finding her watching me, her eyes wide.

"Hi," I mouth.

"Hey," she replies.

Alex catches on because he looks between the two of us with a heavy silence. I let it slide for now—I'm not here to cause problems, but I won't run away if they arise.

"Archie!" Kayla calls out. "Do you want the black death thing you call coffee?"

"Sure. Thanks." I force a smile on my face as I keep glancing at Leila.

"Coming right up!" she chirps and begins fixing me a cup of strong, black coffee. "I don't know how you can drink this crap. It tastes like garbage."

"Tastes fine to me." I smile again, but it must look too forced, because she pauses and gives me a good, thorough look.

"What are you doing here?" Alex's voice turns cold.

I turn back to face him, knowing where all this is going.

"I was driving by."

"Driving by," he parrots. "Driving by in the middle of nowhere and decided to stop."

"Yep." I nod, straightening my body and prepping for what's to come.

In my peripheral I see Justin lean back in his chair and cross his arms over his chest. "This should be interesting"

Freya punches his shoulder, and he laughs. "What? Something's happening and I'm not involved for a change. Let me enjoy it."

"Idiot." She rolls her eyes, and I agree with her.

No matter what other people are doing around me, my eyes always seek *her*. So naturally I glance at Leila—*again*—which doesn't escape Alex's attention. He looks between us and notices her cheeks turning that pretty shade of pink that looks so good with her ginger freckles. He can't not notice; it's like a flame on her pale skin. The same one she has when I'm fucking her senseless.

"You fucker," he growls. "You fucked my sister?"

And then, without warning—who even gives those during a fight—he punches me straight in the nose. Blood splatters everywhere, and I feel the bone crack. I've forgotten how it feels to have a broken nose, and with all my love for pain, it doesn't feel fuckin' good.

Freya yells. Kayla yells. Some other people start yelling as Alex lands another punch to my face. And then another.

I stumble back but straighten again to meet his next blow.

"Alex!" Leila's voice cuts through the chaos.

"Alex, stop!" It's Freya, and I see her running toward us. I'm about to put myself between Alex and her so I can cover her—I don't want him to accidentally hit her in this rage wave he's riding—when Justin grabs her halfway and pulls her back into him. Finally, he's good for something too.

While I'm watching them, I take another blow to the side of my face, and this one makes me see fuckin' stars. I've forgotten how much damage Alex's fist can do when he really means it.

"Ken! Please!" Leila cries out, and the sheriff steps between us. At a very bad time considering Alex nearly lands his fist on his brother's face. Kenneth's reaction is fast, though, and he ducks just in time...or the blow to land on my face again. All right, I can take a lot of deserved beating, but I'm close to the point of having enough.

Kenneth pushes Alex back and yells, "Calm down."

"He fucked our sister!" Alex yells as he lunges toward me again. I don't back away, waiting for him to give me more.

"Calm down, Alex," Kenneth orders in an authoritative voice.

"No fuckin' way!" He makes another move to rush me. "I'm gonna kill this fuckin' asshole."

"Calm the fuck down, Alex." Kenneth pushes Alex back harder. They're both insanely bulky, but Kenneth has a few pounds over Alex. I don't think that's what causes him to take a step back, though. I think it's Leila who suddenly appears by my side.

His attention switches to her, and he steps toward her and yells, "Why did you do that? Why did you play your fuckin' mind games," he taps his temple, "with *him* too? You took my fuckin' friend away!" he cries.

The diner goes quiet. I don't think anyone breathes after his declaration. That's not what I expected. Not at all. I don't think it's what Leila expected either because her shoulders sag, and she swallows loud enough for everyone on the other side of the diner to hear.

"I didn't play games with anyone." Her voice breaks at the end.

He rolls his eyes. "We all know you love to play games, Miss Smarter-Than-Everyone-Else."

"Alex," Kenneth cuts him off curtly. He stands straighter, ready to fight.

"Oh no, not gonna fly." His crazed eyes are trained on

Leila's face. She looks so tiny here, surrounded by everyone a head or two taller than her, in this diner where she's probably had breakfast a thousand times. With her family standing around her. Brothers who are supposed to protect her.

"Alex!" Kenneth's voice rises.

"What?" he barks. "He's just her new project she wants to fix. But when she chews him up and spits him out, that's it. We can't be friends anymore. Because he fucked my sister. So much for bro code, man. Right?" He shifts his attention to me, looking betrayed. And I feel him, I really do —I was the one breaking the code, though; it's not her fault. I'm older and clearly more experienced, and I should be the one who suffers, not her.

And bigger than that—we're brothers in arms. We've seen some shit together. It makes what I did worse. Way worse.

But all my guilt fades away when I look at Leila, taking in her small figure and tight fists by her sides. The look of betrayal breaks my heart and mends it back together in an instant.

"Stop it" is the first thing I say.

"What?" Alex looks at me, his head tilted.

"Stop talking to her like that." My voice is firm; I'm not allowing any arguments.

"Really?" he cackles. "Why? She's my sister, and I can talk to her however I want. It's not your place to get involved."

I take a step forward.

"You have to stop, Alex. You're going to regret this soon. Once this urge to destroy subsides, you're going to regret it, but it'll be too late."

Kenneth sends me a brief, assessing look but carefully

steps to the side. Alex has had severe anger issues since he was a kid, but I thought he reined them in recently. Turns out I was wrong.

He looks at Leila and smiles wickedly. "I can see you worked on his already fucked up brain."

I move in front of her, shielding her. With her out of sight, he might direct his anger at me. I don't give a fuck what he throws at me, but his words are doing more damage to her than any physical blows to me ever could. I push onto his chest, and he stumbles back. I haven't fought back yet, and he may have forgotten what we went through in the Navy. While he was the team leader, I was the vicious enforcer.

He was only landing blows to my face because I let him.

"You need to stop, Alex," I hiss through gritted teeth.

"Huh." He looks at me curiously. "Did you suddenly change your stripes? We both know you fuck everything that moves. I just didn't know you have so little respect for me and everything we've been through that you'd fuck my sister."

Good. He's focused on me again. That's what I wanted.

"I resp—"

"Don't, Stephan." A small hand lands on my back.

Alex's eyes shoot to my face, and his lips part. After a moment, his eyes dart between Leila and me for what feels like hours until they eventually fixate on mine.

"What?"

Not many people know my real name, but Alex does. I'd never give it to someone I just slept with, no matter whose sister she is. I accepted a new life when I joined the Navy, and they conveniently gave me a call name right away, so I could forget about that part of my life and my mother along with it.

"I was leaving anyway," she whispers to me, and I nod, my eyes still on Alex.

When her palm leaves my back, all the warmth evaporates from my body and follows her.

The ring on the door chimes, and I know she's safe outside. I glance back just to ensure she's out of sight before I move in one swift motion, landing my fist on Alex's face. He stumbles back and looks at me, shocked. I take a step forward, getting into his face in order to make sure he *hears* what I'm about to say.

"That was for the way you talked to Leila," I say evenly. "I let you land a few punches on me because I deserved it, but when it comes to her, all bets are off, and you'll get what you deserve."

He watches me, looking dumbfounded. "She's your sister too. Why are you quiet?" he asks Kenneth.

Kenneth squares his shoulders, looking at us both. "One brother making an ass out of himself is more than enough for one family." He shrugs and folds his arms over his chest.

"He slept with her."

"And yet here you are, worried about yourself." Kenneth sighs loudly and shakes his head. "I'm disappointed, brother."

Alex rears back as if only now realizing what's happening. When his eyes sober up, he looks around, and the good side of his face turns red. Yes, I've seen Alex go into a rage before, but it was never directed at those close to him. I've seen him be a vicious asshole, but this was next level.

Because he was never close to Leila, she always yearned for his approval and looked up to him, searching for ways to prove herself when she shouldn't have had to do anything. She didn't need to earn his love. She's his sister. He used to tell me stories about how his little sister followed him everywhere, and he was annoyed with it. He wanted nothing to do with her, even though I saw his hidden affection in his complaints. To be frank, Alex never tried really hard to be a part of his family, and I was on his side because we were a team. But all that changed the second I saw that look of betrayal on her face.

"Where is Leila?" Alex looks around, lost, as if he just entered the room and this shitstorm happened without him.

"Alex," comes Freya's voice. "Let's go home."

He turns toward her, blinks the fog of madness away. Freya carefully walks toward him, clearly familiar with him in this state. I'm a little worried about her and glance at Kenneth, looking for any cues for what to do next.

He subtly shakes his head. "Let him go. He embarrassed himself enough," he says quietly.

Freya takes Alex's hand and leads him outside. His head whips around—most likely looking for Leila.

When he's out, the whispers start. Every patron in the diner is whispering, firing up the rumor mill with a story that'll feed the town for weeks, if not months.

"Well, I guess you really do have big balls." Justin comes to stand beside me. "To sleep with your friend's sister."

I give him a death stare.

"What?" He shrugs. "There were a lot of broken noses when local guys tried to date her. Though," he shifts his attention to Kenneth, "I wonder how you haven't tasted the sheriff's fist yet," he wonders curiously.

"Justin," Kayla ambles over to us and smacks him on the back of the head, "just stop already."

They start bickering like an old, married couple, and I tune them out, not interested in hearing it.

"I didn't know he was jealous of her," I say quietly so only Kenneth can hear.

"He's never been," he replies while watching the door as if either of them would come back. "I don't know what happened, to be honest." Then he looks at me. "Are you alright?"

"Yeah. Why wouldn't I be?"

He raises a brow, letting his eyes roam around my face. I'm sure it looks like ground beef now.

"Yeah." I touch my nose. "I'm fine."

"Want me to set that for you?"

"And next week we'll paint each other's nails? I'll manage." I roll my eyes, and he cackles.

"Offer still stands. I could inflict some pain on you." His brow quirks. "You know, the legal way."

"And here comes the real reason for the offer." I let a smile slip.

His face turns serious. "Are you gonna go check on her?"

I roll my lips. "I want to, but I'm not sure she wants to see me now."

"I think you're the only one she wants to see." He smacks my back and walks away. "I'll text you the address."

Chapter Twenty-One

A RCHIE

I'm pulling into the driveway of her tiny house. Everything here is miniature and cute, like a little fairytale. It's funny how small everything is here compared to her large person- ality. I think that's what drew me to her in the first place. She is an absolutely gorgeous woman, no doubt about it, and I'm always hard around her, always. But it's her presence that knocks me down every time I talk to her; every time I breathe the same air as her.

It was naive of me to assume that I would come out of this unscathed. I told her myself that time at the cabin was all we could have, and she agreed to it. I thought I'd just move on, but I couldn't. That's why I'm here, back in this town where I promised myself I'd never come. Alex is married now and moving on with his life—I can't drag him back to the painful past we both share. If he could find the power to forget and move on, so be it. I can't do anything about that. I'm not judging, but I don't think I can forget what happened on that mission that easily. Or ever. In the end, we came back alive while they didn't.

There's a light in one window. She's not sleeping. Obviously. I didn't come here right away after the diner—I couldn't. I was sitting at the fuckin' bridge we met at the first time and remembering her face when she got out of her car and walked up to me—a stranger on the road. Did I have *thoughts* when I was looking at the water? Fuck, I have constant thoughts; they never leave my brain. But I'd be damned if I ever admitted that to anyone. I don't need the judgy looks. I've had enough of those in my life.

I watched the half-frozen river and cold, deep waters, and all I saw was her face. What would she think? Would she feel anything? Would she miss me? It's fucking petty, I know, but I have to be honest with myself at the very least and accept that I'm fucked up. They say it's the first step to getting help. All right, I accept it, but where would I move? There is literally no one out there who will miss me. No one. She told me that there is always one person out there whose life I irrevocably changed. I changed a few lives, all right. I changed them by killing their sons, husbands, brothers, cousins. I changed those lives for sure, and they won't miss me. I'm sure they'd be happy to see me rotting in hell. That's what I deserve.

The light turns off—I've been sitting here too long, so I get out of the car and walk toward her door, leaving footsteps in the fresh snow.

And then I notice other footprints. Clearly male. Heavy feet. I follow them. They go to the door, and the person stands there for a few moments, moving around a bit, and then walks back to the street, where the footsteps disappear into a big vehicle. Judging by the tires and the spread of the wheels—a newer truck. Delivery? It's not unknown to have a delivery, even in Middle of Nowhere, Maine. So, I shove the footprints to the back of my mind and walk back to her door—having someone drop some boxes by the house is less concerning than having someone watching her in the woods in the middle of nowhere.

She opens on the second knock. Her eyes are puffy and red. Her nose swollen and pink. Her big, gray eyes are shinier than usual.

"Hey," I say softly, trying not to scare her off.

"Hey." She wipes her nose with the oversized sleeve of her gray sweater and steps aside, opening the door wider.

I walk past her and take my shoes off. She closes the door and walks to the kitchen.

"I was drinking tea. Do you want some?"

"In the dark?"

She glances at me but doesn't say anything.

"Sure, I'll have some," I say, trying to suppress a smile at how cute she looks right now.

Her small feet pat toward the kitchen, and I can't help but notice her adorable fuzzy socks. I look around. The place looks like her. Mostly neutral, with unexpected bursts of color here and there.

She puts the kettle on—she was *already* drinking tea, sure—pulls two mugs out of the cabinet and busies herself fidgeting with the teabags.

"Are you okay?" I finally ask when I can't stand it anymore.

"Yeah," she answers with a sniffle.

"He didn't mean that."

She whips toward me, eyes blazing fire. "Stop."

"It's true. He didn't."

"Stop, please." She raises her hand in the air. "You know what the worst part is?" She looks at the ceiling and laughs. "He made me so jealous." Her eyes dart to me. "And I feel like shit. On the one side, I freaking hate him for that. But on the other side, I understand it."

"What do you understand?" I hope she can shed some light because I'm definitely lost.

"Because he loves you, and he thinks now he can't be your friend anymore since you fucked his sister. And on the other side—or all sides, I'm not sure yet—" her brows draw together, "he hates me for the same reason. So, see, my brother's choosing you over me twice. No matter how you look at it."

Oh shit. I didn't think that she might see it this way. I don't think Alex meant it that way either, but I can see some logic in her words.

"Leila," I sigh, "he didn't—"

"No," she raises her hand again, "you can't change my mind. I've tried to be his sister for so long, I really did, but I should know by now that I can't move that wall. Not when it doesn't want to be moved."

Her eyes turn misty, and she sniffles again. She angrily wipes her cheeks with her sleeve, looking at the ceiling.

"I'm sorry, Leila. I didn't want to get you hurt."

"You?" Her eyes turn to slits. "Do you think you were the one hurting me?"

I nod because that's what I do. I hurt people around me all the time, and they either end up dead or irrevocably changed for the worse.

"Idiot." She rolls her eyes. "Stop blaming everything on yourself, Stephan. It's not your fault. A lot of things you think are, actually aren't. This is on Alex and his inability to move forward. The whole family has been trying for years, but he's so angry with our dad that he's stuck on the bad. My mom broke her back trying to show him that she loves him just as much as she does me or Kenneth or Aiden, but he doesn't see it. And today I saw his opinion of me and everything I stand for. So, it's not your fault if that's what you think."

The kettle beeps, and she pours the boiling water into cups.

"If I didn't show up there today, it wouldn't have happened."

"It would. Eventually, it would. Some other old offenses would surface, and he would flip. Doesn't matter. His words don't change the fact that he is my brother, and I love him, but after today, I'll just stop trying to prove that to him. He eventually needs to grow on his own." She shakes her head and moves the mug toward me. "Anyway, water under the bridge."

I look at her again. I mean really *look* at her. She's twenty-four years old, yet she has more calmness, logic, and understanding than I ever did. A woman like that comes once in a blue moon, if ever, and I had the honor of spending a few unforgettable days with her.

My heart squeezes with the understanding that I won't have that time with her ever again, and I feel empty, the feeling of loss taking over me. It's even worse than when I lost my unit. Way worse, and I didn't know that was possible.

"He loves you, Leila," I try again. "He warned me off of you when he saw my interest. He knows me too well and didn't want you to get hurt."

"Yeah," she says dismissively. "Why are you here, Stephan?"

I never told her, but I like when she calls me by my real name.

"I wanted to make sure you're okay before I leave."

"No, why are you in Little Hope today?"

She's watching me, expecting my answer. I could come up with some random reason for why I'm here, but I never want to lie to her, so I go with the truth.

"I wanted to see you."

She takes a careful sip of her hot tea—a long sip—clearly using it to think of what to say next.

"I missed you too."

I smile—it's such a Leila thing to say—an arrow right straight to the heart.

"It doesn't change anything, though," I reply sadly.

"I know." She places the cup back on the table. "Where are you going after this?"

"Back to Boston."

"Are you coming back?" she asks quietly.

I shake my head 'no.'

She looks down at her feet. "I like you, Stephan, a lot. I didn't think I would get attached to you so much for such a short period of time, but I did. You make it so easy."

"Easy?" I ask, confused.

"Yes," she shrugs with a subtle smile on her face, "easy. I mean, look at you."

"Too handsome?" I laugh.

"And cocky." She smiles. "But you're so much more than you think you are. I got so addicted to you—"

"To me or my dick?" I chuckle, unable to resist a little teasing.

She punches my chest and rolls her eyes. "Your dick is not that special."

"Really?" I narrow my eyes at the challenge. "Not so special?"

I take that step separating us, and now our bodies are flush against each other. She lifts her head up to see my face but doesn't touch me. Nor do I touch her. She'll feel my touch soon enough.

"No." Her face turns defiant.

I lean into her and take a deep breath, inhaling her sweet smell. "If I dip my finger between your legs right now, I won't find you soaked for me?"

"No." Her neck moves in a swallow.

I push my nose into her cheek, still not touching her with my hands.

"And your heart isn't beating like crazy for me?"

"No," she breathes out and licks her lips.

My nostrils flare because it's hard to control myself when I'm trying to seduce her. My body refuses to listen to me and starts acting on its own accord.

"And your hands don't itch to touch me?" I move my nose along her jawline. "Touch my cock like you did at the cabin?"

"No," she nearly squeaks.

I press myself to her so she can feel how hard I am thinking about our time in the cabin together.

"And your tongue doesn't itch to tell me what I should do with my hands?"

She just shakes her head, unable to utter a word. I press myself to her harder, and she squares her shoulders again, trying not to back down.

"And if I d—"

"Oh, shut the fuck up," she hisses, grabbing my face with her hands, landing her lips on mine.

I don't waste time because I don't know how much I

will have here, so I grab her ass and lift her up. Placing her on the counter, I settle between her spread legs.

She pulls on my sweater, attempting to get rid of it as if she has some personal vendetta against the piece of clothing. She lets out a little growl when she can't manage it, and I chuckle into her mouth. She gives me a jab to my ribs, and I laugh.

"Oh, you be quiet," she hisses, and I help her pull my sweater off.

"Yes, ma'am."

I take a few steps backward and stand in front of her in only jeans. I let her eyes roam my torso. She's watching me like she's never seen me naked. I like her hungry eyes on me, and the way she licks her lips as if she can't wait to taste me. My nipples ache for her touch—she found the perfect way to pull on the rings to make them hurt just enough. I like how her hands land on her thighs, and she starts kneading her skin as if imagining my hands instead of hers.

I've never felt more desired than I do right now. It's total bullshit that men just want to fuck anything that moves. Well, not exactly. We do love sex; that part is true. But we also want to feel needed. We want to be desired like the very last breath. And she makes me feel like that—like I'm the last breath she is willing to take. Not with her touch, but with her eyes. They don't lie.

"Are you done?" I ask coarsely as my dick presses against my zipper, and I can't take it anymore.

"Not even close." Her voice is low. Her eyes keep roaming my body. "Did I tell you how much I love your tattoos?" She finds my eyes. "They're so fucking sexy. I love how they move on your skin. Like they're alive." She bites her lower lip. "Like they're a journal of the events that made you who you are."

She got it. She got what I wanted to do. I ink myself to remember certain moments of my life, and she understands it.

Then she looks at the skin above my left nipple. The space is empty, and it looks ridiculous on my fully inked torso.

"What are you saving this for?" She points at the spot.

I look down. "I don't know. I just haven't found the right one for here yet," I say honestly, pressing my palm against the spot, feeling my heart start beating faster. An idea forms in my head, and my heart responds to it, liking what I'm planning.

She nods and stretches toward me, inviting me to come closer. I take her hand, and she pulls me in.

"I lied," she whispers.

"About what?"

"I'm actually wet." Her lips stretch in an unholy smile, and I laugh in return.

I stand between her legs and take her face in my hands. "I want to fuck you so bad, Leila. So fuckin' bad," I rasp.

She puts her hands on top of mine. "What are you waiting for?"

I sigh. "I don't want to give you the wrong idea."

"That this is something more?"

"Yes," I whisper.

"It's a goodbye fuck, right?"

I nod.

"Okay." Her voice is barely audible. "I understand."

"Do you, Leila?" I hold her face in my hands and look into her eyes, praying she'll understand me. "If I could ever be with a woman forever, it would be you. You're not just a fuck to me. Do you understand?"

She nods.

"But I can't be with anyone. I'm not built that way, and I respect you too much to drag you down with me."

She watches me, unblinking.

"And I don't need saving. I don't deserve it. Nor do I seek it. Do you understand?"

She nods again.

"I won't make the first move, Lei. I can't. I can't live with that, knowing I dragged you down with me."

"Okay," she whispers. "I get it."

And I know she really does. She doesn't say it just to say it, but she does. And it breaks my heart that I'm losing the only woman I'm capable of loving. I'm losing her before I even had her. I don't give a fuck about what Alex thinks. Or anyone else, for that matter. She's more than them. She is more than anything. She *is* everything.

And that is precisely why I can't be with her.

"Can I make the first move then?"

I nod, expecting to burn in hell for it.

She gently presses her lips to mine—it's not sexual, but soft. They start moving along mine gently.

She turns her face a bit so her lips find the perfect angle to mold with mine, and I open my mouth, inviting her in. I wasn't joking when I said I can't make the first move.

Her tongue carefully probes my lips, a little shy, and I take it as the first move, so I let myself go.

I let my arms wrap around her and pull her tighter into me while I snake my tongue into her mouth. Her hands drop from my face and move to my shoulders. I know she loves them since every time we fuck, she holds onto them, digging her fingers into my flesh. I love it. She loves it. Perfection.

The kiss is slow. We're molding into each other, remembering the feel of us together, knowing it can never happen again. Her hands move to my back as she traces my muscles with her gentle fingers. They jerk under her touch, excited.

I pull away for a moment, annoyed at her sweater standing between us, preventing me from feeling her completely. I tug on it, showing her that I want it off. She lets me help her out of it and then out of her bra. And now she's in front of me in all her glory. Her pale skin and pink, puckered nipples make my mouth water, and I swallow roughly.

"Pants off," I rasp out, and she slowly starts kicking her jeans off her legs.

When one leg is bare, she stretches the other one toward me, and I grab the material and slowly pull it off, leaving her in nothing but her gorgeous hair and red, lacy panties. She always wears sexy underwear, and I honestly want to keep these whole but can't. When I see her wearing these sexy pieces, I want to rip them off her body. So, I do just that—I step closer, grab her panties, and pull them aside, snapping them in half.

She lets out a chuckle and pulls one leg up, placing her foot on the counter, showing me just how happy she is to see me.

A lot. She is really happy to see me.

She points at my jeans, and I obey her silent command. Pulling them off, I stand in front of her with my twitching, hard dick pointing up.

She smiles and crooks her finger, inviting me in.

I step back and land my lips on her neck. Knowing I'll never have the pleasure of doing so again, I mark her skin as hard as I fuckin' can. Sucking and biting, leaving a bruise of ownership, hoping it will last forever.

It will not.

She takes as good as she gives.

Her mouth bites and sucks just as mine does. Her hands roam around my body and then drop between us as she grabs my twitching dick in her hand, spreading the precum over the head. Then she aligns it with her pussy and starts rubbing the head over it. It's so wet and so hot.

I nearly come on the spot, so I pull her to the very edge of the table and replace her hand with mine, trying to save myself from embarrassment.

I press into her, and we both stop breathing.

I push deeper, and she grabs me harder.

I retract and push all the way in, and she digs her nails into my back. I start moving. She wraps her legs around my torso and meets my every move with one of her own. We're in such a perfect balance, it's painful.

"Harder," she whispers into my ear, and I oblige.

I start pumping harder and squeezing her tighter. She bites deeper, and her nails scratch harsher.

Her shuddering breaths in my ear make me nearly lose my footing. "Harder."

I shudder and increase the tempo. Judging by her moans every time I go in, she loves it.

I'm close. She's close too—her thighs are tight around me, her breathing is quick as her inner walls pulse around me.

And then she does something I don't anticipate.

"I love you, Stephan," she whispers into my ear.

And I come like a fuckin' fountain. Unable to wait for her. Pump after pump, nonstop. And she follows me right after.

Riding wave after wave, I come back down to earth. To the truth of her words. To the fuckin' scare of my life.

I pull away and start feverishly collecting my clothes scattered on the floor.

Leila quietly gets off the table and pulls her sweater and jeans back on. By the time she's done, I'm halfway to the door.

Before I open it, I hear her voice behind me. It's not judgmental. It's not accusing. It's firm but gentle.

"I can't be your crutch, Stephan. I don't think anyone can. But I will be if you need me to. Every time your mind gets clouded with thoughts I don't appreciate, I want you to remember what I just said. I mean it, and I stand by it."

I want so badly to turn around, but I can't. My hand is on the doorknob, my heart is bleeding, and she keeps talking.

"I'll always be here if you need me. I'm that person whose life you've changed. Irrevocably for good."

My eyes itch, my nose tingles. I squeeze the doorknob, angry that it'll separate me from her forever.

"Just remember that," she adds quieter. "Just remember me."

I open the door and run outside like all the demons of hell are chasing me. I get in the car and let myself go. Hitting the fucking wheel over and over again with my fist, I squeeze my eyes closed so they won't fuckin' leak. I want to go back. I want to open this door and run back inside her house, to the warmth of her presence. I'm a short breath away from doing so.

My phone rings, and I grab it to turn it off, but I accidentally press the 'accept' button before fumbling it, dropping to my feet. My mother's cold voice rings through the Rover like thunder.

"Is that you, Stephan?"

Fuck. I duck to the floor, trying to find the phone in order to shut her voice up, but it fell under the seat, so I can't reach it.

"Well, it's your mother, Stephan. I have a charity event, and I need you present. Quite frankly, I have no idea why people want to see you here, but they do. Saying you're a hero." An evil laugh follows.

Fuckin' shut up.

"After you being dishonorably discharged," she says offensively. "I prefer not to tell anyone that you're my child, but people remember. Unfortunately." Her cackle grades on my nerves. "Anyway, I haven't heard from you in years. I hope you didn't find some poor American girl to get pregnant. God knows the earth can't handle another one of you. You've done enough damage to your family and those poor soldiers that served with you."

I find my phone but don't press the button. I don't know why, but I keep listening to her.

"Anyway, I expect you to be here on the twenty-ninth. Make sure you look presentable and cover those god-awful things you call art."

And she hangs up. It's like that with her every time. I pick up for some unknown reason, and she spreads her poison.

But she also just reminded me why I can't go back to Leila. I love her too much to ruin her life with my presence, so I put my emotions on hold, start the car, and drive away without looking back.

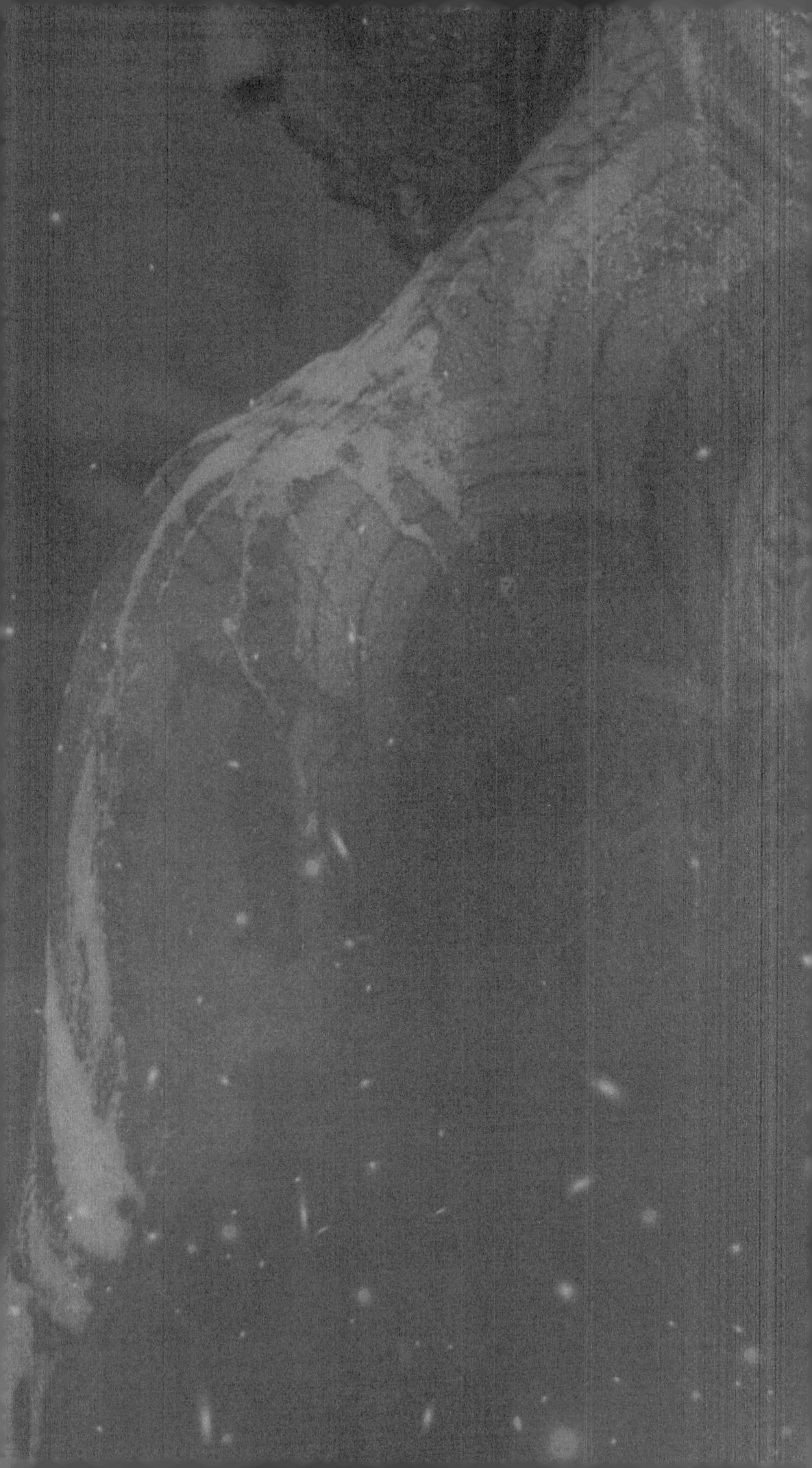

Chapter Twenty-Two

L^{EILA}

Since he left three days ago, I've been moving on autopilot. I knew he wasn't going to stay, but it hurts nonetheless. I wasn't lying when I said that I loved him. I didn't think I could love anyone other than my family, to be honest. I always thought a little differently than people around me and felt a little less, so I figured love wasn't in the future for me. I was wrong. Stephan, appearing in my life, made everything change. Everything. Even my understanding of the world. I always thought if I'd be lucky enough to find someone I could love, I'd never let them go. But turns out, if you love someone more than you love yourself, you set them free.

He is not the type to be caged. By anything or anyone. But I couldn't let him go without letting him know how I feel. I don't regret it.

The moment he left, I went to bed without taking a shower, hoping to preserve his scent around me as long as I could. The second day I planned the same, but I smelled a little gross. *Fine, a lot.* So, I had to wash away all the evidence of him being here the night before. I cried in the shower, a rare occurrence for me. I cried the day before too, but because of my brother. I mourned the idea of him accepting me as his sister. I cried over the years I've wasted trying to prove him that I loved him. I cried over Stephan losing his friend and brother in arms.

But the day after, I stopped crying and decided to figure out how to help the person I loved the most. Unfortunately, the person who could help me is a jerk, so I had to find a way to get around it.

And I'm still waiting, two days later, thinking over how I can get the information out of him.

And the information comes to my doorstep on its own on day four.

A soft knock on my door draws me back from the heavy research I have currently splayed over my worktable. I peep outside and find Alex nervously moving from foot to foot. I open the door two inches and look outside.

He swallows before speaking. "Hi."

"Hi," I say calmly.

"Can I come in?"

I open the door wider, silently inviting him in. He steps inside and looks around. This is the first time he's been in my house, and I've been living here for two years. To be honest, he's never bothered to really get to know me. And I'm just seeing it now, looking back at all the years I've been running around my big brother, desperate for him to notice me.

"It's nice here."

I ignore the compliment and lean against the wall with my arms crossed over my chest.

"Look," he puts his hands into his winter jacket, "I'm sorry. Alright?"

I raise a brow. *That's all you've got?*

He chuckles and wipes his face with his hands. He does it when he's nervous.

"I'm an asshole. I didn't mean what I said. I don't even remember what I said, honestly. Freya told me." He swallows and looks to the side. "I didn't mean it, Leila. I really didn't."

I sigh because I know that he has anger issues. Real, clinical issues where his brain can't contain his emotions, but I also know that people tend to tell the truth when their reins break, and that's why I'm on the fence. Not because he offended me, but because he really thinks all of that, and I don't know how I feel about it just yet.

He lets out a loud sigh and squints at me, trying to make a funny face. "What can I do to make you forgive me?"

I narrow my eyes at him. "What *can* you do?"

"Anything." He places his open palm over his chest. "Absolutely anything."

"Tell me about your last mission."

His face pales. "I can't, Leila."

"You can. It's been many years, Alex."

"I can't." He shakes his head and starts backing away to the door. "I can't."

"I need to know the truth, so I can help Stephan."

He tilts his head, confused. "Help him?"

"Don't you see it?"

"See what?"

"He's suicidal." For the first time ever, I say the word out loud.

Alex thinks about it for the first time ever too, because he pales even more.

"What do you mean?"

"Can't you see that he's driven by guilt?"

"It's survivor's guilt; we both have it."

"No." I shake my head. "His is different. It's deeper. I think he blames himself for something that happened there. I don't see any other reason he would be like that."

"He's not suicidal," he states firmly, trying to convince himself, I think.

"But he is." I meet his eyes and hold them. "And deep down, you know it, but choose to ignore it because it hits too close to home, bringing your own guilt to the surface. That's why I want you to tell me the story so I can help him."

His jaw squeezes shut. The muscles in his cheeks moving under his skin from how hard he's grinding his teeth together.

"I want you to know that I forgive you without this story. You are my brother, and no matter what you say, that fact won't change. But if you decide to tell me your story, I'll dig out the truth. I don't know what I'll find, but I strongly suspect that you both were wrong to blame yourselves all these years."

He clears his throat. "How do you know?" he rasps.

"From what I've found so far, there was a sudden change in commanding officers during the period you got injured and were in the hospital. A whole lot of them. Every time stuff like that happens, they're cleaning something up. But I have a few pieces I can't put together, and that's what I need to know. I just hope one day you'll be able to talk to me about it. I know how to listen."

His eyes are guarded. His throat moves in a rough, loud

swallow before he speaks. "I can't, Leila. I can't talk about that."

He turns around and walks away.

"I still love you," I say to his back.

He pauses, his shoulders hunch, but he pulls the doorknob and walks out.

A sense of strong déjà vu washes over me. The second person to walk out of my house with their back turned to me in the past week. I must be breaking some unspoken record.

I sigh to myself because no one else is here to listen, lock the door behind him, and go back to my research.

A few hours later, a loud knock on the door startles me, and I jump from the couch. I must have dozed off while reading this god-awful article. Another knock, louder this time. I look at the clock—it's twenty minutes past ten. Who would be here this late in our small town unless someone is dying?

I quietly tippytoe to the door and look through the peephole. Alex stands there, eyes crazed. I unlock the door and open it.

"What happened?" I ask.

He looks around, pointing at the fresh footsteps. "Have you had a guest over?"

"No." A chill runs through my body.

"Did you get any deliveries?"

"No."

"Lock the door," he orders and takes off, following the prints in the fresh snow.

It's not the first time in the past week I've noticed it. It's the same shoe print and the same size. They always come from the road, stand on my porch, and leave the same way. I was seriously considering installing the security camera. I know it'll look ridiculous in this neighborhood, but I feel uneasy more and more every day. At this point, I must drop the idea of it just being a stupid prank.

"Leila, it's me," Alex's voice sounds through the door a few minutes later.

I unlock it and let him inside.

"Did you find anything?" I ask.

"No." He glances at me. "It's not the first time it happened?"

"No." I shake my head.

"Do you know who it might be?"

"Not really." I had my suspicions, but they turned out to be false when I texted the person who knows everything again and who was one of the reasons I'm in this situation right now, and he confirmed that the subject is still in prison.

"Okay. I'll get you a camera tomorrow morning." He nods to himself.

"Thank you," I say quietly.

He bends over and starts unlacing his boots.

"Are you staying over?" I ask with a raised brow.

"I came here to give you an interview."

My heart skips a beat. "Interview?"

"Yes." He looks up at me and nods. "Yes, interview. About the night this," he points to his scarred face, "happened."

I blink a few times and then, out of nowhere, find myself launching at him. I wrap my arms around his neck. "Thank you. Thank you, thank you, thank you!"

"Yeah." He awkwardly pats me on my back until I unwrap myself from him.

"Thank you, Alex." My heart is full of love and appreciation, knowing well enough how hard it is for him to open up and talk about this. "Do you want something to eat or drink?"

"I want a bottle of whiskey in one go, but I'll refrain. We want the facts here." He chuckles and walks to the couch.

"Do you want to go on record?"

"Yes." He nods. "It's time."

"Okay." I pull out my voice recorder and start. "Today is January seventeenth; Alex Crawley is present to tell his side of the story. You can start, Alex."

"How do I start?" he asks nervously, scratching his chin.

"We can start by stating the facts about your unit."

"Alright then." He chews on the inside of his cheek and asks, "Can you turn it off for a second?"

I nod and hit 'stop' on the recorder. He looks around, looking uncomfortable again.

"What's on your mind, Alex?" I ask carefully.

He shifts his attention from the very interesting coffee table in front of him to me. "So, you and your new boyfriend broke up?" He raises his brows and rolls his lips. He looks adorably hilarious. And super uncomfortable—after all, we've never discussed our relationships. As far as I know, he doesn't know if I've ever had any. And judging by the way he jumped into the question, he's not going to beat around the bush.

"We were never together to begin with to, you know, break up." I force a weak smile.

His face clouds as his hand squeezes the pillow he's holding. "So, he just fucked you and left?"

"No." I state firmly, preventing him from boiling over again. "We had an agreement. We weren't together. We just spent the time we were given together."

"And he was okay with that?" His forehead wrinkles.

"Do you see him around?" I mockingly look around. "He'd be here if he wasn't, right?"

He watches me for a few moments before speaking. "Are you okay with that?"

"I guess." I shrug.

"Oh fuck." He scratches his cheek. "Did you fall in love with him or something?"

I throw him a funny look. "Or something?"

"I dunno." He looks around as if looking for an escape, and I chuckle to myself. "Do you want me to beat his ass?"

I let out a laugh. "No, Alex. I'm a big girl, and we really had an agreement."

"That's good. Okay." He nods a few times to himself. "I should still beat his ass, though."

"I thought you wanted to beat my ass?" I narrow my eyes.

"What?" He rears back, looking scared. "I'd never do that."

"Hmm." Let him sweat a little, so he knows his actions always have consequences. Always. "Should I remind you that you blamed me for taking your friend away?" I ask, lightly tapping my chin.

His neck and face redden, and his eyes dart away. "Leila," he sighs, "I didn't mean that." He sits back in his seat. "You're both my family. You're my sister, and even if I don't show it, I always feel it. You know what I mean?"

He waits for my nod and keeps going.

"And I always worry about you. But I worry about him too. Leila," he leans forward, placing his elbows on his knees, "what we've been through together—" He shakes his head, looking for the right words. "It binds people, you know. Not only years of service but losing our team and surviving. Only us. You know. No one else. Why are we alive while they aren't anymore? That's the question I'll be asking for the rest of my life."

"That's a lot of survivor's guilt," I tell him. "It must be hard."

"It is, but it is what it is. I'm used to living with that. But —" he cuts himself off. "But our guilt is different," he says meaningfully.

"How is that?"

He sighs and looks at the ceiling. "Because I was a team leader, and they died under my watch." He rakes his hand through his already messy hair. The gesture nervous and uneasy. "But Archie might be the reason why they're dead."

He meets my eyes, probably voicing his fears for the very first time in his life. I'd be lying if I said I didn't feel a tug of disappointment, but it actually makes sense—the guilt he's carrying, the suicidal thoughts, everything. There's only so much a person can take, and he reached that point. Everyone would.

A feeling of tranquility settles in my chest, and I smile at Alex. I'll dig for as much information as I can, and yes, I'm a reporter and I write facts. No matter what I find, I'll help him get through it. I will not leave Stephan alone. Besides loving him as a man—yes, I've admitted and accepted the fact—I love him as a friend. He introduced me to a feeling of real connection with another human being. The sort of connection that comes from within. He's a part of my life now.

"What I just said didn't change the way you feel about him, did it?"

"No," I state firmly.

"Cool." His short nod is one of silent approval. "Then let's get this over with so you can write this article. I sure hope you'll find something different from what we've been thinking all these years."

I sure hope so too, Alex.

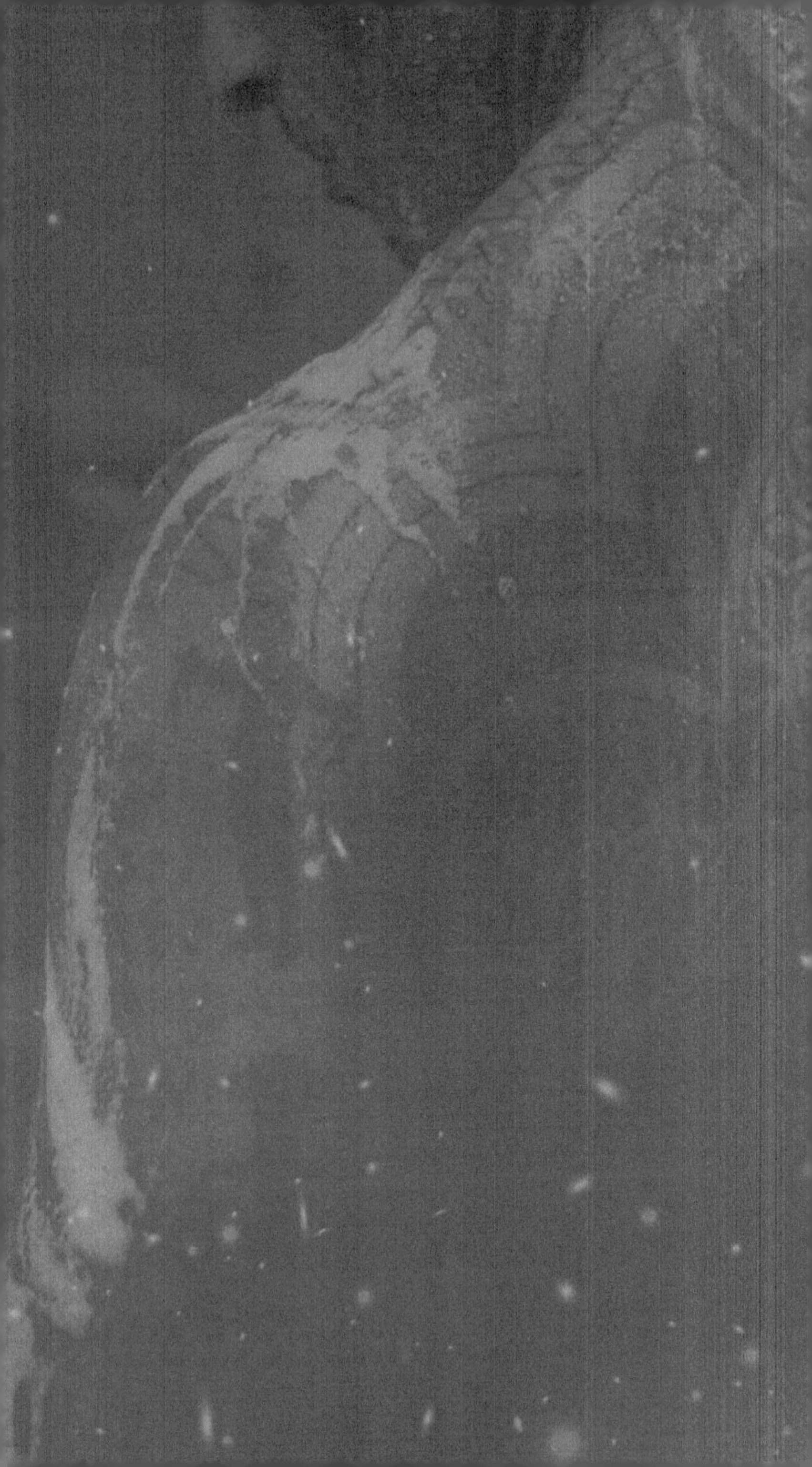

Chapter Twenty-Three

L EILA

The trip to Boston is long. Thank goodness Kenneth lent me his truck, because I hate driving in the snow, and his big vehicle seems safer. Yes, I know I live in Maine and we've got tons of it. Still not a fan. Plus, I'm a nervous wreck. The article in my purse seems to weigh a ton. The paper itself weighs nothing, but the content is heavy. I started this story without his permission. I didn't tell him that I was going to do it, but Alex was a participant too, and his story is just as important.

Besides that, I've found something that might put a target on my back. Not that that was anything new to me. So many things were happening around their unit around the same time, and the focus was lost. It was my job to find it. But what I found was way more than I anticipated, and now I don't know what to do with the information.

My publisher is set to release the story tomorrow morning, and I have the draft copy. I want Stephan to see it first. He might never forgive me for it, but that's okay. As long as he forgives himself.

I drive to his house first. Kayla gave me the address and packed me a huge lunch to go. She's adorable, and I'm very grateful for her, but I couldn't eat a bite—too nervous to swallow anything but coffee.

As I pull into his driveway, I whistle. His house is not just a house, it's a damn Victorian masterpiece. Huge. And I mean *huge*. I'm pretty sure even Freya's whole PTSD center is smaller. Bushes covered in snow, line the path all the way to his door. Massive evergreens frame his property. And the building itself is gorgeous. Made of red brick with a huge double door, it reminds me of a castle from the fairy-tales. A beast's castle. Despite his house being absolutely breathtaking, it doesn't give me homey vibes. Quite the opposite—it puts me in a foul mood. Once the beauty settles in, the grim starts creeping in.

I park and get out of the car. Looking around, I notice that there are tracks from only one car, most likely his Rover. I walk to the door and ring the bell. I ring it a few times, but no one comes to open it, nor do I hear any sign of life. I knock with the same result.

I didn't want to call, giving him a heads up and a chance to escape, so that is out of the question.

All right then, Kayla gave me the parlor address too, so I go back to the car and take off.

It's five p.m., so it should be open. Kayla mentioned that they work different hours than other businesses.

I find his parlor on one of the busiest streets in the city. My friends and I used to go here when I was in college in

Boston: the street is alive during the day and at night, with tons of bars and tourist traps.

His parlor takes up half of the first floor of a huge building—color me impressed, but that's a lot of success for a tattoo place. A pang of pride sparkles in my chest for what he's accomplished as a businessman.

FRAGILE LIVES. The black, neon letters with a red shadow greet me as I open the door. How very fitting.

"Hey, how can I help you?" A young woman, covered in tats and piercings, greets me from the receptionist table.

I walk straight to her. "Hi. I'm here to see Archie."

Her face falls. "Sorry, but he doesn't take clients."

"I'm not a client. I'm a friend, I guess."

Her brow raises. "His 'friends' usually come later at night."

Is she being a judgmental bitch? Well, yes, she is. My eyes narrow at her. What sort of friends is she talking about?

She must have seen it written all over my face, because she smirks and gives me a sinful smile.

"So yeah, wait your turn, 'friend.'"

I'm a levelheaded person with a lot of patience, I repeat the mantra, but right now, I want to smack her head into that table she's tapping her long-ass nails on. But my mother raised me better than that, so I say as politely as I can, "Would you mind telling him that Leila is here?"

"Listen—" she starts, but a big bald guy with trunks instead of arms saunters over.

"Leila?" His voice is full of wonder.

"Yes, that's me. I'm here to see Archie."

"Thank fuck," he sighs and touches my shoulder to direct me to follow him.

"Hank! She can't go there," the receptionist raises her voice.

Hank turns to her. "Sasha, you've been here for two months, and I'm positive today is your last day." Then he lightly pushes me forward. "Let's go. She's been driving me bananas."

"I can see why." Then I remember his words. "How do you know me?"

He gives me a funny look. "I might have heard your name being mentioned a few times."

I quirk a brow questioningly, but he just laughs it off. We walk through a corridor with a few doors on each side. The buzzing of tattoo guns accompanies soft music and quiet laughs coming from the rooms. The atmosphere is relaxing, something that I didn't expect from a place like this. Well, to be fair, I've never been in a place like this. I got my ears pierced in my pediatrician's office when I was four-teen, and that's about the extent of my adventures.

"There." He points to the door on the left. "Good luck, honey." And he disappears.

I take a deep breath and go to open the door when a soft, sexy chuckle comes from the other side. I freeze. Maybe it's from one of the other rooms, so I turn the knob and push the door open.

Stephan's sitting in a leather chair, his feet propped up on the mahogany table in front of him. A bottle of alcohol in his hand. He takes a sip right as I show up. His eyes turn wide, and he spits the liquid out.

Beside him, with her butt on the same table by his feet, is one of the most gorgeous women I've ever seen. Her legs are crossed, and the huge slit in her red, leather skirt reveals a little too much of her sexy stockings she's wearing. Her white, tight shirt is missing a few buttons, and I can clearly see her red corset underneath it. Her hair falls on her back in soft, blonde waves with colorful stripes here and there. It reminds me of Kayla and her constantly changing strands of hair that match her mood. This lady's mood is pretty good though. At least, it was. Until Stephan sprayed her with alcohol.

She jumps on the floor and starts yelling, "Are you out of your mind?"

"Leila?" Stephan stands too and blinks a few times, watching me and completely ignoring the gorgeous woman in front of him, who whips her whole body around, her eyes wide.

"What are you doing here?" he asks, looking guilty as he puts the bottle on the table and takes a step to the side, away from it and the woman.

I glance between them both before I pull the gazette from my purse. Then I slowly walk to the table and carefully place it on top.

"I thought you should read it first. It releases tomorrow." Then I glance between them again and murmur. "Sorry for intruding; I didn't know you had company."

Her eyes are round, and she keeps blinking, her jaw hanging open slightly. She doesn't make a sound. I feel uncomfortable and betrayed, which is illogical since we never even put any labels on our time together. And I totally understand—logically—that he can do anything and anyone he wants, but I haven't. I guess I was hoping he would do the same. Naive of me, I see that now.

"It's—" he says, but I turn to walk away. I've done what I wanted, and I hope he will have some peace.

I raise a hand in the air, hating to be in the situation I promised myself I'd never be in.

"It's okay." I point at the paper on his table. "Please, read it."

And I walk away, leaving the gorgeous woman in the

same pose, her eyes darting between the two of us. He's frozen in his spot, looking even guiltier than when I first saw them there.

I walk past the receptionist, who shoots me a disgusted look, and out to my car.

And this is where I let the first tears slip through.

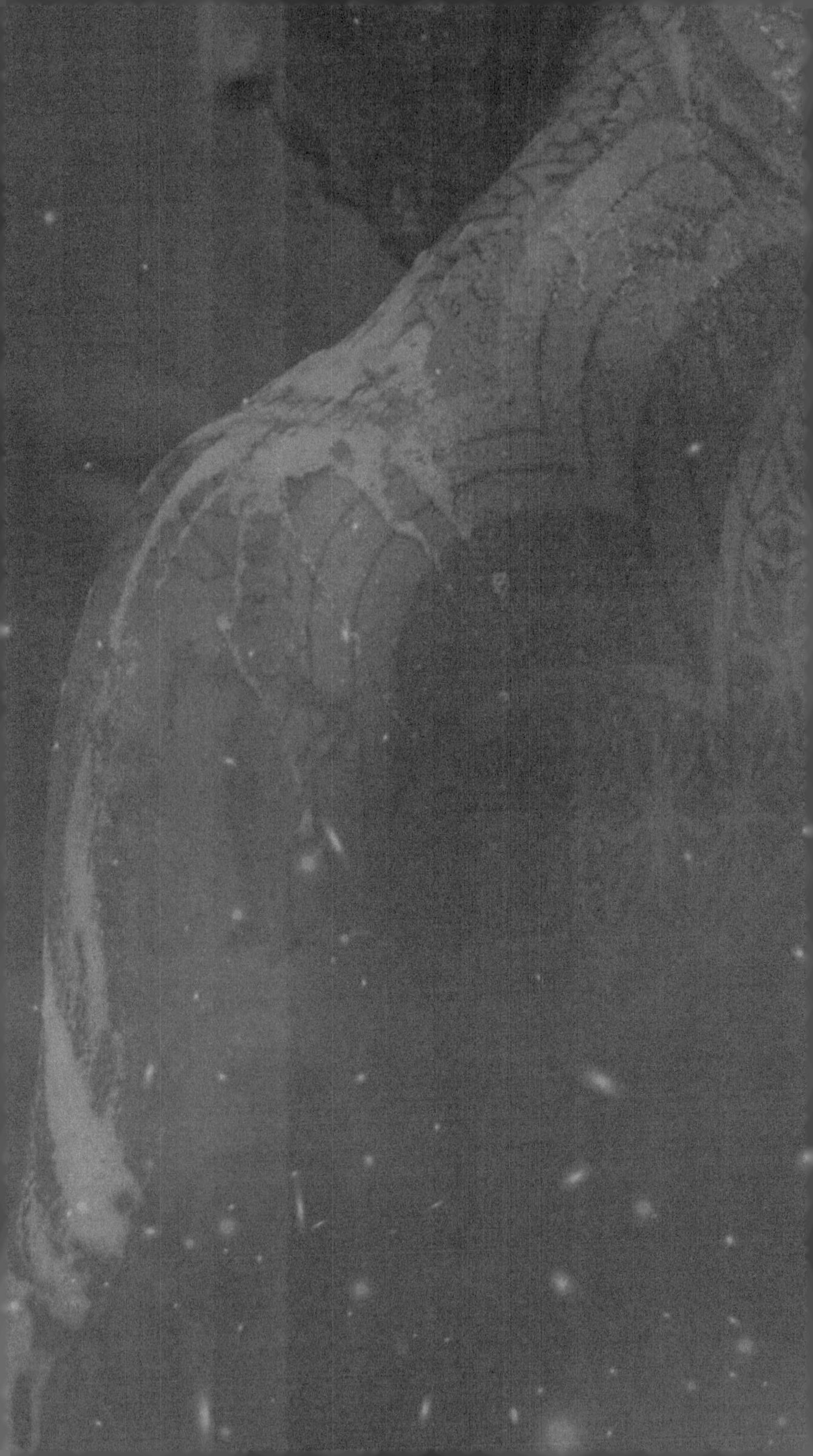

Chapter Twenty-Four

ARCHIE

I blink at the door, still not understanding what just happened. Was she really here, or did I drink myself into a hallucination?

"Fuck, Archie, was that her?" Cherry mumbles from the other side of the table.

"You saw her too?" I look at her hopefully for confirmation that I'm not going crazy.

"Yeah. You didn't tell me she's fucking stunning." Her wide eyes turn to me. "Like stunning, man. I'm crushing so hard."

I shift my attention back to the door. "Why did she leave?"

"Are you an idiot?" She looks at me, a stunned expression on her face.

"What?" I ask, confused.

"She thought we were doing something here!"

"What do you mean *doing*?" My brows furrow as I stare at her.

"Like fucking, I dunno." She shrugs. "Petting. Flirting."

"What?"

"Yeah." She rolls her eyes. "I was sitting on your table," she points at it, "and you were drinking yourself to death," then she points at my chair, "with a happy smile on your face. Of course, she thought we had something going on."

"Why would she think that? You're Cherry." It's so obvious to me drunk, maybe sober me will understand it better tomorrow.

She quirks a brow and crosses her arms. "Does she know that?"

"What?" I blink.

She rolls her eyes and mumbles, "You truly poisoned all your brain cells with alcohol."

"Cherry!" I cut her off, losing patience.

"She doesn't know my name!" she yells. "Dumbass! She saw a woman next to your drunk ass. Do you get it now?"

Understanding slowly dawns on me. Fuck. *Fuck!*

"And besides that," she starts picking at her cuticles, "you looked guilty as fuck. Like we really were doing something." After a massive eye roll, she adds, "You're so dense sometimes."

"But I was." I glance back at the table. "I was ashamed she saw me with a bottle again, that's why I backed away."

Cherry's eyes soften. "Oh, my poor Archie."

Not waiting to hear what she wants to say, I rush through the door, through the parlor, and run outside, but she is nowhere to be found. I run along the sidewalk, looking at the parked cars, but don't find hers. I take my phone out and start calling her, but it goes straight to voice-mail. *Fuck! What have I done?*

I promised myself that if I ever saw her again, I would ask for another agreement. If she wants a day, I'll take it. A year—I'll take it. Anything she'll give me—I'll take it. But I would only do that if fate brought us together on its own, and I would not seek her out on purpose because that would be wrong and unfair to her. I can always find her, always, and forcing myself in her life would give her very little choice. The insane chemistry we have is both blissful and toxic at the same time. For someone young like her, it might close off all future possibilities, and I respect and love her too much to do that to her.

I was hoping this day would come eventually but didn't count on it since I promised myself to never visit Little Hope, so the odds would not be in my favor. What I didn't anticipate is for her to show up here, at the only other place in the world that used to bring me joy before I met her. But for the past few weeks, it hasn't brought me anything but disappointment.

Every time I came here looking for relief, I didn't get any. Every time I expected endorphins to hit when I heard the buzzing of iron, I got none. The more I wanted it, the less I got.

My mind was taken by her. Completely and utterly taken. I've never had this feeling before. Ever. I didn't know I was capable of this depth of obsession with someone.

So, I started drinking heavier than before—the very thing she gave me shit for. I came to work in an Uber, already drunk, and I left in one, too wasted to the point of not remembering my own name. But not once did I think about another woman. Not once, and there were plenty of opportunities. Women love me and they love my money, and before, I'd enjoy every single one of them, but not anymore. Something in me shifted after that time in the cabin. Hell, it shifted way before that, on the bridge.

But she doesn't know all of that, and I can see now how she might have thought something was going on when she saw us together. When Leila opened the door, Cherry was trying to convince me to go to get my shit together; go to rehab before I find the balls to go to Little Hope to talk to Leila. I told her that Leila had my balls in her hands just as she opened the door at that exact moment...

She told me she loved me. I'll never forget that. When I was balls-deep in her, she told me she loved me. I thought it was just the orgasm talking, and she'd take it back when she'd come down from the high. But she didn't. She sent me running for the hills with parting words of love. Words I don't deserve and never will. How can she love me? A monster responsible for the lives of his brothers? How can she do that?

I look at the parlor and decide not to go back because I can't handle Cherry's looks and supportive words. I know she means well, but I'm beyond saving, and we both know that.

I'm about to get into an Uber when Cherry cries out my name. I turn toward the voice and find her running to me in her high heels, shaking a newspaper in her hands. She nearly falls on her ass, and I make a move toward her to help, but she straightens herself and continues her run.

"Wait up, Archie." She waves the paper in her hands. "You forgot this."

"Shit, yeah. Thank you." I take it from her. "Did you look inside?"

"No." She shakes her head. "Something must be so important in there that she drove all the way here from

Maine to hand-deliver it. I think you're the only one she wanted to read it."

"Thank you, Cherry." And I mean it.

"Archie," she sighs, "she's the one."

"The one?" I try to laugh. I've never had this conversation with her before. I mean, is she talking marriage?

"The one who'll give you a reason to live." She places her gentle hand on my chest and holds my eyes as she speaks. "Please, Archie. Let her help you."

"I don't—"

"Don't say it." She punches her fist into my chest. "It's me. Don't offend me with the lies. Please."

I shut my mouth and listen. For once. She's been trying to cure me for many years now, just like other women tried. Cherry is family though, so it feels different, but I'd never responded to any of it. Until now.

"Please, let her help you."

She pats my chest one more time and starts walking backward. I watch her until she disappears inside the building, and a loud horn sounds to my right. The Uber window rolls down, and the guy yells, "You comin' or not?"

I glance toward my shop once again and get inside the car, careful not to ruin the newspaper in my hands.

On the way home, I try calling Leila a couple more times, but it goes straight to voicemail. Shit. I'll sober up tomorrow and drive there.

Wait, maybe I should go there today. Just take a taxi. But then I get a whiff of myself—I smell like a fuckin' distillery—she doesn't deserve that, so I decide on going home for now and making myself presentable.

A cold, empty house greets me like it does every single time. No amount of furniture can fill it with joy or homey feelings.

I call Leila one more time with the same success, and my mood drops even lower. I'm gonna be sober tomorrow, but today I drink.

I grab a bottle of bourbon and move to the couch. Not bothering with a glass, I down a third of the bottle, and my head instantly heavies. I'm used to alcohol in big doses, but maybe this was a little too fast. Since I decided to change my path of self-destruction, I should probably slow down, so I place the bottle on the table.

Right next to the newspaper. The newspaper she wanted to hand-deliver, and I fucked up the moment. I grab it and unfold it. The headline on the first page makes my heart stop.

Heroes who have been deemed villains, got redeemed.

I open the next page with shaking hands.

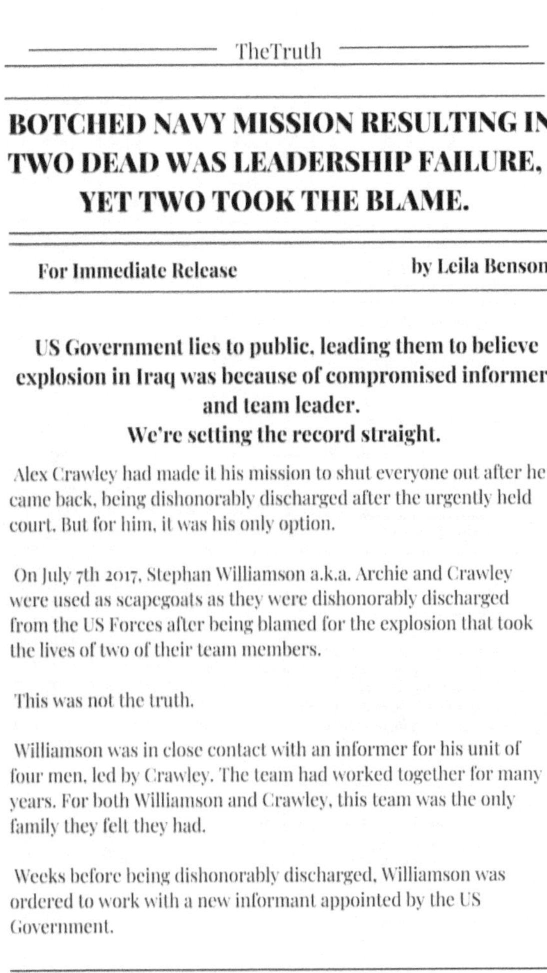

———————— TheTruth ————————

BOTCHED NAVY MISSION RESULTING IN TWO DEAD WAS LEADERSHIP FAILURE, YET TWO TOOK THE BLAME.

For Immediate Release   **by Leila Benson**

US Government lies to public, leading them to believe explosion in Iraq was because of compromised informer and team leader.
We're setting the record straight.

Alex Crawley had made it his mission to shut everyone out after he came back, being dishonorably discharged after the urgently held court. But for him, it was his only option.

On July 7th 2017, Stephan Williamson a.k.a. Archie and Crawley were used as scapegoats as they were dishonorably discharged from the US Forces after being blamed for the explosion that took the lives of two of their team members.

This was not the truth.

Williamson was in close contact with an informer for his unit of four men, led by Crawley. The team had worked together for many years. For both Williamson and Crawley, this team was the only family they felt they had.

Weeks before being dishonorably discharged, Williamson was ordered to work with a new informant appointed by the US Government.

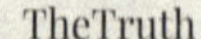

HEROES WHO HAVE BEEN DEEMED VILLAINS, GOT REDEEMED.

"I remember him coming to me in a panic one night," Crawley tells me. "He was nervous. He didn't feel right about the guy. Said the new guy didn't really know what he was doing and seemed shady, but the information he was giving us was important. Or so we'd been told."

Unfortunately, there's not much people in this position can do. Following commands, their team made their way to the location they were told to be at, but were ambushed.

"There was nothing we could do," Crawley says, looking down at his scarred hands. "We were surrounded, but we couldn't make out anyone. Someone knew that we were going to be there. There was no coming out of that unharmed."

That night, two of their brothers would lose their lives in an explosion, Crawley would be disfigured with burn scars down half his body, and Williamson would suffer after all of it would be blamed on him.

"Archie is the only reason I'm even alive right now," Crawley tells me. "I was knocked out in that fire. Under the truck. I was being slowly crushed and burned. Archie tried so hard to save the other men. I was the only one he was able to pull out. We were the only ones who survived."

Except it's not Williamson's fault. It's not Crawley's either.

According to the government, Williamson was well aware of the information being bad. In fact, both surviving men knew, but decided to act anyway, well aware of what was going to be waiting for them.

But the military knew they were in the wrong, and there are several factors that prove this.

...and the list goes on and on as the article continues exposing the night that ruined so many lives.

I'm wiping away the tears I didn't know were running down my face. My nose is itchy, and I try to breathe through my mouth.

I haven't seen their names for many years. Didn't think I deserved to say them. They're dead because of me. Me.

But this article says it's not because of me? I can't believe it. I can't. Because if I do, it means that the system I gave years to fucked me over. That they made me live with this guilt for years. That nothing is sacred anymore.

I grab the bottle and down half at once, hoping to dull this pain in my heart that doesn't let me breathe. But the pain is in there; it's still there. I drink more, but it doesn't work. It's fucking there, eating me on the inside. I drink more, feeling nothing.

I try to rise to my feet, but it works only after a few attempts.

But I have another solution for the pain devouring me. I walk to the kitchen and grab my gun from the top of the cabinet. It's loaded; I don't know why I keep it there, but I do.

I'm lying. I know why it's there.

I walk back to the couch with a bottle in one hand and the gun in the other, but I stumble over my two feet and end up kneeling on the floor by the couch. Hysterical laughter bubbles in my chest, and I can't stop. Tears stream down my face, and I lean against the front of the couch so I don't fall. My sides hurt, but I can't stop laughing. All these years of pent-up self-hatred are coming through. I wipe my face and down a chug of bourbon.

The pain doesn't go away. It intensifies.

I slightly pat the barrel, enjoying the coolness of the metal. The quiet of it. The promise of forgiveness.

It can take me to a place where pain doesn't exist anymore.

I take another sip, and suddenly the liquid burns. So I drink more, enjoying this type of physical pain. I'll gladly take it over the mental fuck I'm having right now. Physical pain is familiar, that's how I get rid of the guilt.

I drink more, and it burns hotter.

I grab the phone and dial her number, not even knowing what to say if she picks up. I just want to hear her voice.

But the call goes straight to voicemail. She might have turned it off because she thinks I'm a cheating asshole and hates me. I'm about to disconnect the call, but then her sweet voice tells me to leave her a message, and I'm mesmerized by it. I realize how much I've missed her, so I talk. Well, I mumble nonsense, and when I comprehend that I spoke too much, I hang up. *Shit, why did I tell her all of that?*

And then I start hating myself, remembering the look on Leila's face when she learned about the pain. It only took her a second to figure out why I do that, and I'm fuckin' ashamed of it now. I smack the bottle on the floor next to me and lean my back on the couch.

Did I really think I could have something with her? Would I really do that to her? I can only drag people down. The article said I'm not a villain, but I don't know how not to be one. I've been living in this cycle for so long, I forgot other ways existed. And I can't offer her anything but my fuckin' money. Nothing else. I'm a shell of a person I once was.

Who am I kidding? I've always been like that. When

my father took me to live with him, the damage was fuckin' done, and I'm no good for society anymore.

I'm not good for her.

I pick up the bottle and down the rest of the liquor. It burns good. Then I take the gun. My thumb strokes the safety lever. My heartbeat finally slows down, agreeing with the decision. I have a will—everyone I care about will be taken care of.

I raise it—

Chapter Twenty-Five

L EILA

Three hours ago

My tears have dried out by now. There weren't many to begin with because I didn't let myself cry. We ended our arrangement, and I can't hold him responsible for wanting a life for himself. If I caught feelings, that's my problem, not his. He's not responsible for me or my imagination.

Does it hurt? Hell yes. Hurts so much I can't breathe. It's hard to focus on the road as my mind keeps replaying the picture I saw. My chest feels tight, and I can't take a full lungful of air. My shaking hands grip the wheel with all my might—which is not a lot.

Would I change hand-delivering the gazette to him, knowing he'd moved on? Absolutely not. I wanted him to get it from me. This article is a big invasion of his privacy—dirty laundry about to be aired for the world to see, but it was needed. I chose the lesser of two evils because he refused to talk about it. I'm still shocked Alex agreed to give the interview, but I'm very grateful for it.

I'm thinking of pulling over somewhere just so the level of adrenaline in my body subsides and I can stop shaking. Once I pull into a gas station and park, I go to check my phone. But it's dead. Dang it! I forgot to charge it, and it died.

What if he called?

What would I do? I don't know how I would react and what I would say. If there is even anything that needs to be said. Maybe he wanted to talk about the article? Oh crap, he needed me in such a difficult moment, and I wasn't available.

I plug the phone in and will it to start turning on faster. I have a new voicemail. From him. I'm about to click it when my phone starts ringing. Unknown number. I so don't need a call right now about how to lower my monthly electric bill or hear a creepy person's breathing in my ear like a couple calls from the last week, so I send it straight to voicemail, but the same number starts ringing again. Could it be something important? The area code is from Massachusetts. I hit accept and put it on speaker.

"*Oh gosh, thank fuck you picked up!*" A feminine, sultry voice fills the car.

"Who is this?"

"*It's Cherry.*"

Cherry? Oh, Cherry! Stephan's friend.

"Yes?" I ask cautiously.

"*Look, I'll get straight to the point. You saw me on his table. I have a bad habit of sitting on every table I come across. Yeah, that's me."* She takes a deep breath. *"I'm not sure if you actually know who I am, but I'm his friend and almost sis—"*

"I know who you are." And with that knowledge, my heart begins beating steadier, and my hands shake less.

Her sigh is loud even in my car. *"Cool. Saves me the trouble. Are you far from Boston?"*

"Yes."

"You need to come back."

"Why?"

"I have a bad feeling." She swallows loudly. *"Like a really bad feeling. When Archie left right behind you, he wasn't...himself."*

"What do you mean?" I ask carefully, not knowing how much she knows and how much I can discuss.

"Dude, he was in a real bad state of depression even before you showed up, but when he thought that you thought he's cheating on you..." she lets her words trail off, *"You know what I mean?"* She pauses again.

"I do." Unfortunately. And I just added more crap to his already full pile with my article.

"I thought so. I went to his place, but he didn't open up. No surprise there. Even though I saw the light in his window. I've been asking for a key to his place for years, but knew he was never gonna give me one—for situations like this. He probably got super drunk and passed out, but I really want you to check on him."

"Why?" I'm already starting the car to drive back, but I still want to hear her thoughts. She's someone close to Stephan who is still somewhat of an enigma to me.

"Because you're the only one who can get him out of this, and if you think otherwise, you're probably not as smart as he says you are."

So, he talked about me.

"Okay, I'm driving back now."

"*Cool.*" She lets out a sigh of relief. "*Please let me know when you talk to him.*"

"Will do. Thank you, Cherry."

When I hang up, I'm dreading his voicemail. And when his voice fills the car, I understand that Cherry was right to call me.

"*Hey...*" A pause. "*It wasn't what you think, you know.*" A shuddering air intake. "*I would never do that. Even though we agreed to go our separate ways after the cabin,*" a sad chuckle, "*I never could, you know. You're all I can think about.*" He laughs sloppily. "*You know, I always laughed at guys at the base when they said they fell in love at first sight and got married a month later. But I get it now.*" A sniffle. "*I get it. It's crazy how much you consumed me after such a short time. You're deep here,*" a sound of a hand hitting something. His chest? That was loud. "*So deep I can't get rid of you. But I must. Because it's so fuckin' toxic. I'm dependent on you, and you don't need this fuckin' burden. I'll only drag you down. You're so young and so pure.*" A deep sigh. "*Thank you for what you did. The work you've done...*" he pauses, "*is tru...tram... huge.*" He laughs. "*Sorry, I'm drunk. Can't speak. You've given me the biggest gift. I'm too deep though, for it to change me, but I am grateful to you. And I love you, Leila. I want you to know that.*" A sad laugh. "*Fuck, I'm mumbling. Such a pitiful sack of shit. Anyway, I'm happy I met you.*"

By the time the line goes dead, my cheeks are wet and my eyes blurry. My heart stops, my palms begin sweating, and I hit the accelerator, willing the snow to disappear so I can drive faster. In fact, I've never driven this fast before.

I'm a grandma behind the wheel, but instinct tells me to rush, because every minute counts.

That voicemail…That sounded like a goodbye.

I push the pedal deeper and pray I'm not late.

I reach his house faster than I could have dreamt of. Without even turning it off, I rush to the door and begin knocking. Nothing. I ring the bell. Nothing again. Alternating between ringing and knocking and yelling for him to open the damn door, I kick it for good measure and run back to my car. A good reporter knows how to pick locks (*don't tell anyone*). I grab the tools from my bag (*yes, I have them, and again, don't tell anyone*), and run back, slipping on the snow and landing on my ass. I'll have a few bruises, but the tiny tool bag is firmly in my grip.

I kneel by the door and pray that his locks have the same key—that will make my life easier. It takes me a couple minutes, but I hear the orgasm-inducing sound of an opening lock. I carefully try the doorknob, and it moves! Just one lock!

I open the door, and it bangs against the wall from the force. I rush inside.

Only to stop in my tracks.

He sits on the floor, leaning on the couch. An empty bottle on the floor. A gun in his hand.

His head slowly turns toward the sound, and he starts blinking without a clear understanding of what's happening.

I should proceed slowly—that's what every book would tell you—but I can't. I succumb to my emotions, and my feet carry me toward him.

Once I'm by his side, he lifts his head and blinks again.

"Are you real?" he croaks.

"I am," I whisper and kneel by him.

"What are you doing here?" His voice is coarse like he's been yelling at a stadium for hours.

"I got your voicemail."

"Oh." His cheeks pinken.

"Yeah, and I came to tell you that I love you too." I carefully put my hand on top of his. The one he's holding the gun with.

"You still do?"

"I always will." I carefully move my fingers on his grip. "May I have this?"

He looks down at our hands, as if only now recognizing that he's been holding a gun all along. He lets go, and my fingers wrap around it. I quickly stand up and move it to the cabinet in the kitchen. Then I rush back to kneel by his side.

His eyes are trained on his lap, his hands fisted on the floor by his sides.

"Stephan," I call his name quietly, but he refuses to look at me. Instead, his fists squeeze tighter, his knuckles turning white. "Stephan," I repeat in the same soothing voice.

No reaction.

So I put my finger under his chin and turn his face toward mine. When he faces me, my breath hitches. I can see the turmoil on it. A raw, unretouched painting of agony. His pain is here, I can touch it with my fingertips.

My heart bleeds for this man. And for everyone else out there. I can *feel* the pain he's going through, and I can share it with him. But how many out there don't have anyone in their corner. I understand him now. I truly do.

The edges of his face are sharper, his lips tighter.

"Stephan." The name comes as a plea, and his whole, large body shudders.

"Go home, Leila." He hides his face in his hands. "Please, go."

"I'm not going anywhere."

"I can't use you as a fuckin' crutch." He's still hiding his face, so his words come out muffled.

"I'm happy to be your crutch as long as you need me to be." I cover his hands with mine and gently pull them away from his face. "Look at me."

He finally lifts his eyes to meet mine. They're raw and unhinged, with no barrier or pretty mask to hide behind. He is what he is—a broken, wonderful man who became a part of me.

"I can't face you, Lei." His voice is tired.

"Why?" I whisper, grabbing his hands in mine and not letting him pull them away.

"Look at me." He takes a shuddering breath. "I'm a fuckin' mess. You don't need that in your life."

"It just so happens that a mess is exactly what I'm lacking." I smile.

"No." He shakes his head. "Not like this. Look at me. Drunk out of his mind, on the fuckin' floor with a gun in his hands. I won't even be able to look you in the eyes ever again."

I drop his hands and grab his face instead. I move mine closer to his.

"Look at me now then, so we don't have this problem after."

He tries to pull away, but I squeeze his face tighter, holding him in place.

"Look at me, Stephan!" I raise my voice. "Look in my eyes because I'm not ashamed of what I see. I'm proud of you for stopping. You had a moment to choose, and you chose right. You chose life. And you chose me."

He starts pulling away, but I'm on a war path, so I speak even louder, almost yelling.

"Look at me! Do you think I can live without you? You selfish prick!" His eyes widen, not expecting that. "How would you feel if you found me with a gun at my head?"

His pupils dilate, and his nostrils flare.

"Would you feel ashamed if you found me like that and stopped me?" I yell in his face.

"No!" he yells back.

"So, why do you think it changes the way I look at you?" I ask quieter. "I'm just happy you're here." A tear slips down my cheek. Is it an angry one or a sad one? I don't know.

"Don't cry," he croaks.

"Don't tell me what to do!" I bark back. He lost that right when he decided to leave me alone.

"Okay." His chuckle sounds wet. "I won't." He wipes the tear away with his finger.

"No, you won't."

"I won't," he parrots with a smile.

"Stop repeating everything I say!"

"Alright," he chuckles once more and brings his hands to the sides of my face. "I've missed you, Lei."

My heart beats like crazy after all the adrenaline of today. I drop my hands from his face and snuggle myself into him. "I've missed you too."

We sit in silence, clinging to each other. His heart is palpitating under my cheek, and my own matches his tempo. I like feeling him like this: raw and real. I just wish his 'real' would change a bit. I could use some less life-changing events in my life.

His strong arms are wrapped around me, and even though he smells like a distillery, I still dig my nose into his neck, enjoying the scent of home I've missed so much. Those short days in the cabin changed me and the way I see the world. I'd always thought I'd end up alone because I didn't know I was capable of this feeling of real, crazy love. The kind where you can't breathe without the other person, and I wasn't ready to settle for anything else. My daddy didn't give me much assurance with his cheating antics, so yes, I lost some faith eventually.

When Stephan left Little Hope, it didn't feel like home anymore. And I used to love our small town and adorable gossip-folk. Not anymore though. Everything annoyed me, and everyone was aggravating. Little things that brought me pleasure before stopped working. I couldn't be around my family I absolutely adore, or even around my whole house because every time I lift my eyes, sitting on the couch, I saw us having sex or his back as he was leaving right after I told him I loved him. He invaded my home, making it feel unwelcoming. And that's when I understood that my cozy house stopped being my home. Instead, home was passed onto a man with a gorgeous body covered in beautiful art with the most handsome face in the world, and a huge heart he doesn't even know he has. Such a package—I couldn't resist.

How do I tell him that I'm ready to marry him and have his babies right now? Is two months too soon? *Nah, it's alright, right?*

"What do we do next?" he asks, looking for the real answer in my eyes.

Shit, did I say anything of my mental mumbling out loud? Well, that would be truly embarrassing.

"What do you mean?" I lift my head to look at him.

"You agreed to be my adorable crutch, and I'm not letting you go now."

"Right," I snort so hard, and he laughs.

"Told you—adorable."

"Yeah, you told me that before and changed your mind." I roll my eyes.

"Leila." His voice turns serious, and he pushes away a little so he can see my face. "You are mine. You were mine then too. It's just now I don't have to pretend or hide anymore."

"How do I know you won't change your mind?" Insecurity I've never felt before slowly creeps on me.

"You don't, but you can trust me." His eyes dart between mine. "I know I've said shit before, but can you promise that you will try at least?"

I watch him for a minute before nodding. "Yes. But you need to promise me something too."

"Anything," he says without hesitation.

I start to worry, not knowing how to form the right sentence. "If you ever feel like you did today, can you promise to talk to me right away? No matter where I am or what I'm doing, you have to find me. Can you?"

His lips thin before he gives me a quick nod. "The deal is active only while you're alive."

"I'm younger than you." I roll my eyes. "I'll try to make it to my nineties."

"Works for me," he says with a smile and pulls me onto his chest.

"I love you, Stephan. You know that, right?"

"Why do I feel like there is a 'but' coming?"

"That's because you're right." The muscles under my cheek turn to granite. "But you smell like shit, dude. You need a shower."

His chuckle is one of relief. "Care to join?"

Chapter Twenty-Six

L EILA

"Your house is insane." I say as I lie on my back in his extra-super-duper-king bed. The sheets are so soft, and the comforter is extra fluffy. He has so many rooms, I don't even know how many total, and every single one of them is tastefully put together by a really good designer. It's still a little cold here. It's beautiful, and the house has so much potential, but it's not...home.

"It's alright, I guess." I can feel his shrug next to me.

"You guess?" I pop my weight on my elbow and look at him. "The house is a work of art. Why did you buy it if you don't like it?"

He chews on the inside of his cheek before speaking. "This house belonged to my father's family. Then they lost it, and I bought it."

I peer into his eyes. "Don't you like it, though? It's gorgeous."

He lets out a loud sigh and brings his hands under his head. "It's beautiful, but it's just...empty, you know. It's not home."

Oh, my poor Stephan. I know the feeling all too well.

"I had the same feeling when you left." I lie back and stare at the ceiling.

"What do you mean?" He sits so he can look at me.

"When you left Little Hope and my home, it stopped being home. It felt like...you took the home with you, you know?"

He watches me for a few meaningful moments before speaking again. "I actually do."

"Good," I say with a smile. "I'm hungry."

"We can order something. Perks of living in the city." He winks and climbs off his giant bed.

"We've ordered every single meal for the time we've been here."

"Yes, because we've had a three-day sex marathon and didn't have time to cook." His lopsided smile aims to make me forget how to think, and he knows it, because he uses it every time I need some extra convincing.

"Don't give me that." I point to his face, barely able to contain my own smile.

"Okay." He throws his hands in the air defensively. "What is your plan then?"

"I can whip us up some breakfast." I shrug.

"From what?" he asks, laughing. "I have beer and bourbon in the fridge."

"Hmm, good point." I lean against the headboard and pull the comforter over my body because if he sees me naked, we will not be getting any food, and I could use a break. To be clear, my coochie could. The man is insatiable and, quite frankly, not small. Far from it, and by day three of constant shagging, I can sure use a break. Like maybe a warm bath with a gallon of lidocaine in it. "Let's order breakfast, but we should go shopping after to stock your fridge and pantry."

His brows shoot up to the sky. "You want to stock my pantry?"

"Why do you make it sound so dirty?"

His laughter is light and carefree—I love the sound of new Stephan. He pulls me into his embrace and rests his chin on the top of my head. "Okay, we can go to the store later."

My face nestles into the left side of his chest, right where he used to have an empty spot, now filled with new ink.

"Did I tell you how much I love it?" I give it a quick kiss.

"What?" He looks down at me.

"My name on your skin."

"How do you know it's your name?" He bites his lip, trying to suppress a smile, threatening to burst.

"C'mon," I chuckle. "Why else would a person in their right mind put a damn ginger squirrel above their nipple?"

His body shakes with laughter. "I wasn't in my right mind. But honestly, no self-respecting tattoo artist would ever put the name of his partner on his body—it's like a call to the universe to deliver a painful breakup."

"Seriously?" I cackle at this professional superstition—everyone has those.

"No jokes. We don't do names on the body, and I made it a rule in my parlors even if anyone asks for it—I don't want that shit on my conscience."

I giggle. "It's so absurd."

"Maybe," he shrugs, "but it's true. That's why we always find a way to find the right representation for the person we want on our skin."

It sounds so dirty...but so right.

"A squirrel?" I lift a brow because c'mon, couldn't he find a lion, or I don't know, a sexy panther.

"That's my little squirrel." He leans to kiss my nose. "It's because I knew you as Squirrel even before I knew you. Does that make sense?"

I look in his eyes and find the truth I've been searching for. "It actually does."

The smile he gives me is heart-stopping and mouthwatering, and I just know my coochie will cry later.

"C'mere," I pull his face to mine, "I need a kiss."

He obeys with a laugh. "You are a very insatiable squirrel."

An hour later, we order breakfast and eat at the small table in the sunroom. It's a very vintage-looking place with old-fashioned flower curtains and wooden stools. I'm a little surprised he decided to keep it—it's so not his style. To think of it, the whole house is a mix of styles. His room is very futuristic, and the living room and the kitchen are as well, but some areas still hold that feeling of old times. And I absolutely love it. I think after his bed, this little table is my second favorite place.

By the time the clock hits two p.m., we drive to the grocery store. We don't have a list because he needs literally everything. He wasn't joking when he said he only has liquor in his house. Even though for the past three days, I haven't seen him touch or even look at the bottles once. I don't think alcoholism is healthy, but in his case, I'm sure he had a reason for it so I don't push (much)—he used it to dull the pain. Hopefully, he'll have less of that now, so the need will subside eventually.

At the grocery store, I get everything I can get my hands on and drop it in the cart he's pushing with the ever-present smile of a jolly fool on his too-handsome face.

We've got groceries for at least two weeks. And since we haven't talked about how long I'll be staying, I figured I'll leave when I start feeling the tension.

"Oh, look at that!" I point at the plates with ugly flowers that sort of match the curtains in the breakfast nook of his house. "They're adorable!" I rush to grab a few.

"They're ugly," he deadpans.

"They are not." They are, but I still level him with a stare, causing a small smile on his lips. "I like them."

"Then we're taking them." He leaves the cart and goes to pick up all the plates from the shelf.

"We don't need that many."

"We do," he replies and places them into the already overflowing cart.

"We need a matching set then," I chime in hopefully.

"Lead the way." He starts pushing the cart with the determined look of a man on a mission.

We grab *not* matching mugs and bowls, check out, and load groceries into the car. Then he says he needs coffee, and right around the corner they sell his favorite blend in a small, local coffee shop.

We walk there, holding hands like a cute couple from a Hallmark movie. I've never thought that would be me, but here I am, perfectly content with the simple pleasures in life.

Then the moment happens. You know the one you

might see in a movie when the sun shines, and something reflects in the light, and it's so bright and yada yada yada? Well, that moment just happens to me. In one of the windows of a small store, a piece of jewelry winks at me. The sun reflects from the surface of the cutest emerald ring on the plant and blinds me. I freeze for a second and watch the ring in stupor. It's never happened to me before. I'm not vain. I don't buy expensive jewelry or clothes. I wear what everyone around me does. Besides the lingerie—that's where half of my paycheck goes. But that ring cried out my name. A ring? A little too meaningful in my opinion, and a little too early. God, I hope Stephan didn't notice.

Giving the ring a side-eye, I pull Stephan's hand away from the shop as fast as possible.

"What just happened?" he asks, a hidden smile in his voice.

"Nothing. I just slipped on the ice. Let's go," I mumble, embarrassed, hoping he'll let it slide.

He sends a doubtful look my way but switches the topic, and I'm forever grateful for it.

We get two orders of his favorite coffee and walk back to the car. Once he starts the engine, he starts patting his pockets.

"Shit, I forgot my wallet in the coffee shop."

"Okay, let's go." I reach for the door handle to open it, but he places his hand on my elbow, stopping me.

"Nah, wait here. I'll be right back."

"You sure?"

"Yeah," he waves me off, "I'll be right back."

He gives me a quick peck on the lips and leaves. I answer a couple of emails by the time he comes back. He gets inside the car with a force, bringing the cold air and the warmth of his presence with him.

"Did you find it?"

"Yeah, it was there," he says, pulls me in for another quick kiss, and switches the gear on the car.

We drive home, where we put everything away together like a decent couple, and I start prepping dinner. Stephan starts the coffee machine, and once it's done, he pours me a cup with the perfect amount of sugar and cream and props his fit butt on a tall stool at the island.

I put music on my phone and start shaking my ass to the rhythm when I notice a hot stare on me. Totally assuming Stephan's thinking about sex, I give him a sultry smile.

That he doesn't return.

"Is something wrong?" I ask as I carefully put the spatula on the table.

He shakes his head.

"Then what just happened?" I'm searching his face for any cues. To be completely honest, I'm still a little on edge, not knowing what to expect from him. I think he doesn't know what to expect of himself either, since this guilt-free life is completely new for him.

"I think I like this house now," he says quietly, and that wasn't even in the top fifty things I expected him to say.

"Alright?" I ask carefully.

He looks around as if seeing it all for the first time. "Since you've been here, everything is the same…But not, at the same time. Does that make sense?" His brows pull together.

I walk around the table and stop between his spread legs.

"It does," I whisper. "You like having me here." I don't ask—I state.

"I do. I think that's what I was missing." Then the

familiar mischievous look lights up his eyes. "A hot woman in my kitchen, cooking me some raw meat."

I smack his shoulder with my fist. "Then go find yourself any hot woman."

"I should." He bites his lips.

"You should." I mimic the gesture, and his eyes dip to my mouth.

"I don't think I can find someone hotter, though." His voice turns hoarse.

"You probably won't," I whisper and put my hands on his shoulders.

"Then I should settle with you." His large hands land on the sides of my waist.

"You should." I lick my lips, knowing it drives him crazy.

And on cue, he pulls me into him with a *thud* and his lips land on mine. My hands move to the back of his neck, one of his most sensitive places. I know he likes me taking charge from time to time, and this is how I can control the kiss.

But this time, he doesn't want it because his palm grabs the back of my neck, and he moves my head to the side, controlling *me*. Then his mouth lands on my neck as he starts sucking on the skin. Then he bites—a little painfully— and I gasp. He kisses the sting away, but I'm a little shocked. I'm always up for some fine line between pain and pleasure, but this bite stepped a little over it.

"Ouch," I say and pull away.

"I'm sorry, Lei. I had to do that." There's no remorse on his face.

"Why?" I ask, dumbfounded.

"Cherry called today and said I have to come to the

office tomorrow to sign some things. And I will have to leave you there hanging out by yourself for ten minutes."

"And?"

"Ten minutes in a place like mine for a woman like you is a lot."

"A lot for what?" I can feel my forehead wrinkling.

"For snatching you. Obviously."

I begin laughing. "That was a good one." I think he's joking, but he's dead serious.

"I'm serious. You are clearly into tats and bad boys, and there is plenty of that there. I don't want to risk it."

"And that?" I point at my neck.

"That's my insurance that everyone will stay the fuck away."

He's dead serious, and I want to laugh. Like laugh to the point I'll start crying, but his face tells me that it's a bad time for joking. So, I sober up, come closer to him, and put my hands on his shoulders. Tactile contact always helps to deliver the message better.

"Why do you think I'll jump ship the moment I see some other hot dude?"

He swallows before speaking. "Because I still can't believe you've chosen me."

"Stephan," I whisper, surprised at how insecure this wonderful man can be. "I can't believe that you chose me either. I'm a small-town girl, a boring sample of rural life, and you're a city millionaire with an empire you've built yourself. With a body and face of a Greek god. I'm sure there are thousands of women willing to warm your bed, and yet here you are, playing house with me. Do you think I'm not scared?"

"You shouldn't be." His eyes move between mine as his

hands squeeze my waist. "You should never fear I'd choose someone else. That I'd even look at someone else." He chuckles. "Hell, that I'd even think about thinking of looking at someone else." He takes my chin between his fingers. "You are the only thing holding me together. And the whole world knows that. If you ever leave me, I'll fall apart."

I rest my forehead against his. "How did it all happen?" I feel his warm breath on my skin. "Yesterday, I was a single girl with no feelings for anyone and no prospects, and now I'm here, with you. It already feels like we're a unit."

He chuckles and rubs his nose against mine. "I like the way you think. We're a unit. I've always felt like there was a piece of me missing. I just didn't know it was you."

"We fit."

"We do."

"You might want to deal with Alex first, though." I smile and feel him smiling back.

"This time, I'll fight back." He thinks for a second before adding, "Actually, I might punch first this time."

"I sure hope you will." I lightly kiss his cheek. "I happen to like your face the way it is."

"You won't believe it, but I happen to like it too."

"Are you wearing eyeliner?" I whisper the question into his ear, and he laughs. A full belly, good-natured laugh.

"Et tu Brute?"

"Your eyes are very pretty." I shrug shyly.

"No, I'm not wearing eyeliner. I have my father's eyes." He pulls me back into him. "In fact, I look a lot like him."

"Do you have any pictures of him?"

"I do." He nods. "I can show them to you."

"After dinner."

"Alright."

We eat dinner in a very nonformal way, meaning I'm

wearing his T-shirt with no panties on because he still managed to fit in a quickie before we ate, and he's wearing my favorite gray sweats. Love that piece of clothing. Definitely created by a woman—a very smart one—we all should praise her every time a well-hung man's junk flops around in those.

We talk about pretty much everything, and I feel like since the veil of guilt was taken from his eyes, he sees the world differently. And I like this new person a lot.

The next day, as promised, we go to the same parlor I had visited him at before. I felt awkward coming here again, especially when I was met with a nasty look from the same receptionist. When she saw us holding hands, her nostrils flared, and I swear I saw steam coming from her ears. *Huh, someone has a crush on her boss.*

The same guy who showed me in before gives me a nod of obvious approval as we pass his station. A few people say hi, and as Stephan predicted, a few very curious, flirty smiles are sent my way. I return them all with a polite smile of my own and grip Stephan's hand tighter.

When he opens the door into his office, the same woman, Cherry, is sitting at his desk and arguing on the phone. When she sees us, she lifts her fingers in the air and keeps fighting with the person on the line. And I'd say she's winning.

Once she's done, she aggressively clicks the screen, drops the phone down, and pulls on her hair. "Fucking asshole!"

"What happened?" Stephan's voice turns concerned, and I see his protective side begin showing. I've never thought of myself as a jealous person, but maybe it's because I haven't found someone I was scared to lose, but even knowing their sort of relationship, I feel a little twinge of the green creature. I try to suffocate it because Cherry was the one who saved Stephan's life. If she didn't call me when she did...I don't even want to think about it.

"The vendor is being a dick. They delivered the wrong colors, and now he's telling me it's our fault because we haven't placed the order correctly." She throws her hands in the air angrily.

"Want me to take over?"

"Fuck no." She waves her slender hand dismissively. "You do you. Or her." She winks at me, and I smile in return. She is rude and crass, and I love her. "I'll deal with the fucker."

"You sure?" He doesn't sound convinced.

"Duh. Of course." She rolls her eyes, and I finally understand their dynamic. She does more for him than I initially thought. She's not only his friend and his family, but she's also his confidant and the person who's holding his business together. Quite literally. An instant rush of gratitude overcomes me, and I, despite me being...well, me, rush to her side and envelope her in a hug.

She freezes for a moment, but then she gets her wits together and wraps her arms around me, giving me a hefty squeeze.

"Do I want to know what's happening?" Stephan asks, confused.

"No!" we cry in unison, and only then do I pull away. But not before I give her another squeeze.

"Thank you," I whisper.

"No," her voice hitches, "thank *you*."

We understand each other, and I go to look up, finding Stephan with a small smile of satisfaction on his face.

As they chat business, I look at the pictures of the tattoos on the walls.

"Those are awesome. Who made them?" I ask to Cherry's satisfaction, because her face turns into one of a cat who just ate a canary.

"Those are made by the very hand of your boyfriend."

Boyfriend. We haven't put any labels on our relationship, but after all the talks, I'd assume he is.

"All of them?" I ask with raised brows.

"Yep," she pops the p, "all of them. He had style."

"Had?" I ask in confusion.

"Yep, had." She glares at Stephan. "Now he won't ink anyone. Doesn't even draw shit."

I turn toward them. "I want you to ink me."

Both of them look shocked. Yeah, I didn't see that one coming either, but roll with me here, please.

"I don't ink anymore." He shakes his head vigorously, visibly slipping into the dark state of mind.

"Alright." I shrug. "I'll ask someone to ink me then. I want a tattoo on my ass."

"Fuck no!" Stephan exclaims as his neck strains and turns red. *Hook, line, and sinker.*

Cherry snickers as she takes a step back. "Let's ask Hulk. He lo-o-oves ass tats. Very good and," she clears her throat, "hot blood. But his hands can do some real magic." She takes another step back. Her face full of mischief while Stephan's face turns redder.

"Who's Hulk?" I play along.

"That young stud you saw when you walked in here." She points her thumb behind her back, a wide smile on her lips.

"Cool," I shrug, "let's ask him."

"I said fuckin' no!" Stephan's voice booms in the tight space, nearly deafening us all. Then he adds quieter, "I'll ink you."

"Sure," I reply calmly, while sending Cherry, who's trying to hold herself together and not burst into laughter, a grateful smile.

"Wait here." Then he turns to me and adds, "Don't come out."

"I won't," I promise, widening my eyes innocently.

Once he disappears from the room, we start laughing. I've never seen him like that, nor did I know he could be such a caveman. Do I like it? No. I freaking *love* it. I've always known I wanted a relationship to consume me. I wanted another person to breathe me, and I wanted to do the same. I just didn't know it was achievable.

"I love it," Cherry says between hiccups. "I've never seen him like that. Oh-h." She grabs her side. "Ouch. Haven't laughed like this for ages."

"Thank you," I say, knowing what she means.

"Thank you too." She nods. "But we'll never speak of it again, alright?"

I nod in return, happy that she chose this way. She worries about him, but she also knows and respects him enough not to talk behind his back. She just became one of my favorite people.

A few minutes later, Stephan comes back with a tray full of things needed for inking, I assume.

"What do you want?" he sits in his chair and asks gruffly, still grouchy from us tricking him.

"Surprise me." I give him my best megawatt smile I know he can't resist. If he learned I say 'yes' every time he gives me a bad-boy smile, I totally figured out his vice.

His face brightens as he pats the table in front of him. "C'mere."

"And this is where I leave you to it. Remember," Cherry lifts her pointer finger in the air in a warning while she walks outside, "the walls are thin."

"Ready?" he asks me with a boyish smile. His face is free of worries, and now I see why Cherry wanted him to ink again—it's his place of happiness. He might not notice, but he transforms into real Stephan. Archie's mask of a tough guy drops, and he is just Stephan. I think I'll be walking with ninety-nine percent of my body covered in ink if it would put that happy smile on his face.

"I am." I prop myself on the table, lie on my stomach, and pull my pants down.

"You weren't joking about the spot, huh."

"Nope." I accept the pillow he passes me and put it under my face. "Told you I want it on my ass."

A few painful hours later, when he starts cleaning the tattoo, I hop off the table and walk to the mirror. When I see what he's done, my eyes go all watery, and a tear slips down my cheek.

"It's perfect," I whisper.

"I know," he says with a proud smile in his voice.

Here is this arrogant man that charmed everyone.

Myself included.

A tattoo of a tiny, black panther gently touching a tiny squirrel with its paw looks back at me from the mirror. The details are amazing, considering the piece is small by itself. He truly has amazing talent.

On the drive back home, Stephan holds my hand the whole time. It's cute and adorable. I bet people who see his mask—Archie—wouldn't expect him to be so sweet, but he is. So sweet and so very gentle.

"What was that about?" he asks, referring to our hug. I think.

"Nothing. Just two women bonding."

"With Cherry?" He sends me a quizzical look. "I love Cherry. Adore her. She is my family. But she's a total bitch, and she doesn't like anyone. I haven't seen her bonding with someone right off the bat. What did you promise her? Our firstborn?"

I chuckle, "She's cool."

He sends me another quizzical look and keeps driving. He doesn't know the extent of things she does for him, and I'll make sure she gets noticed more, because I think she's been that person who'd been holding him together before me.

Chapter Twenty-Seven

A RCHIE

To say things begin moving fast would be a major understatement. And to say that I'm happy with that would be the same. I'm fucking ecstatic. And very scared that one day I'll wake up and realize that all these positive feelings and fullness in my life have been a dream.

Every day since she's come here, my head is brighter in the mornings, and my heart lighter every time it beats. I like to watch her sleep, like I'm doing right now. Her mouth is always ajar, and she makes cute noises while she sleeps. I tried telling her about that yesterday, but her nose scrunched while she tried to prove me wrong, her eyes full of horror as if making sounds at night is something shameful. It's not, and she's adorable.

This house feels more like a home than just the giant monstrosity it was before. All she did was throw her socks everywhere, and chip the new cup we bought, and the house suddenly became cozy. We go to some department store and buy cheap stuff that we definitely don't need. She puts it everywhere, and the level of coziness increases before my very own eyes. She replaced my designer pillows with some bright plush ones, adds throw blankets to every chair, and bought fake house plants. She wanted the real deal, but I convinced her that the poor plants would die when I'm out of town. Even with everything out of place, it all works somehow. My designer, Josie, would have a stroke if she saw the house right now, but it's never been cozier for me.

Maybe it's her presence and not just the little things I notice everywhere now. Or maybe it's both. Regardless, I'm in a state of constant terror every single minute of my life, terrified that it will be ripped away from me because someone out there will remember that I don't deserve any of it.

She stirs and stretches her arm out, looking for me even in her sleep. I pull her into me and make her my small spoon. My dick stirs too, of course. How could it not when her plump, warm ass is pressing against it. I bury my nose into her hair and breathe her in. Her scent became so familiar and so calming. I'd be an idiot if I thought I could be cured from all the shit that's been happening in my head in a week. The truth about the operation and my involvement in it hit hard, but it also relieved some of the guilt. Only some of it—I'm still here and they're still not. But it's easier to breathe now. I can say their names without reaching for a bottle and maybe, one day, I will be courageous enough to talk to their families.

Leila's been here for a week, and I feel like it's been a year. I don't want her to ever leave my side. Kenneth called me yesterday, laughing that she hijacked his truck and asking if I'm ever planning on returning his car and his sister. I told him no. He called me a motherfucker and asked to take care of them both because it took him a hot minute to save up enough to get the truck, so he's expecting it back, but I could keep the sister though—she's for free. I know it's a joke because he loves her to death, but his approval means more than I care to admit.

I know that it would be selfish to keep her all to myself—she's young and she hasn't seen the world yet. But she sure as fuck won't see any other dick—I'll make sure she's so satisfied she can't even think of sex. Especially, with someone other than me.

I don't know how to do relationships, and it's not because I'm some Casanova asshole like some people think I am, but because I've known for a long time that my life wouldn't be long, and I didn't want to put it on another person. So, I stayed alone and stuck to my one-night stands. I didn't know what I was missing though. Now, I'm a different sort of addict, and I don't think I can let her go.

"Mmm," she mumbles and turns her face to kiss my forearm.

"Good morning, my queen."

"Queen?" She giggles. "Since when are you calling me that?"

"Since now, I think. Because you're my queen."

She giggles again, tickling the hairs on my arm and wiggling her ass, completely waking up my cock.

"You've got some morning wood there."

"I've been awake for a long time—it's a 'my queen's ass is against my crotch situation.'" I reply, grouchy, even though I'm anything but. The morning is perfection.

"Do you need help with that?" She turns to face me. A

playful light in her eyes makes my dick jump. "I take that as a yes."

She sits up, the covers rolling off of her to reveal her gorgeous, naked body and fresh tattoo. Only my hand will ever ink her. Mine.

Then she slowly shifts toward my feet, and my breathing quickens.

"Hands under your head, soldier," she orders in that tone of hers she's mastered by now.

"I'm not—" I follow the delicious routine with a smile.

"You are what I say you are." She bites her lips and rakes her nails over my thighs. My poor—*happy*—dick jolts again, weeping with precum.

She slowly moves her nails higher up my thighs and spreads her palms over my stomach. The muscles under her touch begin jerking, and a look of satisfaction sweeps across her face. Then she slowly lowers her head and gives it a long, torturous lick. And then another. Then her mouth ends up on the head, and she covers it with her wet, hot mouth. My balls draw, and I will them to stand the fuck down.

I want so badly to dig my fingers into her gorgeous mane and move her head up and down, but I can't. I'm bound by her order to keep my hands away. I like these games we play —I like to give up control occasionally, especially when she seems to like taking it so much.

Her mouth slowly moves down my cock, and the head hits the back of her throat. She gags and pulls away. Saliva drips from her chin. It's so fucking dirty. It's so fucking sexy.

She makes another attempt to take me in, but she can't, and we both know why. I want to tell her that I'm happy with anything, even with her just looking at me, but then she tilts her head a little so she can see me. Her mouth is full of my dick, and I don't think I need her to fucking go any further, because I'm going to come just from the view.

She does a few slow pumps while her hands move over my lower stomach, scratching my skin with her nails. She lets go of it with a pop, licking from the base to the tip while maintaining eye contact. And then she puts her mouth on it again, swallowing half of it until it hits her throat.

"Lei." My voice is coarse. "Lei," I try again as she keeps moving her head up and down. "Please, come here." I'm not above the begging. Who the fuck cares if that works for the both of us?

She smiles with my cock still in her mouth and pulls away. She climbs on top of me, positioning my slick dick at the entrance of her pussy, and slides in.

That's it, I'm in heaven.

***

After another round—we're like rabbits, constantly fucking —we sit and eat the breakfast that she's made from the groceries we bought like a real family and just chat. Then her face darkens, I prepare for the worst: she'll tell me she's had her fun, and it's time to move on with our lives. But I don't have a life aside from her anymore. I'm like a fucking psycho at this point, and I'm loving it.

"I need to go back to Little Hope, Stephan." She stands up to pour us more coffee. "I've got things to do there. And Kenneth really needs his truck back—he can't keep driving the police cruiser around."

"Okay, I'll go with you." I shrug, dreading her answer.

"What about your business?" She sits back in her chair and taps her chin with her finger. "To think of it, I think we need to talk logistics. I'm there, and you're here. I don't know how we can work around that drive."

"I can get a house there," I suggest hopefully.

"Why would you need a house? I already have a place."

My heart skips a beat in hope.

"Okay, then what's the problem?"

She places her mug back on the table before speaking again. "How long can we do that? You know, live in a car, driving back and forth." Her face turns sad.

"Do you want to move to Boston?"

She looks around. "I like Boston and I like your house, but Little Hope is where I'm supposed to be," she says, so sure of herself, leaving no doubt that that's exactly where she's supposed to be, and she believes it.

"Then I'll move to Little Hope and will come back here for business."

"You can't leave everything behind for me." She looks around, uncomfortable, as if thinking I'll miss this house and the city. Well, maybe I'll miss the city a little, but who cares about that when she'll be by my side every single day. "It's not right."

"Leila," I take her hand in mine, "without you, there won't be anything. You need to understand that. I'll move anywhere for you."

"What about your business?"

"I was thinking of asking TJ," she gives me a ques-tioning look, "Kayla's old boss," I explain, and she nods. "So, I was thinking to ask him if he wants to do business with me or something anyway. I forgot how much I love inking and how much I've missed it. And it's about time I offer Cherry to be a partner, or someone will snatch her from me."

Her face brightens at the news, and I ask, "You really like Cherry, huh?"

Her smile is sad and understanding. "She is your family, Stephan. No matter how you look at it, she's been there for you, and I'm very grateful to her for taking care of you."

That makes me pause. I guess if you look at the situation between me and Cherry like that, she's been watching out for me.

"You have a very light hand. I didn't feel any pain."

"Liar," I laugh.

"Maybe a little." She winces and shows a tiny space between her thumb and pointing finger. "A bit. But I've seen your drawings, Stephan, you should do more of them. People need someone like you to express their feelings in art when they can't do it themselves. I sure can't, and you made the perfect thing for me."

Yeah, since the moment they tricked me into inking Leila, I've been thinking about that. My hand's been itching to take a pencil and draw. I can almost feel the vibration of iron in my fingers. I've missed it, and I've missed the feel of freedom that comes with it. It's an unexplainable feeling when you leave a permanent mark on someone's body. You transfer your energy to them. And that was one of the main reasons I stopped inking—I wasn't enough of an asshole to transfer my shit on people. But now I feel that's changed. That I can actually work with people without giving them my negativity. I need to talk to TJ about possibilities, if there are any. Hell, I'll even be okay if he hires me as a guest artist for a day a week. I could totally open another shop under my own name there, but I don't want to step on his turf—he's spent years building his business there.

"Then it's settled." I take her hand again, pull it to me, and kiss her wrist. "I'll start building a house in Little Hope. I need to call my designer ASAP. It'll take months, so it's better to start earlier."

Her brows shoot up. "Building a house, huh? You sure don't waste time."

"I've wasted enough," I say seriously. "I don't want to waste a minute. Plus, I don't want you to change your mind." I shoot her her favorite lopsided smile.

She laughs, shaking her head, as if the possibility of that is hilarious. I sure hope it is.

Today is Saint Valentine's Day, and I'm going to propose. Yes, I'm very basic. Yes, I'm crazy—we haven't been dating long, but it's enough to know that I want to spend the rest of my life with her. I might need some liquid courage before since I'm sure there is a high chance she'll say no. But I'll keep trying.

We've been living in two cities for nearly a month, and it sure is difficult, especially for her. Her whole family is here, and I see how much she misses them. How often she talks on the phone with her mom, Aiden, and Kenneth while she's in Boston; I guess they're the closest to her. She mentioned that they talked with Alex since he detailed the story about our last mission in the Navy, but I haven't seen her talking to him on the phone. Nor have I. He hasn't made any attempts to reach out to me, and neither have I. After Leila's story, I wanted to make sure I'm in the right state of mind when we talk—we have so many topics to discuss, the first one being him never raising his voice at my woman again.

I bought her a new car, a very large red SUV with the latest safety features since she's so scared of the snow. It's hilarious how tight she grips the steering wheel every time a snowflake shows up in the air. When I gave her the keys, she refused it. Of course. I expected that. But after a few hours of 'tight convincing' (ahem), she gave up and accepted it. I want to spoil my woman and will do just that, and even said woman can't stop me from doing so.

We've been staying in her house for a couple of days, I love it, but it's tiny. Plus, I want to give something to her, so as I planned, I spoke to my designer Josie about the new house. I didn't tell her where I wanted to build as to not shock her—she lives in New York, and I'm sure she won't be thrilled to spend months in a small town. She loves to oversee her projects, so she'll want to oversee this one since I'm willing to put a lot of money into it—my woman deserves the best.

Speaking of said woman, she went to the tiny shop across the street to get some gifts for her family, because apparently, they gift some cute nonsense to each other on this holiday, while I go to get a coffee from Donna's shop.

I'm carrying two to-go cups and step on the street when the hairs on the back of my head stand up. The air electrifies, and everything turns slow motion. I look around but don't see a reason for any of it. Yet still, my instinct screams 'danger.' The same instincts that kept me alive during years in the Navy. And the feeling is exactly the same. Danger is nearby. The same feeling I had in the woods, but never since then. So I got sloppy, thinking it was a fluke and my paranoia talking.

I search for Leila and find her walking out of the shop and striding toward me. A big happy smile on her. Her humongous puffy jacket swallows her whole as usual, strands of her wild, unruly hair poke from under her white beanie. She pulls the phone out of her pocket and looks at it. Her face changes instantly: it darkens, and her eyes shoot around.

My heart slows down. My head whips around, looking for danger.

And then I see him.

A man in a black jacket and a cap low on his eyes.

And everything clicks in place. All my feelings of being watched. Instincts screaming that someone had been at her house. Constant footsteps of never-ending deliveries in her yard.

He pulls a gun out. I don't have time to take him down, nor do I have a weapon, so I lunge, praying to God and everyone who will listen that they'll help me to get to her on time. Coffee splashing everywhere as the cups hit the asphalt.

"Leila, down!" I yell, hoping she'll understand.

She doesn't see him, but he sees her. His gun is trained on her.

Her scared eyes are wide open. She keeps listening to whatever is being said on the other side of the line. She doesn't understand what's happening around her but looks around in shock and fear when she sees me going crazy.

"Leila, duck down!" I yell again. "The gun!"

I'm ten feet away.

He fires. I jump. Another shot. The world stops. The sound of another gun shot.

I knock her down to the ground, covering her with my heavy body. Too heavy. I try to move and see where the attacker is, and it takes everything I have to move a bit to the side, so I don't squash her with my weight while still covering her with my body in case he tries again.

My lungs burn. The taste of metal plagues my mouth. It's hard to breathe. There's a wheezing sound. Darkness overcomes...

I succumb to the tiredness and close my eyes, praying she is all right.

Chapter Twenty-Eight

L^{EILA}

He falls to the ground.

In front of me.

I can't breathe.

But I have no wounds. No nothing. And I still can't breathe.

I look at Stephan, his body still half on top of me. I try to carefully flip him onto his back, and my heart suddenly stops beating when I see blood spreading from under his back. That's why I can't breathe. He's hurt.

He's hurt!

I get myself together and kneel next to him, pulling his head onto my lap. He opens his heavy eyes.

"Stephan, please, baby. Stay with me," I whisper to him. "Please."

"Are—" he coughs blood, "you okay?"

"I'm okay." I try not to cry. Not now. "You saved me."

"And he—" He can't finish the question, blood dripping from the corner of his mouth.

I nervously look around, only now remembering that the shooter might still be around. I pull my body on top of his, and he tries to push me away. But he has no energy left, so his hands drop quickly, and he loses consciousness. I bring my shaking hand to his nose, hoping to feel him breathing. It's barely there, but there. I let out a relieved sigh.

Then I go back to my task of finding the shooter, still shielding him with my body. Now that he can't fight me, I can cover him all I want.

And then I see the shooter. On the ground, and Jake, the local ex-cop and Justin's brother, pushing the gun out of his hand with his foot. He crouches next to him and presses his fingers to his neck. His face sharpens as he rises to his feet and jogs toward us, pulling his phone out on the way.

"We need an ambulance at the corner of Main Street and Eighth. A civilian has been shot. Two bullet wounds. The suspect is down." Then he mumbles something else and hangs up.

Stephan coughs again, and more blood spills out. His breathing slows.

Just as mine does.

"How is he?" Jake croaks as he crouches next to me.

I shake my head, blinking away the tears.

Jake unzips Stephan's jacket and checks his wounds. His face darkens the more he sees. Tears start streaming down my face, and I grab onto Stephan, scared of what Jake will say.

"Two exit wounds."

"It's good, right?" I ask hopefully. "They're not stuck inside, right?"

He glances at me but doesn't say anything.

Suddenly Stephan lets out a loud breath, and his whole body shudders. He opens his eyes, and I feel relief because they're clear. Hope blossoms in my chest.

"I—" he swallows thickly, "love you, Lei."

A beautiful smile stretches across his face, and a waterfall of tears start running down my face.

And then he sighs deeply.

And stops breathing.

"Stephan?" I call out. "Archie?" Maybe he likes that name better, but just never told me that.

"*Stephan!*" I cry out louder. "Do you hear me? *Stephan!*" I yell and start shaking him so he wakes up.

"Leila, stop." Jake calls me, but I refuse to hear him. "Leila!" he barks again when I don't stop shaking Stephan's shoulders.

"Leila!" He grabs my forearm, pulling me away, and barks an order, "Move!"

I blink rapidly, trying to comprehend why he's asking me to move. Why he's asking me to leave? Why doesn't he let me spend these last moments with him? I'll die after anyway. I don't want to live without him.

"Leila, fuckin' move!"

He pushes me away, and I fall on my ass. He stands on his knees next to Stephan, takes off his jacket and arranges it under Stephan's head so it's a little higher than it was before. Then he starts doing CPR. He keeps pushing on his chest a few times and then blows air into his mouth. With every breath, Stephan's chest expands, and then Jake goes back to pushing on his chest.

And I'm just sitting here, useless, while the love of my life is dying.

Dead. He is dead.

Stephan *is* dead.

I begin comprehending what just happened.

The slow feeling of dread descends upon my head and moves down my body, settling deep in my belly. My heart begins aching, and my chest is getting squeezed by an invisible force. I try to take a breath and can't. Just like Stephan can't. The crimson line from the side of his mouth drips down to his cheek. His eyes closed.

And I will never see them again. Never.

A sob erupts from deep within me. And then another.

The pain is unbearable, and all I want right now is to die with him.

I finally fully understand how he felt all this time. When the desire to live dies along with the people you loved the most. That's how I feel. I need him to breathe.

I need him to.

Because if he doesn't wake up, that's it. I'm done too. So, I pull myself together and move toward Jake.

"Jake. What can I do?"

"Call fucking nine-one-one and tell them to hurry the fuck up." The words are rushed out of his mouth while he's pushing on Stephan's chest.

I crawl to my purse and fetch the phone. Right as I'm dialing the digits, Stephan's back arches from the ground, and he takes a loud, shuttering breath. Jake instantly pulls his torso up and presses the jacket from the ground to the wounds on his back.

My hands are shaking. I drop the phone and begin touching Stephan's face.

"You're back," I whisper. "Back. Please, stay." I start

peppering his face with kisses. "Please, Stephan, stay with me. I can't live without you."

"Nine-one-one. What's your emergency?" my phone reminds that I managed to dial for help.

"It's officer..." Then he stops abruptly and curses, "*Fuck.* It's Jake Attleborough. We have a civilian shot, and we need a fucking ambulance at the corner Main and Eighth Street. Or he's going to die." Jake's voice turns authoritative.

"The ETA is two minutes."

"Tell them to make it one, or he won't make it."

The phone clicks, but the line remains open. The voice comes back. *"They'll be there in a minute. I'll stay on the line."*

I keep kissing every inch of Stephan's skin I can get. Trying to imprint his taste in me. I'm touching his cheeks and forehead. He's sweating despite the cold weather, his breathing uneven. He's fighting to keep his eyes open, and I know the moments I'm getting with him might be the last I'll ever have.

The siren sounds ahead, rapidly moving toward us. Once the vehicle stops next to us, two paramedics rush out and run toward us. They check Stephan while Jake's repeating the events of the last few minutes to them.

One of the medics places a huge needle between Stephan's ribs while another tapes the wounds. Then they place a mask with a breathing bag over his mouth.

Another siren sounds nearby, and a few moments later the sheriff's cruiser stops next to us. Kenneth jumps out of his car and rushes toward us just as the paramedics load Stephan onto a stretcher and start moving him to the ambulance.

"Leila! Are you alright?" Kenneth's voice hitches as he stops next to us.

"I am," I answer quietly. "Stephan covered me with his body."

Kenneth's eyes move at Stephan, and they sadden when he sees the condition he's in. He was conscious only for a bit right after Jake performed CPR, and now he's out.

"What happened?"

"I'll tell you. Let her go with him," Jake says, and Kenneth moves his confused gaze toward him as if noticing his presence just now.

"Jake?" He sounds surprised.

Jake nods. "I saw everything."

"Where is the suspect?" Kenneth searches around.

"There." Jake points to the bush where the shooter was hiding.

"Alive?"

Jake shakes his head.

"You got a weapon on you?"

"The state of Maine deemed me sane enough for that," he answers defensively, and I can't deal with that now.

"I'm just asking, Jake." He switches his attention to me. "I need to stay here. Will you be okay until mom comes to the hospital?"

"I'll be fine when he wakes up," I reply automatically and climb inside the ambulance.

"I'll come to you as soon as I can."

One of the paramedics starts the IV while the other asks me, "Miss? Are you family?"

"Yes." I stare at him, daring him to say otherwise.

"Alright." He nods. "The nearest hospital that can handle this type of wound is forty minutes away, and we don't have resources to deliver him faster or to a better hospital. So be prepared."

I nod and pull my phone out of my pocket, grateful that I told myself to stick it back in my pocket before. Finding the right contact, I hit 'dial.'

"*Are you okay?*" A familiar male voice asks.

"He was already there when you called."

"*Fuck.*"

"My fiancé was shot." A little white lie to speed up the process. "And I want to ask for a favor."

A deal with the devil would never feel more justified than right now.

"*Done.*" His voice turns serious as usual when he feels the situation is not to joke about. "*What do you need?*"

"I need a chopper to meet us on the road not far from Little Hope and fly us to the largest nearest hospital."

"*When do you need the chopper?*"

"Five minutes ago."

"*Hmm.*" He clicks his tongue. "*I'll call you back.*"

I drop the phone on my lap and squeeze Stephan's hand. Feeling curious stares on me, I look around to find both paramedics looking at me with wide eyes.

My phone rings and I hit 'accept' and transfer it to the speaker without dropping Stephan's hand. I don't think I'll ever want to leave his side now.

"*I pinged your phone. Keep driving. The chopper will meet you down the road in about ten minutes. There is a big opening in about two and a half miles. I found someone already in the air; they're on the way.*"

"Thank you," I say, relieved.

"*Good luck, little Leila.*"

The phone goes dead, and I look up to find even more surprised stares on me.

"Do you know what we could do with those types of resources?"

"I know," I answer and move Stephan's hair out of his eyes.

One of the guys explains the instructions to the driver, and in about two miles, the sound of a chopper sounds nearby. As promised, it's waiting for us at the large opening on the hill. They transfer Stephan inside, and one of the paramedics jumps in the helicopter with us.

When we're are at the hospital ten minutes later, a huge team of medical staff is waiting for us on the roof. They all come close when it's time to transfer Stephan to the bed they brought with them.

"Hey. You must be Leila?" A tall gentleman with a kind smile and full head of starch white hair addresses me.

"Yes?"

"I'm Doctor Liberman. You must have friends in high places if I'm here right now, specially taking me away from lunch with my wife." His eyebrow quirks up as we all move toward the elevator. Well, the two of us are moving slowly, but the rest of the team is rushing. I made a move to go with them, but they quickly stopped me and directed me to Dr. Liberman's side.

"I'm sorry," I reply automatically, not feeling an ounce of remorse.

"I'll take care of him."

"Thank you."

He disappears inside the elevator with the team, and I stay on the roof.

A hand lands on my shoulder and gently nudges me

toward the elevator. "Let's go. I'll walk you to the surgery room."

I turn my face to find the same paramedic. "Do you know this place?"

"Yes." The doors open, and we walk inside. Then he presses a button. "It's a very good hospital, and they have a good trauma center here. And you scored Liberman." He chuckles.

"Is he good?"

"One of the best surgeons on the coast. Also, one of the biggest assholes."

I let myself smile. "I'm okay with that as long as he makes Stephan live."

"If anyone can save him, it's him."

I feel a little better and lean my back against the wall, waiting for our floor. My phone pings, and I pull it out. The message is from the devil himself:

> It was free of charge. It was a fuck up on
> my end. I owe you one. Good luck.

I figured it's because of *him*, the devil, that we've got the best surgeon. I don't know how *he* managed it in such a short period of time, but *he* did, and I'll be forever grateful. However long it is.

He called me right before the shooting to tell that his sources were wrong, and the man I wrote an article about was roaming free. It was him stalking me this whole time. My article ruined his life, took away his business and his family, and he came to Little Hope to make me pay. The man on the phone sounded so remorseful and so pained for dragging me into that, because *he* was part of that article too, just on the other side of it. A good one, for a change... But it was too late. No amount of remorse will help Stephan now.

***

The surgery goes on for hours and hours, and I've had a few nervous breakdowns by now.

Once I took my spot by the door, I answered my family group text, as my whole family has been bombarding me with texts, and let them know where I am.

A couple hours later, Kenneth and Jake storm the hallway and never leave my side.

Then mom and dad arrive almost at the same time as Freya, Alex, Kayla, and Justin. Aiden texted me that he was coming too, but his car got stuck in the snow. Mark and Alicia came about thirty minutes after my parents. They all took turns sitting next to me. Some of them probably wanted to take my right too, but Kenneth planted himself in the chair there and didn't leave my side for a moment. I glance at him from time to time, getting the feeling that he got closer with Stephan than even Alex was. His arms are crossed over his chest and his brows are furrowed as he stares ahead without seeing anything.

More hours go by, and still, nothing.

When I can't take it anymore, feeling my body begin to shut down with every passing second, a big hand wraps around my shoulders and pulls me into a warm brotherly hug so I can let myself go.

And I cry. And cry and cry. I don't think I can stop at this point, letting all the fears out. Fear of never seeing him again. Fear of never touching him again. Fear of not being able to tell him over and over again how much I love him and how much he became a part of me, and how dull this world would become without him in it.

But then, finally, the doors to surgery open, and Dr. Liberman comes outside. He's clearly wearing the same med coat from the surgery because it's covered in blood. Stephan's blood. My body begins shaking, but Kenneth squeezes my shoulder and helps me to my feet.

Dr. Liberman finds me in the crowd of worried faces and strides toward me. Well, not strides, but slowly walks. His feet are tired, his eyes sunken.

My heart is about to stop. I don't think I'm breathing.

The doctor sighs heavily before speaking. "It was a hard surgery. Two exit wounds in both lungs, and they kept collapsing. He's lost a lot of blood—one of the bullets hit a major blood vessel. We had to do a few transfusions during the surgery." He wipes his sweaty forehead with the paper towel he has in his hand. "He's in a medically induced coma now."

I don't understand if I should breathe a sigh of relief or cry in fear.

Kenneth must be feeling the same because he asks, "What is his prognosis?"

Dr. Liberman finds my eyes and shakes his head, silently apologizing.

I fall to my knees, unable to breathe. Lost in this fear, enveloping me in its scary embrace. I've been living in hope for the past few hours, and now it's been taken away from me.

I weep on the floor of the hospital, and no one can help me. Surrounded by my friends and family, the closest people in my life, I still feel so alone. None of them can possibly understand what's happening inside my shattered heart. None of them know what he means to me. None of them had been there that night I found him with the gun—the scariest moment of my life.

I thought that would be it. No more scares. How wrong I was.

This, right here, is how it feels when the world collapses around you. When all you're left with is piles of broken dreams, hopes, and feelings because you are still breathing for some unknown reason. When you finally understand how small you are and how fragile life is but can't change anything anymore, because you just tasted how easily it can break.

Strong hands wrap around me and pull me into a warm chest. Kenneth doesn't say a word, but he lets me *feel* it all, offering his support and understanding.

I don't know how long I spend on the floor, wrapped in the arms of my big brother, but when I can't cry anymore, and only dry hiccups come out, I pull away and look up. His sad eyes are red-rimmed. I look around and find everyone mourning a person who's still alive, and Alex is the worst of them all. He's staring ahead, eyes absent as he's silently sits in his chair. He's taking it hard, but has no one to share it with.

I take a deep breath and rise to my feet. Looking around, I find Dr. Liberman still in the room with us.

I wipe my face and ask him, "Can I see him?"

"The nurses are prepping him for transfer. Once he's settled, they'll come get you."

"Thank you."

He gives me another look and says, "I'm sorry." He looks around, searching for someone. "The medic said there was someone at the scene who did CPR." It wasn't a question, but an answer is expected.

"Jake was there," I say quietly and point to the ex-cop with a bad history who's been hiding in the corner the whole time. I don't think anyone has talked to him the whole day—or is it night?

"Good job." The doctor gives him a quick nod of appreciation. "He wouldn't even be here if it wasn't for you."

Jake averts his eyes and chews on his lip. But the doctor's words sure draw everyone's attention, and they're all staring at a rapidly pinkening Jake. The doctor doesn't notice the tension and keeps going.

"I don't know exactly how long he'd been dead—"

My heart skips a beat at his words.

"—but your action saved his life. You should be proud, young man."

Now, Jake's cheeks are totally red. He nods at the doctor and quickly looks back down at his shoes.

With that, the doctor departs. I start walking toward Jake.

"Leila?" Justin calls out, but I don't care.

When I reach Jake, I throw myself at him and wrap my arms around his torso, squeezing him as tight as I can.

"Thank you," I murmur into his chest. "Thank you so much, Jake."

He clears his throat before he speaks.

"Sure." His voice comes out gruff.

"Thank you," I repeat again and finally pull away. "Thank you, Jake."

He nods and takes a careful step back. I take a deep breath, smile at him one more time, and turn to face my family. They might mourn him because they know the old Archie, but I know Stephan, and this man has something to live for. I don't want anyone's pity because there is no reason for it—he will live.

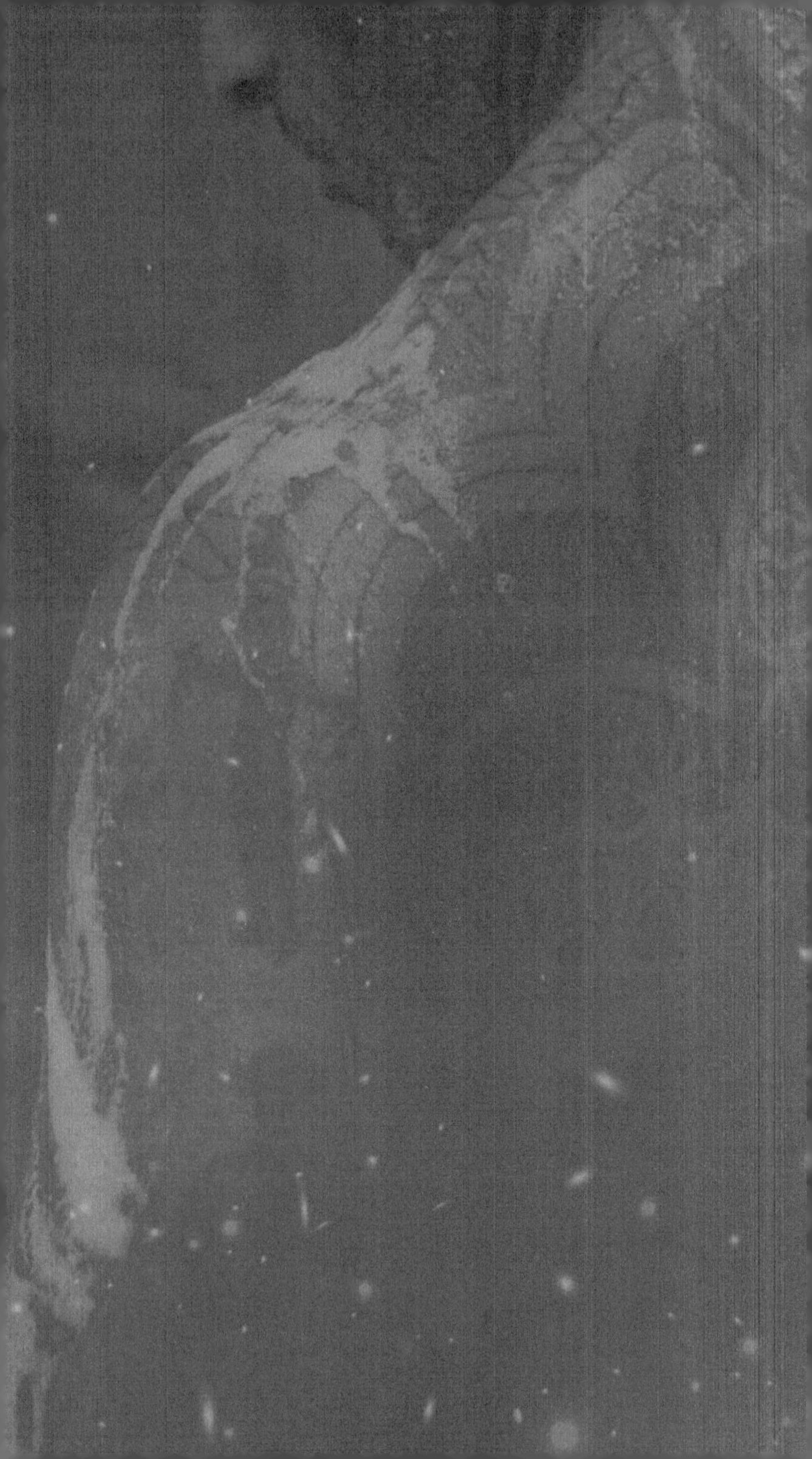

Chapter Twenty-Nine

K ENNETH, the brother, who is loyal to everyone.

My sister's face changes after that hug. I don't know what they said to each other, but she changed after that. I see our old Leila back. This woman is determined and single-minded when it comes to her goals, and she just set one for herself. I just wish I knew which one that was.

While she marches toward me, I glance at Jake. He's uncomfortable as fuck here. He hasn't been anyone's favorite as of recent, and people don't like to be around him, and I can understand why since we had a few unfortunate situations while he was working for the department. He's been deemed the local asshole, and I don't know how he'll be able to redeem himself in everyone's eyes.

Alas, him going on a long leave of absence from the police department. The dude was abusing his power, so he was told to take some time to clear his head. I know he went to some sort of rehab after the shooting, but when he came back, he didn't change much. So yeah, he was forced to take the leave.

Truth be told though, I wasn't surprised to find him on the scene holding Archie together. Quite literally. I'll never forget his determined look as he held the scraps of clothing to Archie's back and front, trying to put pressure on his wounds. He probably knew the bullets hit his lungs, and he was trying to prevent them from collapsing. Jake's always had a good heart, but he was steered in the wrong direction at some point. I still don't know what happened with him—I tried asking as a boss, but he quickly shut me down, and the problems started right after.

Also, there's another thing I'll never forget—my little sister on the ground with Archie, that haunted look on her face, her body shaking. I've never seen Leila so lost and so scared. She's usually so calm and collected, but she was anything but. I think at that exact moment, I understood what Archie really meant to her. I figured they were deep when I found him loitering by the diner, peeping in the windows, but it never occurred to me that their connection could be so strong and so mutual, to be honest. Leila's never processed feelings the same way most people do. She's so closed off and sometimes shy, even though she'd say otherwise. She always does—it's a hobby of hers to piss off her big brother. But I know my sister and I didn't know she could fall so deep.

As for Archie, I've always felt—well, for the span of the months I've known him—that when he falls, he falls till his last breath. And to be frank, I'm fucking happy it's Leila. I know he'll be loyal and responsible, and my sister will always be taken care of. What else could a brother dream of? I was a little scared for the same reason though—

knowing Archie and seeing how much he's struggled with life, I wasn't sure he could survive my sister.

But I think he gets her like no other man could, and there is no danger of them ever separating...if he survives this.

But I'm fucking happy I was wrong. They're perfect for each other—he makes her feel, and she makes him not.

"I'm staying here until he wakes up." She stands by my side, facing our friends and family. "You can go or stay; it's up to you. I understand everyone has their lives, and that's okay. I appreciate you coming here. I'm sure Stephan would appreciate it too."

Fuck this shit. *Stephan.* Why does she keep calling him Stephan?

Then it dawns on me. I haven't even done a background check on him. He's been with my sister—dare I say her boyfriend—and I haven't even checked him out. I'm getting sloppy and too trusting.

"But," Leila continues, "if you're going to be sitting around here with sad faces, burying him before he's even gone, please, leave. I can't handle it right now. All we need," she said '*we*,' "is your support and positivity, not Debby Downers."

Our father chuckles, "That's my girl."

"Jake," she addresses him, voice firm; everyone's breath hitches, "you saved his life, and I will be forever grateful. Thank you."

He nods shyly and rolls his lips, not knowing what to do with all the attention he's getting. Positive attention, for once. The old Jake would bask in this, but this Jake is on the shyer side. Maybe therapy really did him good.

I glance around the room—everyone's looking between Jake and Leila, understanding that she just publicly accepted him, and they better not have any problems with that. The only hot, angry stare comes from Justin, and I feel a pang of surprise. I'd think it would be Kayla, since she was the one who suffered the most from him, but turns out, Justin hasn't forgiven his brother for nearly ruining his relationship. Even though he did eighty percent of it on his own, if you ask me.

I move a little to her side, showing that I'll always back her up, even if I have to smack someone around. There's more than a decade between us, and when she was born, I always treated her gentler than my friends did their sisters. I've always felt closer to her. I still remember sleepless nights when I lulled her to sleep when she was teething and our mom was exhausted, or finding her in my bed when she had a nightmare and came to me; even as kids, she knew I would protect her.

And now I feel calm, knowing that I trust Archie to protect her.

And now he might not make it.

Fuck it, life is so unfair to the best of us.

About twenty minutes later, a nurse comes in and says that she can take one person to his room and the rest can visit once everything's settled. Of course, it's Leila. No one even questions her on that. She follows the nurse with a look of determination on her face, dead set on resurrecting him if she needs to.

Once she leaves, everyone collectively lets out a sigh.

Alex walks toward me, glancing at the door she just disappeared through.

"Was it bad?" he asks, his voice tight. I noticed that he

looked bad himself, but I was too focused on Leila to offer Alex any support, hoping that he'd be fine on his own. Judging by his ashen face, I'm not so sure anymore.

I nod, unable to talk. I've seen those scenes before, but never with my sister and my friend involved. It's hard.

"Do you think he'll climb through?" His voice is even tighter.

"I fuckin' hope so."

He chews on his lip while watching his shoes. "I never made amends with him."

I glance at Alex, not knowing if he expects reassurance or for me to somehow take away his guilt, but I can't give that to him now.

"I was so fuckin' angry that he'd disappear from my life that I said all that shit I didn't mean."

I find his eyes and hold them. "He would disappear without her, not the other way around."

He gets what I mean. His throat works in a loud swallow as he nods in silent agreement.

"I've been there a few times." His voice is rough. "When I came back, I'd been there." His eyes dart away—he's not present here, I don't think. "It's a tough place, and I think I missed the signs because I was too focused to go back there."

I place my hand on his shoulder. "Don't you dare carry this burden too. He's good now; he's got Leila."

His gaze shifts toward the door where the nurse took Leila, and he flinches. "That's another fuckin' thing I've missed. If I just pressed the issue when I saw those fuckin' prints around her house, he wouldn't have been there."

"That one is on me." I squeeze his shoulder harder. "You told me about that, and I fucked it up."

"You are n—"

"I can take one more person to his room now." The nurse appears in the doorframe, and I jump into action, happy for the save.

"We're not done." Alex holds my gaze and steps away, letting me be the one to go inside. Weird, I thought he'd want to be the one since Archie was his friend first.

The nurse shows me the door and tells me I have about ten minutes before the doctor comes in to check on him.

When I carefully push it open, I find my sister quietly talking to Archie. I want to close it and give them privacy, but one phrase catches my attention, and I can't stop listening now.

"I *understand* now," she whispers, leaning in close to his face. "And I want you to know that if you leave, I'm not staying. Call it childish, call it stupid. But you heard me—I am not staying."

Dread settles in my stomach because I know what she's talking about.

The next few days are pure chaos. People come and go. Archie's friend and basically adopted sister Cherry came and stayed in the hotel next to the hospital. She tried forcing Leila to go take a shower at home, but the stubborn mule refused. She says that she's scared to let him wake up without her. I talked to his surgeon, who turned out to be one of the best in the States, and he doesn't have any hope. How this surgeon happened to be in this hospital with a freshly printed license to operate is another question I'll be figuring out.

The more I come to his room, the more I agree with the doctor. I'm not a professional, but I can see him slowly deteriorating. His cheeks become more sunken, and the circles under his eyes darken. My sister took on the role of caretaker for her significant other at the age of twenty-four.

And I couldn't be prouder of her.

As the days go by, people start visiting less, but it's not for lack of trying. Cherry had to go back to Boston to manage the businesses he still owns. Justin and Kayla come to visit on the weekends since it's about a good hour away from Little Hope. Archie's artists from a few parlors on this coast came to visit a few times, and as far as I know, one of the artists from California is flying in this week.

Alex comes every other day to quietly sit in the corner. I know he and Leila talked, but I'm not sure how their situation got resolved—I know better than to get between siblings. Freya came twice, but since she's become more pregnant, car rides have been making her sick. Our father drove our mother here a few times with her homemade meals for Leila. I think her presence hurt Leila the most because her doting almost drove her to the edge. The last thing Leila needs right now is pity. Even from her own mother.

By now, Leila has pretty much moved in. Nurses tried shooing her away at first, but then just accepted her as a permanent fixture in his room. They even bring her snacks and treat her with more and more respect. And pity.

She works from here too. Since that article about the military exposure, she's getting more and more requests. Being a freelancer, she can choose what kind of jobs she takes. And so far, she has only taken those that she can research from this very room.

One day, I came to visit them and found Jake quietly sitting in the chair while Leila leaned her ginger head toward him with a quiet whisper. When they saw me, she shushed her voice, rushed to finish whatever she needed to say, and then Jake walked away with a silent nod of greeting.

When I asked what that was about, she only smiled mysteriously and said that he was sent on a secret mission. I just shrugged and let it go—they're allowed to have secrets, even if I don't like it.

Fine, hate it. I know about everything in my county.

I haven't been here since yesterday because we had an emergency in town, but today I came to cheer my sis up.

"Knock-knock." I acknowledge my presence, and she lifts her head from the laptop where she's typing, her fingers fiercely sweeping over the keyboard as if it personally offended her. "I come baring gifts." I lift the large to-go cup of her favorite coffee from Little Hope. It's probably cold by now, but the gesture is what matters, or so they say.

"Thank you." Her face stretches in a wide smile. "I could use some caffeine."

"Thought so." I walk toward the bed where she's sitting at Archie's feet, propped against the pillows, looking very comfy for a hospital bed, and pass her the drink.

She takes a sip, and her smile becomes wider.

"My life just got a lot better." She sighs loudly and leans back on the pillow, her eyes closed. "Hospital coffee tastes like shit."

"You could always go grab one outside. There's a good coffee shop right down the street."

Her face darkens as her brows pull together.

"You probably *should* go and get something from there. You look even paler than before. Even your freckles are paler. Wha-a-at?" I step closer to look at her nose. "In fact, that big freckle on the tip of your nose," I point my finger at her face, "that you're so proud of, is nearly gone."

She rolls her eyes, but smiles. We've been teasing Leila about her freckles since she was little, and when she discovered that big ginger dot on the tip of her nose, she paraded it around the house, talking about how proud she was of creating such a big one. I think she was six then. Ever since, we constantly joke about it.

"Mew," comes out of nowhere, and I can feel my eyes widening. "Mew." Louder this time.

I glance at Leila, who sends me a conspiratorial smile.

"What the hell was that?"

"That's Midnight." Leila's smile is so wide, it threatens to split her face in two.

"Who the hell is Midnight?"

"He's our cat." From the way she smiles—so wide and proud—I think she has fifty teeth instead of thirty-two. My sister is a little shark.

"What the hell is a cat doing in the hospital?" I begin feverishly looking around, trying to find where the constant mewing is coming from.

Leila drops to her knees and peeks under the bed. "C'mon, Midnight boy, come to mommy," she coos to whatever creature is under the bed. A black, skinny, and ugly as fuck cat slowly crawls outside. And when I say 'ugly' I mean it. It's missing its left eye and ear, half of its face scratched to hell and back, and there are scars all over his body. But then he looks up, right into my eyes, I can clearly see the unbroken spirit in those green of his. He's defiant and strong.

I instantly love the ugly bastard and crouch next to him on the floor, stretching my hand for him to sniff.

"How did you bring him here?" I ask as I make a move to pet the skinny thing, but he lets out a loud hiss and jumps on the bed. Settling on Archie's stomach, he forms a furry ball and starts purring.

Leila's chuckle soothes my worried soul—I haven't heard her laugh for a long time.

"Midnight loves only Stephan. He tolerates me but loves him." She makes at attempt to pet the ungrateful bastard, but he lets out a loud hiss, and she drops her hand with another laugh. "My powerful friend owed me a favor, so he made a huge donation to the hospital, I guess. So they let me have the cat."

Huh, the same mysterious person who arranged the doctor and the chopper. I need to look into him when I get a chance.

Leila probably senses my thoughts because she sighs loudly and says, "No, don't waste your time. It's someone powerful I did a favor for, so he did a favor for me in return. Nothing to dig there, honestly. He lives very far from us and is not a threat. In fact, he is probably one of the good guys." Then she adds sheepishly, "I think."

"Was he connected to the shooting?"

"Yes and no." She chews on her lips before responding —a habit she's had since she was a toddler. "He gave me some insight that put a few bad people in jail. One of them got out, and here we are." She spreads her arms.

"So he is responsible for it." It's not a question, but also, I'm not sure what I'm dealing with here.

"Not really." She fixes the pillow under Archie's head and tucks the blanket into his sides. "I sought him out for that information because I needed to know the truth. And the truth turned out to be very convenient for him, so he didn't mind sharing."

The man responsible for Archie's wounds, was working alone. And he indeed was Leila's stalker who wanted to punish her for ruining his criminal life. We found evidence of everything in the motel room two towns down where he'd been camping since the article about him came out.

Alex told me about the feeling he had when he went to her house, but I didn't pay it enough attention. Archie being shot is one hundred percent my fault even if I didn't pull the trigger myself. But I can't go down that road now, not when Leila's smiling for the first time in forever.

"Where did you even find that ugly thing?" I jerk my thumb at the purring cat.

"By the cabin in the woods. The other day when Jake was here, I asked him to go to the cabin and look for the cat. And here we are." She shrugs, and I won't lie—I'm surprised to learn about her asking Jake. And a little offended. But I guess they connected on some sort of different level that day, so maybe it's a good thing for the both of them.

"Stephan said," she continues, "he'd been coming around to sit on the porch with him before I got there, and then he became jealous and disappeared for a few days." She turns to me. "Stephan was worried sick. Legit was checking out the window every ten minutes to see if he came back."

"What's that thing with Archie and Stephan?" I ask before I forget.

"Ask him yourself when he wakes up," she answers with a smile and turns back to look at the motionless man and the cat who suddenly looks up, letting out the loudest mew of all of them.

The monitor beeps, and we both jump. Leila jumps higher. In fact, she flies across Archie and lands by his side, peering at his face.

"Stephan," this fucking name again, "are you awake?"

A nurse comes rushing in and orders Leila to get out of

her way. My sister moves, a scared look on her face, her eyes wide. Another nurse rushes in, followed by a doctor.

"His BP is dropping," one of them reports, and they start firing medical terms at each other.

I glance at Leila—her lower lip begins trembling, and I'm at her side in an instant, quickly pulling her into a hug. She doesn't say a word, nor do I offer any words of hope. I don't know if they'd be truthful.

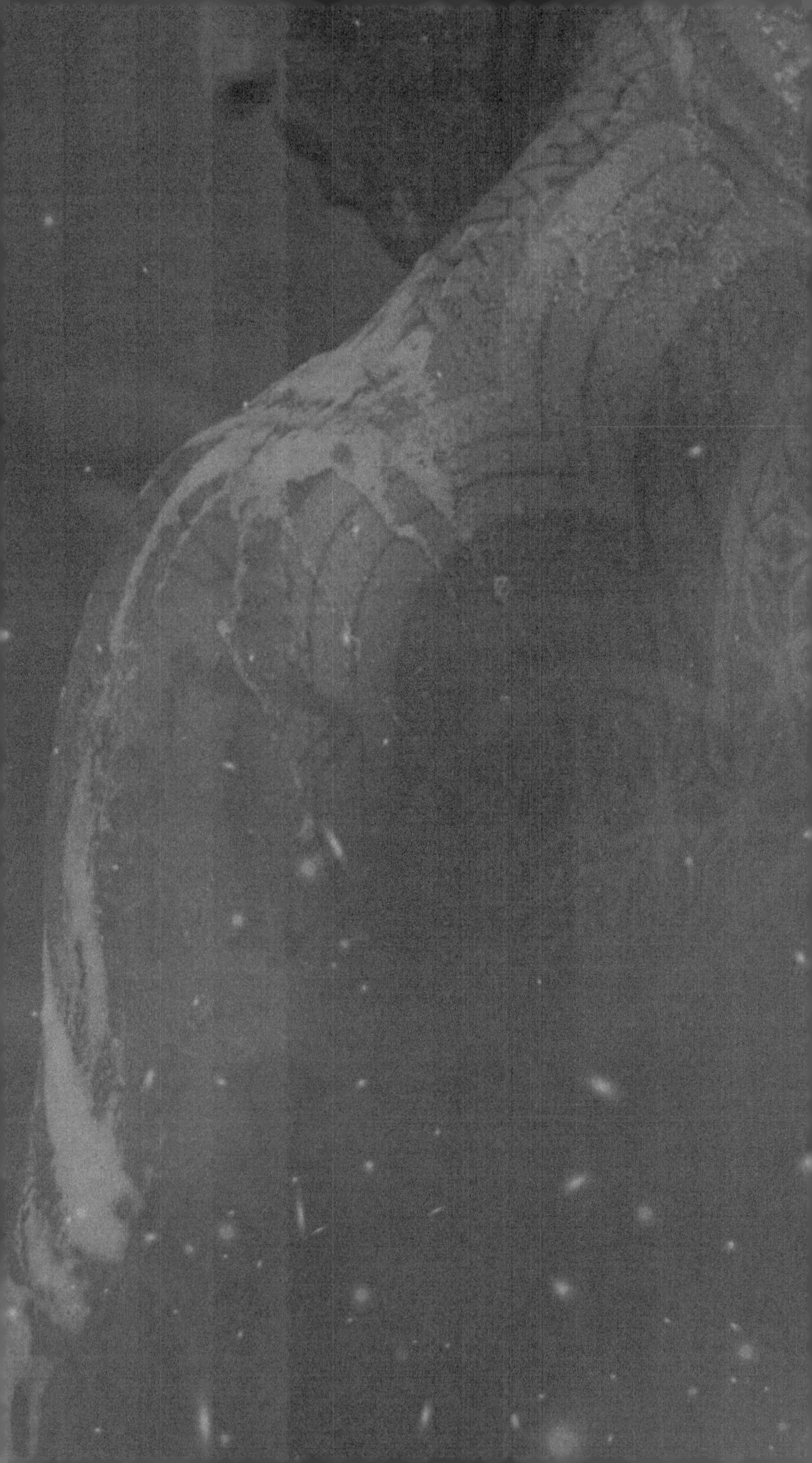

Chapter Thirty

A RCHIE

"I understand now," comes the whisper of the voice that's been holding me together for the past couple of months. *"And I want you to know that if you leave, I'm not staying. Call it childish, call it stupid. But you heard me—I am not staying."*

That's not right. I don't know why exactly, but I get a feeling deep in my bones that it's not right.

To think of it, I don't feel my bones. I don't feel anything. I'm in an ocean of nothingness, and it feels amazing.

Every time I let this ocean swallow me, I hear her voice, and it pulls me back in. Over and over again. Over time, I stopped letting the ocean take me. I fight, but it's useless. The ocean is stronger. It's never-ending, and it's just me here, alone.

But I'm not alone. I feel her presence. To be frank, I think that it's the only thing I feel. I know she says she's holding my hand, but I don't feel it—I don't have hands. I have nothing, just the freedom of not feeling anything.

And I'm ready to go.

But every time the thought enters my mind, I get another feeling. A deep ache in my chest if I had one. It pulls me right back in.

The guilt. I feel a lot of guilt. But this one feels different than the one I've been living with for many years. This one tells me that I'm leaving someone behind. I've never had this feeling before, but I know I like it.

I suddenly feel another presence around me. A friendly one. Like it's someone close to me, and I know she feels it too, because she relaxes. I'm good. She is near, and she is happy.

But then she's stressed, and I'm back to worrying. My heart begins palpitating, and I can't breathe. My throat begins contracting, and I suddenly become all too aware of my body. I can feel it.

There is a warmth under my ribs. Another beating heart and a constant, soft buzzing sound, like a tiny tractor, has climbed into my ears.

I feel more warmth spreading through my limbs. I'm more aware of everything.

I can't open my eyes, but I feel someone talking rapidly.

"His BP is dropping."

She's on the verge of tears. I can feel it. The one who's been holding me together.

I need to fix that.

I try to pry my eyes open, but they don't listen. My chest aches more, and the chatter around me gets louder and faster. They probe and poke my body, and I can't stop them.

"Stephan." Her desperate plea makes my heart stop. The beeping intensifies, and she starts crying.

Fuck it, I'm outta here.

I gather everything I have left and force my eyes open.

And they listen this time.

I find her watching me with wide, teary eyes. Kenneth is hugging her shoulders. His face solemn. I'm clearly in a hospital room, because people in medical scrubs surround me, poking everywhere they can. I try speaking, but something is in my throat. I try to find it and pull it out, but the doctor grabs my hand.

"Let us do that. It's a breathing tube. I'm gonna pull it away, and your throat might hurt."

Might hurt my ass. It feels like he just pulled my esophagus out with the damn tube. I begin coughing. A nurse brings a glass with a straw and brings it to my lips.

"Take one small sip."

I do as I'm told and begin coughing again—the water feeling like burning lava down my throat. She waits till the cough subsides and gives me another sip. This one goes down smoother, and I feel my throat starting to feel like my own.

"Fucking hell, man." Kenneth laughs. "I didn't know if you'd make it."

I brave myself to face Kenneth. I avoided looking at him because I know Leila is by his side. I don't know why, but I'm scared to meet her eyes. Something big has clearly happened, and I'm still out of it. I just hope I didn't fuck up like I always do.

"Welcome back, Mr. Williamson." The doctor draws my attention back to him. He listens to my heart, shines light into my eyes, and pulls away with a satisfied smile. "I'll order some tests to see what's going on with your body, and then we can go from there." He pats my shoulder with a smile. "You just beat the odds. Made me proud."

With that, he departs, followed by the nurses.

Kenneth walks up to me and squeezes my hand. "I'm fucking happy to see you back, man. Welcome to the family. I don't think you have a choice now—you're stuck with us." He lets out a chuckle. "You're going to regret it at some point, but we don't issue refunds."

He smacks me on the shoulder and leaves. Why is everyone smacking me?

I watch him leave, dreading facing Leila, who hasn't made a move to come closer. I probably really fucked up. But she is here, right? So it can't be that bad.

When I'm finally man enough to turn toward her, I find her standing in the same spot, her fists by her sides. Tears stream down her face. Her lower lip starts trembling, and she bites into it.

"Lei." My voice is coarse, and it's all I can really manage. It's the most important word in this world—her name.

And she falls apart in front of my eyes. Her whole body quakes with shudders, and she covers her face with her hands, falling to her knees.

"Lei," I say, stronger this time, "baby." It hurts to speak, but she needs to hear me.

My words do the opposite, and she shakes even more. Her shoulders sag as she digs the heels of her hands into her eyes.

"Baby," I say again. "C'mere."

She picks herself up from the floor, and in one big jump, she throws herself on the bed where she climbs on top of me, digging her hands under my shoulders. Her thighs land on the side of me, and I can feel that she lost a lot of weight. How long was I out?

My arms barely listen to me, but with sheer willpower I manage to force them to lift and wrap around her back, holding her onto me as she cries. If you could call it that. It's more like a soul shattering exorcism of all her fears.

When the shudders subside, she pulls away from me but stays sitting on my legs. Her beautiful face is puffy, her nose is so red I can't even see my favorite freckles. She wipes it with the sleeve of her white shirt and smacks my chest with her tiny fist.

"Never do that again, jerk!" A loud sniffle. "I thought I was never going to hear your voice again. Don't do that to me anymore." Her eyes well up again before she adds, "Please."

"I won't." I croak. "Wha—" I cough, and she leans over to the table to grab the glass. She gives me another sip so I can keep talking. "What happened?"

"You don't remember?" Her brows pull together.

I shake my head in denial.

"You saved me." One more sniffle. "There was a shooter, and you covered me with your body. You took two bullets that were meant for me." Tears start running down her face.

What's wrong then? You are alive, that's what matters, I ask her silently.

She understands, of course, she's always got me, and she smacks me again. Harder this time. That one hurt, and I make a face. She gets scared and starts rubbing the spot she hit. "I'm sorry!" she mumbles. "I didn't mean to actually hurt you." I've never seen her more distressed and disheveled.

She begins rubbing more vigorously, making the sting worse, but like hell I'll say anything to her. If it makes her feel better, I'm all for it.

"You were out for five weeks. Five weeks in a coma, Stephan!" Her lips begin trembling again. "The next time you pull shit like that, I'll kick your ass."

I smile, recognizing my Leila. Then I remember the shooter, and my face changes.

"Jake...took care of him," she says, understanding my silent question without me actually voicing it. "He won't hurt anyone else ever again."

Even though it should be good news, I recognize guilt when I see it. And that's what it is—guilt written all over her face. I wish I could speak normally now, but I'm not there yet, so I try to croak what I can, "Not your—" a cough, "fault. His actions," a cough, "his choice." Then I add firmer. "Not your fault."

I force my hand to move and land atop of hers. "Not your fault," I add again with a squeeze, and she gives me a small nod. I know we'll be revisiting this topic a few times, and I'm ready for that. Who is more equipped to talk guilt more than I am.

Right now, I'm happy to be alive. Never thought I'd say that, but I am. I can't imagine leaving Leila alone in this world where she's supposed to be protected by me. It's the sole purpose of my existence now.

"Mew."

What's that?

She sees the question in my eyes because she pats the space beside us and calls out to someone. "C'mon, Midnight. Say hi to Stephan."

My eyes go round as a skinny black cat jumps onto the

bed and starts purring. He settles by my shoulder and starts licking his paw.

"Remember Midnight?"

I nod in wonder—she got my damn cat here, to the hospital. I knew there were no limits for this woman.

Her familiar scent invades my nose, and I understand how much I've missed it. Even in the nothingness of an ocean I'd been swimming in, I got a whiff of it from time to time. She was right there, pulling me back.

We have a lot of things to discuss, but right now I just want to be in this moment. Where I can truly enjoy being here, with a beating heart and the woman, made for me, in my arms.

Who needs heaven when it's better on earth?

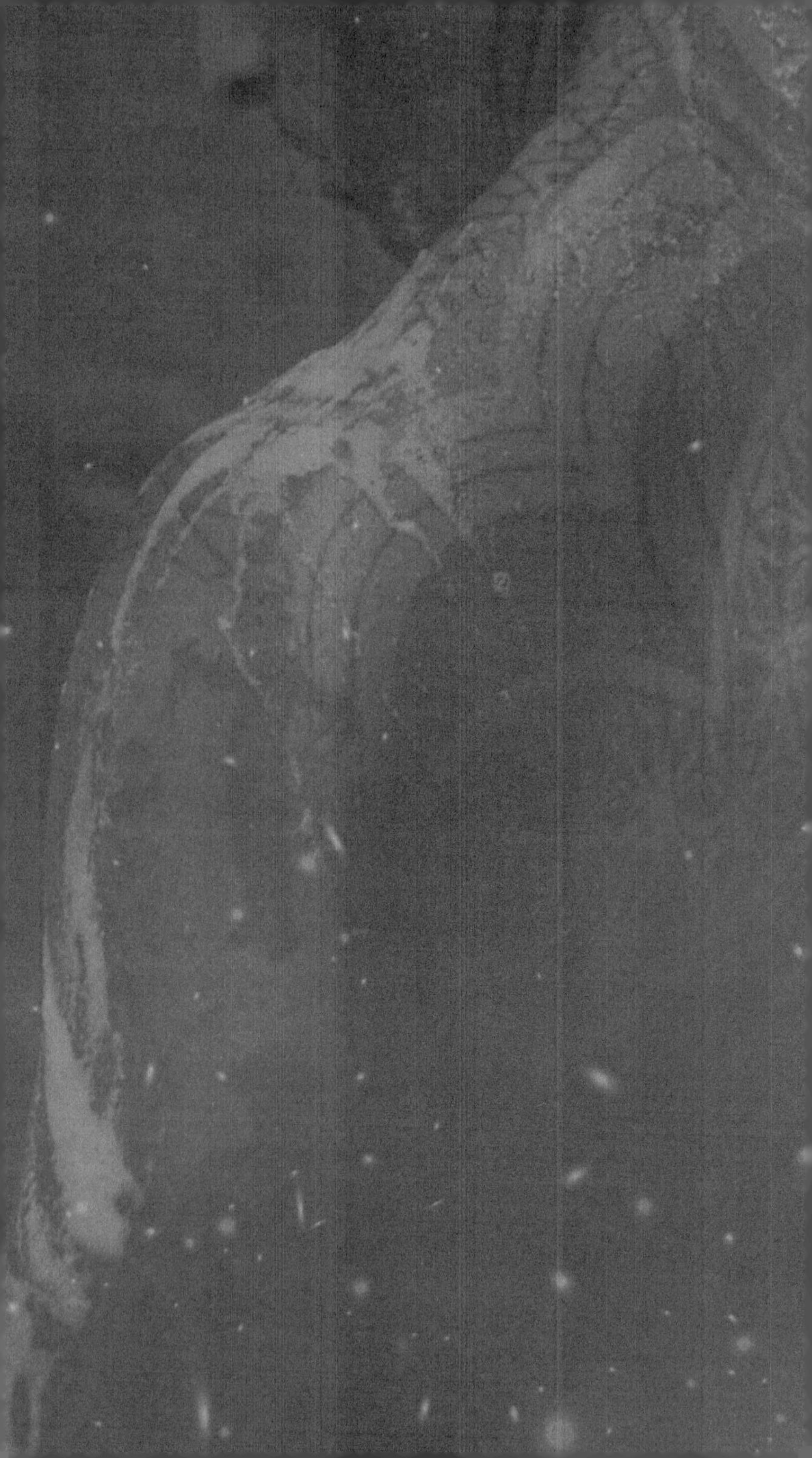

Epilogue

A RCHIE

Two months later

All I want is to go home to Leila and bury my face between her legs, but Kenneth is having some sort of midlife crisis, so I'll be a good friend and get him drunk in a bar.

We didn't take a car because we didn't plan on coming home sober. Yeah, I can drink without getting shitfaced. Well, I'm going to get shitfaced, but it's for a good cause.

For half of my life, I thought of myself as a highly func- tioning alcoholic. Maybe I still am, but when all the guilt was finally taken away, I was left with this intense desire to live I wasn't familiar with. Then I got life with the very person who is the literal center of my universe, and it turned out that life isn't so bad, and I don't need alcohol to get me through every day.

To be absolutely honest, I still feel guilt, just not to that extent anymore. And maybe it's a different sort of guilt—a survivor's guilt. I came back but they didn't. I just know that it might not be because of me anymore. My life is lighter, my head is brighter.

Do I have *those* thoughts now? I do. Not much anymore, but I do. I don't think I want to act on them, but it's hard to change your way of thinking after years of living in the same circle of hell. But now I have my Leila and a mean therapist —excuse me, a person. That's what they call themselves at Freya's PTSD center.

After years of self-loathing and drinking myself to death, I finally decided to climb out of my hole. I just need to get my body on board with that. Years of abusing it didn't do me any good, and besides therapy, I also went on some sort of super healthy diet, and Leila's been watching me like a hawk the whole time.

Knowing that there probably won't be many options taxi-wise, I asked my woman to pick us up later that night.

It's closing on nine, and we're going with the plan of getting hammered.

"I dunno, man," Kenneth says, leaning his chin on his fist. "Just something, I dunno, is missing."

His speech is slurred. We've drunk the same amount of alcohol, but over the years, I've built up a tolerance—my brain is foggy now, but I can think.

"You need a change." I snap my fingers.

"A change?" He raises a brow. "What type of change?"

"I've got an idea." I try to smile as innocently as I can. He'll definitely kill me later, but he'll thank me at some point.

To my utter surprise, we manage to grab a cab, and ten minutes later, we arrive at TJ's place. He's Kayla's ex-boss and was the first one to discover her talent. We chat from time to time, and I'm thinking of buying his place since he wants to retire in Florida. I called him from the bar and asked if I could use his parlor for something for my friend. TJ lives in the same building as his shop, so he said he'd open it for me when we get there.

As we stumble out of the car, TJ is already unlocking the shop.

"Where are we?" Kenneth looks around suspiciously.

"We're helping you to take the first step into your new future," I smack his shoulder, "my friend. Let's go."

He looks at the parlor's sign and narrows his eyes. "I don't know about this."

"Oh, you'll love it. C'mon." I push him inside where TJ is pulling a bottle out from under the receptionist's table.

"I guess you'll need this if you're about to do what you told me."

"What is that?" Kenneth nervously looks between me and TJ.

"A piercing." I smile evilly.

"No-o-o." He begins shaking his raised hands. "I can't walk around Little Hope with a ring in my ear."

"Don't worry," I smile, "the ring won't be in your ear."

"Where will it be?" Once again, he looks between us for answers, and on cue TJ and I both look down at his crotch. "What? No!" He covers it with his hands, his voice higher.

"I promise you, your life will be changed forever after this," I announce, dead set on convincing him to change something in his uptight life.

"Yeah, when my dick falls off, I bet it will." He starts backing toward the door, sobering up every second.

"It feels real good," TJ chimes in while he pours whiskey into three plastic cups.

Kenneth pauses for a moment. "You've got one?"

"Yep," he downs his glass, "and my wife loves it."

I quirk a brow, surprised at this piece of information. Not surprised that he has one because TJ is a badass, but surprised he decided to share—the man seems tight-lipped.

"Alright, good for you." Kenneth slowly walks back, "I'm not doing it, but I'd love to hear a story. Or two."

I exchange looks with TJ while we both barely contain our laughter, and he pushes the full cup toward Kenneth. "Sure, I've got a few."

Thirty minutes later, we're shitfaced. Myself included. But not TJ—that man has the tolerance of a horse.

"So, what do you think?" he asks Kenneth. "Want to change your life for the best?"

"Ya know what?" Kenneth smacks his open palm on the table. "I do."

I pause, the cup midair. "Really?"

"Pff, yeah." He rolls his eyes. "I could use a change, ya know."

I know, because I've seen Kenneth getting stuck in that circle of hell where only good boys go.

"Let's do it." He smacks his palm again, knocking my cup off. "But you won't do it," he tells me and then points his wavering finger at TJ. "You, though, look sober enough for it. I don't want to end up with holes in my balls if he touches it." He waves his hand at me dismissively, making me chuckle. I've never done a piercing wrong, but I've also never done one while intoxicated like this.

"Deal." TJ's turn to smack the table.

What the hell is wrong with people constantly smacking everything? Don't they know how to deal with emotions another way?

TJ hurries to the back of the parlor to collect the needed supplies, clearly in a rush so Ken wouldn't change his mind.

"Ya know, my mother likes to throw her proper friends' daughters at me in hope that I'll finally settle." He chuckles and rubs his hands together with an evil look on his face. "I bet they'd be surprised to find ma dick pierced."

"They sure will." I smile but feel bad for him. He doesn't have my demons, but he has his own. The oldest of the family, he was born to be the good one and to take care of everyone else. People forget that sometimes, even the oldest kid needs to be taken care of too.

TJ comes back and preps the table. Then he pats it. "Hop on it and pull your pants down."

"With pleasure." He laughs at his innuendo and follows TJ's instructions. "You've got some painkillers?"

"Sure we do, boy." TJ grabs the bottle and passes it to him. "That's your pain medicine."

Kenneth chuckles and takes a generous sip. It's the second bottle TJ produced from under the table, and I wonder how many more he has in there. Then he puts his gloves on and preps...the area.

"Ouch, it's cold."

I roll my lips trying not to smile—if he's complaining now, he sure won't like what's to follow.

When the needle pierces his skin, he cries out and grabs my hand, squeezing it hard.

"Don't be a pussy," TJ says as he tries to pull the wand

through. I'm not allowed to say anything, but TJ sure as fuck can laugh at him. At this point, I'm super tipsy, and the situation seems very comical to me. Knowing Kenneth, he'll come to kill me tomorrow. I can't wait.

At TJ's words, Kenneth starts cursing. "Ya didn't tell me the shit's so painful."

"It's your dick," TJ deadpans, cleaning the area. "What did you expect?"

"I dunno." Kenneth shrugs while still squeezing my hand. "Not that for sure."

I bite the inside of my cheek the whole time TJ gives Kenneth care instructions, knowing I'll have to make sure he looks at them tomorrow, sober. Once we're all done, I call Leila and tell her the address of where to pick us up. She's running errands in Springfield, so it'll only take her about ten minutes to come pick us up.

I'm having a strong case of déjà vu, but this time around, I'm allowed to openly lust after my woman, not scared that her brother might deem me unfit. In fact, his approval means a lot to me. More than I expected. I guess I really like being accepted into a big family, and gaining not only my future wife, but brothers.

We chat as we wait for Leila, and at some point, Kenneth asks the question I was waiting for.

"So, what about you?" He nods toward me.

"What about me?" I smile sweetly, playing dumb.

"Do you like yours?" He nods at my crotch.

And here's the moment I've been waiting for. "I don't have one." And my face stretches into the widest smile.

TJ laughs but tries to hide it with a cough.

"You motherfucker!" Ken yells in something close to a falsetto, and TJ and I can't hold it anymore and start laughing.

Ken lunges for me and punches me in the shoulder, nearly knocking us both down on the floor in our drunkenness. But I'm saved by the bell. Well, a phone call. My device starts beeping, and then I see Leila's car parked outside. When she notices me watching her, she gives me the most brilliant smile and waves. I go all sappy when I see her like that and lose focus, so I get punched again, and this time it hurts. Well, I deserved that one.

"Stop, stop!" I raise my hand in front of me in defense. "You don't want to punch this pretty face; it needs to give you cute nieces and nephews!" It's the first time I've thought of kids, but once I do, it's all I can see. Leila with a belly full of my babies, in our house we're building. A big family of happy people who don't treat each other like shit and constantly put each other down. I'll raise them well and I'll be a good husband. I know I can.

"A punch in the face won't ruin your genetics, idiot." Then he pauses midair. "Wait a minute. Are you pregnant? I mean..." He nervously looks between me and Leila's car outside. "Is she pregnant."

"Nah, relax. She's too young for that. But it's in the plans." Then I level him with a stare. "And I'm not asking your permission."

He snorts. "So defensive. But if you did," he turns to stare me down, "need my permission, I wouldn't object."

I nod with a secretly happy heart, keeping my face level. I wave at TJ, who's watching our bickering with a cup next to his mouth. "Thanks, man."

"Anytime." He laughs and adds, "And that deal we talked about? Send me your proposal. I want my place to be in good hands."

I don't show him my surprise since he's been sending

me around the block every time I bring up this topic. "I will." I wave, and we walk outside.

TJ accepting my offer to buy his place means more than anyone knows. I've always wanted to build a work environment where people felt like they came home to, and TJ managed to do just that. This parlor is his life, and him saying that he wants to sell means that he sees the same potential in me and he trusts me not to let him down. I don't know what he just saw, but he did. And I refuse to overthink any of it. I'm just going to accept it.

When we sit in the car—I'm in the passenger seat and Ken is in the back—I pull Leila to me and my mouth lands on hers in a hot kiss. I haven't seen her in a few hours, and I've missed her. I want to pull her pants down and move her to my lap so we can...

"Staaaahp it, my eyes!" Kenneth complains from the back seat, and I remember that we're not alone.

Leila pulls away, her cheeks red, and her lips swollen. She pointedly looks between me, Kenneth, and the parlor. "Do I want to know?" she asks.

"No," we answer in unison, and she shifts the car into gear.

"Alright then."

A few minutes later, Kenneth is snoring away, and I enjoy the quiet moments with my woman.

"Marry me," I say out of nowhere.

"What?" Her head whips toward me for a moment. "Let's talk about that when you're not drunk to tears."

"I might be drunk, but the decision has been made a long time ago when I was very sober." I dig into my pocket on the inside of my winter coat she makes me wear and pulls out a black velvet box. "Pull over."

"Stephan—" She gives me a wide-eyed stare.

"Pull to the side, please."

She gives me another look but pulls to the curb. Once she's parked, I click the button on the box and show it to her. When she recognizes the ring, her mouth falls open.

"Stephan," she whispers.

She saw this ring in the window while we were walking to get my favorite coffee when she came to Boston the first time. She subtly looked at it, but I knew she loved it. It's just like her—unique and beautiful. It's not flashy, but very classy. It's made of white gold with three emeralds, the center one being the largest, with a few tiny diamonds around them. If it was up to me, I'd get her the biggest fucking diamond I could find, and she would be walking around with that rock on her finger to let everyone know she's mine. But it would be that—just a rock. And this ring is so her.

"Stephan," she repeats quieter, and my heart begins sinking.

Fuck, fuck, fuck.

Did I misread the signs? Fuck! How can I change her opinion now?

I look to the back seat, wishing Kenneth would disappear so I could pull her pants down and start convincing her to change her mind, but he keeps snoring away, oblivious to my turmoil.

"You don't like it?" I brave a question, and her eyes well. "Fuck, you don't want to marry me." My happiness deflates in an instant.

"No, you idiot!" she cries out and punches me in the shoulder. She's about the only person I can tolerate it from.

But that's it. She told me she doesn't want to marry me and that I'm an idiot for even entertaining the idea. She's always felt my mood swings, so she must have sensed this one as well, because her eyes go round, and she starts talking rapidly.

"No!" She rolls her eyes. "You're really an idiot! Of course, I want to marry you!"

"Then I don't understand..." I blink, trying to figure out what just happened. "Why are you crying?"

"Because you've waited so long!" She throws her hands in the air. "You've had this ring for what? A whole three months?"

The understanding finally dawns on me, and a wide smile stretches across my lips. My woman is angry that I waited a whole three months to propose. I think we'll get along just fine.

"So, is that a yes?" I give her that lopsided smile I know she likes, and she instantly turns to goo. The apples of her cheeks pinken, and she smiles shyly.

"It's a yes."

"Fucking yes!" I cry out and pull her in for another kiss.

"Not again." A loud groan from the back seat once again reminds me that we have an audience.

I pull away from the kiss and give him the stink eye. He flips me off and buries his face into the collar of his wool sweater. "Just get me home before you eat each other's faces again."

He's going to be my official brother soon, so I turn back and flip him the bird, making sure he sees it. He rolls his eyes and looks outside. The corners of his eyes wrinkle in an attempt to hide a smile.

I have a family now. A big and instant one. I'm a lucky bastard.

Bonus story

Want to see a day of Frank's life? Yes, the moose. Yes, Frank the Moose.

Please find MY NEWSLETTER tab in the following link and follow the instructions.

https://linktr.ee/ArianaCaneAuthor

Afterword

As I typed so much, I got so emotional that I had to go and delete everything because it turned out to soppy. Here is the second try.

Thank YOU for reading! Welcome to Little Hope if you are new! And welcome back if you've been around! Thank you for picking my book among millions of other amazing books.

Can you guess who will be in the next book? Yes, Kenneth! A sheriff with a good-boy complex who tries to help everyone. He is quiet and oh so good, but he's got something 'bad' inside. He just needs someone to show it to him:) You can PRE-ORDER his story here!

Stay tuned for his story! In a meanwhile, you can check out my other books at <u>arianacane.com</u>.

And this website address https://linktr.ee/ArianaCane Author has all my Social Media if you want to stay tuned!

Thank you!
~with love,
Ariana, Frank, Ghost, Midnight, and all the bears of Maine

Also by Ariana Cane

<u>**The World of the Fallen Gates series**</u>

Dystopian, paranormal, urban fantasy romance series

Tale of the Deceived, Book 1 of the duet

<u>Story of the Forsaken, Book 2 of the duet</u>

-vampires, werewolves, faes

-true enemies to lovers

-the life after the World has ended

-super slow-burn

-one bed

-true series

-scorching tension

-tons of secrets

<u>**Little Hope Series**</u>

Small town, slow burn, contemporary romance stand-alones.

Haunted Hearts, Little Hope Series, Book 1

Alex and Freya,

-one bed

-grumpy-sunshine

-strangers to enemies to lovers

-an ex-navy veteran with PTSD

-woman on the run

-woodchopping

-cabin in the woods

-damaged MMC

-all the bears of Maine

Guilty Minds, Little Hope Series, Book 2

Justin and Kayla

-true bully romance

-groveling

-tattoo artist-waitress/mechanic

-miscommunication for a good reason

-wildlife of Maine

Broken Souls, Little Hope Series, Book 3

Mark and Alicia

-fireman and author

-strangers to neighbors to lovers

-hurt/comfort

-trauma recovery

-man's best friend

-protective MMC

Fragile Lives, Little Hope Series, Book 4

Archie and Leila

-enemies to lovers

-one bed

-cabin in the woods

-age-gap

-brother's best friend

-the most beloved character

-wildlife of Maine

-trauma recovery/PTSD (MMC)

-lots of tattoos and piercings (MMC)

<u>Book 4, Kenneth's story, is coming soon…</u>

Acknowledgments

It's been quite a ride for me. I hope you enjoyed it too. I tried to give Leila and Archie justice because in my head, they are perfect for each other. I couldn't imagine a better partner for Archie. Once Leila, quiet and observant Leila, talked to me first, I knew it will be her.

I will try to make all of it short, otherwise, it will be another whole book because there are so many wonderful people I'm grateful for.

As always, thank you, Sarah. I don't even need to say anything at this point—you know it all. Thank you! And I'm sorry for being grumpy!

Jennifer. Yes, you. Yes, YOU! Yes, Bookaholic79. You're in every book, LOL, and you will stay in them!

Steph, for always keeping me on my toes. And your research, of course. I don't know what I would do without your certain posts.

Tracey J., I'm so happy you found my books.

Meaghan, my fellow stalker, thank you for being with me.

Darlene who always helps me to brainstorm. Can't wait to receive your messages as you read.

Tessa, your heartbreaking messages make me feel like I'm not wasting my time here.

Alexandra Hale, thank you for helping a friend out all the time.

To my whole ARC and street team. Thank you! If you

have been with me since the very beginning—a double thank you goes your way. For also taking a chance with me.

If for some reason (the only reason is that my distracted self forgot to type it) you don't see your name, you are still here! I truly am very forgetful and trying so very hard not to forget everyone, but forgive me if I accidentally do.

My lovely team! Hailey, Andrea, Preet, Crystal, Cheryl, Josie, TracyB, Erin, Sovaria, Anshul, Christina, Rhonda, Rose, Jenn, Echo, Trinity, Retrogirlreads, o'mama, Samantha, TaMara, Melissa, Michelle, Michelle A., Samantha C., Zakerah, Molly, runofthemill, Jennifer, Jen, Heather, Lindsey, Marisa, Samantha H., Cynthia, and Lisa.

Thank you all!

And the READER! You! Thank you for picking up the book and welcome to Little Hope! Or welcome back:)

~with love,

Ariana, Frank, Ghost, Midnight, and all the bears of Maine

"You're the only thing holding me together. And they all know that."

www.ingramcontent.com/pod-product-compliance
Lightning Source LLC
Chambersburg PA
CBHW051312190726
48290CB00001B/118